HUNT HER

HUNT HER

COME FOR ME, BOOK TWO

KELLY FINLEY

Hunt Her

Kelly Finley

© 2021 Kelly Finley Publishing, LLC

Visit the author's website at www.kellyfinley.com

ISBN: 978-1-7374516-4-8 (eBook)

ISBN: 978-1-7374516-5-5 (paperback)

This is a work of fiction. Names, characters, places, brands, media, and incidents are either the product of the author's imagination or have been used fictitiously. Any resemblance to actual persons, living or dead, events, or locales is entirely coincidental.

The author acknowledges the trademarked status and trademark owners of various products referenced in this work of fiction, which have been used without permission. The publication/use of these trademarks is not authorized, associated with, or sponsored by the trademark owners.

Edited by Tiffany Tyer and Kat Wyeth (Kat's Literary Services)

Proofreading by Meredith Sweet (Kat's Literary Services) & Deborah Richmond

Cover by Caroline Johnson

 Created with Vellum

ALSO BY KELLY FINLEY

COME FOR ME SERIES

Protect Her, Prequel Novelette

Pierce Her, Book One

Hunt Her, Book Two

Chase Her, Book Three

ALL FOR YOU

After Him, Book One

With Him, Book Two

And More To Come...

FOR YOU

Want a free copy of *PROTECT HER*, the Come for Me Prequel Novelette?

Join my monthly news tease for this special gift, bonus scenes, sneak peeks, and more. I share it all!

Join at KellyFinley.com and this gift is coming your way.

To KA,
Thank you for holding my hand and telling me everything
will be okay.

HUNT HER PLAYLIST

"I'm Afraid Of Americans" by BONES UK
"White Flag" by Bishop Briggs
"Forever" by Labrinth
"Love Again" by Dua Lipa
"Blinding Lights" by The Weeknd
"Rain" by Ro James
"Miracle" by CHVRCHES
"PILLOWTALK" by ZAYN
"Just Breathe" by Pearl Jam
"One Way Or Another" by Until the Ribbon Breaks
"Falling Like The Stars" by James Arthur
"Black Sea" by Natasha Blume
"everything i wanted" by Billie Eilish
"The Fear" by The Score
"Sign of the Times" by Harry Styles

Listen to the HUNT HER playlist on Spotify

ANONYMOUS

Anonymous

It's her.

Out of the corner of my eye, she always had my attention. How that woman's shoulders would stand strong while she laughed with the girl, protecting her.

And that damn face of hers. The smile, disarming. The strands of golden hair, alluring. Those speckles across her nose with her pink lips sounding with rolling laughs, inviting. My gaze would trail down the vein in her neck, tempting me.

But it's her marine eyes. How they aim for you. How they pierce right through, claiming their target.

Defiance trails the air around her. Even her chin resists my rule. Either it's up, challenging me, or it's down, calculating her next move against me.

The urge. To follow her. To take her. To end her. It

never really took me. Too many other things attracted my attention before.

But now with this viral spectacle, with the video and photos connecting her beguiling image to that global celebrity?

The glorious revenge will horrify millions.

The cost? The sacrifice to pursue her? Worth every risk.

A scent drops, the first spot on a trail, twisting my soul with a hunger driving me to have her.

The hunt has begun.

CHAPTER ONE

CHARLIE

I'm Afraid Of Americans by BONES UK

Charlie

"Are you ready for this, Charlie?"

Ready for what, I wondered. The hard cock urging between my cheeks, or the bundle of lit dynamite I was about to throw on my life?

Fuck it.

I'd do both.

His baritone British accent pressed into me, not asking about the meeting—the one in an hour that would have the world aiming for me. Adding one more maddening predator, the press, hunting to claim my sanity. And my life.

No, he was asking for more of me. His brute body steamed against my back under the rain from the shower above, hands caressing my wet cheeks, spreading them, gliding his eager, hard lust between them.

"Daniel Pierce, I don't know how you're ready again," I said.

We'd just fucked two hours before.

No. That round on the bathroom vanity was making love, bringing tears to my eyes at his gasps of love for me.

Because as of this morning... we were finally free.

Free to be together. Free to tell the world. Free to love.

And our ecstasy lasted that blissful, orgasmic moment before it was shot away by the text *ping* that beckoned me to check my phone charging on the hotel nightstand. While Daniel started our shower, my index finger touched the screen.

And summoned hell.

Now, I was thankful he couldn't see my face. Lust and fear were smeared across it. A guise I wore daily since I'm with him, loving him.

His fingers descended between my thighs, expertly strumming me closer. To pleasure. To the edge. To him.

"I'm ready for you and our life together, Charlie Ravenel." The words hummed from his lips across my shoulder. Standing behind me, his truth was tempting. "It's all I want. You. Us. Our love," he said, "and no more hiding."

I was never supposed to do this. Months before. When I was hired to protect Kierra Williams—a sixteen-year-old actor someone was stalking on the set of the smash show *The Druid*. My mission was to keep the girl safe and to find out who was leaving notes, tormenting Kierra with haunting tactics.

But I fucked up. And fucked the one man I shouldn't.

Daniel Pierce.

The lead actor on the show. The A-list celebrity with sixty million followers. The one with a panty-melting face.

The one with a profile of masculine perfection only a bit more recognizable than his I-don't-care-if-my-dad-catches-me-fucking-him perfectly sculpted muscular frame. And don't get anyone started on his amazing ass.

Our first fuck was an atom bomb of love dropped on my lonely life.

And now his hands wrapped around me, coaxing me, reminding every cell in my body this is where I belong, even if it means giving up everything to be with him. Not that I was the kind of woman who gave up a damn thing for a man. Fuck that. Never.

I had no choice. Not after the last forty-eight hours.

Nope. I told myself. *That's bullshit. This whole gorgeous, hot mess started months back.*

True. Daniel and I were a secret until that famous shot connected the two of us.

That shot? That video?

It was the one when me, Daniel and Rob, my best friend and colleague, were at a gym in Madrid, Spain.

To the public eye, we were just friends. Friends who shared workouts and our work on *The Druid,* filmed at the massive studio nearby. Daniel was the famous face with constant cameras on him. Rob and I were his colleagues, cast security for the show.

All would have been peachy until a loud noise cracked the air like gunshots across the gym. Some guy had dropped his heavy bar, but the sudden sound had dropped me to my knees in a PTSD blackout, shooting my mind back six years to when I was a Marine.

And shot three times.

Witnesses in the gym had recorded the spectacle with their phones—#danielpierce rescuing a woman passed out in his arms.

So yeah, that video? It struck fucking media gold.

Because I was no average damsel in distress.

Posts of the video went viral, revealing my distinct scars. The bullet graze across my right cheek. The shot through my right shoulder. Hashtags, rumors, and comments started. Millions of them. And fans and press have been hunting the blonde draped over Daniel Pierce's biceps ever since.

And now this.

A stand-off.

A lethal chess game with the sadistic stalker I caught trying to rape Kierra Williams. The stalker was none other than Kierra and Daniel's co-star.

The beautiful. The famous. The evil. Mason Hunt.

"You can't fight me, Charlie." Daniel's digits focused me on this indulgence. One I needed like fire needs oxygen. The only thing that grounded me—that kept me sane—was his love.

His lips nuzzled down my neck, knowing my "hell yes" spot, the heat of his wet body, every part of it firm, and one even harder for me, wanting in. A whisper steamed over my ear, "I can't get enough of us," while thick fingers plunged into my thirst, the others teasing my tingling nipples.

Frisking hands grabbed my desire with another beckon from his lips, "you're so fucking beautiful," in that velvet, bass voice. It could sell sand in a desert. A gentle kiss landed on my cheek. "God, I love you, babe. Come on. One more time to celebrate. We're finally free."

No, we weren't.

I read the text minutes before joining Daniel in the shower. It slung me right back into a prison cell of fear, crashing me into the concrete wall of reality.

Unknown

I'm standing in line. Thinking
about fucking with you.
Today & always

It was a fatal secret I'd surely keep from Daniel to protect him. He never knew such threats. I'd already been shot by such a man and survived. Never would I let harm come to Daniel, the rare gem of love I found again.

The last words I had said to the stalker? To Mason Hunt while he licked his evil "fuck you" words up to me, promising he wasn't done? Tormenting. Stalking. Raping.

I had stood over Mason, after I kicked his ass, before the detectives came to whisk him away in cuffs. Squatting down, confronting his eyes and threat, I said, "You'll be standing in a long line if you want to fuck with me."

Now Mason's white-pretty-boy-celebrity-rich-ass made bail, paid a sycophant member of his posse to buy a bag full of burner phones so he could let me know... he was standing in line and waiting...

To more than fuck with me.

Warm water rained over me. Resting back against Daniel's cement chest, my tormented mind took this spot as a buzz of Xanax to my anxiety. If only for a short life. Or a night. Or a moment. Daniel was my harbor in a hurricane and my squalling storm... all at the same time.

He stood behind me with more than desire. It was love. Love wrapping around me, asking to lavish me. And I wanted this. Needed it. Given how long I pushed love away. Feared it for six years. Until Daniel.

Could I really do it? Drop all my defenses given how many were gunning for me now?

Resistance twisted my shoulders. Fear deployed through my nerves.

"How do you reckon we're free now?" I asked him. "I'm about to lose my job and step out into white lights on a red carpet with you for the entire world to see and fuck my life sideways."

"Charlie." His shocked voice and gentle hands turned me around. Hurt by my comment burned in his aqua eyes. "You don't have to go to the premiere with me. I would never make you do a bloody thing."

Shit, I didn't mean to fire at him like that. My damn mouth needed a silencer sometimes. The fucking text from Mason had sentenced me to a vengeful mood.

Daniel wouldn't let go. "What's going on with you?" Confusion dripped from his face. "We talked about this yesterday. How we're doing this together. Are you having second thoughts?"

His hulking shoulders rose under his steel jaw, veins and sinews down his neck tensing in my sight. He said, "If we do this, there's no going back. Our lives. Our careers. Nothing will be the same." A small measure of his power squeezed my bicep. "I love you and I won't have you resenting me. What do you want, babe?"

"Daniel." My hand scratched over his sexy stubble. "I *want* to go to the premiere with you. I love you, and I *want* you to fuck me *and* my life sideways."

No smile back. He didn't buy it.

"I'm serious, Charlie. Don't muck about." Little droplets were clinging to his dark chest hair, while drip by drip, falling from his coal-colored waves. Even angry. Or hurt. He was the sexiest man to millions and the most beautiful love I'd known. "We don't have to go public."

"We already *are* public, Daniel. Your obsessed fans are connecting the dots as we speak. My scarred face and body passed out in your arms in a Madrid gym months ago. It's all over social media. And last night? The same scar across my cheek, on the Comic-Con stage walking behind you and Kierra, clearly security for the cast of *your* show. The connection is made." Certainty washed down my face, staring back up at his. "Tick fucking tock."

Was it his fault?

No. We both had a legacy of guilt.

He was an A-list celebrity at the pinnacle of his career whose feet couldn't hit public pavement without notice. Without risk.

I loved him. But hated his life.

I was an addict for protecting others, mainly girls and women. Years ago in the military and now as my job. My instinct kept us safe but always told me—*hide. Never seek the spotlight unless you're saving someone.* Only then, like before, would I stand in the fire.

He loved me but had no idea what we faced.

In four days.

I would take a swan dive into his celebrity life.

Exposure to the level of fatal, I feared.

His hand cupped my cheek. Goddamnit, it always disarmed me, and he knew it. "I know we're running out of time, babe," he said. "It's why we agreed to do it this way. On our terms. Out our relationship before the press or Mason can."

"I know." I held his hand caressing my face. "We're in this together. I promise."

God, how I wanted to tell him more. We had more to worry about from Mason than him leaking to the press that Daniel Pierce was dating, fucking, whatever, a member of cast security for his show.

That was salacious gossip. Nothing to fear.

The text this morning? To hell it was **Unknown**.

My instinct read it and stared down the next week, months, hell maybe the rest of my life. Knowing...

Mason Hunt was sinking his sadistic teeth into me now. Vicious because I busted him stalking Kierra. Obsessed with revenge for the ass-beating I gave him when I stopped him trying to rape her. Fixated upon a new target for his demented psyche—the woman who ruined his career.

I knew the minute I set my sights on Mason Hunt five months before that he was a predator.

And now... *I* was his prey.

But if I told Daniel, we'd both be robbed of peace. And I meant it. I loved him. Because, dear God, the man dropped to his knees and loved me so much in return.

Yes, on paper, I was the hero, the one who sacrificed. The one who gave her service and almost her life to help others. And I would till my dying day.

But what the world didn't know about Daniel Pierce was that behind his facade of hero, celebrity, and beauty, you find a man capable of a love so great it tore down my every defense.

He could fuck me. Fuck my private life. Fuck my safe solitude all up.

It fired my DNA up—*protect him, always.*

From the terrifying truth. From my haunting, lingering instinct. It was always right. Warning me...

Mason Hunt isn't the only one gunning for you now.

CHAPTER TWO

DANIEL

I was supposed to focus on my job, posting stories about my interviews at Comic-Con for *The Druid*. Finding this odd place in my ego telling me to talk to a device in my hand like I'm chatting directly with you. And you. And you. To my sixty million followers who apparently gave a shit what shirt I wore, what weight I lifted, or what I ate for breakfast.

I used to ignore the feeling that plagued my soul. That any of it fucking mattered.

Now... I couldn't.

Because I stared at what *did* matter to me. What would until my last breath.

Charlie Ravenel.

The legs of her jeans were sticking to the lotion on her thighs. Making her muffle curses at apparel that wasn't cooperating. Making her do a cute dance, hopping, and twisting into her white jeans. She lost her struggle against her foes—denim and Lycra—falling against the side of the bed in an even louder, laughing curse.

Chuckling at her spectacle, I easily pulled on the black T-shirt my stylist suggested for the day's attire. "Need some help?"

This was a complicated question.

No. The woman I loved could take care of herself. The proof was written down her body. Scars of her capability. Hurting more than flesh. The pain they left behind deserved someone to care for them.

I swore... I would.

"Yes," she said. "Go stand at the bottom of this hotel building and hold these damn jeans out so I can jump from the roof into them." The button finally lost the battle, fastening her jeans tight.

"With the way your bum looks in them, the fall would be worth it."

Sliding on my own, I sympathized. My jeans had to be tailored to fit over my legs and backside without gaping at my waist.

Her lips cocked up in a smile. "Are *you* ready?" she asked, pulling a white tank top over her head.

The wince in her cheek registered in my adoring gaze. I knew her body. How every time she lifted her right shoulder, residual pain from the bullet shot through it, screamed through her bones.

"Fuck yes, are we having another round?"

Because I could. I'd muck up the schedule for the cast and media circus waiting on me to take ten, maybe fifteen quick minutes to make love to her again.

Because that's what this was. Love. Finally.

Yes, there were moments in my thirty-seven years when I thought it was. For months. Once for a year. But never like this. This was a union I'd drop everything for. Over and over again.

"You wish, Sex God." She secured her black wrap sweater in a knot. "Damn, they need to bottle your boner power and sell it to millions."

"The source of my boner power is you." The *clank* of my leather belt sliding into my jeans and the direction of this conversation twitched everything below it. "You're petite, not small enough to fit in a pill bottle, but perfectly tight for my thick cock. I'm getting hard just looking at you."

Fuck, how I wanted to bend her over the bed now, kick her ankles apart, and drive into her sweet pussy while my fingertips thrilled her clit. Bloody hell, the way she came so hard was my undoing.

"Ha, smart-ass," she said. Our naughty banter made her grin, making me even more horny. "You know what I mean. Are you ready for the meeting? For the reveal?"

"Yes. But you're the one who should get ready."

Schedules be damned, I crossed the room to stand by her side. "I can be with whomever I want and suffer little consequence. Demand what I want, and others make it happen." Brushing my hand across her silky strands. "I worry about *you*. You're the one risking your career for us to be together."

I risked nothing to be with Charlie, but I was changing everything.

The day before, I rearranged my entire career for her. Canceling press events and photoshoots. Telling anyone making demands they would have to wait. Because this love was more important than my career.

And this love, I had to protect it from Mason Hunt.

Also, the day before, Charlie caught Mason stalking Kierra.

All season, she built a case so strong against him that no court could deny his guilt. Police took him away in hand-cuffs, but given Mason's celebrity, he was probably already out on bail with an ankle monitor.

At least Mason would be leashed, unable to hurt anyone anymore... unless... he fired his mouth.

That mouth would aim for Charlie. Telling the whole world how she violated the ethics of her job as a protection officer. How, while she was protecting Kierra, she was also falling in love with me, Kierra's co-star—a career-killing move.

Charlie would never forsake her job. Not even for me. Her priority had never wavered, always protecting the girl first. But few would care fuck all for that truth.

For me? Mason couldn't hurt me, not by outing our relationship. It'd be a blip of press and done.

My fans would never abandon me. They always wanted more. And I gave it to them. Selfies on the sidewalk. Autographs outside a pub.

Fuck's sakes, I once stopped for a fan in Sainsburys. A midnight craving for a mint chocolate Cornetto turned into a five-minute chat in my pajamas, jacket, and beanie. And taking a photo with the fan, of course.

I earned a devoted following that wouldn't turn on me, regardless of who I loved.

The risk though... it was what my fans would do to Charlie.

Millions would love her, celebrating our relationship with cute memes and reposts. But some would vilify her, spewing lies, damning conjecture and jealous rants.

But Charlie could take it. She had survived far worse than evil words fired her way.

Still, terror twisted my insides.

What did I fear more than fans? More than Mason Hunt's mouth?

My past, the one hidden from scrutiny for so many years. It would devastate Charlie and our love. I'd take all the bullets in the world to protect her from my dark truth.

She smoothed her hands over my chest. "Hey, where'd you go in that pretty brain of yours?"

"I was just thinking about all I'm changing and all you're risking." Even inches below my gaze, her eyes pinned me to a wall, a captivity I craved. "And how I love you so bloody much for it."

"Well, I might be risking my career, Daniel Pierce, but let's be clear." Her marine eyes arrested me here, in my heaven. "I'll stop when time does."

"Well done, Ravenel." I lowered my lips to the smart ones I adored. "Keep your sexy wits about you. We're going to need them."

A gentle suck of my lips over her top one unleashed her moan. I did it five more times, our bodies melding to the other's curve.

A knock at the door startled my kiss away.

"Keep this urge between your thighs." I cupped my hand across the crease I craved, making her moan more. "I'll satisfy it over and again tonight."

CHAPTER THREE

CHARLIE

S itting in front of my laptop in Daniel's hotel suite, I waited to confess. To my boss. And to Daniel's.

My sexy accomplice sat beside me, hidden from the interrogating camera.

No more tactical gear and garb for me. No more working cast security. Not just for *The Druid*. For any production. My face was too recognizable, a liability now.

My new uniform? A pair of jeans, a tank, and a sweater.

A cool breeze from the air conditioner chilled over my long strands still wet from the morning's shower where I was on Daniel again.

Once we had talked it out. Once I saw the love straining in his eyes—I had to have him. He didn't complain, happy to take me hard against the shower wall.

As fucked as our lives seemed destined to become, it didn't matter. Our love was greater.

At least, I hoped.

Finally, our three parties connected on the video call, exchanging pleasantries.

Daniel's boss, Lorraine Morris, called in from New York. She had taken the red-eye flight back to the city after the Comic-Con panel the night before.

My boss, Jeremy Bennett, joined the meeting from the HGR London office, clicking his pen as usual. I'd worked for his company for five years. We were contracted by the biggest studios, charged with protecting high-profile actors.

And I was still in San Diego, the bruise and cut on my face from the fight the day before with Mason shining back at me on the screen. Proof I did my job. Proof I'd protected sixteen-year-old Kierra Williams.

The problem was my painfully ethical integrity fucked up along the way.

I put the sword to my gut to fall on it.

"I'm proud of our work. Kierra is safe and the evidence against Mason is solid." Talking to the screen split into thirds, I spoke on behalf of the security team for the show. "Thank you both for your confidence in us."

"It's an honor working with you, Ms. Ravenel," Lorraine said. "You know I build teams of women for my cast and crew. I want you on my shows, every time, and back next season on *The Druid*."

"Thank you, Ms. Morris. I know Jeremy would love to reduce the security budget to a detail of one—me." The two bosses chuckled. I didn't. "But I have to respectfully decline your offer."

Their eyes widened in surprise.

It was logical I'd stay on the show. I grew close to Kierra. Why would I leave her protection detail?

I drew a deep breath, exhaling guilt and the admission. "It's no longer appropriate that I remain on the show. I deeply apologize for the breach of ethics and lack of disclosure until now."

Tears threatened.

Shit, I hated betraying my integrity. Never was I supposed to get involved with a cast member. But I did more than get involved. I fucked up and fell in love... with the star of the damn show.

Suck it up with a guilty straw.

"I'm in a personal relationship now that prevents me from working in any professional capacity on *The Druid.*"

With no apology on his face, Daniel turned the laptop, sharing the camera with me.

Lorraine howled back in surprise, slapping the desk in front of her.

Jeremy's pen stopped clicking at the sight of Daniel's celebrity face beside me, his hand reaching to hold mine.

"Blimey!" Jeremy exclaimed.

Daniel said, "We hope we have your blessing."

"Blessing?" Lorraine laughed. "Daniel Pierce, I couldn't have ordered up a better woman for you myself, and trust me, I've considered it with some of your antics."

Colleen, Daniel's assistant, sat across from me, taking care of everything "Daniel Pierce" with a tap of her fingertip on a tablet. The nod of her head in passionate agreement with Lorraine's judgment made me grin.

Lorraine beamed at us holding hands on-screen. "You more than have my blessing. I'm so happy for you both."

I watched Jeremy; his normally calm demeanor looked ruffled by the news. "What about you, boss? You okay with this, or am I fired?"

Jeremy leaned back in his office chair. "Ravenel, it took the god of gods to make you abandon your duty," he said, enjoying his cheeky reference to Daniel's blockbuster role as Zeus. "Yes. I'm all right with this. But I better bloody not lose one of my best protection officers."

"I promise, sir." The burden lifted off my heart. "We'll figure out how I can still work given what will happen."

We all knew it. My career would take a hard right turn once the story of our relationship went public. I wouldn't be able to hide in the shadows anymore.

Daniel chimed in, noting the time before the interviews awaiting him. He filled them in on our plan for handling the coming storm of press because of Mason's arrest.

Mason would be a liability to the show. Though his character was dramatically written off at the end of season two, he wasn't done. His mouth would be gunning for us soon.

The plan was I'd be Daniel's date to his film premiere in Manhattan in four days. He shot the rom-com *Swipe Right* the summer before and had a press junket this coming week. Using the media event and opportunity, we'd reveal our relationship before Mason could.

"It's the only shot Mason's got at us," Daniel said. "Once we take it away, we're safe."

Daniel's wrong. My eyebrow twitched. After Mason's covert text to me this morning, I knew... Mason was a loaded .22 with fourteen shots left.

"We're going to use Charlie's name from when she was married and in the Marines." Daniel's thumb rubbed over my hand. "It honours her service and her late husband."

Yes, it honored Kai, my late husband, but that wasn't the only reason I'd suggested it.

In what little public information there was on me, almost all of it was under "Captain Charlotte Roberts," my former married and military name.

After my husband was killed serving in Afghanistan

and I came home shot from the same service, I sought solace and safety in my maiden name—Charlotte Sophia Ravenel.

But I was no fool. Mason would figure out the ruse or someone would discover my name change. One day.

For now, debuting as "Captain Charlotte Roberts"—a former Marine dating a celebrity—shined the perfect spotlight on us. PR fucking gold for Daniel's sparkling career.

If Mason tried throwing shit on my image and service, it wouldn't stick, only slide down with stink on him.

What if Mason finds out the real reason you've been hiding?

My instinct taunted, sitting beside me, squeezing my other fist until it blanched white with fear.

Guess you never plan on telling Daniel either? Good idea. He'll think you're fucking crazy. PTSD will be the least of your worries if you tell him what you really fear. Why you really hide on your secluded home island, or in the secure shadows of a studio set, or behind a popular Southern family name that goes back centuries with its own shameful history.

I swallowed hard, feeling like a paper silhouette target at firing range—hanging there, exposed for anyone's ripping aim.

You're so fucking brave protecting others. But you're too chicken shit to tell the man you love that another fear haunts you. One that's warned you long before Mason Hunt...

Someone else is coming for you.

Instinct hissed in my ear, making my stoic cheek wince.

What the fuck are you thinking, bitch? Dating a celebrity? How many damn targets do you want on your chest now?

"Sounds like a smart plan to me." Jeremy's assessment broke my mental detour through hell.

"Yep, control the story before it controls you," Lorraine

agreed. "You two enjoy your time together. And perhaps, Ms. Ravenel, I mean, Ms. Roberts, you can join us as Daniel's guest for the premiere of season two this December. We wouldn't be here without you."

"We'll see." I smiled at the compliment. "December feels like a lifetime from this July."

And now... I'd be damn lucky to live long enough to see it.

CHAPTER FOUR

CHARLIE

"Bye, babe." Relief permeated Daniel's plush voice, minty breath, and supple kiss. I tried breathing it in across our lips, desperate to share it.

It didn't work.

His kiss. His body. Our fucks. All so damn hot—and what I'd be seeking this night—but it wasn't our heat blazing through me then.

I smoldered with fear, closing the hotel suite door, embers glowing with the familiar burn of goodbye. The inferno of farewell had destroyed my world too many times. My parents. My husband. Almost my life.

Daniel's departure left me in terror... standing here with my forehead pressed to the door.

He, Kierra, and Anders—the remaining principal cast of *The Druid*—they had to make up for the interviews missed the day before because of Mason's attack on Kierra.

None of which the press knew about. Yet.

And oh hell, when they finally did, with one spark of a

press release from the studio, our world would burst into a raging wildfire.

My bottom lip bore the brunt of my anxiety. I chewed its tender flesh as I moved about the suite. The distractions I tried to find before settling onto the sofa, not here.

Colleen sipped her tea from across the coffee table, considering me over the edge of a white porcelain cup. She set it down. "I know it's been a difficult few months for you both, but there's grace in it all. I've never seen Daniel like this." Her manicured tips swept through her silver hair. "He's quite in love with you, dear, to the detriment of his career."

Holding a bag of ice to my cheek, I curled up on the cushions.

Dozens of photographers would snap hundreds of photos of me that would post to millions of screens within days, and my right cheek looked like it had danced with a sledgehammer. Coupled with the six-year-old bullet graze scar under it, I worried it was all cameras would focus on and not Daniel, the star of the film.

"I don't want him to kill his career for me. I just want us to be safe."

"I know. And let's face it. The man has millions of pounds in the bank and millions of fans. He'll be just fine to set different priorities in his life. Finally."

"He's gonna miss you."

Colleen pinched the space between her tired eyes. "There's never a good time to retire, but I must. Daniel's like a son to me. I've suffered with worry for him for years. But he'll be fine. He has you now."

Freezing drips melted down my cheek. "Oh, I'm not gonna be his assistant or his mom." A cold drop landed on my shoulder, trickling over another scar. "I love him, but I'm not that kind of woman."

"That's exactly why I won't worry about him. He has enough people doting after him. What that man has needed is his equal. One who loves him—flaws, fame, and all."

I respected Colleen's wisdom. Daniel didn't need more people fawning over him. Smoothing the uncomfortable out of his life. Paid to anticipate his every need. Hired to tell him what he wanted to hear.

Something crawled across my brain. At what Colleen said. "Why do you worry so much about him?"

"The usual stuff." She adjusted her tortoiseshell readers. I clocked it—Colleen's nervous twitch. "And celebrity nonsense." Her eyes, hiding behind lenses, darted for the window.

I dropped the bag of ice into the bucket. "Colleen, I can't protect him if I'm in the dark." The sleeve of my sweater wiped the moisture off my cheek. "Are there threats to Daniel I need to know about?"

Something in Colleen's stare. Evasive. Concerned. An elegant bang of hair dropped in front of her eye when she turned back to my question, hiding half her gaze and the truth.

"Nothing I'm too concerned about anymore, dear," she said. "I care for him, and I adore you, but you know my role here. I'm not at liberty to discuss it."

I huffed, resting back against the blue gingham-print sofa.

Yeah, I knew.

Colleen was muzzled by nondisclosure agreements and loyalty to Daniel. All while Daniel wore rose colored glasses over his smoldering eyes—assuming every fan, every event, and everything would be just fine.

We feared otherwise.

"You know if I ask him, he won't tell me." I reached for what I could have, pouring a third cup of coffee from the silver carafe on the table.

Colleen mirrored me, reaching for a sip of tea. "Daniel learned the hard way, dear. Secrecy is his default setting now. It keeps him safe. Denial gets him through the rest. Not a day goes by without someone wanting something from him. You'll need to be patient to break his habits."

"I hate how he does it," I said. "How he gives it all away to his fans." The steam from the coffee threatened to scald my tender lips. "He stops anywhere for them. When he's at home. Or in a restaurant. Even behind rope lines and barricades. He's a sitting duck. Letting them take selfies. Signing autographs. Indulging groping hands."

I'd reviewed the evidence online taken of Daniel in public.

Hell, it was everywhere. Shots snapped feet away of Daniel walking the streets of London. Videos of him at the season one global premieres for *The Druid*.

They made me sweat watching how Daniel violated safest practice. Letting people reach across the barricades, grabbing him, holding him close for selfies. He—or any security trying to protect him—had no idea what was two-people deep behind the desperate fan.

He was supposed to be careful. Stand back. Let security flank him. Yes, if he had to reach for the picture to autograph, take it, sign it, hand it back, standing at least two safe feet away.

Damn the fucking selfie hugs everyone wants. Take their phone. Hold it high. Still two feet in front of the barricade with the elated fan in the background.

And please, God, would he quit stopping for every

crazy-ass Tom, Dick, and Horny Harriette wanting a photo with him?

After twenty years in the limelight, Daniel's admirers never feared his refusal. His chin would always turn to smile for their camera.

I loved that about him. How Daniel's big heart and body got oh so close. To me. And what I hated about his life. How his celebrity stood way too close. To his fans. To danger.

"Well, perhaps you can talk some sense into him," Colleen said before letting her sips build a foreboding silence.

That's not it. You're thinking with your brain. Not Colleen's.

What was Colleen so worried about?

I wanted to press for more intel. Screw an NDA. I needed to know what else was aiming for us.

A *ping* cut across the air, lighting up my phone screen. I glanced down at the text demanding my attention.

Unknown
Did anyone ever tell you?
How your beauty strangles the
life out of a man?

Fuck this asshole. My fingers plucked the phone up.

Yes, I'd strangled Mason until he passed out. That's what a rear naked choke would do. What me and many others in the military were trained to perform without thinking. Repetition bred instinct to act.

Mason was like the rest of them—men who saw me and assumed a petite blonde was harmless.

Fucking idiots.

That's what made me lethal as a protection officer. The best weapons fly under the radar. Sure, big and muscular served its purpose. Those men use presence and pounds for results.

I used practice and patience, sneaking up to aim my weapon or fists.

A massive bomb or a small, targeted bullet?

Either could kill you.

The text dug into my side like a dull butter knife.

Something. Mason is up to something.

His ego was too ravenous to be satisfied with only fucking with me through an almost entertaining stream of texts.

My index finger tapped the screen. To Instagram. To Mason Hunt's blue-check verified celebrity account with over twenty million followers.

His most recent post this morning? With 2.3 million likes and clicking up?

A white flag.

Bolting for the bathroom, my bare feet hit the charcoal carpet, coffee surging up my throat. It spewed from my mouth into the pristine white bowl.

Why?

A white flag didn't signal surrender in Mason Hunt's depraved world.

The thrilling part of this hunt?

The power I have, getting others to work for me.

With one covert message, I can summon soldiers from any global landscape—rural or urban.

All rushing to serve me.

All believing in a cause greater than any risk they may take fulfilling my command.

And once I dangled this bait in front of them?

This beautiful blonde bait?

The only challenge will be holding back their impulsive fire.

Waiting for my signal.

Waiting for the perfect, blood-soaking opportunity.

CHAPTER FIVE

DANIEL

Kierra Williams's emerald eyes sparkled suspiciously. Walking beside her, down the hotel corridor with a carpet pattern that dizzied my eyes, I saw her curious glance.

Her question confirmed it. "So, your room is next to Charlie's?"

A snort behind me.

I turned. Rob, Kierra's new lead protection officer, flexed his nostrils, suppressing a *you're busted* smile.

But how else was I supposed to do this? To keep this secret?

Charlie was like a protective big sister to Kierra. And she was the oxygen in my veins, the love keeping me alive.

After two years on *The Druid* with Kierra, she was like my little sister too. Through long days on set, or chats in the makeup trailer, I tried watching out for her.

So, when Kierra's breathtaking security shook my hand months before, she rocked my world. Concern for Kierra hit me while the woman guarding her dropped me. To my knees. Then on my back.

In love with the most beautiful, badass woman I'd ever met—Charlie Ravenel.

She saved me from my lonely ego, protected Kierra from a perverse bully stalking her, and saved our entire show.

Mason's torment of Kierra? Charlie ended it.

That's what I loved so much about her. How Charlie gave all to the people she loved, the people she protected.

And she never asked for anything.

All I knew in my celebrity world were people immoral with entitlement. Sheltered from true hardship. Privileged and exploiting others. Most of them? Greedy for even more.

Mason Hunt was their bloody poster child.

Charlie humbled them all. In the military, she had sacrificed everything for the two girls she almost died for. And now, she'd do it again for any girl or woman who suffered a man threatening them.

The only greed I knew from Charlie was in bed, shameless demands for sex I gladly met. She unleashed a fearless pursuit for love upon me. Given how long it'd been absent from her life, it was a hunger I didn't know if I could ever satisfy.

But I was the fucking luckiest man alive to sure try.

"Are you going to tell me?" Kierra pestered me, nodding her chin toward our two rooms, mine and Charlie's next door.

The proximity screamed guilty.

"Go enjoy your lunch with Ms. Ravenel."

"Oh, come on, Daniel." Kierra stomped her floral print Converse high-tops. "What's the craic?"

Her Irish lilt tempted me, but I wouldn't dish the gossip.

Rob and Joaquin shadowed behind her. They were Kierra's security detail now, and Charlie's colleagues and best friends who'd known about our relationship for months.

This ruse in the hallway highly amused them. Their faces twisted with grins, massive shoulders shaking as they chuckled at the joke.

Cheeks burning hot with guilt, I stopped in front of my door. Offering her a quick hug, my words lightly grazed over Kierra's copper hair. "Have a good break, yeah. I'll see you at the premiere this December."

Kiera pulled back, eyeing me, cheeky-like. "If ships don't sail sooner," she said.

Her clever meter surged off the charts, using her teen slang for outing what she was about to officially confirm. Fuck, just like Charlie.

Bloody hell, she'd trained her well.

Rob and Joaquin fell in behind Kierra, still chuckling.

The key card beeped in front of my door. I smiled, outnumbered by Charlie and her minions and loving every minute of it.

The door opened to Colleen lounging in an ivory chair. A view of the San Diego bay sparkled behind her. My luggage sat on the bed, half-packed for our flight to Manhattan tonight.

A moment of silence held comfortably between us. We overheard Kierra's excited squeal through the door between the adjoining suites where Charlie met her for their lunch date.

"It's all sorted," Colleen said. "Your charter flight departs at eleven tonight."

Her pursed lips warned more troubled her mind than

the usual logistics of my life. I plopped down on the edge of the bed that Charlie and I shook last night.

This was Colleen's last gesture before her retirement. Elaine waited in Manhattan, ready to take over. My career. My life. I adored Elaine, but grieved Colleen's departure.

"Promise me," I said, "that retirement doesn't mean retreat."

My mum was my home in Cornwall. But Colleen was home everywhere I'd traveled—my second mum—and leaving.

"My love, you know I'm always here for you." Her palms smoothed over absent wrinkles in her trousers. "But it's been a decade. A long ride. Year. And day."

Her tone held my gaze in detention before she said, "You know I haven't said anything to Charlie. And I can tell... you haven't either. But you must. You must tell her *all*, Daniel. That woman loves you. And you're besotted to the point of bliss and blooming lucky to have her."

Her slender knees rose to loom above me.

"But if you're not honest with her about everything, about what happened"—her truth and prophecy held my periphery—"you will kill the best thing that ever happened to you." Her gentle hand landed on my tense shoulder. "This isn't farewell, my dear, but I don't do goodbyes."

I shot up, pulling Colleen into my arms. Damn English formality, legal contracts, and professional dictates. I adored her, was barely able to utter through my stuttering grief, "Thank you."

Her thumb and index finger seized my chin in her grasp. She wore a big smile wet with tears while she shook my jaw. "Done and dusted, my dear. Now keep this tidy and right."

Her navy shoes pivoted on the carpet in front of me, spinning their direction for the door.

As I watched her leave, we didn't say a word. I'd see her again. And I bloody well knew I had better heed her warning until then.

Yes, Charlie was my bright future. But I had to confess to her about my dark past.

CHAPTER SIX

CHARLIE

White Flag by Bishop Briggs

I had fifteen minutes to get my shit together before Kierra would knock at the door.

Colleen had kindly offered me a bottle of water while I sat on the black penny-tile floor of the bathroom, explaining away my sudden sick stomach. "I think I may be a bit concussed from yesterday."

You think, Charlie Girl? Mason did repeatedly slam your head into the doorjamb of the bathroom in the suite, smearing your red blood down the white wooden trim like a pugilistic candy cane.

Colleen had stood at the threshold asking, "Should we phone down to the concierge for a doctor?"

"Let me see how I feel in a few hours. If I'm not better, I'll call one when we get to New York."

In reliable English fashion, Colleen had left me to my

pride and privacy. She had to meet Daniel next door to say goodbye.

I stood up and splashed cold water over my face but couldn't wash away the truth.

What did the white flag on Mason Hunt's Instagram account mean?

Not surrender.

Three years before, Mason Hunt had starred in a cult indie film. The role was meant to shed his Disney child-actor persona. It was a calculated risk featuring him as more than teen eye-candy, garnering him critical acclaim, and a bevy of adult roles.

But the film became more than that.

White Flag was a sick, ironic twist for a title.

The film is a dark tale of an underground society of young men—white supremacists—who target anyone they perceive as threats. People of color. Women. The LGBTQIA+ community. Immigrants. Name it. They hate it.

Mason's character, John White, is the ringleader. A rich teen using his family's white-collar power, money, and name, he builds an underground enclave and arsenal for torment. A white flag hangs from the ceiling of their hideout, surrounded by white pillowcases smeared with the blood of their victims.

The story is a cautionary tale—a comment upon privilege, power, and the evil undercurrents of hate in American culture.

The leader, John White, descends into madness over his pursuit. Hatred overpowers his psyche to the point of incapacity. Karma finally defeats his evil.

The ending fades out to his catatonic face blubbering at dirty white snow melting into oblivion outside the window of his mental hospital window. His nurse, a middle-aged Hispanic woman, resentfully hands him the meds that keep him sedate... and barely alive.

The movie worked for those with elevated hearts and intellect.

And it worked getting Mason critical acclaim for his performance.

It also ignited a cult-like following who heard it as a clarion call. Demented fans worshipped the film and the John White character like zealots. T-shirts, posters, a hit soundtrack, and social media hyped the evil.

As tragedy would predict, a deranged fan decided to turn fiction into horrific fact, murdering a gay Asian male outside a gay dance club in Atlanta. The white flag they found in the murderer's car, stained with the dark blood of his poor victim, was evidence putting that *White Flag* zealot away for life.

The studio pulled the film from screens. The film's creators issued statements. Mason's publicist sat him in front of reporters. He had a script reciting his regret for the misinterpretation of the film, pleading for others to understand; he did not support violence against anyone.

A lie.

Somehow the sinister psyche of the character seeped into Mason's soul. Maybe he was always that way. That's why he embodied the character so well. Or maybe it snapped something in him, twisting his mind with a performance that became personality for him.

Either way, I didn't care.

Mason raised the White Flag on his social media.

The post would raise his clan of followers, asking their leader, "Who is the next target?"

I considered the welt and cut on my cheekbone from my

fight with him yesterday. The circles under my eyes seemed to darken in seconds.

With one digital wave of his white flag, my fight with Mason Hunt had just begun.

He wasn't stupid enough to document his torment. The burner phones he used for texts couldn't be traced back to him. Yes, you could trace them back to who bought them in some cases, but he had a cadre of sick fucks who bought them for him.

And he was way too practiced with his life in the limelight. Never would he actually threaten me. He'd figure out a way to paint a red X on my chest as "next," I was sure.

Who else would he come after? Me? Certainly. Daniel? Probably. Anyone I loved? Possibly.

Bile burned back up my throat. I swallowed it down.

What are you going to do?

Minty mouthwash burned my mouth. In a gratifying splat into the sink, I spat it out. I checked myself in the mirror. No residue from my lost coffee.

I was fine. And knew what to do.

A memory flashed of when I was in college, loading groceries into my car.

A young man, clad in fraternity letters was taunting a teenager in the parking lot. The poor kid working at the store was trying to wrangle the metal carts on wheels together.

One of them had escaped. It rolled down the slight grade, hitting the college asshole's truck. An offense enough for him to unleash gay slurs upon the innocent teen.

The energy in the air cracked over my nerves. Putting the last bag in my trunk, I watched with a side-eye, certain.

This is wrong. This is dangerous.

I'd stepped in, trying to defuse the tirade with jokes

about the dumbass carts. It didn't work. He only taunted the teen more.

So, I started ripping the frat boy a new asshole with my own visceral vocabulary, elevating his rage, turning his fangs upon me.

He reared back and punched my mouth.

I smiled tasting blood on my teeth, counting five witnesses in the parking lot, and memorizing his truck's license plate. The permanent slur on the bigot's criminal record? Worth the quick punch of pain.

You're going to do what no one does better. Bring the fight to you. Bait Mason into a trap so alluring he'll think the snap around his neck is a harlot's hug.

A knock on the hotel door penetrated through the bathroom door.

It was Kierra and time to put this bullshit aside. For now.

After big hugs, we sat on the sofa with room service trays. Thankfully, I'd ordered soup. No way my stomach would tolerate more. Slurping spoonfuls of tomato comfort and taking bites of a baguette quickly nourished me back to strength.

"So, Daniel's room is just next door?" Kierra's berry lips grinned, emerald eyes watching me. "And he wouldn't stop smiling today. All daydreamy through our interviews. Wonder what's on his mind?"

Reap what you sow. You taught her to observe and now you're busted.

"Kierra Williams, I'm so proud. How'd you assess it?"

"I knew it!" Kierra squealed. "I caught him smiling at you on set when he thought you weren't looking. And he avoided you too much. I knew he was hiding something."

She leaned closer. "I'm almost as good as you, using my eyes and instincts."

Kierra paused, then confessed, "You know… it was a girl crush on Daniel. That's why I told you months back that he made me nervous. I mean, who doesn't fancy him? But Daniel feels like a dad to me now. Not that you're old, but —" Kierra stopped.

We roared at the insult she desperately tried not to commit.

"Can I have another badass woman like you on my protection next season?"

"Oh, Taneesha is a badass," I assured her. If the studio approved it, she'd be perfect for Kierra.

We exchanged more hugs, knowing we'd be texting all things Harry Styles and TikTok dances over the coming months.

When we stood, saying goodbye in the doorway, Rob and Joaquin flanked the entrance from the hall. I gave them hugs, cherishing their secret too.

Rob and Joaquin were a couple.

I'd watched from the sidelines. Smiles that lingered. Hands that brushed. Words that toyed. My colleagues' friendship had grown into rich love. A pull they couldn't resist. A rule they broke at work. Just like Daniel and me. It bonded us couples even more.

If schedules worked, they'd make a vacation visit to my home later this summer.

Thinking farewells were done, a warm hand grab mine, turning my gaze back.

"I want to thank you, Charlie. For everything." Tears welled in Kierra's eyes. "For making me brave. For making me fight back. For saving me yesterday. For this whole past season. I wouldn't have made it without you."

Fuck, I almost lost it right. Emotions had gurgled up my throat the whole day. The muscles in my neck tensed, stuffing it down. I'd always be strong for Kierra.

I squeezed her hand back. "No thanks needed, chica. If not for Mason's bullshit, I wouldn't have met you or Daniel. So, it's a fair trade."

"Will I see you back in Madrid next year with Daniel?" Kierra reached for one more hug.

I held her back praying the words were true. "Yes, you will."

CHAPTER SEVEN

CHARLIE

Forever by Labrinth

A drop swelled then tapered from the tip of my finger. I watched its graceful fall, transfixing my troubled mind.

This whirlpool bath was the only body of water I could find stuck in a hotel room.

In three hours, a car would whisk Daniel and me from this hotel to a charter flight, to another hotel. All controlled. All secured spaces. All trapping us in a luxurious prison, keeping us safe.

A hesitant rap hit the door. "Can I join you?" A voice crooned from the other side.

The fact this the man didn't understand he could do more than enter our bathroom... he could take up residence in my every molecule.

He already did.

My one certain joy waited to enter. "Anytime," I called back.

My memory documented the sight but couldn't capture the visceral moment.

How his presence invaded the room. Slowly stripping down. Curves and carves of shredded muscles. A perfect measure of dark masculine hair groomed down his tall torso. A face impossibly beautiful with a tender smile for me. An impressive cock hardening for me too.

Naked of everything, he climbed into the tub behind me.

I anchored between his thighs, nestling my body back into his while water threatened to overflow the tub. My hands memorized the ridges and rise of the muscles across his thighs.

Either side of any ocean, he was my home.

"Please tell me, babe." His question lulled over my damp ear. "I know something's troubling you."

Which was worse? Hurting someone with the truth? Or lying to protect them from it?

Most say truth is best. Most don't know the capacity of its pain. But I'd been plummeted into its hell multiple times already.

Truth was overrated.

"I meant it, Charlie. You don't have to go the premiere with me." His palm soothed over my hair. "I don't need a PR statement or to be Instagram official to affirm that I love you, that we're together."

"It's not that." Drops from my fingertip fell onto his kneecap. "It's just that all my life I sought training, rules, and protocol." I started weaving trails up his thigh, making his dark leg hair form wet waves after my path. "Once my parents died, I needed some form of control. I was too young, too naive to know that the military offered a paradox of control *in* chaos."

His grasp gently stopped my hand, lifting it to his lips. It wasn't an interruption. It was an invitation to share more.

I confessed half my truth. "But as of today, I control nothing. It all feels like chaos. I know nothing about the next few days, weeks, or even months of my life, except that I love you." Swirling over his torso, I turned, hugging his center. "And I'm afraid because I'm completely at the mercy of fate." My lips pressed against his chest, damp with his taste and bathwater. "And all the times I was here in the past, I lost the loves of my life."

His knuckle lifted my chin. "Charlie Ravenel, I swear to you, I know we can't control everything." I surveyed the oath from his lips to the promise in his eyes. "But please know that nothing can control how much I love you."

His lips pleaded for mine to meet his journey. Our deep kiss. Our promise. Taking us over. Bathwater lapped the edges of the tub, splashing down to the tile floor.

He sat up, cradling my jaw and lifting me up. He took more with his tongue intimately lingering over mine, sending sweet shocks down my body, pooling heat between my thighs.

This had been one of the most terrifying days. And all I wanted now, needed now, was him. All hell could break loose, but if we had this, our love and bodies, we could endure it all.

His strong hands seized my ribs, lifting my breast up to meet the tip of his tongue. Its heat traced wet circles over my cool, pebbled nipple. Then his mouth engulfed my tender flesh with hot breath and a perfect, hard sucking pressure, making me cry out, arching for more as he took the other.

His dark waves traveled across the valley between, lavishing back and forth while his warm hands sailed paths across my cooling flesh, forcing my moans at his journey thrilling every inch of my skin.

My hand plunged in the water, grasping his cock bobbing for me. Stroking what I craved so much, my thighs spread, ready to sink down on him.

But he said, "No, babe, I want to drink you," pulling me up to kneel on his massive buttressing shoulders. They rested against the back of the tub while I balanced my body, emerging from the water, bracing my palms against the tile surround.

God, what a sight.

How he cupped my ass cheeks, his grip spreading me open to him, guiding me down to perch over his mouth. Drops of water chilled my rising flesh matching the sensation of the cool air he blew over my clit before the heat of his tongue took it.

Oh fuck, he did it so well, igniting me even more while he toyed, rattling his tongue across the sensitive nub before delivering a firm suck. I cried out again. His long, firm swipes turned into a culling and curling torrent, licking and dipping into my pleasure. Then his thick fingers flexed into my walls with merciless plunges, dragging me to the edge.

Looking down, the vision of it, of his mouth claiming me. It made me sink down, burying him, his muffled moans of delight vibrating through my folds. As if Daniel didn't need air. As if he wanted to only breathe me, desperately inhaling me in before exhaling hot groans into me for more.

A spasm ripped my control. I heaved through its gush over his tongue, his lips, his chin. He lapped up more of me before I let go, sliding down him, mixing my lust with the bathwater.

Splashes and grabs. Lifting me up. Carrying me to the bed. I didn't remember how we got here, but he was on top, clasping my wrists above my head, cuffed together under his sweet grasp while his strong knees splayed me open.

"You're so beautiful like this." He held me here, his strength, his weight, I could take it. "So pink and full and ready for me."

Good God, I was pulsing for him, and he was right here, savoring the sight.

"So are you," I said at his beauty mounted above me. The heft of his erect cock, his insane body, his exquisite face —he was a masterpiece. "Tease me. Make me beg for you."

Lurid fascination took his face. Gliding his tip up and down, through my slick folds, the ache was maddening. I lifted my hips, needing more but he kept playing, pulling back. "Is this what you want, Charlie?"

More than anything.

Have him.

Fuck him.

Love him.

I'd do it all.

Wedging his fat crown in, he barely stroked inside, exciting my entrance, my body thrashing for more. "Are you going to beg for my thick cock?" Pressing in, he teased me, holding right there, pumping, lightly smacking into my lust.

"Yes." With the thrust of my hips, I grabbed for more. "Please, Daniel."

He pulled all the way out, leaving me desperate. "Beg me to fuck the hell out of you, Charlie."

It suddenly hit me, "Daniel, please." It cried out from my heart, my beg morphing into a vulnerability so deep, only he could fill it. It was more than lust. I could hear it in my voice. So could he. I loved him. Always.

His face softened. A groan left his throat as he entered, his eyes enraptured watching my face as his body curved with slow dives into my depths, pushing gasps over our lips with each plunge. He put his lips to mine. We fused, stirring our breath together along with my tangy taste secured by his tongue, swirling over mine.

The clean musk of his lust, as he held my arms overhead, it softly wisped down, marking my senses. The tickle of his soft chest hair across my nipples tensed them to his touch. The urge flexed our torsos together, melding us into the same motion.

The intensity of it, with his gaze on mine, it rushed a convergence of emotion through me. There was no time before, time when I'd lost everything. And no time from now... to hope for anything.

It was only this, with him, the moment shared almost painful to the point of beautiful.

"I promise, Charlie." His breath rolled shallow over his lips, suspended and ready, waiting for me, swearing it all. He clutched my hands—not letting go. "You won't lose me."

Yes, he held me in an unrelenting hold, over my heart, over my pleasure. With one hand still clasping me here, the other lifted my leg over his shoulder, his body urging even deeper into me.

It lured me out, open only to him. To his aqua eyes watching me succumb. To his heft, grinding over my clit. To his hard, stretching thrill all the way inside.

With the lift of my hips at that perfect angle, his generous cock hit the deepest spot in my core, delivering overwhelming strikes against its exquisite sensitivity. Each one thrashing me up, and up, and up to an aching peak, my breath clinging to the verge.

The stare in his eyes saw me dangling there. Filling his lungs, he gave a savage pump of his cock shoving me over.

"Daniel! Please!" It snapped each vertebra in my spine, wringing every tissue in my body so tight until all released, shaking with a sudden throbbing shower over his cock.

He clenched his teeth, groaning back his release, swearing, "I'll never stop fucking you, Charlie." Pounding even faster, making my pussy relish his force, he insisted, "You're going to come so wet for me again."

Yes, I was, the craze of it charging across my nerves.

He let go of my hand, curving over top of me and crushing his lips to my ear. "Do it, Charlie. I'm yours. Mark me up so fucking hard."

I ripped my fear and love across his backside. The primal moan from him, at the pain he begged me for, at his flesh scratched deep underneath my fingernails, it dropped me down again. Twisting my neck open, vulnerable for his bite, my orgasm owned all my senses and the one squeezing tight around him.

With a soft sink of his teeth into my flesh, he groaned. No pain, only pleasure as my walls felt his thick cock pulsing.

"Charlie," his sigh replaced his gentle bite. He was too strong, taking control of our embrace, twisting our bodies to where his wrapped around mine too. "I promise you won't lose me."

Something. What? Held us here. Clinging to each other. My face cradled in his neck to this truth. To finally having love again with him?

It forced a stream of tears from my eyes.

For a hunt to be successful, you study what you track.

How they migrate, when they move, when they rest, even what they eat. Their entire day to their seasonal habits etches into your brain.

Regardless, the best place—often the only place—to hunt is in public. Though it presents additional challenges to the effort, the reward is grand.

You obsess over the terrain. You know every site they may seek cover, where they hide and what baits them out.

The whole world knows where they are now. Comic-Con in San Diego, California.

And with one click, I can find where they're going next.

The *Swipe Right* movie premiere in Manhattan.

A smirk soothes from my lips to my finger sliding over the touchpad of the laptop, searching, sure of one thing that always tempts prey into the open.

The rut.

The frenzied mating season that entices the game, day and night.

So overcome by their animal biology, by their physical desire, they forget their mind. Desire dulls their instinct keeping them safe.

Every cell in their bodies is focused on their union, binding the mates together, offering the hunter two showy targets... if your kill is ambitious.

Mine certainly is.

CHAPTER EIGHT

CHARLIE

Colleen pulled the strings on our lives one final time.

Our private charter overnight to New York was a rare flight I actually slept on. A luxury car met us, whisking us from the airport to the Lotte Towers at the New York Palace—a convenient Midtown Manhattan location for Daniel's premiere and press junket.

Colleen booked the Champagne Suite, spoiling Daniel one last time before he transitioned to Elaine, who waited there, ready to take over.

Before we left San Diego, Colleen made sure Logan MacGregor's London office had my measurements for a dress for the premiere. Daniel was the fashion designer's menswear brand ambassador, making Logan thrill at the opportunity to style both Daniel and his date.

Logan insisted on talking to me for inspiration, saying he had to know more than my measurements. While we flew to New York, Logan flew a suit to Daniel and two gowns to me, arranging for his New York glam team to adorn us for the event.

A world premiere? It kept cracking through my nerves. Indeed, it would be. Of Daniel's film and my life for all to scope.

Dawn filled the sky when we arrived. We soaked in the view from our multi-level suite over the skyline. After a shower, we hid under yummy white sheets for a long nap until the Pearl Jam song on Daniel's phone alarm woke us. Him, for his first interview, and me, for a master plan of my own.

For our escape to my secluded world—Daufuskie Island, South Carolina.

Two months before, the idea of Daniel on my home island washed a tide of terror through me. Hell, the idea of walking a red carpet with him shot through my mind with a percussive, "NO!".

Now, in the absence of choice and in the presence of love, I forced it to feel right.

My lips brushed Daniel's goodbye. The heavy click of the suite door closing behind him found me going for my phone.

The call I had to make suddenly flushed my heart with an unfamiliar joy.

Hovering my fingertip over the names on my **Favorites** contacts, **Pop/Evelyn** appeared at the top of the list.

Their names on the screen brought it all back. How I'd never known a day alive when they weren't around.

When I buried my parents, Pop and Evelyn buried their best friends. They swooped into my life as my almost-parents ever since.

Few memories survived from the week of my parents' funerals. They died in a plane crash. My dad was an incredible pilot, flying with my mom on frequent visits to Miami. But the fuel system in their plane had had a defect.

"Defect."

I hated that one little fucking word. So small. But big enough to take down many lives.

The week after my parents' deaths was a blur of tears and shock. At eighteen, all I recalled from the hell of it was Pop's sanctuary hug, his Old Spice aftershave wafting around me. And Evelyn's silky brown hand, holding mine, strong and glistening with Palmer's coconut lotion.

They'd never wavered since, blanketing me with love like I was their own flesh and blood.

It gripped my throat, telling them about Daniel over the phone.

"I know I made y'all worry all this time about me, like I'd always be alone. But he was worth the wait. Y'all are gonna love him, I promise."

"I'm sure we will." Evelyn's soft assurance was salve over my heart. Hearing the tremor in Evelyn's voice, I cried too. "We just want you happy and safe."

Pop said he'd watch Daniel's movies that week. Not one for screens, he preferred books or the boat, but he needed to know the man with his little girl.

"We'll have the house ready for you," Evelyn said. "I just worry; you sure you're ready for this, Minnow? This is a big step. Might bring up some things for you."

Evelyn worried about more than me bringing Daniel home. I knew. She was asking about that—my PTSD. How my attacks and paranoia could flip my world upside down.

It was bad when I first came home after Afghanistan. Evelyn had nurtured me through many episodes.

"I'll be fine. Please don't worry," I said, all while worrying myself.

How I did have another episode in Madrid, the one that went viral, exposing me to the world. How I didn't tell Daniel this was just the tip of the iceberg.

I had much more terror I couldn't control beneath.

And never would I confess this to him.

He'd question my sanity.

When that call ended, something else washed ashore. Another wave of concern.

If I went home, followed there by one of Mason's *White Flag* fanatics, they could find my extended family. Our lack of a shared name protected them. But if we were spotted together on the island? It would risk the ones I loved, giving Mason's sick shits more innocent targets.

But what are you going to do?

You can't hide in a hotel forever, though it's damn fun trying. Besides, home has advantages. Lots of them. Like your rifle.

I had to take the risk. Better to hunt or be hunted on your own terrain than vulnerable in an unfamiliar landscape.

Daniel returned in time for a lavish room-service dinner. The butler had set the dining room table like a holiday feast, brimming with the Italian dishes Daniel loved.

He updated me on his afternoon taping for a night show. How he had joked with the host, telling stories about antics filming *Swipe Right*, then teasing the second season of *The Druid*.

"Any questions about me or Mason?" I asked through slurps of squid ink pasta.

Daniel sipped his wine before answering, "Not yet."

Guilt clutched my ribs. Like I was cheating on him. Like I was having a twisted affair with Mason. A ridiculous notion. Daniel was the only man I wanted, yes, God, in every way.

But I *was* lying by not telling him about the texts so far. And the one I'd received today.

Unknown
Stroking hard strangling
thoughts of you right now

Mason's lewd reference to his masturbating fantasies made me retch.

Yes, Mason was a hot man. But his beauty reeked with malice. His evil mind was brewing up something lethal, I knew.

"Did you make your calls home? Get it all sorted for us?" Daniel's questions stopped my death train of thoughts.

"Yep. Prepare *not* to be spoiled, Daniel Pierce." A napkin dabbed my guilt temporarily away. "We'll be roughing it compared to the oceanside luxury you're accustomed to. The fanciest structure we have on the island is an abandoned beach resort that's haunted."

"Can we sneak in? I've always wanted to have haunted house sex."

"Ew. I'll fuck you in many places, but a haunted hotel is not one of them."

"Speaking of fucking in different places. I got a call from my mum today."

"How the hell did your mind go from fucking in kinky locations to a call from your mom?"

My crass question made him toss his chin up, laughing.

"Sorry. Missed a mental step. In thinking of fucking in different places, I thought of my new home, of you and me inaugurating it. Then I remembered the call from home, from my mum. We couldn't chat long, but she phoned to tell me that my brother and his husband are bringing their daughter home tomorrow."

Daniel had shared with me months before how they awaited the birth of their daughter via surrogate. She would be the first niece and granddaughter for the Pierce family, making all excited for her arrival.

"I know the plan is to go straight to your home when we're done here." His fingertips, buffed with a gentlemen's manicure while veins popped across his sinewed forearms, reached out for mine. "But would you be willing to make a quick trip home with me? To meet my niece and family first?"

Hell to the No!

I wanted to hide forever with him. On terrain I controlled. On a very small island I could surveil for incoming threats with near-perfect aim.

The last thing I wanted was to fly from this fucking island of millions to another island of millions where all would be searching for us by the end of the week.

But, Charlie Girl, the way he's looking at you? He could broker permanent peace across warring nations.

"Okay."

No turning down his grateful hand, pulling me up, leading our path to the bedroom.

I'd make sure he showed his appreciation well this night.

CHAPTER NINE

DANIEL

"What's today?" Charlie tempted under the thin bedsheet hiding everything I craved.

Like I didn't hate a grueling press junket enough. Having to leave her to do it? I really resented it now.

All I wanted to do was crawl back into bed with her and inch by inch peel back the sheet with a trail of kisses and never leave.

But discipline won out like it always did.

I didn't get this far, in this shape, with this industry status without an almost manic level of sacrifice. Snapping the white button-up off the hanger from the rack of clothes my stylist had sent over, I donned threads tailored specifically for me.

"I start the press junket downstairs this afternoon, and have a cover interview this morning with *GQ* at the

Baccarat. Scott, my publicist, he put this on the boil months back. Since the Logan MacGregor fiasco, I have to answer for that bloody mess."

My eyes flicked up at hers.

Fuck, Pierce. Why did you bring that up?

She knew the exact mess I mentioned. It broke us up for a month. Why?

Because Logan and I got plastered before Logan's fashion preview party in London, and my ex-girlfriend, Kathy, had circled on the red carpet there, waiting for me to appear.

Kathy worked for the same PR firm that repped me. She was the account director for Logan's brand. It was how I met her.

For two years we were hot and cold, most of which was me admittedly jerking her around. I was never in love with her. I just didn't want to be alone.

And she was convenient, embedded in the industry, understanding my world, and most of the time not demanding more than what already ripped away pieces of me.

I had arrived at Logan's party that night pissed drunk, aching over Charlie who was having cold feet about our secret relationship. And Kathy had wrapped around me in my drunken haze. In her grasp, I lost time and place, barely remembering the sodding mess.

The embarrassing debacle went viral. My red eyes and lips on Kathy matching the red carpet. My hands grabbing her bum with a smirk for the cameras.

But once we were inside the hall, while Kathy professed her love for me, I remembered myself, and who I truly loved... Charlie.

The soft lines on Charlie's face now told me the past reference didn't trouble her. "Is there a photoshoot for the interview too?"

"Not yet." I looped a black leather belt into my jeans. "We're getting that sorted. I was supposed to stay next week for it, but after Mason, plans changed."

She sat up, her blonde mane tousled from last night's fervid fuck, holding the sheet to her chest like she had to be modest in front of me. Fuck, it was beyond seductive, another bloody gesture making me want to abandon it all for her.

"Daniel, I don't want you shirking your obligations because of me. We can stay here longer."

"It's fine. If we are off to London next week, maybe we can do something there. Logan wants to feature his new Savile Row store anyway." My foot wedged into one black leather Chelsea boot, then the other. "If you don't mind, of course."

"Me? Mind?" Her cute chin tilted to the side. "I'm riding the Daniel Pierce train now, remember? You're in control."

I laughed back. "That's bollocks! I control nothing about Charlie Ravenel." The temptation too strong; I leaned over for a kiss. "But I'll be back for a quick lunch. Will you ride my train then?"

She grinned back, inches from my lips. "All aboard."

THE DRIVER PULLED into the underground parking lot of the Baccarat Hotel. Simon, my guard, got out before opening the door for me. Scott, my publicist, met us in the lobby of the hotel. An easy introduction to the reporter was made before we turned in the direction of the Grand Salon for our reserved seating nook.

I took five steps across the lobby of the hotel and—

"Excuse me, aren't you Daniel Pierce?" A forty-something woman in stylish yoga apparel approached. "I'm so sorry to interrupt, but my husband and son are big fans."

I gave the slight gesture to Simon—a low right-hand brush. This was okay.

"Thank you very much." I stopped. "I appreciate that."

"I feel like such an idiot, but can I get a quick video?" Her phone was already in her hand, aiming for my face. "It's my son's twelfth birthday next week. It'd be the best present for him."

I gave a birthday greeting to the camera on her phone. Then a quick thanks and turn away. I knew better than to linger.

The interview went over time. Scott gave the reporter a polite one-hour notice, but I answered more questions. Really, I hoped to explain away my cringe-worthy bender in London and later in Menorca where we were filming.

To the reporter, I chalked it up to blowing off steam through a hectic production and a joking love for Spanish rum.

Not true.

It was a destructive pity party I had over missing Charlie, fearing I'd lost her forever to the Kathy quasi betrayal.

I wrapped up the interview with a sense of humor, sharing how I'd sworn off rum in preparation for the grueling training regimen for my next role.

Over ninety minutes later, it was time to depart. Simon escorted me to the main entrance of the hotel. The driver had to meet us on Fifty-Third Street. The entrance to the underground parking deck was temporarily blocked by fire trucks responding to an alarm at the steakhouse next door.

The second my boots hit the public pavement under the black cantilevered stone awning shouts erupted.

"Daniel! Daniel!"

Necks snapped left.

A group of fans, five women, and two men, stalked by the front of the hotel.

Fuck, Pierce. Your yoga fan inside dropped a #danielpierce *location pin on you.*

Simon pounced, taking position between me and the approaching group. There were no barricades to stop them. A luxury black sedan waited for us, idling on the street. The distance was too far, a rude dismissal if I didn't say hello.

I stopped, mid-sidewalk, giving them what they wanted: autographs, selfies, and waves for videos. Simon kept covertly pushing me along, moving me closer to the awaiting safety of the car.

"Hey, man, I'm such a big fan," the biggest guy proclaimed, lurching for me, snaking his arm around my shoulder with a phone in his other hand.

Something about his approach. The snap of his reach. The control he tried wresting over me.

Heat fired my pulse up.

Simon caught it too, wedging the guy off me. The fan resisted. Both my elbow and Simon's hands had to push him off, creating an inertia that made both me and the fan stumble back like bowling pins to Simon's polite strike between us.

"Thank you." I waved, covering the last couple meters to the car quickly with Simon sheltering behind. "Fuck's sake," I huffed once we found safety in the waiting car.

We glanced back. The group of fans stood, noses down, posting the quick spectacle to social media.

One #danielpierce and instantly... millions would see it.

CHAPTER TEN

DANIEL

My heart rate calmed as the elevator rose to our suite.

Charlie had texted me; she was enjoying the hotel gym. Wishes of joining her were futile. We couldn't be spotted together yet.

The butler service had lunch out. I loaded up a plate with salad and steak before heading to the terrace.

Two bites in and I phoned my mum back with the good news. I was coming home.

And not alone.

She spent the first five minutes gushing over the arrival of my niece. Baby Adelaide was home with her dads and doing well.

"Those two won't know sleep for years." My mum chuckled. "When are you here, love? I'm gathering everyone round."

"Let's do something at my home," I offered. "I'll phone ahead, have it ready. We get into London Sunday morning."

"We?" The lilt of my mum's voice rang up.

"Yes. I'm bringing someone home that I want you all to meet."

"Does she have a name?"

Her tone made me grin. "Yes. Her name is Charlotte Ravenel. I met her on set this past February, and we've been together since. She's here in New York with me now."

"Daniel." She exhaled my name with a beaten sigh. "Can we *not* simply have a family gathering with no girlfriends? Need I remind you of the last one you brought round? She botched the whole thing."

No, I didn't need reminding. And yes, she made it sound like I brought stray pets home that pissed on the rug. I didn't blame her.

The most recent drama?

When I brought Kathy to my father's birthday party the year before. At first, Kathy seemed at ease. An hour passed before I noticed how Kathy didn't offer help. Even when all prepped for the party, she sat, drinking wine, speaking only about herself. And she kept clinging to me like a bloody life jacket on the Titanic.

Later, Kathy commented on my mum's wedding ring. How it looked like an estate piece. It was. From my father's family in York. Then Kathy asked aloud if there were more Pierce estate rings to be placed on fingers.

The disapproving glances from my entire family had sliced my way, their glares silently wondering why the bloody hell I was with this woman.

That was the beginning of the end.

It took me another six months to steal away from her. Another few months, after meeting Charlie, to finally confront Kathy, confessing it was done long before.

"Mum, I promise. I know my taste has been questionable in the past. But not this time. You're going to love Charlie."

"Do you?"

"Yes. More than I ever imagined possible."

"Have you said so to her?"

"Yes, a ridiculous number of times a day. I love her, Mum. So much."

"All right, then." I knew that tone too. She was smiling on the other end. "This is new. I can hear it in your voice. She's more than welcome."

"Can we plan for a party next Tuesday? Everyone at my house?"

"I'm Gran, so, yes, all will be there when I summon them."

I dusted off the rest of my lunch while we planned the details.

The July heat had me venturing back inside where I sat surrounded by two stories of glass. Here I called upon my team to prepare for the party and trip. All while something gnawed at me.

What Colleen had said. How I needed to tell Charlie about my past.

I did.

I was about to fly home with her, descending into generations of a wonderful family but not great moments of mine. Some my own foolish fault. Some the price of celebrity life.

But how did you tell the one you love, "Oh, by the way, this is how I cocked up in the past. Horribly. Oh, and this is how fucked up my life can be. Insanely. But ignore it and love me anyway"?

It was like telling a new houseguest to ignore the dead body propped up in a chair, rotting in the corner. Impossible.

The click of the hotel door snapped my chin up, ending my last call. I expected to see a smiling face appear.

Instead, anger marched in and across her beautiful face. Not even the sexy black leggings and sports bra she had on kept me from noticing shoulder blades wrenched up to her ears in fury.

Charlie Ravenel wasn't a yeller. She didn't do temper and drama. That I was thankful for.

Though maybe this was worse.

Her rage was an iceberg, 10 percent above you could see, 90 percent below you should fear, the entire mass of it wrecking your world.

She stood stoic, silence freezing the molecules around us.

First play? She made it mine.

"Babe, what's wrong?"

Only her chin moved, slightly up, and challenging me. "Tell me how that happened today."

What was she talking about? Then I remembered. Who I loved. How she was wired. And how my life was never private in a public space, #danielpierce stalking my every move.

Clearly, she saw it on social media. How fans had swarmed me outside the hotel. And the eager one who got too close.

"We handled it," I said. "The garage was blocked by fire trucks, so we had to leave through the main entrance."

"Why didn't someone run advance and notice they were out there waiting for you?"

"It was me and Simon. Scott too. We walked out together and there they were."

She shook her head. "You need at least two on your

detail, Daniel. One for advance and one for cover. That shit could've gone sideways so fast."

"No, Charlie. I'm not walking round with an entourage of muscle around me. I'm not running for bloody office. And look at me. I can protect myself."

"Not here, Daniel." The strain in her voice rose. "This isn't London or Madrid. He could've had a gun."

Wisdom told me to parse the situation. Quick.

Yes, she was right. Here in the States guns were a risk. But I knew how to be safe.

Yes, it was her job. One she couldn't turn off, especially since three bullets hit her years ago in Afghanistan. It made her sensitive. I respected that, but I wouldn't overreact.

She grew impatient with my silent reasoning. "You take too many risks, Daniel." Plopping down on the sofa opposite me, she pressed her fingertips to her temples.

"You let them get too close. When you're not working, you go out with no protection. And when it's a public event? You're reaching over stanchions. Getting too close for selfies. Hell, I've seen video of arms grabbing for you. And you relent, giving hugs. Do you not realize a threat could be one person behind that fan? What they could do to you in a quick second with a knife or worse?"

"Charlie, I respect it's your job to see it that way. But I have mine too. I can't simply stroll past a rope line of fans and not stop and do the dance—the autographs, the greetings, the photos—it's part of the job."

"Yes, but you do it more than others. I love that about you, how kind you are with everyone, but damn, it's too much. You have no idea what's waiting out there for us."

Her voice panicked, like she blurted something she shouldn't.

"What do you mean, 'Waiting for *us*'? Are we talking

about my fans, or something else?" Something on her face. Brow tensed down. "What are you scared of, Charlie?"

"Everything." Her gaze cast out the window. "This is what I meant by not being in control. If you were my mark to protect, it'd be me and Rob on your detail at the least." Her eyes wouldn't meet mine. "I'm scared for both of us. Once everyone knows about us... shit will go down so fast our heads will fucking spin. We must change how we do things. Now." Her marine eyes shot back at me. "Trust me."

My palms opened, willing to hear her out. "Then what do you propose?"

"When we fly, we use private charters or the VIP service. No way we walk through a public terminal. When we can, we use Simon and other hired detail. I can be backup, but only if you listen to me. Don't protect me like a girlfriend. I know it's your instinct but shove it down along with your ego and let me do my job. I can help cover us both, at least for private trips. And no more stopping for fans in public. It's too risky when locations get dropped, and then we're fucked."

"All right. That's reasonable, to a degree. I know what you can do. Just know that I will pound someone's head to mash if they hurt you."

"Fair." The muscles across her frame relaxed. "For the premiere, you need Simon and one more detail on the rope line. Stay two feet back. No more side hugs for selfies. You're in New York, not London. Be extra careful."

A premiere she would attend with me, the thought filling me with pride. It calmed our confrontation into an understanding, respecting each other's jobs. Especially with the way she was determined, not dramatic.

I stood up, in awe of her expertise. It drew me nearer.

To her. "Any other commands I must submit to, Ms. Ravenel?"

Fuck, it turned me on. How badass she was. How protective she was over me. How I did indeed know she was a formidable force, small and lethal, like a dose of ricin poison in water. One drop of her and you were down.

I certainly was. For her. For whatever she demanded. Especially when she looked so fucking fit with her commands, anger diluting to desire upon my approach, lording over her.

She grinned up at me. This argument was done. Passion cracked the air around us now.

Leaning back on the black leather sofa like Chief Executive Fucktress, coolly bossing me around, she said, "Take off your pants, Pierce."

The tip of her tongue trailed across her back teeth; lips parted. A destination I desired. Now.

We knew we'd find my hard appreciation of her rule when my trousers and briefs met my ankles.

I started unbuttoning his shirt. "Unbutton it, but leave it all on," she insisted.

Her fetish for half-clothed sex drove me wild, like we were too starved for each other to even undress. Most of the time, it was true.

She demanded, "Kneel over me."

My knees sank into the sofa cushions, straddling her face, the heavy length of me throbbing inches from her petal-pink lips. The sight of her gorgeous face, innocent freckles with those devil eyes and this sexy blonde ponytail in front of my cock—it was porn-worthy.

"Are you going to cover me now, Charlie? With this naughty, wet mouth of yours?"

The wicked smile on her lips took it next level. "Keep talking dirty to me, Daniel, and find out."

And I did. Through moans at her tongue teasing up my shaft, through her tight, dripping descent down to my base, through the filthy words from my mouth dropping equally inspired.

"Do you like sucking my cock, Charlie?" Talk about a rhetorical question. The vigorous pump of her fist and lavish of her tongue answered over and over. It wasn't words in her reply I craved. "Show me how much you like it, babe. How much you love sucking me off."

With a lift of her hips, she pulled her leggings down before fingering herself, making the sound of her slick smack of lust hit my ears. I about lost it. Fucking her mouth while she moaned, my praise grew lewd.

"I love fucking your tight little mouth and pussy, Charlie. You're so fucking naughty about it, aren't you?" She snatched my hand, moaning, guiding it to grab her ponytail. "Yes, babe. You're so fucking fit and naughty for me."

The sight controlled me while she let me control her deep *gluck* and gentle gag drooling over my cock.

"Bloody hell, you do this so well." How she could take me, almost down to my base, I didn't know, but it ravaged me, every thick inch. "Makes me want to fuck every part of you, Charlie."

With a hard shove, she pushed her leggings down over her knees. The plunge of her hand between her spreading thighs jerked harder, telling me she wanted it too. I'd claimed her pussy and her mouth. One more tight hole remained. Next, I'd beg for it to be mine too.

The promise of it, and the pleasure now, it shook tremors across my lips, down through the muscles in my abs, my thighs. I was close, so fucking close, panting, and holding back. But not without her. Never.

"Come on, Charlie."

She gazed up at me. Fuck, the pleasure she moaned with, giving it to me, just like I did to her. It was a goddamn opiate in the veins between us, always lusting for more of each other. Her eyes threatened to close at the weight of it.

"You like my cock in your mouth, don't you? I can hear it. I can see it too. It's on your fingers fucking your sweet, wet pussy like my cock's going to fuck you so hard tonight. I'll fuck you so long, Charlie, I'll make your pussy rain your cum all over me."

My words took us. Her eyelids dropped, moans vibrating over my shaft while her back arched with an orgasm spilling over her hand and the sofa.

I bellowed "Oh fuck!" at my spurts rocketing into her mouth. She swallowed so much of my lust that my cream escaped over her lips. As I recovered my breath, her generous mouth kept adoring my satisfied length with tender kisses.

"Don't ever doubt me, Daniel Pierce." She leaned back, mouth glistening with my cum, grinning because she was right. "I've always got you covered."

ANONYMOUS

It's too easy, hunting people online. It erases the fun.

In fact, it seems there aren't many people who don't have a toe in the digital sand.

But her? She's a challenge and not easy to find. There's nothing on her.

Ah, this makes her such an alluring target. How she hides. How she resists exposure, like she's afraid of it.

She makes the hunt thrilling.

Him, on the other hand? Millions of footprints. He craves attention. It's easy following his trail, knowing his next step.

The pattern is clear—track him to find her.

Like a buck to a doe when the mating begins, he is locked down to her and won't leave her side.

Daniel Pierce is one magnificent stag with a showy rack, a prize leading directly to the smaller target I scope for.

CHAPTER ELEVEN

CHARLIE

Love Again by Dua Lipa

We went to bed early for obvious reasons. Afterwards, Daniel collapsed into slumber. So did I... until something woke me hours later. Tomorrow. The premiere.

My mother used to say you can't jump halfway off a cliff.

Well, I was about to take a running leap off the rim of the Grand Canyon in a matter of hours. A fall sure to kill, even if the journey down was majestic.

Months before, I'd had that nightmare. When Daniel and I were on vacation in the Seychelles.

He'd grabbed my shoulder, snatching me out of sleep, out of the terror. He told me I was kicking his shins, gripping the sheets, and crying out. When he asked what it was, it wasn't my usual nightmares of war.

That nightmare was of bright white lights, holding Daniel's hand, letting it go, and falling. Falling, certain I'd never get back up.

Tomorrow I'd step into that terror, holding Daniel's hand under the deluge of blinding light.

My mind couldn't take the premonition.

Because I had already fallen. Once to three bullets. Twice to love. What more could possibly happen?

Heart thumping, pulse racing, I lay perfectly still in a lush bed beside the gorgeous man I loved.

Can you believe the fucking irony? You're living every woman's dream.

Yet for you... it's pure hell. Well, half hell. Not him, just his life.

Sleep mocked me now, the nerves firing through my limbs its accomplice.

Sliding out from under his arms, I grabbed my sneakers and socks off the floor, plucking up leggings and a sports bra tossed on the chair from our evening romp.

I got dressed in the bathroom. Grabbing one of Daniel's T-shirts off the bathroom vanity, I put it over me like a short dress. Yanking my hair back in a ponytail, I slipped our door fob into the small pocket in my leggings, and quietly snuck out.

Agitation paced me like a caged leopard, growling to escape as the elevator lowered, floor by floor. I had to get the hell out of here, at least for an hour.

The night concierge in the lobby offered a polite greeting. For safety's sake, I told him I was going for a run, to expect me back in an hour. The doorman did his job with a generous smile.

And I took off, running up Madison Avenue, starting at Fifty-First Street, gunning for at least twenty blocks, if not more. However far it took to escape this fucking feeling.

On a Tuesday night in Manhattan, no, the city never sleeps, but chaos quieted at the late hour. Restaurants closed. Sidewalks emptied of the working crowds moving like cattle across the concrete strips during the day.

My breath took cadence with the pound of my sneakers on the pavement. Thoughts intruded. I shoved each away. But one I couldn't shake. It returned at the end of each block.

Mason Hunt.

In the past three days, my phone lit up with over fifteen texts from **Unknown**. Most were annoying. A couple were specific. Hints to the identity of the digital stalker blowing up my device.

The ones this afternoon while I sweated in the hotel gym? They taunted me. Another reason why I put my fist down with Daniel about his security.

Unknown
Which do you prefer?
White, red, or black?

Unknown
Tough call. Right?
All big scores

Fucking asshole, referencing paper targets to sight a firearm, and referencing hair. My blonde mop with sun-bleached white streaks. Kierra's red waterfall of strands. Or Daniel's black waves and signature tendril.

You know which you prefer, Charlie Girl.

Mason's pretty-boy face in the sight of your rifle. You never miss the shot, bull's-eye through that bastard.

Fury had me sprinting, occasional faces blurring by. Taxis and cars honked in the distance. All I could hear? My rhythmic inhale, cycling in through my nostrils, flowing out of my mouth.

I'd been checking Mason's Instagram and Twitter. Three times a day. No need since I put notifications on his account, but my obsession made me click anyway.

Nothing since the white flag.

That post had five million likes and over forty thousand comments. A few hundred—yes, I scrolled through all I could—asking who has the white flag raised on them.

The next post would be his signal. A covert red X marking the target. Would it be a picture of Kierra? Daniel? Or me?

Fuck Mason Hunt. He's threatening everyone you love.

He thinks it's a game.

It's not.

It's war.

I gambled he'd make the classic mistake. Like most men. He'd get comfortable, arrogant, firing his impatient munitions.

And like many women have observed, comfortable men become careless. He'd slip up, revealing his identity. Then I'd have him. On cyberstalking, intimidating a witness, possibly conspiracy to commit a felony.

My weapons were as usual: patience and time. The problem? You never really knew how much of either you had in the chamber.

Twenty blocks up to Seventy-First Street and I turned right and right again onto Park Avenue.

Damn, the smell of New York City on a sweltering July

night. It blasted through my rage. Piss, garbage, asphalt, auto grease, and food filled my nostrils. The stench melded well with my disposition.

Tomorrow I must be the lady on a gentleman's arm. For Daniel, I was proud to do it.

A small part of me wished I could be like most women. Focusing on what I'd wear. How I'd look. How everyone would finally know... yes, I was Daniel Pierce's girlfriend. Basking in the spotlight of his fame, most craved the attention.

Not me.

Hell, I even hated the word "girlfriend." What an insulting term.

Hell if I was a "girl".

At thirty-three, with a college degree, military rank, and a few fucking bullets through me, I was a grown-ass woman. Though accolades and scars weren't required. Once my parents died, I was an adult in one horrific moment.

And "friend"? With the way Daniel and I loved each other? The way we respected each other? With our passion that made us fuck like erotic rabbits? There was nothing friendly about it.

But watch, the cynic in me knew. Twenty-four hours from now I'd be "Daniel Pierce's girlfriend." What the world did to so many women—erasing their identity with the life of a man's.

Good fucking luck trying to erase me. I didn't give a shit for what people called me.

No matter what, I'd always make myself known.

Through it all I'd be holding the hand of the man I loved. What that one simple gesture meant to me.

All the years I'd walked alone, my hands shoved into pockets, no one holding them. The solitude soothed at first.

Then the ache set in, raising a bruise on my heart I didn't know I had until Daniel Pierce touched it.

And goddammit, I was in love again.

I huffed a chuckle.

If only my parents could see me. All those years my dad made me take etiquette classes and dance lessons for cotillion. Well, they'd finally pay off.

And my mother would swoon at the dresses that Logan MacGregor sent over. Logan's team would do my hair and makeup, and the final fitting. Still, I didn't know which dress to wear.

Either way, it had taken thirty-three years, and I'd finally be the belle of the ball my dad always wanted.

The irony amused me, distracting from the hamburger wrapper that kicked over my foot. And the asshole taxi driver who honked at me when I flipped him off because I had the right of way.

I could play the lady, but this was my element. July heat drenching me. Daniel's T-shirt hanging like a soaked shower curtain off my frame. Cussing, sweating, running, real and raw—this was me. I'd rather be sprinting across a sandy beach, but anything bringing breath, exertion, sweat with a little pain, it brought me pleasure.

Yep, same way you like your sex.

My smart-ass musings lifted my spirits.

I glanced up. Fifty-Eighth Street in the distance. It looked like cops pulled someone over just beyond. I ducked right onto Fifty-Eighth, avoiding the commotion.

A line of people corralled in front of a club behind a barricade covered with black signs reading "LAVO," music thumping within. The throng of bodies dressed in summer's fiercest fashions pushed against one another to get in.

I nimbly ran past. Pausing at the corner, jogging in

place, I waited for the pedestrian crossing light to give me the green to turn left, running back down Madison Avenue.

Suddenly, halfway up the block in front of me, I clocked them.

A man and a woman in a fight. Arm gestures flying. Chins craned forward. Voices screaming. A cup in the man's hand, thrown to the ground before he yanked the woman by the top of her head, trapping her, screaming, by a fist full of her long black hair in his grasp.

Adrenaline dumped heat. Firing nerves. Heating muscles. Eyes wide with a glance right. No traffic. Bolting across the intersection, down a half block, my arms slicing like knives, elbows at an angle, I sprinted toward the attack.

"Hey!" I shouted. "Let her go!"

The man glanced up at my command, still with the woman cowering low, shouting, "Stop!" at his dragging snatch of her hair across the sidewalk.

I halted. Five paces back. *What's in his pockets? His right hand?* In New York, no telling.

"Fuck off, bitch!" His right hand swatted the air to intimidate me away.

Two empty hands. No weapons. It's on.

But the woman blocked my path like a small, shrieking barricade, preventing me from leaping upon the attacker.

"Help me, please!" the woman cried, her face locked down, staring at the pavement, trying to wrest her strands from his clutches, but she couldn't break free.

Fuck this.

"You heard me, you motherfuckin' dumbass." I ran around her, shoving his free shoulder. "You and your pathetic little limp dick." Bringing the violence to me. "Wanna a real fight? Let her go."

It worked. The man let the woman go before grabbing my wrist. I screamed at the woman. "Run!"

Then I stepped toward the man. Toward his blanching clamp over my wrist. Squatting low, getting closer to him, I snapped my trapped elbow in toward his. It forced his wrist into a torque it couldn't hold, freeing mine from his grasp.

But his other hand went for my throat. Slamming me back against the glass "2200 Sq. Ft. Available" sign. The woman was running back down the block, back toward the club for help.

I didn't need it.

Once his right hand strangled my throat, lips spitting "fucking cunt" in my face... I was set.

With a lightning pivot of my heel, my hip and right shoulder delivered power to my palm striking against his forearm. The force knocked his hand off my throat, momentum causing him to fall forward, toward me.

My right arm snaked fast, wrapping around the back of his neck, trapping him in a guillotine chokehold. But he was too big, too drunk, flailing at his view of the pavement.

Contracting the strength in my core, snapping my shoulder down to collide with my right leg rising, I slammed his face, crushing his nose against my sharp kneecap.

He went down, blood gushing from his nostrils.

Bouncers and a small crowd ran toward the scene. It took an hour for the police to arrive. To get my statement. To let me leave after convincing the officer that the bruise on my cheek was not from that fight or violence within my own relationship.

Once I explained my job, with a scar proving it, we shook hands, and I was free to go.

By the time I jogged back to the hotel, it was past two a.m. Pushing through the glass doors of the private entrance to our hotel, I saw Daniel standing there, phone in hand, talking in a frenzy with the night concierge. He wore jeans, a T-shirt, disheveled hair, and worry carved into every line across his brow.

He glanced up. It all washed away in his rush to me. "God, babe. Are you okay?" He crushed my face into his chest. "We were worried sick."

I gave him a quick explanation, apologizing to the concierge for the worry I caused.

Once we stood alone in the elevator, Daniel pulled me into another embrace. "Fuck's sake, babe. I woke up. Thought you were in the loo, but after a while, nothing. I got up, searched the suite, the hotel gym, and the bar for you. Finally, I asked the bloke at the desk, and he said you went for a run. But it'd been over two hours and he was worried too. I was about to phone the police."

"I know. I'm sorry. I should've left a note, and taken my phone with me, but I hate running with it."

"What got into you? To go running through Manhattan at midnight?"

With a *ding*, we were inside our suite. I made a beeline for a glass of water in the small kitchen. After I guzzled it down while Daniel patiently waited in the doorway, I answered him.

"I woke up scared about tomorrow. I mean, today, and the premiere. I felt trapped. My heart started racing. I didn't want to wake you, and I knew the only thing I could do was run it off."

He grabbed a fistful of his dark curls. "That's it, Charlie. Plan's off. You're not going with me to the bloody premiere. It's stressing you out too much. I won't have it."

"No. I'm going. For all the reasons we planned. And I'm going to have fun, dammit." I stepped toward him, puckering up for a quick kiss. He reluctantly bent down, accepting it. "Besides, I feel better now. The run helped. And kicking some fuckwad's ass helped too."

A grin lifted the corners of his pillow lips. "Is that all you need to feel better? A daily ass kick and grapple?" His hand snuck around my sweaty waist. "I'm happy to oblige in that regard." He urged me back against the countertop. "Want to grapple now?"

"No." I pushed him back with a playful forearm to his throat. "That's called 'fucking' because that's what we'd end up doing. And I need a shower and then sleep. I'd rather not have dark circles under my eyes *and* a bruised cheek for your big premiere."

CHAPTER TWELVE

CHARLIE

We awoke in time for brunch. I nestled beside him on our lavish bed, my gaze contemplating the buildings outside.

New York City was not my cup of tea. Too much noise. Too much concrete. Too low of a decent person-to-asshole ratio. As evidenced by last night.

Even in five-star hotel suite, the opulence didn't quell the nerves mocking me again.

Though I'd worked numerous premieres for *Fated,* the show I worked on before *The Druid,* I drew breath now like a fish out of water.

Vulnerable. Gasping for air. Moments from death.

Years before on *Fated,* I'd been protecting Juliette, the show's star.

Who's protecting you now, Charlie Girl?

I sat up, checking my phone on the nightstand.

Unknown
You know what I prefer.
White

Of course Mason preferred white over red or black, the racist asshole. And he preferred blondes. No news flash here.

I set the room service tray on the nightstand, pushing my phone away. Something needed to take my frustration. Shredding my cuticles helped.

You'll be standing in the line of fire again. The focus of cameras tonight; everyone aiming for YOU.

"Hey, beautiful." Daniel pulled back the curtain of hair blocking the fear swimming in my eyes. "What's going on? You're a million miles away."

Pushing his robe open, I rested my head down on his chest, the spot I loved. "I'm nervous again about tonight."

"Charlie, I promise"—his lips grazed over my hair—"even when the car pulls up, if you change your mind, I'll understand. I'll step out alone. We'll sort it. Release a statement. Or have Scott call some paps and leak where we're conveniently having lunch on a patio or walking in a park somewhere tomorrow. Or we can even make it bloody Instagram official. I don't care."

Promising an escape helped. That, and his gentle squeeze and words.

"I love you, babe." He soothed. "Your cute stories and mouse voices. Your stubborn, razor tongue. Your frustratingly big heart. I want you happy, not scared."

My nose nuzzled into the soft hair over his hard pecs. With all his might and muscle, he could be so tender. It was my only relief now.

"I love you too. All your 'bloody fuck's sakes', sweet

surprises and cocky smiles. *Even* how you like carrying me all over the damn place." A chuckle shook his chest under my sigh. "I'll be all right. I've suffered worse than a case of stage fright."

"Well, I wanted to wait until later today, but I have a little surprise that may help."

That word popped my head up. "What is it?"

This man was a gold medal triathlete in romance, sex, and surprises. Oh, this would be damn good.

And the sight of him in a thick open robe? Another elixir soothing my nerves. Damn, white towels or robes were man lingerie. Second best—his proper, English business pants, commando underneath, of course.

Tell those damn texts and nerves to shut the fuck up and enjoy this.

He grinned. "It's not a surprise if I tell you."

"You brought it up, you big tease."

"I was hoping you'd use some Marine grappling tactics to whip it out of me." His fingers reached for my robe.

My grasp snapped his wrist in a fast pinch. "Tell me first, and then I'll reward you, Pierce."

"The surprise arrives this afternoon. But I think you'll enjoy the day more if I tell you now." His smile faded. "I want to make this fun for you and not another part of my life you have to suffer."

My heart warmed. How he was changing his life for me too. How he tried making up for my sacrifice, knowing mine was about to be made unrecognizable after this night by being in his.

Yep, you'd endure a drug-free appendectomy with a dull knife for him.

"Well, what is it?"

"My surprise, for which I hope to be indecently

rewarded for *is*... that Juliette is coming to the premiere tonight to be here for you, for us."

"What?" I jumped up on my knees. "Are you serious?"

"Yes, I'm bloody serious."

Daniel invited my best friend to his premiere? Juliette would be my hilarious tour guide through popping lights, bullshit small talk, awkward photo ops, and hopefully some damn fun.

Juliette Jones's fame burned as bright as Daniel Pierce's. This was her territory too. With Daniel on one arm and Juliette on my other, I had nothing to fret.

Excitement shoved fear out of the seat, plopping it to the floor. "Is Juliette bringing a plus-one?"

"Yes, I don't know who, but she's bringing someone. They're meeting us here for cocktails at five."

"Daniel." I cradled his jaw in my hands, coaxing him up to his knees, cherishing every fleck of aqua and teal in his loving eyes. "Thank you so much."

My words followed my lips to his, desperately wanting to shower him with more than gratitude.

I freed his robe of its bind. Latching my grasp over his cock, I gifted him with hard, grateful strokes. My aggressive pump dragged a moan up his throat. I stopped to strip our robes off before pushing him back on the bed.

He reached between me thighs. "I love it when you take charge, Ms. Ravenel."

"I love it how you always know exactly what I need, Mr. Pierce." I trapped my palm over his gliding through my sex, starting my wanton ride over his fingers.

Holy hell, here it was again. This fierce new hunger for him. Now that we were free to be together. Free to do whatever the fuck, however the fuck, it possessed me. An appetite I wouldn't apologize for.

I had starved for this. My heart, my flesh, my desire, famished. In so much pain for so long, I demanded the pleasure. Trusting him, wanting him, I'd more than earned this.

"I want to try so many things with you," I confessed. Shame. Shyness. They found no place between us. "I waited so long for this, for you."

"Like?" His fingertip dipped, teasing inside.

"Like everything."

"Like toys and naughty games?" His eyes glimmered with our shared imagination. "Risqué outfits? Videos and voyeurs? Cuffs and spanks? Tell me what you want, Charlie."

"Just us two, trying it all." His fingers curved hard, deep into me, pushing a gasp from my lips. "Will you?"

"Will I?" The look on his face? Not amused. It was captivated. "I'd give my life to try everything with you, to do anything with you."

I climbed on top of him, guiding his hand up, slick with my desire, to pinch my nipple, hard.

My force parted his lips, forcing his question. "Do you fancy trying a hard, naughty shag then, Charlie?"

He followed my lead, pinching and playing with my nipples while I straddled him. "Hell yes." I teased us with my slippery folds gliding over the wide ridge of his cock, but not letting him in.

God, he looked so fucking hot, enthralled under my soaking grind. It slacked my jaw, breath sighing, "Do you feel how wet you make me?"

"I know I can make you fucking drown me." His hips thrust up. "I'd commit crimes for this tight pussy of yours."

"You're spoiling me tonight," I said with his fat tip begging in. "How can I spoil you?"

The pinch of his fingertips kept twirling over my nipples. "Any way you want." He twisted harder.

The sweet pain dragged a "fuck!" from my throat, carving my fingernails into his chest. His torso flexed into my scratch, seeking more.

"You almost said it yesterday." My fist clenched his cock, swirling his tip barely inside while I jacked off his shaft. "What do you really want to try with me?"

His muscular frame twisted at the torture. "Goddamn." His hands captured my breasts, clutching like he held on for life. "Give me that fucking pussy now."

"Say it, Daniel." My lust glossed my fist, pumping his cock, wedging his screaming hard crown inside, stirring it around. "What do you want to do to me?"

My taunt clenched his jaw. His aqua eyes urging wild with lechery, abs flexing at my challenge, pecs drawing up to strike, veins in his neck straining the words over his snarling lips. "I want to fuck your tight ass, Charlie."

I took his confession with a concurring kiss, sucking his bottom lip, then his tongue, brutal and lush while he moaned at my lewd whirl above him. Drifting my lips over his, I purred, "You're *my* reward, Daniel Pierce."

With a twist of my knee, I climbed off and turned around. Throwing my leg back over him, his cock roaring hard for me, I watched over my shoulder.

He looked amazed, like he was watching a pornographic fireworks show begin, eyes in awe, hands out in wonder, lips anticipating.

Perching my ass over him, I provoked, "If you want it, tease it first, Daniel." Sliding down slippery onto his hard saddle, I started my greedy ride.

He growled, "Fuck yes," while his hands reined my hips from the new angle. "Lean forward, babe, and let me see."

Giving him a shameless view of what he craved, I braced my hands against his shins, my body folded over his thighs, cantering my pussy up and down the length of his thick cock.

"That's it. Spread open for me." The sensation. Behind me. Him pulling my cheeks open. "Show me where I'm going to fuck you."

All modesty gone, we were racing over new borders, no more boundaries. The thrill of how far I wanted to go with him? Obscene rapture. To my very end.

His fingers dipped into my pussy beside his cock, taking a smear of my lust. It made me moan at the painful stretch before he pulled them out.

"Will this be mine too, Charlie?" A wet trace circled, flirting next with a slick, gentle probe of my ass. "Am I the only one?" His thick finger pushed in.

Fuck, it made my pussy rush for him. "Yes, Daniel." So many things I'd missed, but would try now, only with him.

My hands sweat over his knees, my body shuddering at the pressure, the sliding in and out. Then another finger nudged in, tissue spreading, not far, just enough for a little pain and a storm of pleasure.

"Do you think you can take my big cock fucking you like this?" He wouldn't relent, giving me a preview of a much bigger, salacious show. "Pounding you like this?

"There, Daniel," I gasped, "that's all I can take."

His hips bucked. "Then ride the fuck out of me now." His thrust made my pussy trot up his cock, into a full gallop over him. The lush pleasure inside of me, feeling full of him, his words taking me too. "Just like this, babe. I'm going to have every part of you." His fingers, stretching, pumping hard inside, dashing my pace.

I couldn't speak. The dual sensation of him taking me,

the obvious quake in my thighs, shaking my hands over his shins, lost in his voice, drowning in the pleasure, my eyes closing, I let him in.

This was how much I loved him, trusted him. He was more than my gift. Our connection. Our passion. It was my final paradise. From his tender embrace to his delicious intrusion, he was everywhere inside me.

"Fuck, you're so tight." Breath thrummed heavy in his voice. "Your pussy is so full with me." The awe in his tone. What he must see, I groaned so deep.

That made him ram even harder. "You like me in your ass, don't you, Charlie?" Lust stole my breath and I didn't want it back. "I love it too, babe. I'm watching you. Come on. Do it. Come so wet down my cock."

I did, crying out, jumping down his cock with a soaking hurdle. I wouldn't stop, couldn't stop riding him hard for two more, letting my body indulge and my heart revel, marveling at the gift of him.

He was a slew of curses, holding on to me until he could take no more of our race. Seizing my stride, hands bruising my hips, his back arched, straining my name with a rattle of gasps escaping his throat.

I looked over my shoulder. "Consider us both spoiled," I said, smiling at his panting face, grinning, sweaty and satisfied back at mine.

CHAPTER THIRTEEN

CHARLIE

I stood like a mannequin, letting Logan MacGregor's seamstress finish the last stitch. My hair and makeup were done, though the makeup artist performed magic to perfectly cover the bruise and fading cut on my face.

A knock on the bedroom door made my thin nerves jump.

"Hold your horses, Daniel." I chuckled at the dirty pun to my cowgirl ride this morning.

"It's not Daniel, bitch." A familiar voice called back from the other side.

Joy surged my heart. "Bitch, get in here!"

Juliette rushed in, closing the door behind her.

"Oh! My! God!" She exclaimed, taking in the vision of me all gussied up. "Charlie, you look mint!"

The seamstress stepped back, clearing the path us to embrace.

"I'm so glad you're here." Wrapping my arms around

Juliette, I choked back tears. "This means so much to me, Jules. Thank you. I'd cry, but don't want to mess up my damn face. I've never worn this much makeup before in my life."

I didn't want a big fuss so I left my hair down and natural. Logan's stylist only added more volume to the waves skimming my waist. But the makeup artist played up my eyes with a smoky teal, bronzing my tan skin and freckles to a glow. I'd never seen myself like this before.

"Get used to it loving Daniel Pierce," Juliette said. "He'll parade you across every carpet looking like this. You've come a long way from ball caps and tactical boots." She cradled a champagne flute in one hand, the other caressed the silky fabric over my hip. "Where did you get this ensemble? It's to die for."

"Logan MacGregor. He sent over two, but I fell in love with this one."

The other dress was an aqua lace gown with a plunging neckline, embroidered with pearls. I picked this more daring choice—a strapless midriff bodice top covered in tiny pearls, paired over a dark-teal full skirt that flowed like water just above the floor.

The exposure of the fabric tingled my flesh. It revealed inches of my abs while showcasing my naked shoulders and arms. The other dress would have covered my scars, so I picked this one. Never would I hide them again.

The seamstress packed up her kit, giving a quick approving nod. I thanked her before she quietly left.

"Daniel's not going to be able to keep his hands off you."

Like Juliette had room to talk, looking dead sexy in a strapless white-gold metallic fitted dress that fell to her knees with a long slit up her right thigh. She was a sex kitten ready to romp, making me joyfully suspicious.

"Bitch, you're dressed for some hands on you tonight too. Who's the lucky person I'm about to meet?"

I slid on nude kitten heels with pearls across the straps. I'd flatly refused high heels, disappointing Logan. "I won't be able to think straight in them," I told him when he called for inspiration on the dresses he sent over.

A cat-that-just-ate-the-canary grin rose on Juliette's face. "My date is Alistair."

Shock widened my eyes. "What!"

Juliette Jones and Alistair Campbell went back years. Cast for the first season of *Fated*, they spent five years on set together—the whole time as friendly colleagues.

Alistair was the same hot-as-hell actor who had crushed on me. When I arrived on set, tasked with protecting Juliette, Alistair's gaze had lingered on me.

He was one of the few men who ever tempted me after my husband was killed. But I politely turned Alistair down. I hadn't been ready yet, to date... or to risk my career. And my desire still slept at the wheel.

That all tailspun the second I set eyes on Daniel, careening me into this current ditch of delight and doom.

I froze, astounded by the news. "When did you two hook up and why the hell didn't you tell me?"

"We didn't hook up." A guilty smile wouldn't leave Juliette's face. "I needed a quick date when Daniel called me to surprise you and I knew Alistair would want to support you too."

I squinted through the altruistic reason.

Yes, all three of us—me, Juliette, and Alistair—had become good friends. Juliette and I were joined at the hip. And Alistair was a sweet guy, taking my polite rejection in stride.

Of course he'd do something nice for me. Alistair also

knew Daniel well. He co-starred with him in the second *Zeus* film, playing Apollo, the handsome son of the gorgeous god.

But horny dripped from Juliette's infamous wide-mouthed smile and sculpted cheeks. My best friend could conceal her feelings from me like plastic wrap. Transparent.

"You are so full of shit." I chuckled. "You want to be more than friends with Alistair now. And he is your type, boo. You do like those hot fuckboys, and no one looks it more than Alistair. Does he know?"

"I don't know. We've been in the friend zone for so long. But it feels different between us, especially tonight."

A courteous tap hit the door. "Charlie, you sure do know how to keep a man waiting... again."

Yes, Daniel had waited weeks for our first kiss, and a slow tease of months before we had all kinds of hot sex. And he could patiently wait for me to finish getting ready too.

I focused on Juliette. "Well, I've got my detail cut out for me, don't I?" Giving her a swat on the butt. "Moving your ass from friend zone to fuck zone with Alistair."

She tossed her tawny strands over her shoulder. "We shall see."

"Keep your fingers crossed and legs open, chica." I grabbed a pearl clutch from the bed. "Are you two staying here at the hotel?"

"Yep. Daniel booked us two rooms, but hopefully we'll only need one." She tipped back her last sip of champagne, opening the door. "You have my full blessing now, Daniel Pierce," Juliette cooed to him waiting in the hallway. "She's all yours."

A long sigh dropped from his lungs when he saw me. "Good God, Charlie." Closing the distance between us, he wrapped his hand around my bare waist, hooking his knuckle under my chin and taking a deep kiss. With his lips glossing over mine, he professed, "You look absolutely ravishing."

"Save the ravishing for later, Pierce." I twirled his tendril. "For now, I need three shots of Tito's and ten of whatever appetizers you ordered out there."

The path to him is a digital map. Press releases. Media posts. Teaser trailers.

Search the area of #danielpierce and you can almost pinpoint his current and usually his next location to...

A film premiere at Lincoln Square, at the movie theatre off Broadway.

Zoom in on the satellite image and map the building in advance. To a fourth level balcony. Right across the street. A median of trees offers perfect cover to aim through.

It's a perfect stand with an adjacent parking deck next to it, allowing easy escape.

The night will be spectacularly public.

Hundreds of witnesses to the big show. A sea of press shooting every arrival, smile, and wave. Fans screaming for the man they love.

I smirk, knowing... Daniel Pierce isn't the only reason they will scream tonight.

The security at the event will be tight. But nothing in open air, in the public, is truly secure.

How many times, America, does it have to happen for people to learn the fatal lesson?

Seems entertainment still bests safety every time.

CHAPTER FOURTEEN

CHARLIE

J uliette and Alistair arrived on the red carpet before us. The fans piled behind the barricades screamed, shocked that the principal cast from *Fated* reunited for a movie premiere—and as a couple.

Peeking over the passenger seat of the car, I witnessed the delightful spectacle.

The press clamored for pictures of this boon of a guest list. Most assumed they were here because Alistair had worked with Daniel, that they became close filming *Zeus 2*.

No one knew the real connection—me.

Juliette and Alistair gave their waves to the fans and photographers, strolling inside for drinks.

Next, Daniel's co-star in *Swipe Right* arrived in front of us. Eve Mitchell.

I loved Eve cast in the film. It was about time more studios cast mixed race couples in a big release rom-com. Daniel said it was one of the reasons he took the role. It caused buzz for the film already.

And Eve was stunning—a former model with great comedic timing and romantic chemistry with Daniel on screen. Eve stood with her husband, giving photos before starting her interviews, waiting for Daniel's entrance.

Our silver car pulled up. Stomach flips hit me again, but joy at sharing the night with Daniel and my friends surged stronger.

He took my hand, holding it firm. "Hey, beautiful"—he dusted his lips over mine—"I love you."

I smiled back, swearing every word, heart brimming, "I love you too, sexy."

Daniel was an orgasm in a tailored suit.

Logan sent him one in the same dark-teal-to-black hue of my skirt, fitted to perfection over his skyscraper shoulders. The shirt underneath matched my bodice, shimmering in a pearl color, unbuttoned for a peek at his chiseled chest, driving me and millions mad.

"Ready?" he asked.

The click of the door handle signaled our entrance. Simon and another HGR officer sent over at my insistence guarded outside.

Humid air rushed in when Simon opened the door. Elaine, Daniel's assistant, waited there along with his publicist, Scott. His team stood poised, anticipating him and the big night.

"You can't jump halfway off a cliff." I gave him a playful push. "Let's go."

He stepped out to his name being announced through the loudspeaker, inspiring a cacophony of high-pitched squeals and shouts of "Daniel! Daniel!" Pausing for a few waves to the crowd, he turned, offering his hand to me.

Here you go, Charlie Girl. Fingers wrapping around his. *Get ready to lose all gravity.*

Jump!

Oxygen punched from my lungs. Thoughts flew by too fast to think. Feet touched pavement. Stepping into open air, my ankles wobbled weak. Muggy air weighed my bare shoulders. Nervous thighs shook under a flowing skirt.

Holding on to him, my hand trembled, but his strong, soothing grip... it could lead me anywhere.

It landed me in bright white lights and shrieks, blurring my senses.

The bind of his palm against mine, my only support. Together, our stride, guided by security, his team, and a slew of publicists for the event, led the way. The squeeze of his hand—*I love you*—ushered me down the red carpet under the massive black tent over the huge *"Swipe Right"* backdrop.

Our path halted on the first mark. Proud and petrified, I stood beside him, tightening my grip that dampened in his. Giving away smiles to the blinding lights and shouts of "Daniel, over here! Daniel! This way!" Again and again.

Every effort I sacrificed for this one simple performance.

How hard could it be to stand, smile, and hold the hand of the man you love?

Excruciating, when your trained eyes scanned the crowd, past the loud lights. Brutal, when your mind was deployed out of your body, screening your periphery for threats. Torture, when your heart contracted with fear, then relaxed with love. Terrified because you knew someone, *no, more than one*, was out there.

Hunting for you.

Open your eyes.

His hand let go. The void pinched my breath.

His touch returned, caressing the bare skin across my

back, securing its guard around my waist, conjuring tiny goose bumps along the journey. It turned my gaze, meeting his.

The cleft of his chin leaned down, asking for mine to join him. Our lips, turned up in smiles, softened for a sweet, slow kiss.

This simple gesture. It declared love.

The.

Press.

Went.

Ballistic.

Glaring pops of light. Yelling. Shouting. "Who's your guest, Daniel! Who's your guest!"

No answer. Only his smile at me, beckoning for another kiss.

When his supple lips met mine again, they seized my breath, making camera shutters click so fast I felt surrounded by rattlesnakes under solar flares burning through my eyelids.

The safety of his touch pulled back, turning to the line of press, answering their demand.

He said, "Charlotte Roberts."

My world?

A tsunami washed it away.

CHAPTER FIFTEEN

CHARLIE

Done.

They had my face on camera. They had my name—my former military and married one. Like everything in this world, they consumed it and started using it for their profit, for their pleasure.

"Charlotte! Charlotte! Daniel! This way. This way. Charlotte! Over here!"

Dizzying my balance, the barrage of shouts slammed my brain. A minuscule nerve twitched in my neck at the exposure, though a smile graced my face the entire time.

The ground beneath me tilted. The hammer of my heart stole my focus. A ringing stabbed my eardrums. A prism of light shifted over my vision. The present moment threatened to leave, summoning my past hell.

No! Stay here, Charlie Girl. My clammy palm clenched his. *Don't you dare fall.* His flesh, my anchor. *Hang on to him. Now.*

Daniel's steadying grip never wavered, securing me to

him. To more stops and pictures. Minutes of more torture. Vulnerable in my stance. Open for all, aiming their cameras and phones, claiming pieces of me. My name. My scars. My sacrifice. My love. It all lay open for the world to plunder.

He leaned down, mouth grazing over my ear. "You okay, babe?"

"Yes," I lied.

"Our fate is sealed."

His voice? Always able to pierce the dissonance of my hell. His tone warmed with devotion, but the reality sparked terror in my heart.

Hear that? That's the crackling bonfire of the bridge back to safety burning.

And I did it.

Standing in the inferno with him, I watched it all burn to ash in the white-hot flames of fame with each searing flash in front of me.

Though the late July heat owned the air, a sudden chill bit my soul.

Over the crowd. Look!

Through the oak trees in the street median. *That building.* Diagonally across the street. My eyes counting. Scanning one, two, three, four stories of glass up. *The rooftop balcony—*

"Ms. Roberts?" A publicist for the event stepped in front of me. "Come with me, please."

I turned. Daniel kissed my cheek. This was the plan. I was free to go inside. He had to give away more.

Following the pull of the publicist, I glanced back. I had to be sure. Yes, Daniel fulfilled his promise, working the rope line with his two guards, staying two feet back from fans and the boom mics looming over his head.

He'd be busy for a while with quick interviews and

pictures with Eve, his co-star, other cast members, and bigwigs.

Alistair reached out for my hand, leaning down to peck my cheek where Daniel's kiss still tingled on my skin. "You made it through the gauntlet." He and Juliette had waited in the theater lobby, drinks in hand, ready to save me from the next ordeal.

I wanted to douse my fear with the vodka tonic Alistair put in my grasp, but twists in my stomach canceled that impulse.

Guests pounced on my friends, asking about their attendance.

"We're just here to support our friends and to enjoy the film," Juliette said with her practiced smile and dismissive reply, her hand covertly reaching down for mine. It was almost as small but a big comfort.

It took a few minutes and funny "remember when" stories between the three of us for me to feel a smile cool my cheeks. Joking with my friends, I patiently waited for Daniel to join us.

Juliette's hand took my elbow, her ruby lips whispering, "Let's pop into the loo before it gets mad again when Daniel gets here."

I followed her lead. This was Juliette's arena, not mine. Alistair said he'd hold ground and wait for our return.

Juliette's path wove a deft needle across the room, tossing hellos over her shoulder to all who tried stopping us. Putting our noses down, we made it through the crowd.

The VIP restroom guard smiled at our approach, unhooking the velvet rope from the stanchion for us to pass. We pushed through the door, delighted to have the facilities to ourselves.

I asked from one stall to the next, "Any action between you two in the car?"

Toilet paper clunked on its roll along with Juliette's laugh. "No tongue yet. But he did give me a good lip lock before the door opened. Fuck, he wets my knickers."

Flushing filled the air before I replied, "It's only a matter of time. Depends on how long you two want to tease the hell out of each other before your hands are all over him."

I smoothed my skirt before pressing down on the door handle of the stall, pushing it open.

To see.

Her.

Standing there.

Kathy Fields.

Kathy offered a smile and an introduction, like I didn't know who she was. It amused me when Kathy said she was Logan MacGregor's PR director. Omitting the obvious.

She was also Daniel's ex-girlfriend.

"You both look smashing tonight." Kathy offered while I smiled and washed my hands in front of the mirror.

Was she complimenting Daniel and me? Or me and Juliette? The obscure remark twitched the corner of my lips up.

While Kathy continued, "Logan's going to be over the moon at the photos," I clocked her in the reflection.

How Kathy's relaxed tone didn't match her flexed knuckles, tense over the velvet clutch in her hand. How her eyebrow arrowed up in challenge. How the air reeked of French perfume and a fight.

Juliette emerged from the other stall, surveying the situation. She also knew who Kathy was. Juliette was there when Daniel had stumbled drunk down the red carpet at

Logan MacGregor's London party with Kathy, returning her kiss.

We always got each other's back. Juliette had told me immediately about that horrid, heartbreaking night.

"Thank you." I poured authenticity into my reply. "Logan was very kind. Both dresses he sent were gorgeous. It was hard choosing which one."

The smile on Kathy's face stayed too long. "Yes, it can be hard to know what's appropriate if you're not accustomed to such occasions. It's an easy mistake to make between two choices, but alas, one must be had over the other, even if it's the wrong one."

Oh, Charlie Girl! She's clever. An elegant backhand insulting your station, fashion, and status with Daniel.

Chalk three points on the board for her.

But nope. I wasn't tempted.

Getting sucked into a tacky cat fight with a woman? I'd hang upside down by my toenails before losing dignity over a man. Even if he was the hottest one alive. Even if he was the love of my life.

My interest in fighting Kathy? Zero.

"Well, Logan's a talented designer. I hope he's pleased with my selection."

"Are you pleased"—Kathy's red manicured fingertips gathered her auburn tresses over her shoulder—"with your easy selection?"

Smack! Another point on the nasty board. Interest at 20 percent now.

Juliette washed her hands in the sink behind Kathy, chiming in, "Charlie could make a hessian sack look like haute couture. She looks mad fit tonight, as always."

It turned Kathy's seethe toward Juliette. "Indeed," she

said. "How do you two know each other? Seemed quite cozy when I came in."

The focus on my friend twinged my trigger finger. I'd always protect Juliette.

"We worked together on *Fated*. Juliette, Alistair, and I," I answered, pulling the malicious attention back to me and away from my friend. "Small world that Alistair knows Daniel as well."

I dropped Daniel's name as a cherry on top for Kathy to enjoy.

It squinted her brown eyes. "And just how long have *you* known Daniel?"

The insinuation? I took Daniel from her. It was bullshit. I didn't know about her, and Daniel hadn't spoken to Kathy for two months before I met him.

The notion pained pathetic. Two women fighting over a man? Like we had no value and men were our only worth? Like grown men had no responsibility for their actions? Like they were passive pawns exchanged over the desperate scratches between needy women?

I refused the sad, sexist cliché.

I turned, confronting her. "Kathy, I'm not doing this. I'm not the kind of woman who fights another."

Kathy's steps clicked toward me, her glare burning through the air of her exhale.

"No, you're just a scarred-up whore who spread her trashy Yank thighs and Daniel jumped in. You just want the fame. I hope you can handle it—the paps, the press, his fans. They will rip your low-class life apart. I'll see to it." Her lips snarled up. "And if you wait long enough, your bestie behind me will be his next unfortunate slag."

Interest at 90 percent now.

I saw the flinch in Juliette's shoulder, standing behind Kathy, ready to strike. I shook my head no. To all of this.

And 100 percent control.

"Jump between my thighs and call me what you want, Kathy. I don't give a fuck." Speaking slow so my words would brand the woman's soul. "I got these proud Yank scars helping others, so I'll help you too. I won't fight you because I feel sorry for you. All you talk about is Daniel and fame. Get your head out of your privileged ass and see there's more important shit in this world."

I seized the ground between us, not feeling the height difference with Kathy perched over me in heels. I stood higher on much more.

"And get a good look at my scarred-up, trashy whore face." I aimed my glare at her, memory conjuring a bloody war. The threat from a jealous ex-girlfriend? A joke. "And ask yourself, Kathy... if you attack me again or some other slag I love, how the fuck do you think I'll answer you next time?"

Fear shot across Kathy's eyes.

Then they rolled as she turned on her heel, pushing past Juliette and charging out the door.

Juliette yanked a paper towel for her hands. "You are far too kind, Charlie. I would have gutted her."

I reached into my pearl clutch for a tube of pink-tinted balm. "Me against Kathy?" Smiling, I rimmed my lips in the mirror. "Not a fair fight."

CHAPTER SIXTEEN

DANIEL

Blinding Lights by The Weeknd

My hand reached for Charlie's. "I thought I'd be the one keeping everyone waiting." I stood with Alistair in the lobby, drink in other hand, an adoring smile for her.

To say Charlie looked ravishing was an understatement. She could be a runway model if not so petite. Everyone on the carpet asked about her. Asked if she was my girlfriend.

I kept answering, "She's my love, yes."

I hated the word "girlfriend," understanding why Charlie disliked the term too. It diminished her and our love.

Having her here tonight... I always wanted this. Like the few in my elite cadre, I'd wished for someone on my arm who made me proud, and everyone swoon. Not judge. Not question. Not shame. And instead of a calculated PR move, to have this be real? Loving this woman beyond any measure I'd ever known?

Yes, Charlie was media gold. Yes, we'd pay the price for it. And yes, I'd bleed all accounts dry to keep her by my side.

"We were a bit delayed," Juliette said, "by Kathy Fields."

That name clenched my jaw. "What happened?"

"Nothing I couldn't handle," Charlie said. "I'll tell you about it later."

Right on cue, Eve Mitchell, my co-star, and her husband came over for a toast. We started up a lively conversation, descending the group into easy banter.

The rest of the night sailed by perfectly. Only one awkward moment when Kathy approached me leaving with Charlie. Giving us thanks for repping Logan's brand so well, she offered me a polite peck to the cheek. Then she turned for Charlie, doing the same.

Watching her lips retreat from Charlie's scar, I didn't miss it. The sneer in Kathy's eyes. The pity in Charlie's.

Once we found ourselves alone in the safety of the car driving back to the hotel, I had to know. "What went on between you and Kathy?"

"She tried insulting me, tried baiting me into a pathetic cat fight but I wouldn't scratch."

"What did she say?"

"The usual stuff. Whore insults. Shaming my dress and scars. She thinks I stole you from her." Her eyes rolled. "Shallow bullshit."

"She didn't try to hit you or something?"

The thought dropped fear through my veins. Not for Charlie. She could flatten her foes. I feared Kathy.

"No." Her jaw cocked curious. "Why? Did she hit you when you were dating?"

Fuck, Pierce.

You've got to be a psychological chess player if you're going to hide something from her. Anticipating she'll be two moves ahead. Checkmate.

"No. She never raised a hand to me. Nor I to her, never to a woman." I gazed over her shoulder at the posh shops rolling by. "But she's got a streak in her. I can't describe it."

"Try." Her tone held little patience.

"Things she said. Almost sinister. And her behavior sometimes. Just odd."

"Be more specific."

"Like the first night she stayed over at my townhouse. I woke up and found her going through my wardrobe. I asked her what she was doing, and she said, 'Knowing everything about you.' Months later, I caught her snooping through my phone, deleting old girlfriends from my contacts, then copying the rest into hers. I don't know how she unlocked it. Must've watched me enter the code, which was dodgy, I know. When I asked her why she did it, she said she'd help me stay focused on my career."

"Daniel." Charlie's tongue snapped my name like a towel. "Do you need blood to bleed down the walls to know when a woman is a horror show?"

"I broke up with her, didn't I?"

"After two years of that control. I would've shown her the door the minute she started snooping through my shit. Did she have a fucking cape with the letter S hanging from her pussy or something?"

It made me laugh—the image and her crass mouth.

"No, you have the super pussy, Charlie. I was just a

gullible arse who went for the ready access. Believe it or not, it wasn't easy for me to meet women. Ones I could trust. I assumed because Kathy was in the industry, and right there working with my publicist on the Logan brand, that she was a safe choice."

"How safe do you think she is now?"

"She'd never do anything. Just be petty and mean-spirited. But you can take it. We both can."

"Anyone else I need to know about before I land in your past?"

Here it is, Pierce. Your chance to tell her. All that Colleen said you should. A golden fucking invitation.

I looked into her eyes with the truth sitting on the tip of my tongue.

The way she asked me. It thinned my breath, her beauty staring back at me. Trusting me. Loving me. I couldn't do it. I couldn't hurt her. Not tonight. Not ever.

"Just some nutter fans." I divulged the obvious. "Ones who send things. Post stuff. Or make claims."

"Like what? Like you're gay or the father of their kid?" Her grin assumed it was preposterous.

Careful, Pierce. Don't you dare bloody lie to her, not to her stunning face.

"Yes. Stuff like that. Or that I've slept with them."

"But you used NDAs to muzzle that up, didn't you?"

Yes, I did.

My entire industry was wallpapered in nondisclosure agreements. Like everyone carried five contracts in their back pockets, sealing secrets and mouths with threats of expensive penalties if anyone disclosed the truth.

"Most of the time," I said.

Good, that isn't a lie, Pierce.

"Why didn't you ask me to sign one?"

"Would you?"

Members of my team already gave me hell about this. How I never asked Charlie to sign an NDA. The risk of insulting her with the request and losing her was far greater than any risk of what she could divulge about me later.

"I've signed them for work and other clients. I'd sign one for you if it makes you feel better." Her sculpted shoulders shrugged. "I have no interest in hurting you. It's not in my nature. And I value my privacy too much to go blabbing my mouth to a damn soul."

"I know." I lifted her small hand to my lips. "That's why I never asked. We don't need one. I'll disclose all to you."

Careful, Pierce. That's what your heart feels.

But your head knows... that's the half of it.

Is a half-truth a lie?

Sometimes I didn't know anymore.

After twenty years of protecting my privacy, secrecy was hardwired in my brain. NDAs were my DNA. When asked about details of my private life? My mind parried every question, guarding my truth.

The fucking irony.

How I'd craved the spotlight, but once its blazing glare burned through my life, all I wanted to do was shelter in the shadows.

I had millions in the bank and not one pound of it could afford full candor or fact.

She was the only one I trusted. Of course, I did my family too. But my family wasn't a relationship with the intense intimacy I shared with Charlie.

No one ever saw me. This true, naked, and raw. But she did—from the moment we met.

And I tried. Tried stripping it away for her. I wanted

her to know all but fear stopped me, terrified if I revealed my past... we'd have no future.

The screech of the tires turning into the underground garage of our hotel lifted my eyes from gazing at her. Juliette and Alistair's car pulled in behind us.

Time for the after party.

I'm not pleased.

My soldier didn't take the shot.

He only reported back that he couldn't get a clear target on her. That press, staff, and Daniel Pierce had blocked his aim.

Yes, I will take him down too.

Their hero will fall, his defeat sealing the story. Making it a legend. A Hollywood horror show.

But I want her dead. First. Bloody. And sure.

Change of tactic.

No more long-range scopes with distant aim.

Next time, we kill closer.

CHAPTER SEVENTEEN

DANIEL

The sun wasn't up but my alarm and cock were firm alerts. One buzzed behind me on the nightstand, the other, I urged into her cheeks. "You sure do make it hard for a man to get out of bed."

"I can feel your massive struggle." She nestled against my body. "But your fine ass better get going or you'll be late."

I had a live second-hour interview on a morning show, followed by press all day.

"Enjoy breakfast with Juliette and Alistair. Give them my best, yeah." With a kiss to her cheek, I forced my body to roll away from hers.

No complaining about this junket schedule. I arranged it this way, grueling but fast, getting us out of New York and home.

Once I arrived at the network studio, coffee revived me along with a lively interview with my co-star, Eve. The afternoon pushed us through interview after another, repeating the same jokes and stories.

Still, no questions about Mason, Kierra, or Charlie.

Exhaustion weighed me down when I returned to our suite. After a late dinner with Charlie on the terrace, she rewarded me with a massage that only tempted me for more. Smelling like almond oil and sex, we fell asleep early in each other's slick arms.

I met Eve again the next morning for our final interview with Ginny Smith—an icon of morning talk shows, infamous for her cheeky questions.

A statement from the studio about Kierra and Mason had been released early this morning as I was warned it would be. I spoke with Ginny and her producers in the green room before the show about how I wished to handle it in our live interview.

Sitting next to Eve in our directors' chairs, I laughed with Ginny and her audience about our antics behind the camera. The movie centered around a camping trip for the lovebird characters, so gags with fake snakes and spiders were rife on set.

Then Ginny moved to the next prompt as planned.

"Now, Daniel, I know you wanted to comment on a statement that Showz released this morning about an incident between Kierra Williams and Mason Hunt, your fellow cast members on *The Druid*."

"Yes, thank you." My palms smoothed my tan trousers. My spine sat up tall. "I, along with the entire cast and crew on the show, care for Kierra immensely. She has nothing but our full support. We remain protective of her privacy, knowing that in time, she will share her story and that it is hers alone to tell."

Ginny signaled for her audience to clap in support of Kierra before asking, "And what about Mason Hunt?"

I gave a measured pause before answering, "I hope Mason gets the help he needs. We all believe people can change, and I hold the same wish for him." A light round of applause followed.

Ginny leaned back in her chair, tapping her cue cards against it, launching her signature mischievous grin.

"Now, I understand on a much happier note that *you*, Daniel Pierce, were a little busy yourself this past season."

Though I hadn't discussed this with Ginny, I knew what came next. A photo of me kissing Charlie at the *Swipe Right* premiere appeared on the monitors and screens in the studio.

The audience clapped while Ginny fanned herself at the sight of us.

The genuine smile that surged my face couldn't be stopped. I glanced at the picture on the monitor. "Why, yes, I have been a little busy." Heat flamed up my neck to my cheeks.

Fuck, Pierce, you're thirty-seven years old... and blushing.

"Now, Daniel, you can't show up to your premiere with a beautiful woman on your arm and not tell us more. In fact..." Ginny paused. The screen split in two. One half, the photo of me kissing Charlie at the premiere. The other half, me carrying Charlie passed out in my arms at the Madrid gym months before. "I'm feeling quite a romantic story here."

Ginny's prod filled the studio with applause.

I smiled at the eager crowd then turned back to her.

"Well, Ginny"—I could feel it, my pulse racing, my skin

flaming while my lips hitched high talking about Charlie—"the story is I'm the one who's been swept off his feet."

"Aws" and even more applause erupted from the audience.

Ginny leaned back, licking up the sweet scoop of news she'd just scored. "Well, Daniel. I must say I approve. Of course, it would take one of our very own to do it—a United States Marine."

What? Bloody hell. You weren't expecting this!

My eyes shot to the monitor.

Charlie's battalion photo appeared on screen.

I'd never seen this picture of her. It stopped my racing pulse, seizing my heart. A younger Charlie wearing fatigues stared stoic at the camera, her hair held tight in a bun, her cheek with no scar.

Pride welled up in my eyes for her about to sacrifice so much for her country... for two girls in particular. It almost fell over my lashes. My mouth forced me to confirm the truth in front of my face and the world.

"Yes. She served her country in Afghanistan. She is a proud veteran and former United States Marine—Captain Charlotte Roberts."

The audience jumped to their feet, thundering in applause while Ginny and Eve clapped along in admiration for Charlie.

Ginny patted my knee. "That's fantastic." Score one hundred for her ratings. She turned to the crowd. "Let's thank Eve Mitchell and Daniel Pierce for joining us this morning. Go see *Swipe Right*. It opens today..." and Ginny wrapped her show.

I sat in the car afterward, Midtown buildings a blur on the drive back to the hotel. Under my gray jacket, sweat poured down my back while clammy hands wiped down the legs of my trousers.

I'd done this before in interviews, answered questions about women I dated. Though press were under strict directions from my publicists not to ask, it didn't stop some. I was always discreet, brief in reply.

But this time? Talking publicly about Charlie? It was entirely different—in my head and my heart.

Reason told me why I had to answer the question. It was a story of our own making. We cooked it up for the media to devour with a giant digital spoon.

Taste this—a celebrity dating a Marine.

Even better? It's a male celebrity dating a female Marine.

Delicious, right? The man who plays the hero is dating a real one, a woman.

Hungry for the whole meal? The male British celebrity who plays a hero, praised for his perfect face and body, is dating an actual one—a female Marine veteran, proud with scars of sacrifice across her beautiful face and body.

This was a feast.

THIS WAS THE STORY.

Our future. Our fate.

It was a destiny I cherished with a love for Charlie that jumped off the screen, impressing any viewer's heart.

But trouble knotted my brow, churning my stomach, making fear drip from my pores.

When I had stepped outside the studio door onto the Manhattan sidewalk after the interview, a new sensation bombed me. I felt dangerously exposed.

Greeting the fans waiting outside, signing their photographs and paraphernalia, I stopped, black marker poised over a shot of my face. My right shoulder twitched, flinching my hand about to sign a *The Druid* poster of me for a fan.

I swore I heard Flynn, my dead twin brother. It was his voice telling me...

Get out of here. Go!

I bolted for the car door handle, yanking it open before Simon could.

Meet danger, Pierce. No escaping it now.

CHAPTER EIGHTEEN

CHARLIE

It was a blissful forty-eight-hour reprieve from Mason's texts.

Unknown

I crave white with a pink gash

And now he was back, taunting me after his red, black, and white double entendre, exploding into my world with another one.

White for my hair like his last text and now a pink gash.

Was he referencing the pink scar on my face, or was it a perverted sex play on the word "gash" for my pussy?

I knew—both.

The flatscreen on the wall lifted my attention from the one in my hand to Daniel's live interview. I propped up on my elbows to watch it, glad he had a chance to support Kierra. The man volleyed questions with perfect answers like a Wimbledon pro.

Then the storm.

The lightning—*flash*—a photo of me and Daniel at the premiere.

The sonic thunder—*boom*—the woman from the premiere was the same one passed out in Daniel's arms months back.

The squall raged overhead. Not one second between the lightning and thunder—*blast, crack*—the same woman in a U.S. Marine Corps battalion photo.

The connection? Almost instant.

I wasn't naive. Anyone's past was a few clicks away. Once the press had my name, with clearly a bullet wound through my bare shoulder, standing proud on the red carpet, genius wasn't required to suspect I may be former military.

It was all an abstract plan until now. Surprise didn't strike me but something else jolted through.

Watching Daniel live on screen was surreal. It wasn't the sweet man who teased me the night before, nuzzling into my neck, making me giggle.

Fucking hell. Shaking your world like a snow globe... it's you!

The famous Daniel Pierce is on the screen talking about you!

I ripped my gaze from the spectacle, rolling to my back. Rib cage heaving. Thoughts streaked like lightning through my brain.

You're exposed now. Press will find you. Fans will target you. Anyone can hunt you.

Panic blurred the ceiling in my vision. Dread dove into me, making the mattress below me spin. Shock hit my heart so hard it wanted to crack my ribs open and climb out, running away.

No, no, no, no. Calm down. Now.

I closed my eyes, focused on my breath. Counting each inhale. And exhale. With all my discipline... slipping, slipping... only light and water around, I meditated. Into calm. Into nothing... into...

A memory of my dad.

The first time I shot a gun, I'd begged my dad to. I even did my chores with a smile for an entire month to earn the privilege.

Dusting the bookshelves in my dad's home office, I eyed the weapon hanging on the wall. My grandfather's Springfield sniper rifle. The gleam of the walnut wood on the weapon, it called to me.

But when I stood, twelve years old at the outdoor range with my father, protective lenses over my eyes, ears muffed for the blast, my hands trembled. I had the aim but feared the fire.

My dad came around, squatting beside me, his palm pressing the muzzle down to the ground before he gently pulled the muffs off my ears. "You afraid, Charlie Girl?"

I'd rather eat lima beans, a gag-worthy food, every day for the rest of my life than admit to my father I was afraid. But love crinkled around his ice blue eyes. "Yes." The word came out of my mouth; tears threatened next.

His hand cupped my cheek. "Fear is only a feeling. It's not a fact. Never let it make your decisions." His massive palm mussed my hair as he stood, tapping my right shoulder. The one braced for recoil.

I pulled the muffs back over my ears, taking aim again. Confidence poured through my tense muscles, liquefying the solid barrier between me and the weapon, welding my aim to the target. With one call after my exhale. "Pull!" The trigger. Clay exploded. Target, hit.

I was born to do this.

A soft touch graced my cheek. "Wake up, beautiful." A voice from above. Eyelids opening, sunlight and a silhouette glowed over me. I focused on an adoring smile, on a handsome face.

Wake up. That hot actor? Daniel Pierce from the Ginny Smith Show?

He's standing over you while you're in nothing but your bra and panties.

Does this shit ever stop feeling odd?

He bent down. "Are you okay?" He pressed his lips to mine, his tongue searching too.

I sank deeper into him, into the mattress. "Yes," I sighed, letting the power of him tingle through every part of me, particularly *that* one.

He sat down beside me, nodding toward the flatscreen. "Did you watch?"

I sat up. "Yeah."

His hand glazed over my knee. "I wasn't expecting the other photo. Your battalion one. It shocked me. I tried hiding it, but I don't think very well."

"It shocked me too. Scared me actually. But it's done. The world knows who I am, so we're in this together now, Pierce."

"I have a couple hours before my lunch meeting." He stood back up and started unbuttoning his shirt, revealing a dusting of chest hair and chiseled muscles, damp with sweat underneath. "Do you want to join me in the hotel gym?" Tossing the shirt over the chair, it landed, drenched. "Because now we can be spotted together."

I answered his invite with a naughty grin.

It made him laugh, stepping out of his pants. "I don't have much time, Ms. Ravenel."

"A hot quickie is fine with me."

I sat up on my knees.

He stood naked in front of me, half liking the idea now, I could tell.

"A quickie's not fine with me," he said. "Not after this morning and those photos. Now that we're public, we'll celebrate tonight. First, with me taking you to dinner."

"Tell you what. You cover business; I'll cover the games for tonight. Deal?"

His devilish side grin agreed.

They took the game next-level, blessing me with a rain of shots.

Her with him at a film premiere. Her in the U.S. military. His celebrity confirming on live TV what some suspected all along. Patriots and fans are falling in love with their romantic union.

The story is splashing across screens. Posts are populating feeds. The reports from almost every global news outlet fill searches.

They.

Are.

Everywhere.

America lauds their beautiful new heroine. Like a warrior goddess for all to worship.

And the world's hero is in love with her.

Well, aren't we all?

Comments posted amuse me.

As if they know them. As if they are invited into their

lives, into their bed. As if they can taste a small drop of the ocean of their paradise.

Indeed, they are a couple in love.

A sexy, captivating one prime for paparazzi pursuit and fan obsession.

Captain Charlotte Roberts and Daniel Pierce...

A couple of high-value targets.

And my soldier had tracked him, following him in a cab, leaving the Midtown studio where his live interview was foolishly (reliably) announced in advance.

To an elite hotel nearby.

Between her beauty and military rank and his celebrity status, the reward will be RICH. The public spectacle of their murderous ruin GRAND.

Any price I pay for hunting them now?

Worth the grisly score.

CHAPTER NINETEEN

CHARLIE

Daniel kissed me goodbye. He had a late lunch with a director at Bagatelle. A final meeting with his manager at The Polo Bar for a review of next offers. Then finally, he was off. Off work and off grid for two months.

And my career was off too... on an indefinite hiatus.

His silver sedan pulled away. I followed, striding out of the parking garage onto the sidewalks of Midtown. I parted my hair down the middle, covering my scar, securing it into place with a Greek fisherman's cap.

I had several shops to visit before Daniel returned this evening. My body demanded a walk to them. It was a hot summer afternoon and other than my run and the premiere, I'd been cooped up in hotels for over a week.

Relieved to find my phone empty of Mason's texts, I reached out for a man who could lift my spirits any day.

"Sup, fucker!" I pictured him on the other end, first glass of Sangria for the evening in hand.

"Sup, fucker!" Rob's voice filled my heart. "Where you at, boo?"

Over five years we'd worked together and not one shitty fight between us.

"I'm in Manhattan, shopping for Daniel and sex toys." I caught the horny grin from the businessman passing by. "Where you at?"

"Damn, bitch. I'm still in Madrid. Getting turned on by visions of your man and sex toys. Need recommendations?"

"Nope. I got a credit card ready to burn down a list of kinks I crave." We shared everything, bonding over more than dirty banter and a love for men. The same war, same service, same PTSD connected us forever. "We're off to London before we head to my home, so I'm stocking up on some naughty buys."

"Sounds like you two are going to fuck your way around the world."

"We're gonna try." A glance up, two more blocks before my first stop. "His love and fucks are the only things keeping me sane and happy right now."

I told Rob about the unknown caller texts from Mason. Since I was sheltering Daniel from the torment, I had to share it with someone.

"That's some fucked up shit. Not surprising though," he said. "Given what Mason did to Kierra, it's textbook target transference that he's focused on you now."

"Speaking of, how's my girl doing?" The week since I'd seen Kierra felt like a month already.

"She's all happy with sass like you taught her. Her family goes home to Galway on Monday. Everything's secure. Joaquin and I will chill here with his family for a couple weeks and enjoy our time off. You're not the only one planning a fuckfest for a vacation."

The cosmic stars aligning thrilled me. How I found love and so had Rob—falling for men at work when we shouldn't have.

It bonded the four of us together even more.

"It doesn't feel like a vacation," I said. "Not with these damn texts exploding into my day."

"What's your plan, then? Offense or defense?"

"Right now, it's a waiting game."

Rob laughed. "And you're a gold-medal bitch in it. Mason's good at evil, but no one beats you in that event. Need anything from me? A trip to California to shut him up forever?"

"Tempting, but no. If anyone's muzzling him for good, it's me."

I stood in front of the first store. A group of teens idled outside, phones in hand, eyes darting my way. Did they recognize me? Or was it my imagination?

Fuck, this was crazy making—having a public face.

Now I didn't know... was it ego or instinct talking.

"Just be on standby for me," I said. "I don't know what the hell is coming our way."

"You know I will, boo. But don't let that asshole Mason get into your head and bed and ruin this. You waited too long not to enjoy that hot-ass man of yours. So, the only thing that deserves to be coming is you. Tonight. Many times. With him and some nasty lingerie and toys. Send me pics."

"Maybe. Love you, fucker." Call over.

Rob's right. If a flamethrower's gonna torch my private life, I might as well enjoy my smoking-hot companion until it's all scorching white ash.

I left fear waiting on the sidewalk while I stepped inside the flagship store for American Threads.

Elaine, Daniel's assistant, had offered to shop for him, but I knew better. Elaine wouldn't have an eye for how to dress him. More like disguise him. But I could turn England's proud son into a South Carolina Lowcountry boy.

Yeah, right. Hiding Daniel Pierce's handsome face and eye-popping frame is like hiding a July Fourth fireworks show on a clear night.

Still, safety insisted I try.

The camouflaging bounty included cargo shorts, logo tees, swim trunks, board shorts, baseball caps, and, of course, three pairs of flip-flops.

This should do it. I sent for a car from the concierge at the hotel to take the heavy bags back to our room before walking to my next destination.

On to the real shopping fun.

CHAPTER TWENTY

DANIEL

Rain by Ro James

What turned me on more?

The sexy texts from Charlie saying to meet her in The Gold Room, our hotel's restaurant of opulent metallic walls and ceiling wrapped around chocolate leather everywhere?

Or was it the crowd of posh hotel guests and Manhattan society seated around? All who would witness her entrance, joining me at our table for two in the back.

Was it the public display of our love that pleased me?

Temping, but no.

It was the seductive game she was playing, making me twitch in my trousers at this sexy sport.

For tonight. For forever, I prayed.

The cocktail menu made me laugh at the memory, at the cosmic irony of the restaurant's signature drink. The

Mrs. Astor—vodka, Campari, lemon, strawberry, and balsamic—the flavors of their first kiss. I ordered one for Charlie.

There was a cabernet sauvignon from Napa I wanted to try. And I had fun with the shared plate menu too, ordering dishes from our homes—fish 'n' chips and fried chicken.

A sensation blanched my skin.

I glanced up.

A woman was trying to take discreet photos with her phone. People put their eyes on me the second I walked in and hadn't left stopped.

I didn't give a flying fuck. Nothing would keep me from enjoying the freedom of my first public dinner date with Charlie.

This was our last night here before a flight tomorrow to escape. Escaping for a week in my world. Then I'd immerse myself for much longer in hers—in every sense of the word.

In the past, I never bent my life or location for a woman. They followed me, my schedule, my career. Now, I welcomed Charlie's world circling mine in infinite measure.

While the sommelier poured the wine, my eyes turned toward the door, my gaze always fated to find her. An audible gasp escaped my lips at the approaching vision.

From the toe up, I didn't recognize her.

Clicking black stiletto heels aimed my way. Matching glossy stockings under a hard-core minidress with a sweetheart neckline. Wild waves of a blonde mane spilling over her shoulders.

Fuck's sake, the sight of her fit body bound tight in black leather stalking toward me made saliva pool in my mouth.

Me and my cock stood, greeting her with a "I want to fuck you right now" kiss with all eyes of the high-brow crowd on us. I pulled the chair out for her. She sat, crossing her legs, revealing stockings clasped into lacy black suspenders.

A moan growled down my throat while I sat across from her. But my cock didn't. It stood, hard and impatient, under the table, wanting to toss it over and fuck her now on the parquet wood floors.

"Ms. Ravenel, thank you for the pleasure of your company this evening."

Instead, I raised a glass to her sexy efforts. *Clink.*

"Mr. Pierce, I assure you, you will enjoy a lot of pleasure in my company tonight."

Bloody hell, toast to that and any rituals required to keep this woman in your life, Pierce.

I watched her pink lips sip the drink, savoring the taste of our first kiss. Her lashes closed. A surprised smile spread across her gorgeous face. That lush mouth professed "you've got to be kidding me" as she found me smiling at my surprise for her.

"The memory is on the menu," I said, "so we must be fated to be here now."

Our plates were placed in front of us. Laughter at my dinner choices quaked her cleavage and my soul, lust and love tumbling through me.

"How long do I have to sit here in this dazzling torture?" Wine poured over my lips. I licked them before adding, "Now that we're in public and in love, I want to bend you over this table right now, lift up that dress, spread your thighs and let them all watch just how much."

"Let a lady enjoy her drink first." Batting her lashes at me, "Or two, actually. I love the taste," she was a tease on two fit legs. "Second only to your creamy flavor."

"Show me mercy. You've got me in a hard state. There will be no discreet exit as three phones are on us right now."

We managed to behave through dinner.

Of course, she made a smart-ass comment about million-dollar fried chicken that had me rolling. Over a second round of drinks, I told her about my day, my next films and projects. She didn't mention her afternoon.

I was curious. "I see you've been shopping." The dress and lingerie were new to her wardrobe. I guessed Bergdorf's.

"I made quite a few purchases today. I bought your entire wardrobe for Lowcountry life."

"Entire wardrobe? I have plenty of casual clothes."

"No, you don't, Oliver Twist. Trust me in my neck of the woods. Your Southern accent is improving, but you're too fucking pretty and recognizable. Just wear what I bought and please don't talk."

"Speaking of fuckable and wardrobe." I took the last sip noticing she had taken hers too. "May I beg of you that we make our exit now while I'm in a presentable state?" I rose, offering my hand.

She smiled, eyes on my crotch. "Better hurry."

Taking my hand and heart, she stood up beside me. I relished it, proudly wrapping my arm around her tiny waist clad in butter-soft leather.

This moment, walking beside her as we worked our way through the crowded restaurant, I never felt so proud. Not just proud. It was pure. Pure joy. Pure love. For all to see.

Two women at the table to my right recorded us. Three others in front took pictures. Sod it all.

I was too focused upon taming my stiffy long enough to make it to the elevator.

FROM THE SHOWER, I heard a hard-core playlist throbbing through the speakers downstairs. After drying off, I slid black trousers back on with nothing underneath.

Descending the curving staircase into a dark living room with floor-to-ceiling windows, the city lights guided me. She wasn't here. I smiled, spotting the open glass doors to the terrace, following her scent.

The sight of her thrummed my every muscle tense. An hourglass clad in tight ebony leather. A perfect profile, confidently gazing out over the city with a drink in hand. My bare feet pursued the vision, capturing her waist in my grasp, always loving the ask across my lips. "May I have this dance, Ms. Ravenel?"

She spun around, inches from my lips, "Always, Mr. Pierce," before setting her drink down.

Music poured through the air. My grip secured her body against mine. With one hand lacing through the tresses at the nape of her neck, my other thrilled over her ass, curious about what hid underneath. Silky strands tickled my nose, inhaling the mouth-watering praline spice of her perfume.

Nothing I wanted more than what I held in my grasp. She was a gift I couldn't stop coveting.

Her fingertips skated down my naked back. The ache for her right then flexed my breath, but I surrendered to the honour of worshipping her all night.

"Did I tell you how ravishing you look, Ms. Ravenel?" Gentle bites I took down her neck as the tune morphed into another singing of lust. She arched open, sinews soft for my possession.

"Did I tell you no one else can ravage me but you, Mr. Pierce?"

"Can it always only be me?"

"Perhaps."

She directed my hand to the zipper of her dress. One long pull parted the gold chain. Gliding my palms over her shoulders, it fell to the deck.

Holy fuck, the sight seized my eyes. Lights glowing around us cast shadows over lithe muscles and curves. Of her body adorned with a black lace suspender belt under a black G-string with a matching lace demi cup bra.

"Is this all for me, Charlie?" My hunger shredded her into delicious pieces. One at a time, I'd devour them all.

"Take what you want, Daniel."

Crashing my lips to hers, I charged her back fast against the glass window of the terrace. A large ivory umbrella cantilevered over us, barely concealing our salacious spectacle.

I dropped to my knees. "I'll have all of you"—starting at her arched ankles in heels, I caressed up her silky calves, over her carved thighs, swearing—"and I'll never get enough."

But I tried.

With the light touch of my fingers and heat of my mouth, I teased time and again where nylon and lace met her flesh. Steaming through knickers over her soft mound with my breath, her musk raided my memory.

With my lips pressed to her damp lace, nose taking in her intoxicating scent, I insisted, "Tell me what you want, Charlie."

I craved her command. How her breath shallowed when she said it.

My ears burned greedy for her consent while my eyes watched her lips, nose inhaling her desire, my body waiting for permission to unleash.

Upon her command I heard, "Eat my pussy, Daniel," and I did.

Ripping the knickers down to her ankles, fingertips spreading her open before burying my mouth, my tongue licked, feasting on what I thirsted for.

She cried out. Clasping her hands through my wet waves, trapping me here, she bent her knees. "You fucking love eating my pussy, don't you?" She writhed hard over my face.

Her aggression made me moan, responding with my own, relishing her with a fierce, darting tongue and then lush, thick licks. God, she tasted so good. My fingers eased into her slick tunnel before I slid my knuckles back and forth against her walls while I sucked her clit.

Thighs trembling, she was almost there. My eager mouth waited, needing to drink her, driving my digits as hard as she pulled me in.

Her body seized, gasping my name. Yes, and her tight contractions wrapped around my fingers, her lust drenching down my wrist, her body shaking over my lips devoted to her fresh salty pleasure.

I stood up, serving my two drizzled fingers to her mouth. "Taste what I do to you, Charlie." She sucked them like she did my cock, hard and hungry. "Since the world knows you're mine now, I'm going to fuck you for all to see how much."

Dropping my trousers, desire possessed me, right here, on the terrace, in the dark, hot air of the Midtown skyline. The night gave us enough shadows, but the public risk intoxicated me. I wanted the spectacle.

"Do it," she insisted, kicking her knickers away.

Her ribs still heaved for breath as I seized her firm ass cheeks, pinning her against the glass. A craze took me and my cock, making her cry out while I drove into her dripping want with abandon.

Care for the world outside left. Desperately, I only needed the one inside her. Yes, her always, could I ever get enough?

Then... I could sense it—someone watching us.

It only drove my urge harder, craving the shameless declaration. I loved this. Loved her. Let them watch. Let them record it. It didn't matter. Nothing did. Only her. We were going. Together.

"Daniel, stop." She panted, hanging on to me, to our edge. "Take me inside."

Kicking my trousers away, I walked us through the doorway to the low chaise lounge. She told me to lay her down, directing me to kneel beside her mouth.

A groan lulled up my throat, watching her tongue skim my glistening shaft, licking off the glaze of her lust along with my first milky drops.

She clamped my hand between her open thighs, making me brace my other against the cushion behind her.

I worshipped the sight—her body, writhing in black lingerie, her hungry mouth taking my length while my hand claimed what dripped tight for me.

"Yes, Charlie. You're so willing for me, so fucking wet." I tried making it last. "Fuck my fingers while I fuck your tight throat." It did until that made her moan, feeding on my cock, her spit drizzling off my crown. Oh God, I was there. "Yes, you're so fucking dirty for me, aren't you?" My naughty taunt, this lewd view of her, my climax, it scorched up, swelling for fast release. "Fuck, babe, I'm coming."

She pulled her mouth off, offering her tongue to my sweet spurts. I lost my mind, praising her name and the obscene sight, shuddering at my creamy spasms over her lips causing her sex to clamp around my fingers. The arch of her body, coming at the taste of me and the shameless show she gave, it shook me with a final spasm over her tongue.

"My God, Charlie." I sank to the floor, on my knees, bowing to rest my head on her huffing taut belly. I had to find my breath while she found hers, softly caressing through my waves.

Both of us knew... our ritual wasn't done for the night.

CHAPTER TWENTY-ONE

CHARLIE

The glide of his hand tickled my back. "I hope I make it up to you," he said.

"Make up what?" I asked, my toes still encased in silky nylon, drawing them over his bare feet.

"How it will never be the same for you. No more privacy. There will be pictures from our dinner tonight. Of all our dates, our walks, our shopping, wherever we go, we'll be watched, photographed, gossiped about."

We took in the view of the night skyline, propped up together on the sofa by the glass doors, enjoying another drink.

"Does it ever bother you?"

I had to be honest. His forecast was accurate. The storm blowing in over my life because of his fame, it did frighten me. Only in moments like this, folded into his body, did it all feel worth it.

"Not really. I've grown numb to it. But now, when they'll come after you, I'll feel it. I want to protect you from it, but I can't." His arms squeezed tighter. "I just don't want you hating me for it."

"I could never hate you."

He lay quiet for a moment. "We've both lost too much to say 'never' or 'forever'."

Something in his words. There was a depth, a pain I knew but didn't want to believe.

"I'm a grown woman. I can take it." The words came easily out of my mouth. But for the first time, the senti-ment... it faltered.

Could I take it? The stalking paparazzi and fans? The threat of Mason? The haunt of something even worse coming for me that maddened my mind? Did I really love him so much that I'd risk it all for him?

"Babe, you say that now, but wait and see. It can be manic. You don't know yet what it feels like... for years, years of being hounded and followed."

Yes, I did.

I didn't tell him.

Paparazzi and fans would be new.

But feeling hunted? I sensed this long before him.

"You're right. I don't know your world yet." Every muscle on my frame squeezed him tighter too. "But I've known love. And I love you now." I kissed over his heart. "With manic, mad love."

A kiss from his lips dragged across my hair. "You have no idea how much I love you, Charlie. How incredible you are. How every time I look at you, I'm in awe. Every time I kiss your scars..."—his chest huffed—"you're the real hero and I'm the lucky one."

Whatever came our way? I could take it. And take him.

No one was promised it all.

If forever didn't exist. If never could happen. Well then,

time was a crashing wave you couldn't stop, and I'd stand with him in it.

His fingertips tickled down my abs. "But I'll forever remember this glorious vision of you," he said, making my muscles quiver. "I hope you know I find you just as sexy in my sweatpants and T-shirt."

"Glad I kept the receipt, then."

"Don't you dare." He tugged at the bow over the clasp where the garter held my stockings. "This ensemble is a weekly must now."

My hand floated down his happy trail. Whoever came up with that name was right. It was the path to my paradise.

"Hmm, sounds like I should keep the other gift I got for you too?"

"Fuck's sake, there's more?"

When it came to us, there'd always be more. Standing up, letting him drink in the sight, I walked across the room. Bending over for his gaze, I plucked a small black bag with a matching ribbon handle from the floor. I sauntered back toward him, dangling it in front of his nose, offering my other hand.

"I'll never be done playing you, Mr. Pierce."

With an extra sway of my ass for his view, I led him into the dark dining room adjoined by an intimate seating area of low leather sofas overlooking another wall of windows.

I turned around, swinging the bag over the crook of my index finger.

"Do you want this or sweatpants?"

He raked his hand through his hair, smiling. "The lady does make a compelling point."

With a shameless grin I informed him, "This is not a lady's gift, Daniel."

Indeed, it wasn't.

Luscious minutes later, I watched him over my shoulder, struggling to control himself at the sight of his cock sinking into my pussy bent over for him.

His gaze was down, marveling at his gift—a pink jeweled princess plug in my other space of desire, preparing to take his cock one day.

I could hear the strain in his throat, how it mandated every breath of control he groaned for, his eyes enraptured by my display.

He had opened me with gentle fingers and lube, introducing a new ritual into the lustful path of what we'd slowly explore together. The sensation was scary, then incredible. I wanted this with him.

It only bonded us more. The trust I gave. The patience he lavished me with. I never thought it possible, to be this exposed, this defenseless. But with him, I didn't need walls. They all fell for him.

Tame thrusts of his cock kept spiraling me up to a new, ready peak of ecstasy, feeling every sensation of his mass diving into me. The lush, heavy pressure heightened my pleasure, pushing inside me, my walls clutching around him tight.

His hands spread my cheeks wide, exposing me more. "Damn, babe. Look at you." His tempo didn't stop. "Fuck, you drive me mad." He pulled out, leaving me open, aching. Then with a grunt, he plunged back in, hard. "You're my new jewel."

I cried out. His brutal force quaked my thighs, making me weak. I bowed over the back of the leather sofa while he kneeled behind me, guiding me there, stroking me higher, and higher, up to this exotic edge.

"Daniel, God." I motioned for him to hold still. "It's so

much."

He slowed. "You want me like this, Charlie?" Grinding deep circles with his thick cock, his fingers reached around, delivering the same force over my clit. The pleasure seared my nerves. With a scream, I burst with its flooding fire.

His groan thundered the room, holding on, knowing my body. Knowing I had more coming.

With a fierce swirl in the opposite direction, he took one more from me, stealing my voice that could only find breath for a moan as it poured down my thighs, soaking over his.

"Goddamn, Charlie." He didn't stop. "I can feel you pulsing around my cock."

The weight of his chest laid over my back. Pulling my lace bra down, taking my nipple, he matched his thrusts to his light twirling pinch. His lips pressed to my ear. "You love coming for me, don't you, Charlie?"

Barely able to speak, I huffed, "Yes."

"Tell me." His voice coaxed my nerves to thin, his fingertips doing the same to my clit. My God, I was ready to snap with a fire across my every fiber. "Is it only for me?"

It shook me in violent rapture, under the heft of his voice, of his body and the promise of his presence in every part of me. "Yes, Daniel."

More luscious grinding inside. More of his voice in my ear, in my soul. "Your nipples?" He pinched one. "Your clit?" He rattled it. "Your pussy?" He pounded it. "Your ass?" It stretched for him. "Say it. Are they all mine?" With a soft kiss to my back, "To love, Charlie?" with a ferocious hard thrust, he growled, "And to fuck?"

No other sound, no other sensation but him, rushing over me, everywhere. "Yes, Daniel." The highest edge scraped under my fingernails, almost letting go.

With a loud primal moan, he leaned back, thrusting his

thick cock with savage pounds while he pulsed his glossed jewel, to its widest point and back, stretching me even farther. It dropped me.

The coupled sensation, it made us both come in worshipping gasps for each other, losing all light and sound, sliding and slipping down together.

Holding on to me, he laid us down on the sofa in the shared, sweet palpitations of it, of my back heaving against his chest, of his breath in my ear.

I struggled to still my body, to find my breath. Like he did for a while. But I couldn't stop trembling.

His palm soothed over my hair. "You okay, babe?" He sounded worried by my silence and shakes.

"Yes." I took his hand. "I just don't think I can stand right now." A heavy weight of satisfaction, of sleep almost took me.

"Hold on to me." He picked me up, carrying me to the threshold of our bathroom. "I'll get the bed ready while you start the shower for us." He set my feet down.

I closed the door, tending to this new state of my body, spent and satiated. He joined me once he heard water splashing. We lavished each other with soap and kisses under the almost hot water. My eyes couldn't stay opened.

Towels dropping by our bedside, we crawled into the mountain of white sheets and blankets. He covered us, taking his place behind me, intertwining his legs with mine, wrapping his arm around me to hold my hand.

"I love you, Charlotte Ravenel." He kissed my hair, gently squeezing my hand. "I'll give everything away to be with you."

My exhausted lips echoed his love before I fell into the deepest sleep of content.

ANONYMOUS

I often wondered about her scars.

About how she got them.

So did millions. They were in awe of them. In awe of her.

She's on covers.

They're in the headlines.

The world is enthralled by the captivating couple.

Posting and chatting about them, their conjecture is fueled by even more shots of them enjoying a dinner date in Manhattan. It was a proud open display of their love.

One I relish.

The ascension of the adored couple will only make their murderous fall more spectacular.

Zooming in on where bullets had pierced her skin, I smile.

The vision?

How bloody her wounds were.

How much pain they must have raged through her flesh and bones.

How she had apparently survived them.

Not again.

There will be no more scars on her.

Dead bodies don't scar.

They only rot with fatal wounds.

CHAPTER TWENTY-TWO

CHARLIE

Daniel knelt behind me, holding my hair back. "Babe, do you even remember last night?"

"Yes" fell from my lips before another retch. I lost everything this morning *but* my memory.

Breakfast and coffee.

Joy and safety.

I'd bolted toward the bathroom, barely making it before a heave rippled up my spine, wrenching my stomach. It all spewed from my mouth.

Daniel had rushed in after me. "You had too much to drink last night," he guessed.

Yes, I drank more than usual. And, yes, it was a hell of a night.

But something more potent stormed through my insides.

While we had munched on our breakfast served on silver room-service trays, we nestled atop our big bed.

Daniel checked messages, reviewing our travel to London today.

And I checked my phone.

Emails from Jeremy glowed back. He wrote that I needed to digitally sign paperwork for our report to the San Diego Police Department, providing proof of the case against Mason.

The logic was here, my fingertip hovering over the Instagram icon.

Coffee churned my stomach. Acid from orange slices I loved burned my throat. It didn't stop me.

I'd pressed the screen to Mason Hunt's feed.

There? A photo of Daniel kissing me at the premiere. Swipe. A photo someone took of our date last night. Swipe. Another photo. The one from the gym with Daniel carrying me in his arms.

Pupils scanning, I read Mason's comment.

Congratulations to my colleagues #danielpierce
and #captaincharlotteroberts. Ain't love a bloody
grand show?

It choked the life from my throat.

My soles hit the floor, running from its sickening grasp.

No stopping it now.

"Babe"—Daniel asked once there was nothing left in me, wetting a washcloth for me—"should I phone down for a doctor?"

Spitting the last piece of terror into the toilet, I answered, "No. I'm fine. Just no more Mrs. Astor drinks."

I couldn't tell him yet.

Emotions would own him. Rage. Worry. Insanity at the truth—there was nothing we could do about Mason.

Nothing but what I was doing, keeping us safe and hidden.

There was no crime in a colleague posting a picture of another, sharing public photos blasted across social media.

What could we file a complaint about?

It was only America's pretty-boy Mason Hunt, joining in the global adoration, congratulating Daniel Pierce on the new love of his life, Captain Charlotte Roberts.

You're fucked now, Charlie Girl.

Mason's post just aimed the red X. *White Flag zealots will be gunning for you and Daniel now. Goddammit, you played right into his hands.*

Yeah? Well, there was no other hand to play.

Daniel squatted beside me, blessing cool cotton across my forehead.

"Let me at least phone for some medicine. You can't get on a flight to London like this."

He's right. Suck it the fuck up and deal with this.

"Okay."

I rolled over, leaning against the wall behind me. This was as good as it got with me accepting help. I'd let Daniel care of me while I took care of Mason Hunt.

For now... I had a call to make.

FOR A VIP AIRPORT LOUNGE, it sure was crowded. What else should I expect, though, on the last Saturday of July? Seemed everyone had somewhere to go, even celebrities and CEOs.

Daniel dropped into one of two lounge chairs by the window, his phone buzzing this afternoon with calls home.

I took advantage of his distraction, excusing myself to

the restroom. Actually? I found a hidden corner away from prying ears to raise my own damn flag.

"Ravenel. To what do I owe the honour of a Saturday night call?"

The tone of my boss's voice? Always disarming. But make no mistake. Jeremy Bennet was a Grand Master of Security.

I didn't know what he did before that made him so qualified to run an international security firm and I was smart enough not to ask.

Glancing over my shoulder, I made sure ears weren't skulking by. "I'm sitting at JFK on my way to your side of the pond."

"I know you too well, Ravenel, to assume you're phoning to schedule a visit for tea."

Damn, I loved him. And everyone else who jumped past the bullshit and got down to business.

"Nope. I'm not. I need to work with you on something. And it's just between us. No one else."

"Let's have it."

The pen clicking commenced. Every time I called, the man clicked a pen. Like threats fired his synapses *and* his damn thumb.

"I need everything on Mason Hunt. Everything you can find on his active *White Flag* affiliates. And I need your help keeping eyes on them too."

"Will do," he said. "Care to tell me more or am I pissing blind on this one?"

"He's blowing up my phone. Unknown caller bullshit, but it's him. I'll send you a log of the texts when I have a secure line. Check his Instagram if you don't already. The sick fuck posted a white flag days ago. His post today were pictures of me and Daniel."

The loudspeaker overhead stole the volume. "Ladies and gentlemen, British Airways Flight 116 has begun boarding."

Still, in the returning silence, Jeremy said nothing.

I peaked around the corner. Daniel's neck started to crane, looking for me. "Boss, you still there?"

"Yes. I just checked Hunt's Instagram." More pen clicking. "I've got to tell you Ravenel, I don't like this at all."

"Me neither," I said. Daniel stood up, stretching his legs, eyes scanning for me. "Just pull what you can find and when we're wheels down in London, I'll call you."

"All right, then. Safe travels." Jeremy ended the call.

Once we were on the plane, I didn't know whether to be impressed with the first-class individual pod-like suites we were booked in or bummed that we weren't in coach.

Yes, the seating was sumptuous for a commercial plane. The pods had all the comfort bells and whistles.

But it isolated me.

Daniel sat across the aisle, kicking back in his own pod for the overnight flight while I was left alone in mine. The window and my fear were my only travel companions.

Resting my head back on the chair, the dizziness from the anti-nausea medicine kicked in. The airplane floor underneath my seat became a tilt-o-wheel carnival ride.

My eyelids snapped open, finding balance.

A low commotion of the last passengers filed in. My heart seized a beat at the sight.

A young woman in a black headscarf took her seat in the pod in front of Daniel. Her daughter bounced in the aisle beside her, tiny hands held out, impatient, asking for her tablet for the long trip.

The mom glanced my way. Stylish translucent frames rested on full cheeks over a gentle smile. I offered her a kind smile back. Speaking Farsi, the little girl kept asking for her tablet and stuffed turtle.

The memory of a similar sight? Of a beautiful young mother and her little girl. Speaking a different language. One I also knew.

It strangled me, squeezing all air and the six years since from my lungs. Forcing me right back.

To there.

Back to the much younger mother and daughter in Afghanistan. The ones who suffered a brutality nothing but death could free them from. Death of their abuser. A death my soul bore the burden of.

And I'd do it again if it meant that mother and daughter would be safe from him.

If I thought I knew terror, I knew nothing. Nothing compared to what those girls used to endure. Every day. Every night. With no escape.

Until I tried.

Tried to free them.

It was a fair trade—their safety then for mine now.

Because every turn of fate from that day had brought me to this one. Terrified for my life. And Daniel's.

If you had to do it again, would you? Take the job to save another girl, Kierra?

You did it and found your greatest love. And your greatest risk. Living now in a colossal dream and nightmare.

Grief and thirty-three years taught me questioning the past was a fool's errand. I never had a choice. Protecting others defined me.

The only selfish thing I'd done was love Daniel. But if I didn't allow myself this one beautiful indulgence there would be nothing left of me to help others.

Even if it cost me my life.

A sudden stream of tears spilled over my lashes. My face turned toward the window. Hiding my reaction. To my love. My fear. My fate.

"Ma'am, can I get you anything before we prepare to taxi? Champagne?" The flight attendant dutifully hovered above me.

With a quick swipe of the torment down my cheeks, I answered, "No, thank you."

He squatted by my side. "Ma'am, are you okay?"

Hell no, I wasn't okay. "I'm fine, thank you."

But his attention was enough to get Daniel's. He stood up, towering behind the attendant. "Babe, is everything all right?"

The flight attendant looked over his shoulder, immediate recognition of Daniel and then pure pleasure took his face. He rose to greet him. "Can I get *either* of you anything, sir?"

"Yes, please," Daniel replied. "Can you get us two ginger ales and some crackers?"

See, *this* man knew exactly how to care for me.

The flight attendant bowed slightly, rushing away to his task.

Daniel squatted beside me, aqua eyes searching mine, taking my hand. "Are you feeling sick again?" His thumb caressed my hand, and dammit if it didn't rush another river of tears down my cheeks.

What the fuck is wrong with you, Charlie Girl?

Got a pen and paper? You're gonna be jotting down a damn long list.

His palm moved to my soaked cheek. "Do we need to get off the plane?"

"No. I'm fine. Not sick. The medicine is making me dizzy. And this whole first-class thing does not cream my corn."

My Southern sass made us smile.

"Mama, where is my electric cord?" The girl sitting in front of me stood in the aisle, tugging at her mom's sleeve. "The tablet lost its power."

I understood what she said, but the sight and foreign language turned Daniel's head. Taking in the same tender spectacle—the adorable mother and daughter—he turned back to gaze at me.

If one could paint compassion across a person's face it would color his now.

"I see." His hand squeezed mine while he whispered, "Do you want to move seats?"

"Please, no." I'd crawl over glass for miles and then jump in a pool of rubbing alcohol before risking offending them. "I'll be fine. And with the woozy I'm feeling, I'll be asleep in no time."

"I hate being across the aisle in that pod and not able to hold you."

"Me too. Next time, we fly coach."

We chuckled. Daniel Pierce hadn't flown coach since the suffix of "teen" left his age, commercial flights growing rarer still for him. But he bitched about not being a pompous prat, or an entitled polluter, resisting the indulgence of private charters whenever he could.

He patted my hand. "Get some rest. I'll check on you in bit."

"That's what they pay flight attendants for."

He stood up, looking every bit the fucking sexiest man alive and the sweetest man aboard the plane.

"Well, you know how I like to make the skies friendly for you, Ms. Ravenel."

Indeed, he did. On the private planes where we scored

more than miles together. *This* was not an option on a large public aircraft like this.

The flight attendant came back with our request. It amused me. All the high-end food in first class and all I craved was soda and crackers.

The cabin lights and my eyes dimmed. The aircraft climbed while I fell. Deep asleep and into a vivid dream. Remembering...

My mother with long chestnut waves curtaining her gaze. She glanced up, staring over the rim of her turquoise readers, across the dinner table at me.

"Charlotte, eat your pollo guisado. You haven't touched a bite."

"I'm not hungry," I said, pushing the chicken with my fork around the arabesque plate.

"Why not? It's your favorite dish."

The slow drop of my mother's book to the table warned I wasn't getting away with sulking.

"They're all mean to me, Mama."

It was the second week at the school I'd started after my family moved to Turkey. And I had suffered through it.

When I was eight, my parents plucked me from the safe shores of South Carolina to Spain. It became home by the time I was ten, only for them to rip me away again.

If they were handing out awards for "Best Bratty Child," I won the trophy. I was angry leaving our home and friends in Madrid to move here, to Ankara, Turkey, for two more years.

I was almost eleven. Didn't know the language. Didn't know anyone.

"Do you try, Charlotte?" The glasses came off my mom's bronze face. I knew—that meant no-bullshit mom. "Do you try talking to people? In their language? That's why you're at the International School. They're trying to teach you, but you must try too."

"But I sound like an idiot. Turkish is hard."

Asking an eleven-year-old girl to speak a new language in public when a Niagara Falls of insecurity washed over her world should be a war crime of cruel and unusual punishment in my young mind.

"I know it's hard." My mother spoke in English now. We were speaking Spanish. She switched to her non-native tongue, making a point. "It's been hard for me too. People in the States laugh at me, at my accent, but I won't let them silence me."

I recalled years back, clothes shopping in Hilton Head, South Carolina.

How the cashier had made a cruel comment about my mom's rich Dominican accent. Like the mean woman couldn't understand her. So, I'd chimed up with my hand on my hip, swaying my neck with the biggest Southern drawl I could muster.

"My mama said she ain't *got* no fifty-dollar bill. She's wonderin' if y'all can break a hundred instead. But I suppose you don't know *shit* from Shinola 'bout what a hundred-dollar bill looks like, do ya?"

I was seven years old. Knew I shouldn't cuss. Didn't know what the hell "shit from Shinola" meant. I'd just heard my dad and Pop say it all the time, so I threw it in for good measure.

My mom didn't care.

Her arm had wrapped over me in a firm side squeeze, handing over a hundred-dollar bill to the cashier with more grace in her tan pinky than a Southern belle has in her lifetime.

That same hand reached out for mine across the dinner

table. My mom's touch—always a warm dose of vigor and love. And always smelled like coconut.

"If you want to survive, Charlotte, you must talk to people in their language."

I played with the diamond on my mom's wedding ring, swiveling it back and forth across her thin finger.

"Yes, ma'am."

"Perdón?"

My mom made another firm point, switching back to Spanish.

Putting my focus on the delicious aroma of garlic, oregano, and turmeric under my nose, I shoveled a pile of chicken and rice onto my fork, lifting my eyes and chin, answering, "Sí, Mama."

"MAMA! MAMA! WHERE IS MY MAMA?"

Cries from a girl woke me. Dawn light debuted in the window. The commotion dragged my eyes to peer into the airplane aisle.

The flight attendant replied, "She's in the bathroom, sweetie."

But the girl couldn't understand him.

I jumped up and knelt by her pod. "Your mom is in the bathroom. She will be right back. Would you like me stay here until she does?" I spoke the girl's language.

It made her little head cant to the side with a happy smile.

"What's your name?" she asked.

"Charlie. What's yours?"

"Neda." She picked up her stuffed rainbow turtle. "This is Roya."

"Well, hello, Roya and Neda. It's nice to meet you both."

The plane hit a bump. And another. It shocked the girl. I didn't care for it either but wouldn't show it.

The girl's tiny face squinched, frantic. "Where's my mama?"

I pointed to the "Occupied" lavatory door over my shoulder.

"She's right there. She will be right out. I promise." Changing the subject, I distracted her from her mom's absence and the plane's turbulence. "Did Roya have her breakfast yet?"

"No, not yet. Roya likes apples."

Another bounce.

I worried I'd have to return to my seat, leaving the girl alone and scared. Thankfully, with a click and slide, the mother appeared.

I stood up with another drop in the air. The mom thanked me while we had to return to our seats.

Daniel leaned out of his pod.

He had watched the whole thing, reaching his hand out for mine for a quick squeeze before I sat down and buckled up. Seemed we'd rock and roll through a final descent into Heathrow Airport.

Once we landed, taxiing toward the terminal gate, I, like everyone, took my phone out of airplane mode to see what had pinged my way.

Two texts.

One from Jeremy.

I've got an update.
Ring me when you're in &
watch your six

He'd told me that before, each time not mincing words to watch my back. Below his text.

Unknown
Love can be so black & white.
Will it be worth it?

I deciphered Mason's text. White for my hair. Black for Daniel's. Our love. Our now-public relationship in black-and-white print all over the media.

The sadistic fuck deserved a few points for creativity.

Only a few.

Remember what mama taught you? To survive—talk to people in their language.

Thrill stuck a needle in my vein. The taunt seeping through my muscles with liquid elation, seeking the high of the hunt.

I replied:

And yet pain is so black & blue.
And always worth it

Like the bruises of pain I'd put around Mason's neck, choking him out.

Pretty man didn't like it very much. When a woman beat the hell out of his rapist ass.

See how much of that shit sandwich Mason could eat before spitting it—and his identity—out.

Satisfaction radiated through my nerves at the *whoot* sound.

Text. Sent.

CHAPTER TWENTY-THREE

DANIEL

I watched the mum in the headscarf and the little girl. They were first off the plane. When I turned to Charlie standing up beside me, she did the same.

Funny what triggered memories. They weren't speaking the Pashto Charlie had spoken in Afghanistan, but the presence of them—of a young mum and her daughter—it seemed to bring it all back for her.

My hand rested on the small of her back. "Feeling better this morning?"

She beamed up at me, a completely different woman from the one crying hours before. "Much better."

Slinging the backpack over her shoulder, she led our path out of the plane to our escort who guided us to the car where Simon and Matt waited.

This was the security I conceded to. Simon took a flight the day before to meet us in London. Matt, Simon's backup, was already here. They'd escort us safely home today. Afterward, both men were on holiday while Charlie and I were secretly tucked away in my home, later in hers.

And I craved every moment of it. No security. No driver. No team around. Only her in my home and later, with my family... like a bloody normal person.

"So, what's on the itinerary?" she asked, gazing out of the car window at London whizzing by on the M4.

"A quick stop by my townhouse to freshen up, grab a few things and a bite, then a five-hour drive to Cornwall. My mum is coming round tomorrow to prepare for the party. Then everyone descends upon us on Tuesday."

She turned back to me; eyes wide. "Everyone?"

I chuckled. "Just my family. But trust me, they're enough to make any gathering a party."

The grip of her hand twisted in mine. "Tell me again the lineup."

A list of names and relations trotted out of my mouth. My eldest brother, his wife, and two boys. My next eldest brother, his husband, their new daughter, the guest of honour. My sister, Tess. Maybe she'd bring a date. And my parents.

"Only ten or so of us," I said. "Not a lot."

"That's a lot to me. I come from a family of three, now only one, remember?" Her free hand raked through her golden locks. "I haven't even had a chance to get a gift for the baby. I wanted to get her a book."

"We'll go tomorrow when shops are open." I lifted her hand to my lips, ease filling my bones to be home and with her.

Minutes later, white columns and black iron fencing in front of rows of Knightsbridge townhouses filled the vista, signaling we were close.

I reached forward, patting Simon's shoulder. "Give us a couple of hours, yeah."

Simon checked the clock on the dash. "All right. Back at eleven, then."

The car turned down the cobblestone road to my door.

On a quiet Sunday morning, two people were walking their dogs. The path was clear to the quaint garage doors in the line of mews houses that included mine as we approached. Matt slowed the car to my door.

Suddenly, Charlie reached forward, "Don't stop," grabbing Matt's arm. "Keep driving."

"What?" I asked.

"Drive. Now." Her tone barked with might. Matt had no choice but obey. "That man up there." Her chin gestured to a bald guy having a smoke, dressed in black, four doors up and standing by a planter with a sculpted, topiary tree. "He's a photographer."

Our heads turned his way. She was right. A camera with a long-range lens swung on a strap, hidden on his left side. The photographer's stare lifted to us passing by.

"How did you know?" I asked as Matt took a fast left, back onto the main road.

"He glanced up at our car, telegraphing intent," she said. "He was waiting for us. How the hell did he know you'd be coming home this morning?"

Bloody good question.

I was used to paparazzi around my neighborhood. I wasn't the only person of note living in Knightsbridge. They'd snap photos when I was in Hyde Park going for a run. But waiting outside my door? Never before.

"Who else knew you were coming home?" Simon asked.

"Where to?" Matt chimed in. Poor chap couldn't keep driving in circles.

"Straight to Cornwall." I almost snapped at him. I answered Simon, "Only my family and the team knew."

Charlie bent down, grabbing her phone from the front pocket of her bag. "How many is that?"

"The usual," I said, bewildered, counting quickly. I trusted my team completely. Elaine, my assistant. Simon and Matt, my detail. My manager. My agent. Scott, my publicist. My estate manager. They all worked for me for years. None had ever betrayed me. The idea was impossible. "Seventeen or so, including my family. They wouldn't do this."

Charlie's index finger tapped across her phone. "Well, someone did. No damn way this was coincidence."

"What are you doing?"

"Texting Jeremy at HGR. See if he knows the guy. Dressed all in paparazzi black as usual, but those yellow Adidas sneakers may be his signature tell."

Fuck's sake, how did she catch that? I barely assessed the situation. But Charlie had clocked the photographer half a block away, read him as wrong, and remembered what he wore? Down to the shoes?

Pierce, may you never doubt this woman again.

The sent sound of her text filled the car. "If we find out who it is," she said, "we'll offer him a sweet enough deal to leak his source."

Simon took his phone out. "This has never happened before. Not on this team." He started tapping away too.

We found a quick place outside of London to refresh and refuel. Afterward, texts and calls were made. No one we contacted had a clue how it leaked that I was coming home this morning. Or how they knew my exact bloody address.

I phoned my mum, asking if she told anyone outside of

the family. She knew better. They all did, but I had to be sure.

Charlie quietly talked on her phone. Jeremy had phoned her back. I overheard her share the bit about the paps waiting outside my door. Then her face grew eerily stoic. All she uttered for minutes was "Uh-huh."

What the bloody hell was Jeremy saying to her?

"Any insights?" I asked once we wrapped our calls.

"Nothing yet." The set of her jaw. It didn't say "nothing." She had mentioned "telegraphing intent." Well, she telegraphed trouble.

"Charlie?" I pinched back a lock of her hair so she couldn't hide. "What aren't you telling me?"

"We don't know anything yet, Daniel. Jeremy's calling around about the photographer." Her words and reach snapped forward, securing her phone back in her bag. "How much longer do we have?"

I noticed the change in subject and went along with it. For now. "Three hours."

"Well, keep me awake, please. Both of us. Or we will be burdened with jet lag for days."

Simon started a game of trivia on his phone. Between the four of us and with only one more stop along the way; the trip went by fast.

It was a little after two o'clock when the car wound its way down the narrow road lined with tall hedgerows. When the tires turned right onto my cobblestone drive, the biggest exhale escaped my lungs.

"Daniel, this is beautiful!" Charlie exclaimed.

It was. My two-story stone and cob estate perched high atop thirty acres on an open hill sloping down to a rocky shore with a sweeping view of the sapphire Falmouth Bay, shining bright on the clear summer's day. A lush forest was my neighbor to the west and the wide manicured lawn to the east of the house traveled the distance to where a rugged point jutted out into the bay. Complete privacy on both sides.

My chest filled with pride that all renovations were finally done. I'd yet to see the finished product or even stay a night here.

Matt parked the car in front of the stone wall with a large arched double wooden door that protected the courtyard and front door. We all got out. While Simon unlocked the house and Matt started grabbing our bags, I took Charlie's hand, walking with her around to the back of the home, to the magnificent view of the bay.

"My God, it's breathtaking," she said, not taking her eyes off the water.

But mine beamed at her, at the beauty of her standing here. "Yes, it is."

That turned her head. I took her with a kiss that had been a long time coming. To have love in my home? For the first time in thirty-seven years?

It flooded my being. The triumph of my lips over hers, tongue capturing hers, salt and sea filling my nose while the taste of her filled my heart, saturating my mind. All I desired was here with her.

Her lips pulled back, grabbing a breath. "Can I have the grand tour?"

I relented for now. Besides, Simon and Matt were waiting by the car.

Simon stifled a smile at our approach. "I think there's a tradition to be observed."

I agreed, sweeping Charlie off her feet before she could resist, carrying her through the arched door into the courtyard.

"See you in a few months," I called over my shoulder to them. As the car pulled away, I stood with Charlie at my front door painted English red.

Her hands wrapped around my neck. "You just can't resist carrying me around, can you?"

I stepped over the threshold with everything I cherished cradled in my arms. "I can never resist you, Ms. Ravenel."

Our journey stopped here in the grand foyer by a stairwell that curved to the bedrooms above. Taking her lips again, one thought consumed me.

But she squirmed in my arms. "Not to ruin this happily every after scene, but I need a bathroom break."

My lips grazed down her neck, complaining, "This would've been so romantic. Right here. Right now, Charlie. First steps into my home. You're mucking it up."

"Yes, well, sorry that my bladder kills the romance."

I showed her around. First to the guest lavatory. Then to the living room center stage to the view outside. It sat open with a chef's kitchen on the left, sharing the same view, while a giant dining room impressed from their right. An office and library were at the front of the home, along with my gym. An indoor pool sat on the far end of the home in a conservatory so it could be enjoyed throughout the year. Upstairs were four bedrooms and three remodeled bathrooms.

These renovations I'd festered over for years. Walls moved. An owner's luxury suite created. Infrastructure upgraded. Windows replaced. All that had been in my mind's eye.

But what bloomed in my heart was the interior design. Design Charlie had helped me select months back. It was stunning, and she agreed.

Aged oak floors glowed under the plush indigo velvet

sofa we picked out. It sat between matching vintage cognac leather sofas she had suggested to provide enough seating for my family. The white of the walls we chose warmed in the summer light. Muted brass lighting and accents in the living room and kitchen gleamed elegant. All while the Midnight Sky Aga oven beckoned me to make the first cottage pie.

"What's in here?" She lifted the lid to a bakery box on the butcher-block breakfast bar.

I peered over her shoulder. "Looks like my estate manager popped down to the local bakery for us." I picked up my favorite—a scone.

"Let me make something for you." Reaching for two plates, I put a scone on each. In the fridge, I grabbed the fresh strawberry jam and clotted cream that were always on my shopping list.

Charlie nosed around the kitchen until she found the kettle. I smiled. When in Rome. More like, when in England. She made the tea.

We didn't even sit down, didn't want to after our travels. We just stood here, eyes rolling, savoring bites of a true Cornish delight.

She licked the cream off her thumb, declaring, "Okay. That's a far sight better than coffee and doughnuts. What's it called again?"

I swirled a finger in the jar, offering it to her lips. "Clotted cream." Her tongue snaked the dollop off. "Fancy more cream, Charlie?"

The urge kept taking me. From the moment we arrived. I'd been imagining this. With her. How long would she make me wait?

"Someone sure landed home and horny." God yes, her hand started stroking the impatient cock under my jeans.

My palm pressed over hers, helping with the friction. "This is all I want. You. Our love. Here in my home. As many times as we can."

Her other hand grabbed my ass. "We'll have to take a break sometime. Unless you plan on having me upstairs while your family throws a baby shower down here."

Her nipples came out, asking me to play under her thin sport bra and jumper. A swirl of my fingertips over each parted her lips while I confirmed, "Oh, I *will* take you upstairs for a quick, hard fuck. I don't care who's here."

Bloody hell, the thought made me horny. Thought? No. A plan because that was happening. For now, I grabbed her hand milking my cock before leading our path through the living room.

She asked, trailing behind me, "Are we going to try out each bedroom?"

"No." I stopped in the foyer by the hallway table she'd chosen. "Right here. You're the bottle of champagne across the bow of my ship." I started to drop to my knees.

She pulled at my arm. "Daniel, I need a shower first."

I loved her taste no matter but devised another plan, rising, curling behind her, cupping my hand between her thighs. The thin fabric of her yoga leggings with no knickers on? Too easy to tease through.

"Then I'll take you like this." The strength of my fingers pressed, gliding over the singular crease I craved, wanting in.

Her hips arching against my cock told me not to stop. Hooking my thumbs over the elastic band, I pulled her leggings down to her thighs. She kicked off her shoes.

"Lean back on me, babe." I pulled her against me, my fingers spreading her folds, finding their slick harbor.

The grip of her hand reached up, grabbing my waves

with her groan of "yes, Daniel" while my lips threaded down her neck.

My other hand tugged at the hem of her oversized jumper. She took the hint, lifting it overhead and flinging it to the floor before she returned, curving back into me, writhing, bending her knees and opening for more of my generous torrent across her pussy.

God, I was crazed to have her now, as all mine, only mine.

"Is this how you do it, Charlie?" I pulled her thin sports bra up, over her breasts, desperate to take them in my toying grasp. "Is this how you play with your beautiful pussy, getting off and thinking of me? Of all you want to try with me?"

"Hell yes," she admitted with a lusting huff.

Fuck, it was getting me off too. My cock strained under restricting denim, begging for her. But I wanted this first. The erotic blessing of her across my threshold, marking the spot where she invaded every part of my life.

"Do it for me, Charlie." The aroma of her vanilla tresses tickled my nose. "Get off right here on my hand. Shower my floors so that I'll think of this every time I come home."

I meant it. I needed her pleasure now, and the memory of her forever. It filled every part of my body and heart, so it must reside in every room of my home too.

"Only if you're next, Daniel." Her arm reached behind her, clasping my firm length. "Right here in the foyer, I'm going to watch you. Watch you jerk off while I record you."

Fuck yes, my fingers hooked deep inside, taking her with a throaty moan. The kink of it driving me mad, my lips steaming over her ear. "You want to watch me, Charlie? Watch while I have a wank for you?"

My fingers scissored along her clit, sliding through her

rousing serum, teasing with long strokes. Swirling a gentle pinch of her nipple with my other hand, I demanded, "You want to watch me come, don't you? How I think such lewd thoughts of you."

"Oh shit, Daniel." Her knees buckled. "Harder," she demanded.

"Like this?" My foot stepped down on the waistband of her leggings, pushing them down to her ankles. She stepped out, freeing her stance to splay open for my hand.

I took all of her now, fingers jerking against her swollen walls, palm pounding against her clit, my other hand clamping down on her breast, pinching. Just enough until, yes, she gave a wanton moan.

"Come for me, Charlie." My lips didn't leave her ear, giving her the words she always begged to hear. Her body was an instrument I could play with expert strokes. "Be so naughty for me and rain your cum all over my floor."

Her shoulders dragged down my chest, losing strength in her legs. The vice of my bicep seized her waist, holding her up while my other hand wouldn't relent, determined to deliver her desire, urging out the tide pouring from her pussy. A scream railed from her lungs with her shower all over her leggings and my hardwoods below.

The sight of her puddle, it frenzied my mind. She dangled in my grasp. "Give me more." I knew she had it. My hand hammered for it. Her body shook for it. "I want more of this sweet pussy and cum again." I yanked another screaming orgasm from her folds.

"God, Daniel." The words heaved over her lips. She was quivering and spent, for now.

I set her feet down, turning her chin for a thundering kiss before I made quick work of dropping my jeans to the floor. "Get your phone," I said, wanting this too much and holding it back.

She took two steps and long seconds to her bag on the table, then her phone was in her hand, then on me. "Just like this," she demanded. "Stand here. In your home. In your voice. Naked only for me."

I pushed my boxer briefs to my ankles before pulling my T-shirt off, tossing it on top of her jumper.

Fisting my cock, I had no regard for privacy. Or nondisclosure. Or publicity. Or image. Or security. Not with her. She could have this from me. My home. My trust. My body. My love. Everything from me.

She yanked her bra off and stood nude, leaning against my red front door, legs spread open. One hand held her phone focused on me. The other focused between her wet thighs. "Show me, Daniel, how you jerk off thinking of me."

The lurid sight of her. Her fit body with trails of lust from my touch trickling to her ankles. Her tits, firm and awake, nipples hard from my play. Her gorgeous, sexy face and dirty pink lips urging me on. It was easy.

My expert hand jacked with practiced twists at the top. "I do it like this, Charlie." Warning drops fell to the floor, over her pond of pleasure. "For you."

"Tell me what you think about, Daniel." Her fingers smacked between her lips. "And say my name."

Fuck, I couldn't believe I was doing this. Standing vulnerably nude with my boxers at my ankles. My swollen, throbbing cock in my choking grasp. My bare chest heaving, so overcome with lust for her I was letting her record it.

The whole world could see my hardcore display. It would ruin my career, and I'd welcome the wrecking. I'd only submit to this for her. Always and only for her.

So I confessed it all. How I jerked off in the shower thinking about our sex. Sharing our lurid specifics—her promising princess plugs, my fetish for her body stockings, the feathers she tickled over my ass, the oil I lavished over her nipples, my obsession with tasting her perfect, pink pussy—the indecent details took me closer to panting breath.

"Oh fuck, I'm going to come for you, Charlie." I was there. Immersed in the sight of her. Thought of her. Trust with her. Anything with her. Watching her get off too, swelling my cock to full with an even faster pump. Almost...

"Come, Daniel, knowing you're going to fuck my ass in your home."

"Oh fuck, Charlie!" My desire shot the distance at the truth between us. I watched with another gasp as it fell to the floor in a trail leading toward her. One more firm squeeze and I iced over her puddle at my feet.

I struggled to focus on her. How she was coming again, promising, "I mean it, Daniel." Her thighs shook while I stood gasping for breath at our salacious show. "You're the only one."

CHAPTER TWENTY-FOUR

CHARLIE

"**I** see your eyes closing." He called out from the kitchen. "It's only five. You can't fall asleep yet."

"Then come keep me awake." I stretched out on the sofa, way too comfortable under the knitted ivory throw, watching him prepare dinner. After our laughter mopping up the foyer floor and then taking a shower, my eyelids rested at half-mast.

"I can't make cottage pie and keep you occupied at the same time."

He can, however, look sexy as fuck peeling potatoes. Pajama pants. No shirt. And in the kitchen. This is true lady porn right here.

"Pleassseeee." Exhaustion brought out my inner five-year-old. "Just let me close my eyes for thirty minutes."

His chef's knife poised over potatoes. "All right. Thirty minutes. Sweet dreams."

Oh, sweet Jesus, yes. My lids slammed shut. Chopping sounds filled the air. I waited for sleep to rent my brain. But the minute it was free of Daniel's distracting love, Mason Hunt moved in instead.

I couldn't evict the thought. What Jeremy had told me on the phone in the car on the way here.

"There have been four confirmed *White Flag* attacks," Jeremy had reported. "First, the tragic murder of the gay man in Atlanta. That prat is in prison for twenty to life." Pen clicking. I heard it over the hum of the tires down the motorway. "After that, three more attacks. One, a stabbing in Florida. The second, a stabbing in Georgia. No suspects caught. And the third, an open stalking case in Virginia. No suspect either, only white flags left at the scene."

"Uh-huh." I'd listened, gut twisting at the proximity of those locations to my home. Though it was no surprise that Mason's *White Flag* psychos would cull from my home in the southern states.

It was a region steeped in a shameful history of white supremacy, violence, and hate. *White Flag* just gave it a modern, cinematic twist.

I'd wanted to ask about the profile of the victims, but Daniel sat too close. It made me feel dishonest. Like I was cheating on him right there in the car.

Thankfully, Jeremy knew me too well, giving me the intel.

"The three cases where the person survived? The first was a Florida migrant worker at a petrol station. The second was a gay white male at a Georgia petrol station. Unfortunately, his rainbow pride sticker made him a target. And the third, the Virginia stalking case, it's a young woman, a college student and activist. Attractive. Long blonde hair. Twenty years old. Someone keeps leaving white flag threats on her windshield."

I'd replied "uh-huh" like an idiot not able to say more.

Jeremy picked up on it, assuming correctly—this was a secret from anyone within the sound of my voice.

He'd continued, "So you've got threats to your north and to your south when you go home. All, a couple months ago and nothing since. Tread carefully, Ravenel. Hunt's posts are dangerous. He's out on bail with an ankle monitor, can't leave California, but he doesn't need to. Not if these nutters act on his behalf. In the States or here in the UK. His reach is global."

"Uh-huh." I gazed to the window, not able to face Daniel. Fear had slathered my face like my daily SPF moisturizer.

Jeremy shared more intel. "I've got a call into the FBI, for the agent leading the *White Flag* cases—Agent Beverly Cooper. We'll do a call with her. Tomorrow sound good?"

Fuck, no. It sounded like a shitstorm. How could I do a call with an FBI agent while Daniel and his mom stood feet away?

"Yes," I answered. My job. My problem. I'd figure it out.

"All right, then. As soon as I hear back from her, I'll text you the time for the call. Send me the log of Hunt's texts to share with the agent. Can you get to a secure line?"

"Uh-huh." My last reply. Daniel's home had to have WiFi. If it worked, it certainly was secure. He couldn't afford otherwise. "Talk with you soon." The dreadful call had ended.

The whirl now of the mixer wormed into my ears. Still no rest for me while Daniel made mashed potatoes for the cottage pie.

Tactics clicked down my mental to-do list. Get my laptop. Email copies of the texts to Jeremy and the agent without Daniel seeing me. Figure out an excuse to hide tomorrow for the call with the FBI. Keep taunting Mason the next time he replies. Tease his ego until he must be known to me.

And watch your back. Yours and Daniel's.

Oh, and don't forget—keep lying to the face of the man you love because that's a great fucking idea too.

Nope. Cross that off the list. You've got to tell him. He's a grown man with enough power to pummel someone into dust.

I'd tell him. But not now.

He deserved this—a carefree week with his family in his new home. I wouldn't ruin it. Besides, until I talked to the agent, there wasn't much more to tell.

Silence. Then steps toward me. Toasty lips and stubble tickled my cheek. Cedar and bergamot cologne drifted over the tip of my nose. "Wake up, beautiful." A rich voice that could rouse the dead curled over the shell of my ear.

I was awake.

Not for long. After dinner, once he covered us with the duvet on the bed for our first night here, sleep called me, but a hand caressing my cheek enticed me more. I opened my eyes to his. The sweetest adoration radiated from his touch. "What's keeping you up?"

"This." The back of his fingers brushed across my cheek. "You. In my house. In my bed. I bought this place hoping that one day, I'd share it with someone. But I never imagined it would feel this glorious. It's my house, but sharing it with you, the woman I love? You make it my home."

"Do you wanna stay? You've never been able to enjoy it until now. I don't mind. I want to do this for you."

"No, I want to see your home too. This Sunday. I know it's more than a home for you. It's your parents' memory. I'm honoured you're going to share it with me."

"Well, I don't know, Pierce." A grin lifted my tired cheeks. "There's a hefty toll you'll have to pay to enter."

Where this was coming from—desire for him overpowering my exhaustion and fear—I knew now.

Daniel Pierce was my harbor in the tempest.

His love. His care. His sex. Storms could rage outside, but if I could shelter in the safe waters of his body and heart, I had my calm center, one he filled with joy.

He slowly rose, swelling to billow down through me. "Can I pay the toll now, Ravenel?" Lips to my neck, he nuzzled in, tickling my flesh.

It made me giggle back, and him push into me farther with laughter, pursuing me across the mattress until our play turned into love blessing his bed for the first time.

ANONYMOUS

It's an obscene video.

You can almost tell it's them on an outdoor terrace in New York City. Night shadows and an umbrella obscure some of the view, but their lewd act is obvious.

Their honed bodies. His kneeling before hers. Hers shameless for him. Then they intertwine like animals. She seizes him, his backside thrusting hard into her before they disappear inside.

As profane as I find it, it arouses me. Greatly.

I downloaded it. Watched it. Viewing it several times until I couldn't resist the urge, giving myself the pleasure it provided.

Pleasure with their pornographic public show.

Pleasure with how my soldier had followed them, watching them, capturing the salacious display.

Pleasure with how I alone have the video and will keep it to enjoy.

For now.

My soldier reported their departure from the hotel the next morning. A bribe to a bellhop scored the intel that they checked out with a car going to JFK airport.

Where did they go?

CHAPTER TWENTY-FIVE

DANIEL

Not even a bit of jet lag could mar this day.

We set the alarm, going to town for another round of groceries, popping into the book shop for a gift. Zooming around in my Ming Blue Aston Martin—one I rarely got to drive—brought me great joy and small attention. None of it concerned me.

It was Charlie's white-knuckled response that demanded my focus. I had to shift down my zeal so she wouldn't claw my skin off in terror at my speedy turns.

"What's first?" I asked, standing ready in my kitchen to be her sous chef after we unpacked our goods. She had informed me that she was "hell-bent" on making a coconut layer cake for tomorrow.

She plopped a bag in front of me. "Sift this flour, please. Two-and-a-half cups worth."

Our tandem baking efforts delighted me. But as I watched her put the final swipe of icing on the cake, I noticed how quiet she'd been. Eyebrows pinched. Shoulders to her ears. Not even her favorite tunes beating through the Bose made her dance about.

"Hey." I hooked a finger under her chin, turning her gaze to me. "What's wrong?"

"I'm nervous as hell."

"To meet my mum?" The premise shocked me. "She's going to adore you. Besides, compared to others she's met, you're the dog's bollocks."

Her eyebrow arched up. "Who was just before me?"

Fuck's sake, Pierce. Walked right into that. How fucking daft.

"Kathy. Last summer. For my father's birthday party. It was complete shambles. You're positively lovely by comparison."

"Thanks for the low bar."

But that wasn't it. She was too confident to whinge over an ex-girlfriend. Something else troubled her.

"Charlie, I can't read your mind, but I know when something is on it."

She looked away, out toward the water. "It's been fourteen years since I've done something like this. Like the first time I met Kai's sweet family. And then I lost him. Lost all that love. It nearly killed me." She chewed her lip, tears welling in her eyes. "This makes me so afraid that I'll lose you too one day."

I pulled her into an embrace, cradling her head into my chest. I worried—this was too much. Too painful. Too fast for her. The doorbell chimed. My mum arrived, plunging us into the water to swim in this, whether Charlie was ready or not.

But the afternoon washed us gently ashore. My mum came in with her open arms and heart for Charlie, and soon, she smiled. Her sculpted shoulders fell at ease.

And I could tell how my mum warmed to her. A lot.

Yes, the victory was easy over someone like Kathy. But still. The light in my mum's eyes danced watching me with Charlie, joking, giving pecks, helping my mum prepare sausage rolls and cucumber sandwiches for the next day.

Charlie excused herself for a call she had to take from her boss, saying something about her report against Mason to the San Diego Police. Odd because I thought she sorted that already.

She darted upstairs. My mum quickly spoke in her absence.

"I like her, Daniel. Very much." She washed the knives, handing them to me to dry. "Please don't be a twit and lose her. Your heart has always been in the right place. Let your actions be too. Change everything for her. Now."

I pecked her cheek. "I'm on the job, Mum."

She elbowed me with a grin at the double entendre to the hard work and sex I dedicated to keeping Charlie.

"Whatever happened with that Kathy woman?"

Oh, how my mum could wrap a phrase in a bow of disapproval. She never liked Kathy. Or any of my girlfriends. Only two she liked. Charlie, now, and Tilly, my girlfriend when I was twenty-four.

Tilly and I had dated a year, got close to marriage, but it wasn't love, only the expected trajectory of life at that age. Then I got offered a film in LA. Then another.

Tilly's job kept her in London and that couldn't last. The shameless fucking that seduced me stateside didn't help either. It didn't take long for Tilly to catch my guilty tone, my evasive tactics. We were over. Only my family was disappointed.

And I fed them even more in years to follow. One girlfriend after another. Taken to parties or premieres. Hooked on my arm. Each a sexy, young accessory to my celebrity life. I was such a prat. My family? They were never impressed. In fact, they seemed embarrassed for me.

It took one horrific night for my life to change. The consequence, the pain so deep, it dropped me to my knees. I wasn't the same after that. The few relationships I had since were calculated choices with no risk. No harm. And little feeling. On the outside, we appeared perfect. On the inside, I was protected.

Only my parents, siblings, and Colleen knew what had happened. What made me change... and that it was slowly killing me.

That was until Charlie Ravenel dragged me out of those drowning, freezing waters. Her love revived me, saved me.

"I cocked up once, Mum. I got plastered with Logan MacGregor before his party and Kathy was there. You saw the photos where I kissed her, too pissed to know better. But that was it. We weren't together anymore, and I finally ended it."

"I reckon Kathy didn't take it well." She passed me a bowl. "She doesn't strike me as the sort of woman who makes a dignified exit."

Yet... Kathy did.

She never raged at me on the phone when I confessed we were over, that we had been for months. Other than her nasty run-in with Charlie at the premiere the week before, she wasn't making an ass of herself.

Though I wouldn't question my mum's wisdom, perhaps Kathy could behave. We still had to work together. She was the PR account director for Logan MacGregor, and I was Logan's brand ambassador.

In fact, I'd see Kathy this Friday at the photoshoot scheduled at Logan's new flagship store.

A fact I'd yet to tell Charlie about.

Right on cue, she returned from her call upstairs. "Sorry that took so long."

"Perfect timing." I snapped her with the towel before indulging in a soft kiss. "You missed a round of dish duty."

She seemed relaxed now, with my mum, with whatever had troubled her before. Her ease turned into elation at the stories my mum told, divulging every embarrassing story from my childhood.

Like the times I hid with my sister Tess. Playing with her dolls, making up dramas to act out. Until my older brothers caught me. Then it was my fists that responded to my brothers' taunting.

Or the time I came home quiet from school. My mum finally got it out of me over milk and biscuits. How my classmates had laughed at our elderly teacher, Mrs. Gillis. I hated how they mocked her. I saw her as my own gran, so I punched the cruelest boy in the mouth, spending the day in the headmaster's office.

Charlie mused, "Your big heart and fists get you in trouble often, don't they?"

I carefully measured paper-thin slices of cucumber like my mum taught me as a boy. "Fancy you're guilty of the same thing, Ravenel."

"Yep." She cut the crusts off the bread like my mum had just shown her. "I guess ass kickin' dills both our pickles."

That dropped my knife, my ribs cracking with laughter at her lightening quick Charlie-ism.

"Go on then." I wiped hysterical tears from my eyes. "Tell mum some of my favorites." Bloody hell, I needed to record her sayings. They got me every time.

"What? Like 'That man is 'bout confused as a fart in a fan factory'?"

I howled back while my mum gave a cute snort.

"Or 'That man couldn't find his ass with both hands in his back pockets'?" She kept going. "Or my daddy used to say that I was so stubborn I could make a preacher cuss."

I couldn't take it anymore. Racked with laughter, hugging her from behind, I swore, "See why I love her, Mum?"

CHAPTER TWENTY-SIX

CHARLIE

Our banter continued all evening, even after Daniel's mom left.

It was official, I adored her. Daniel's warm soul and a great measure of his beauty came from his mom.

The day of easy laughs and sweet stories let me forget, even for one more night, the torment that frayed my nerves. A distant memory, a sensation returned I hadn't felt in so long. Family. One can forget how they bless your life until they're ripped away.

I felt it, a new belonging, a glowing, making me grin while Daniel and I stood at the kitchen table wrapping the gift I bought this morning.

Pointing to the twist in the ribbon I said, "Put your finger here."

"That's what she said." Daniel obliged. "Wait. No." His eyebrows danced. "That's what *you* said."

The scissors in my hand cut the yellow bow. "Can we even wrap a baby shower gift without you talking dirty?"

"Nope. You look too bloody cute when I wind you up."

"Keep tryin' my nerves with scissors in my hand and you'll see how cute I get."

With a yank, I tied the ribbon. It snagged his finger, blanching it white before he freed the tip with a grin.

"Tell you what, Ravenel. Stop fannying about with this ribbon and give me a go at yours, and then I'll stop."

"How cheeky." I teased, amused, knowing in my tongue "fanny" meant "ass," but in his, it meant "pussy." My body reacted to his taunt. "Which fanny do you want, Pierce?"

It wasn't a question. I could read every naughty thought behind his aqua eyes. "I fancy both your fannies tonight, Charlie." His palm cupped my ass.

Exactly. "Just why are you so obsessed with my fanny and down yonder?" I just needed to finish wrapping this gift.

"Because I could go down on your yonder and wander forever."

I threw the tape at him. "Quit wisecrackin'."

"Speaking of cracks—"

"Dammit, Daniel. We need to finish." I stomped my foot. "Stop it."

"I'll never stop." He wrapped his arms around me, shaking with laughter. "There's nothing, Charlie, that I don't want to do with you."

"Nothing?"

He turned me around. "Nothing."

"Does this mean I get a go at your fanny too?"

Drawing his mouth to mine, he sighed, "Listen to me, Charlie Ravenel." His eyes swore it too. "There is *nothing* of mine that I won't give to you."

That tickled my stomach, tingling between my thighs.

The taboo of it. "Tonight"—my lips skimmed his—"I go first. I want to share this with you."

His eyes sparked. "You're *my* gift." The depth of his voice matched his lush kiss, his full lips serving mine with a tongue seeking my submission. Unwrapping me. Taking my breath before his hand took mine, leading me upstairs.

In the shower, he lathered me up, lavishing me with caresses that put me on my knees. I sucked him off, his praise reverberating off the marble. How I craved it, his creamy orgasm so his next would last longer.

It always got me off too, looking up, watching him. How his mouth gaped helpless at his cock fucking my throat. How my name tumbled from his grateful lips along with his gorgeous climax.

Then he devoured me to a wild state on the bed, insisting, "Tell me how much you want, Charlie."

With thick fingers, two of his, gliding into my pussy and his face between my legs, I couldn't be any more wet for him. At least, it's what I thought so far.

"More, Daniel." I could take all of him, I hoped. Certain, either way, the man would take all night getting me ready to try.

"You want more of this?" Harder, three of his fingers pounded, his mouth sucking my clit, twisting my body into more than ready. I was desperate, glistening over his lips.

"Please, Daniel."

"Roll over," he said, rising from between my thighs. When I did, I saw he was greedy too, his cock roused hefty for me.

The mere act of turning over, lying on my stomach, ass up for him thrilled me even more. He reached, pulling two pillows from the head of the bed, and wedging them under my hips, tilting me open for him.

I knew his plan. I had prepared. A call to Rob days before had helped. He informed me with great detail how to get my body ready. And I scored big at the sex shop in New York too, evidenced by the array of toys and options on Daniel's nightstand.

His hands coveted my ass now like he was making a wish over a genie's lamp. Warm pulling, spreading me open, he stared for minutes with heavy breath at the sight, tingling my exposed flesh. "Fuck," he sighed, "you're so beautiful, so pink." My shameless, vulnerable display raged my appetite for his.

Finally, his lips hummed against my cheeks. "You want me to play here, don't you, Charlie?"

The reason for his kinky request? We both craved the sound of consent, the proud affirmation of lust. "Yes, Daniel." The jut of my hips curved up higher to him, echoing my desire.

And oh fuck, he did it.

His tongue laved in hot circles, ringing, licking wet over what he wanted to claim. Breath pinched my lungs with the pleasure, at the new sensation. Then his fingers, thick like his cock, plunged into my pussy while another practiced digit strummed over my clit.

Every curse I muffled into the mattress while he lavished me with this unrelenting thrill. Every part of me his tongue had teased and probed. Now it toyed over his final destination, lapping another scream from me. Even through the low roar pouring from me, I heard his guttural satisfaction.

"You want more, don't you?" His finger circled my ass again, slick.

More? I didn't know how far, how deep this could go

but I was willing. Ready to plummet to the ocean floor with him, as long as his flesh didn't leave my side.

I turned my face to the side, gazing back at him. On his knees, pillowed lips shining, he worshipped me and the carnal nectar trickling down my thighs.

Taunting him with a shake of his next wish, I said, "Show me what *you* want, Daniel."

His grin disappeared between my cheeks. His rich, milky voice confessing, "More of this," before his tongue did it again, flicking darts over the tiny gap he wanted to fill, driving me mad and ready to come again.

But he got up. Bowed open for him, my body yearned for his return. I ogled his steps to the nightstand for the lube, his erection bouncing long and heavy with anticipation.

Holy hell, the man can sell sainthood to the devil looking like that. I grinned. *But tonight, it's all about shameless yummy sin.*

He returned to kneel at his altar. With a few pumps of the lube, he insisted, "Beg me, Charlie," his fingertip circling, teasing, pressing for permission.

I had no will power, no resistance. "Please do it, Daniel." And fuck yes, he did. One slick finger then two slid in, and my body opened, knowing this probe from him before.

It lit my pussy up, his other hand taking that too. The double sensation of his fingers moving inside, filled me everywhere, stretching me, making me arch for more. If there were two of his cocks, only his, I'd take them both. Just like this.

The ramming sensation he gave me now was close enough, making pleasure shake through every fiber in my thighs. What he gave me? Blinding thrill, urge taking my every nerve, ready to shatter in bliss.

"You like my fingers fucking you, don't you, Charlie?" Oh hell, my name across his lips in that accent, with his naughty question. "Your tight pussy and ass want my hard fuck, don't they?"

I answered like sugar is sweet, another orgasm, an avalanche, rumbling through me, shaking my knees. Good God, I didn't know it could feel like this, making me greedy for more.

"Daniel"—I gasped—"now. Please. I'm ready."

"Not like this." He kissed the small of my back. "I want to see your face, to watch you."

"Lie down, then." We had many positions to try, but this one offered me the most control the first time.

"Get the condom," he said, submitting to my ride, "and the little vibrator."

It felt odd reaching for a condom, to have any barrier between us. My birth control implant, years of abstinence, and his clear tests protected us. But I knew why.

He wanted all of me tonight, my virgin ass and then my pussy. Once his expert fingers rolled the condom on, I straddled him, dousing his cock with lube.

"Charlie"—he reached up, pulling my lips to his, dancing a deep kiss of our taste across my tongue before his nose nuzzled mine—"go as slow as you need." Another sweet kiss he gave me before I noticed the look in his eyes. "I'll wait for you." Expecting. Enthralled. Exclusive. "Always."

It became too real, beautiful, scary to do this with him, only him. It was greater than lust. It was trust I'd never given before. Vulnerability I'd never allowed. It was how much I dropped my defenses to him. Walls crumbling to dust at our feet.

"Only for you, Daniel," I whispered over his lips.

"Only for us," he answered before taking another kiss.

I gripped his length, perching over his tip, and eased down. I'd praised his generous cock before, but now it truly heaved its might into me. It hovered at my opening, straining along with the look on his handsome face.

How he watched me, so gorgeously enraptured by my promising descent. How I wanted him, even if it took all night.

It didn't. His hand fumbled for the vibrator. With one click, he teased its low hum over my clit. The pulsating thrill emboldened me. With an exhale, I took him in, stretching, burning, trying to open for his mass.

"You can stop, babe," he said. But his pleasure pummeling me wouldn't. Toying with my clit. Twirling my nipple to delight. Making desire reign over every other part of my body to permit this. I wouldn't stop. Not with the vision of him under me. He was so fucking beautiful, licking his lips, reining back his greed.

More of him eased inside, the pressure in me building, quaking my thighs, taking deep breaths, I relaxed through the burn, wanting him more than the pain. Slowly lowering, surrendering to him, "Oh God, Daniel," it was all of him.

The tremor in my legs wouldn't stop. My lips shaking for breath, I braced my trembling hands against his chest. The force of him, all of him inside, it was so great I couldn't move.

His voice strained, asking, "Are you okay?"

A slight nudge lifted his hips. His face winced, I could tell, he resisted the impulse knotting across his body. His hulking pecs under my palms tensed with restraint too. He was fighting the urge to fuck me hard like this.

I wanted his full lips, his supple kiss. Something soft from him to balance the iron force of his invasion. "I'm okay," I said. But if I moved... this pressure? It wasn't painful. It was overwhelming, dominating every sense, every nerve in me with primal urge.

"Try this." He clicked the toy twice. It thrummed deep against my clit, the sensation radiating like a glorious lightening show across my pelvic floor.

My body took over, demanding I seek what it promised. Slowly, sitting, lifting up on his length, I chased it back down, losing my fear. Aching for more, slowly, I did again, and again, the pressure turning into pleasure. "God, Daniel, you feel so good."

"Come on, Charlie." Crooning my name in his heavy, satisfied voice, he coaxed my ride. "Yes. Fuck me, babe. Just like this." Igniting my every nerve, climbing me up, I plunged down again. "Fuck, don't stop, you feel so good."

He sat up, dropping the toy, and putting his around my waist, guiding his possession. His body shifted into more exquisite pressure inside me.

How he knew me, the path to my extreme edge. How he could take me there, his dirty commands bewitching his beautiful face. "My thick cock is fucking your tight ass, Charlie." How his hand grabbed my hair with a tender pull, putting my gaze to his. "Does it feel good?"

Every part of him did. "Yes, Daniel." How he knew what to say.

"Say it, babe." The words we needed to hear. His eyes locked to mine. "Say what I'm doing to you."

How his mouth opened, riveted, inches from my answer. "You're fucking my ass, Daniel." Oh God, the surrender, the revel of lust storming inside.

"You love it, don't you?" His clutch. His piston. His claim. How his command lulled into a beg. "You love me fucking your ass, Charlie. Say it."

I climbed even higher. "Yes, Daniel." How I was hanging on to his gaze, his voice, his body, with no fear and going even faster.

His eyes rolled back at my pace, his touch magnetic over my flesh. "Oh, fuck." How he roared, his stare back at me, at my narrow bind taking all of him, at my chase to my end. The beg from his lips. "Say it. I'm fucking your ass. Are you mine now?"

The words hailed from my entire being. "Yes"—the affirmation expanding my body, my heart, forming anew around him—"I'm yours, Daniel." How I wanted him, needed him, loved him.

The pleasure was tectonic. About to detonate every inch of me. So full of him, I was afraid to release it, afraid of my undoing. His eyes witnessed me hanging here, from my highest edge. "Then come for me. All of you, Charlie." He drove me back down his shaft. "You're mine now."

His covetous kiss, his tongue across mine, it freed me.

No time, only him now, the pleasure crashing down, dropping through every piece of me. No sound, just one perfect, annihilating contraction after another, exploding my breath away from his lips. It poured from me with sweet convulsions, drenching him. My only sight? His aqua eyes, blurred by my tears, falling down my cheeks like every part of me for him. His hands cradled my face, watching my end, my lungs grabbing for breath. "I love you, Daniel." I cried, smiling as I shattered over him.

He wrapped his brute arms around me, lifting up on his knees and laying me on my back. With a gentle, slow wince and tug, he was out of me, snapping the condom off and tossing it on the floor.

"Can I, Charlie?" He gently touched my pussy pulsing for him. His eyes heavy, body tight, desperate for release.

"Yes, Daniel." I pulled him on top of me.

And though his request was gentle, his demand wasn't, grabbing me hard like I wanted, unleashing all his restraint. He controlled my hips, urging into me with all his mass, the sound of his urgent breath with his merciless thrusts was music beside my ear. His fuck was so savage, so sweet and so intense with every thrust to my core. With his face next to mine, I'd never heard his grunts drum so hard, or felt his force so strong, so intense.

I wrapped my legs around him. His hulking shoulders in my grasp heaved with one towering shudder after another, his throat straining groans that sounded painful until his breath calmed. "God, I love you." His words sealed warm over my ear after his collapse, confessing, "I'm all yours too, Charlie."

CHAPTER TWENTY-SEVEN

DANIEL

A *ping* from her phone woke us.

Fuck's sake, she was getting a lot of texts lately. Though I'd never complain. It was her work and I was guilty of the same from time to time.

I watched her hourglass figure roll over for a peek at the screen. She held position, replying. Her shoulder blades, the muscles buffering her spine, they all twitched tight, like movement hurt her.

"You okay?" I reached out, rubbing her back, worried last night was too much for her. "Are you sore?"

She turned to me with a smile. "I'm fine." Lingering over me with a soft kiss, she said. "More than fine."

Still, I doted on her all morning. Making her breakfast. Winding her up with more fanny jokes. Keeping her in top Charlie-ism form for my family's arrival. It only seemed to soothe her more.

When my entire family came through the door of my

home—one after another with platters in hand, greetings, and hugs—nothing but bliss buzzed my bones.

Though a terrified moment entered when I closed the door behind my sister, the last guest through the door. It twisted my stomach, fearing that one of my family would forget. That their hearts would open to Charlie... and so would their mouths.

That would wreck my precious world. With my shame. With my secret. With each day, I knew I needed to tell her. But not today. It was too special to ruin it.

My concern was warranted because my father was besotted with Charlie, especially when she kept answering him with "yes, sir" and "no, sir."

"Daniel, I like her!" He bellowed under the afternoon sun on the patio. "She treats me like the knight I am."

Charlie couldn't help it, charming my family with her accent, wit, and beauty.

Even when my eldest brother, Samuel, notorious for nosy remarks, asked about her scars, she took it in stride. Holding my baby niece swaddled in a blanket, she explained the ones exposed by her sundress and ponytail, and the worst one above her right hip hidden underneath.

It didn't escape me. The esteem that lifted their chins up to her story.

"Don't muck this up, gormless," Samuel told me later, slapping my back before reaching for another Guinness from the fridge. "I love my wife. But gawd blimey, you fucking wanker. You get to be sodding handsome, famous, rich, *and* you get a woman like that? You ought to get on one knee for her now before she realizes what a knob you are. What's the wait?"

"I'm not faffing around. I'd get on one knee today, with

you lot here, with Gran's ring I have upstairs, but she's not ready. I don't think she'll ever be."

"You can't know unless you ask."

"She's a widow," I explained. "Like her, her husband was a Marine, killed in Afghanistan one day after she was shot. That was six years ago and a tragedy I can't imagine. I don't think Charlie will ever promise forever to another man. I'm the first she's been with since and that honour is all I'll ask from her. I don't care what we call it."

My brother quieted, humbled by the truth. A truth that caged me in fear. In a future of this. I wanted Charlie forever, but if I asked for the honour of marriage, she'd pull away. And if I ever disclosed my horrific past, she'd be gone for good.

Even my little sister, Tess, adoring Charlie too, chimed in, "If you mess this up, you're barmy."

Later, Tess led Charlie through a roast of my teen years. Of "Daniel's Dishy Ducks," as Tess called the girls who befriended her just to score an invite into our home, hoping to score with me too.

"Do you remember the one who hid under your bed?" Tess asked. "I thought she'd left hours before, but the poor wee girl waited until you came home from rugger practice."

"Emily Pritchard," I recalled, happy to keep the focus on my innocent teen years than the decade that followed. Happy to see Charlie smile with no jealousy, only entertained by my squirm.

"I don't know who screamed louder." Tess snorted. "You, when she crawled out from under your bed. Or her when she saw your naked twig and berries ready for your evening wank." She nudged Charlie. "Poor ol' Emily was so shocked by my brother's wide willy that the whole school heard about it."

The tale had Charlie in hysterics while I confirmed, "Henceforth my reputation preceded me into any room."

"By seven inches by her report." Tess fell over Charlie, both roaring about the gossip of my girth.

Charlie, sitting across from me in a pile of laughter, cried, "Seven inches? You *have* grown since then, Daniel Pierce. Poor ol' Emily would be gossiping to the *Daily Mail* now."

Yep, Charlie Ravenel fit right in with my brood and our bawdy banter.

My brother, Michael, and his husband, Charles, also niggled me with covert praise. Particularly when they unwrapped Charlie's baby present, a kid's book of Aesop's Fables. When she read it aloud to my niece, with her cute mouse voices and bravado, my entire family was smitten.

"My little brother looks troubled." Michael prodded me. We were upstairs in a guest room, giving the baby a nappy change and bottle. "You haven't told her, have you?"

"If I tell her, I'll lose her." I held my niece, infatuated with the little bundle in my arms. "You don't understand. What I did. It goes against everything Charlie stands for. She'd hate me for it."

"I'm almost halfway through this life, gormless." Michael tossed a cloth nappy over his shoulder. "And one thing I've learned is the past comes back for you. You might as well welcome it in."

I let my brother's wisdom wash over me, silencing my heart with guilt.

Michael filled the silence. "Look, I know bugger all of what you've dealt with over the years. But I can imagine. I've had people come on to me because we share a name and a face." He reached out, taking the baby from my arms, and resting her upon his shoulder for a gentle tap. "And I've just met her, but I can tell—Charlie is a smart woman. She's not naive to your lifestyle. So explain it to her. How one time, you made a horrible mistake."

"A mistake that devastated another woman? No, she'd never forgive me."

"You didn't intend to hurt her, Daniel. And you've done nothing but try to answer for it since."

"Well, in all my years, dear brother, I've learned it's not the intent that matters, it's the effect. And that will break Charlie's heart if she ever finds out. And she's been hurt enough. I'm not going to hurt another woman, intent be damned."

I appreciated Michael's faith in the obvious love between me and Charlie, but I couldn't.

I'd endure any torture before wrecking Charlie's life once more. It was my horrific mistake, my damning burden, and I'd carry it in silence for us both.

By the evening, as my siblings gave their goodbyes and stamps of approval, I didn't know whether to swim in pride or shame.

The magnitude of my sinful choices must have burdened my family all these years. I never appreciated how it taxed them with worry until its absence revealed the strain.

For it was all washed away with the evening's tide.

Because now my family was almost as in love as I was with Charlie Ravenel.

CHAPTER TWENTY-EIGHT

CHARLIE

Miracle by CHRVCHES

The day was a blur. A roller coaster of thrilling ups with a few terrifying plunges into reality.

Fearing Daniel's family was ridiculous. They were beyond welcoming. "No airs about them," as my dad would say.

A couple of thoughts kept bothering me though. Troubling my mind while Daniel and I enjoyed a final dinner with his parents after the others left.

First worry—my call with Jeremy and the FBI agent the day before.

Agent Cooper was a sharp tack. She'd been working the *White Flag* cases for a couple of years, leading the investigation into the federal hate crime violence that it inspired.

When I updated Agent Cooper that Mason, the star of the sadistic film, was arrested for stalking and attempted rape, interest in the agent's voice steeped her questions.

Questions about Mason's torment of Kierra, about his tactics. Were they the same as the ones harassing the college woman in Virginia now? Mason couldn't be doing it, but someone was using *White Flag* methods.

I'd hidden with my laptop while Daniel shaved. I emailed Mason's texts so far to the FBI. Agent Cooper agreed on the call that it was Mason sending them. The FBI would trace the texts, but I was right. Mason was too tech savvy to make a stupid mistake. He deployed layers of deception.

After my call to the FBI, I relaxed a bit. I wasn't alone. Another woman was on Mason's case too.

The worry, though? I didn't tell the agent how I was poking the snake. That I was texting and taunting Mason back.

I did it again this morning, waking up in Daniel's bed, in his safe arms to a text *ping* on my phone.

Unknown

Dripping red is the color
I crave from you

It was Mason's reply to my text from the plane. The one jeering about the colorful bruises I put on his neck.

Red meant more than blood to Mason. It meant a mark —the red X that his character, John White, put on a picture of the next target for *White Flag* violence.

What's the next play? I smiled. *Yep. Make him bite.*

My reply:

What's your favorite shade
of mine?

Could I provoke the mansplaining asshole to answer?

On the set of *The Druid*, Mason had never shut up. While I protected Kierra, I suffered his arrogant mouth too. The prick knew it all, an expert bigot on everything.

So if I tempted him with questions, luring him out... it just might work.

Careful. My finger had paused over the send icon. *Lure him out but remember, he's gunning for you and Daniel. It's dangerous protecting two targets at once.*

Whoop. Sent before I could change my mind. Reminding myself to hide my guilty phone in my bag later, I rolled over to what lured me even more—Daniel.

My second worry? My conversation with Daniel's mom.

While I sat there, politely listening to the chat between Daniel and his parents about his house renovations, what his mom had said earlier played like a tune I couldn't shake.

It kept looping.

It was only the two of us cleaning the kitchen when his mother had said, "Promise me, dear, that you'll give him chances. Of all my children, Daniel's heart is the biggest. After we lost his twin brother, he was a magnet for tragedy. That's why he has a talent for drama. And his handsome face causes trouble. You know he works in a ruthless industry, that he's made mistakes. But please don't let them tear you two apart."

The question shot through my mind—what did Daniel do, so bad that even his mother worried he'd lose me?

Maybe it was a mom thing, worrying for her son. Did he have cuts of imperfection? Yes.

So did I.

"Charlotte, dear, Daniel tells me you're an island kid too." Daniel's father turned the dinner conversation toward me now.

The way his parents called me "Charlotte" warmed my heart. "Yes, sir. I'm from a very small island, Daufuskie, just off the coast of South Carolina. Only five by two miles wide. No bridges to it. Everything comes in by boat."

I cut into a round piece of what looked like sausage on my plate. My own dad's stern rules played through my mind, insisting I eat whatever was served. And I loved Daniel so much, I'd even swallow lima beans for his family.

"Has your family always lived there?" His dad was very much a Daniel Senior—same handsome face full of polite curiosity.

Before taking a bite of the strange substance on the end of my fork, I answered, "No, sir. My line goes back to the South Carolina Lowcountry. Some owned a slave plantation at one time. A history that disgusts me. It did my grandfather too. That's why he moved to the island after serving in World War Two, before it even had electricity in the 1950s, and it's been home since."

The glob landed in my mouth after my answer left it. It was metallic with a chunky, gelatinous texture. *Oh God, it's foul.*

But all eyes were on me. Talk about lineage. I summoned all my Southern manners, swallowing the most horrid piece of food ever to pass my lips. And I'd eaten MREs in a ditch reeking of piss before.

My throat fought me, threatening with a gag. But my stubborn will forced it down.

"And I'll see her island home this Sunday," Daniel chimed in, oblivious to my struggle.

One I lost. *No human alive should eat this.* My jolt to the downstairs bathroom knocked my chair over. I didn't even make it to my knees before it retched up my throat into the porcelain bowl below.

"Babe, you all right?" Daniel was right behind me.

Dropping to my knees and spitting the rest out, I asked, "What the hell did I just eat?"

"Blood sausage. I should've warned you. My parents love it. I refuse to eat it." His hands held my hair back. "The smell alone is vile. Why'd you even try it?"

"I didn't want to offend your parents."

"That's not happening. They adore you." He wet a hand towel, passing it to me. "What else can I get you?"

I wiped my face. "Cinnamon gum from my bag, please, so I can burn this taste out of my mouth."

He turned a quick corner for my bag in the foyer. He was gone a bit. Longer than the ten seconds it should've taken.

When his beautiful frame returned, the look twisting his face was anything but. "What's this, Charlie?"

Oh, shit! Your phone!

He found it in my bag searching for the gum.

His reach punched it forward. I could read the screen lit up with **Unknown** texts.

You know my cravings
You know my touch
You know my smell
You know my taste
You know my desire
It's all for you

"It's not what you think." I tried rising to my feet, but his anger took all the space in the small room.

He seethed, "Then tell me what to think."

Don't do it. Not with his parents here. He will blow a fucking gasket.

This was my shitshow. One I wanted no audience for.

I forced myself up into his space, staring back at him. "I'll tell you after your parents leave. We're not making a scene. Agreed?"

One eyebrow up. Not his happy one. This one pulled fury across his face, all the way to down the veins on his neck. "Agreed."

It seemed like forever, but it was only an hour before his parents gave their goodbye hugs, requesting another visit soon.

Daniel's hand was still on the brass knob, closing the front door to their farewell, welcoming in his rage upon me.

"You want to bloody explain it to me now, Charlie?" One step toward me, he traced over the same path we christened with our lust and love. None of that was here now. "Because I've been holding down my own vomit about who the fuck is texting you that shit!"

Go ahead. Stick your curious finger in the mouse trap like you did when you were a girl 'cause here comes the smack of pain.

"It's Mason."

His jaw jerked back. "What? What do you mean, 'It's Mason'?"

"They started the day after his attack on Kierra and his arrest. They're texts from burner phones, but I know it's him. It's fucking obvious."

"That was two bloody weeks ago, Charlie!" The words stormed out of his mouth. "And you're just now telling me?" Wait. One more insult he had to add up. "And you're only confessing because I fucking caught you?"

"Daniel, I'm sorry, but there's nothing we can do about it. Not yet. Not until he fucks up and reveals it's him. And I didn't want to upset you until then."

"I'm not a sodding child, goddammit." His face reddened, veins popping up on his neck. "But fucking hell if you aren't treating me like one, insulting me like I'm not man enough to take the bloody truth!"

Dear God, when he got mad, his tone went from butter rich to bitter rancor. And I just stood here in my pile of fuck-up, not knowing where to step next.

He did. "How many texts? And are you texting him back?"

Hey, Charlie Girl. Take this shovel. Go ahead. Dig the grave deeper.

"Thirty-four texts so far. And yes, I've texted him back. Twice. Starting the day we got here."

His next steps thundered toward me, his voice booming with even more rage. "Are you bloody fucking kidding me? Thirty-four fucking texts!"

Never would he lay a hand of anger on me, that I'd die knowing, but the look in his eyes screamed murder. "What the fuck are you sexting him back with? Fucking love notes?"

I understood. He was pissed as hell and shocked. And hurt. All my fault. But jealousy had no role in this shitshow.

"Daniel, I'm sorry I didn't tell you yet. But I was going to. As soon as I knew more. I talked to Jeremy before we got here. He found the FBI agent who's working the *White Flag* cases. The ones inspired by Mason's sick film. I talked with the agent yesterday. That's why I went upstairs. She's going to help me catch Mason."

His gorgeous tongue sucked his bright white teeth before he sneered. "And you lied to my face about the call to Jeremy and the call yesterday too. And you laid in my bed next to me this morning, secretly texting Mason while I laid naked behind you, touching you, like a fucking sick, twisted threesome."

Change tactic, this was getting ugly. "Daniel, do you love me?"

His face contorted. "Yes, Charlie. You know that I love you. But don't insult me again by changing the fucking subject."

"I'm not. If you love me, then you trust me."

"You're making it difficult to trust you when I catch you lying to me. And never will I trust Mason Hunt not to be an evil twat."

"Well, then, trust me to handle this. Like I did the first time with him and Kierra. I hunted Mason for so long, I know how he works, how he thinks. I know what to do."

"What are you doing, then? What are you texting him?"

"I'm speaking his language, texting him back with cryptic replies to taunt him. Once we prove it's him, we've got him. On cyberstalking. Conspiring to commit a felony. Intimidating a witness. Federal hate crimes. And probably more."

He shook his dark waves, refusing it. "So, you're taunting him to attack you. I know him too, Charlie. I worked beside him for two years. I know how he talks about women. How he treats them. He's a sadistic, perverted fuck. He makes Charles Manson seem like a schoolboy."

"I can handle him."

"Handle him? You're going to have your small hands full of evil you can't control if you keep this up. That's it. No more texting him back."

Nope. That did it. Line drawn.

I stepped to it, right up to his chin and command.

"Daniel Pierce, I love you. Goddammit, so much. But I got shot three times and survived. Hell, I've been targeted my whole damn life by bullies, guys, and guns. It's no different now. So don't fucking tell me what I can't survive. And never tell me what I can and cannot do. Ever!"

"I love you too, Charlie. And I respect the hell out of you. But I don't get a say in this? Fuck that! I'm not bossing you around. I love you and I'm fucking concerned. Because one of us should be. Because clearly you have no regard for your own safety, but I do."

Okay, he was right. I could be cavalier with my life. The three bullet scars down my body from the last time I provoked a man were evidence.

And truth be told, Mason was a snake. One I could charm, but I was no fool. His venom could poison my veins. Daniel's too. Killing us both.

My guilty silence gave Daniel too much time to make the next logical step. Yanking his phone from his back pocket, his fingertip swiped the screen, checking Instagram.

I wanted to grab his hand, stopping him before he saw it, pulling him down into the pit of vipers with me.

Too late.

His fingertip tapped. Mason's account appeared. He selected the most recent post, the pictures of us next to the white flag before it.

When Daniel's eyes lifted to mine, I didn't recognize him.

My mind had predicted it, but my heart wasn't prepared. Not for this. Pure fear. Pure rage. And yes, betrayal maligned his beautiful face.

Betrayal that I didn't tell him days ago—Mason Hunt was hunting *us*.

ANONYMOUS

here are they? Where did they go after New York? It infuriates me.

A probe of her brief, public military record reveals she was married, is a widow now. Her last known address? Her dead husband's in Albuquerque, New Mexico.

And then... nothing.

The trail on Captain Charlotte Roberts ends there. How dare she?

But Daniel Pierce is easy game to track. This soothes my nerves.

Photos of him from over a decade lead a trail straight to London. To one of a few high-priced neighborhoods in the sprawling city.

There are hundreds of shots of Daniel Pierce where one can see even house numbers in the background. It only takes minutes to decipher the street.

The area to filter my search?
It's bliss.
It's obvious.
It's Knightsbridge.

CHAPTER TWENTY-NINE

DANIEL

Rage crackled under my skin. All night, I wouldn't talk to her. Thankfully, she kept her distance.

For there was nothing I knew to say. Nothing that wouldn't blemish our love if I opened my mouth with all that coursed through me.

It knew no direction. No clear, decisive articulation.

Anger at her lie. Fury with Mason. Both whipped my mind with lashes of logic.

Smack! Charlie had lied to me for over two weeks.

She didn't tell me from the morning we made love in the shower in San Diego that Mason Hunt had texted her. Or about the thirty-three times since. Eerie times when Mason had transferred his target from Kierra to Charlie with his stalking obsession.

Thwack! Mason was after us.

I never feared the physicality of the young man. My power loomed over him. That fight I'd win. But it didn't matter. Not with the weapons Mason deployed—his demented fans.

The *White Flag* movie disgusted me. With critics raving about the film, I tried watching it. Couldn't get through the first twenty minutes. Some called it "art". All I saw was gratuitous violence.

I always felt a responsibility as an actor for what I put out in the world, choosing mostly action hero or romantic roles, some with a bit of comedy to give people a laugh.

But the *White Flag* film and Mason's choice to do it? One that opens with his character, John White, torturing a young woman? And all the brutal acts he gets his gang to commit?

No way I'd ever agree to do a film like that.

The fact that Mason's performance was so eerily convincing—it violated my soul.

I could distance myself from a film or a character. When your entire career is built on producing fiction, it's difficult not seeing all as such.

Not now. All I could see was Charlie. Charlie in those scenes. Charlie getting hurt. Tortured. Raped. And Mason relishing every scream of her pain.

I didn't care if I was also targeted in that fucking post.

They could come for me. I'd had all sorts of demented attention mailed to me, posted about me, sick fans whose affection for me turned dark. I was numb to it.

Not anymore. Raw rage and, yes, fear coloured my eyes. Not for me. For Charlie.

She sat inside, reading a book on the sofa while I sat outside. The cigar I smoked couldn't pacify me. But it occupied my fist that wanted to punch.

Not her. Never.

It cracked my knuckles wanting to destroy Mason. The

threat that Mason could hurt the woman I loved? Letting Charlie take Mason on by herself? Not an option. I'd throw all my might and money into ending him.

But how?

Charlie was right. Mason was a sneaky, sick bastard. We had to catch him. But her tactics? Texting and taunting him back?

I didn't know if Charlie was a lethal, talented protection officer, or an addict for the hunt of anyone threatening women, including herself.

I guessed both.

I guessed right.

But I was certain how far she was willing to go. Every time I made love to her beautiful body, the scars down it testified to what she would sacrifice to protect someone else. It only inspired more of my passion for her.

And this was it. What hurt me almost as much as the fear of losing her. Of her being hurt. It was that with all we shared now, she didn't share this with me.

Yeah, well, you're hiding something too, Pierce. Much worse. So jump off your bloody high horse.

"Are you coming to bed?"

It turned my head. The vision almost broke me open. She stood in the doorway of my home in a black silk nightgown. Fuck's sake, her beauty eviscerated me every time.

I tapped my ashes, gauging my rage because even the seductive sight of her couldn't tempt me now. "Later."

"Are you going to talk to me?"

The resonance of her question? Not desperate. It was bold. Like she knew we both were guilty. Of lies of omission. Of fear of harming the other.

"Not now."

I didn't trust my mouth. I wouldn't risk saying anything now that would ruin forever with her.

I didn't speak all night, lying beside her in bed, exhaustion finally beating down my anger. The next morning, I awoke with it again on the horizon—promising another day of this furious weather.

We packed our bags. She made the bed. I updated my estate manager—we were leaving Cornwall, headed to London.

Before, I was excited for the trip, to drive my car with Charlie, taking the back roads and showing her beautiful sights along the way.

Now, I didn't give a flying fuck. Not with the silence taking root between us. It bloomed with a foul stench while we put our bags in the boot of my car. I resolved to endure the misery for the drive back to Knightsbridge.

"Stop," she said, before I turned out of my drive onto the narrow road.

I stomped the brake but wouldn't look at her. "Did you forget something?"

"Yes, dammit. We both forgot something. That we love each other. And I'm not sitting here for five more hours of silence until we talk this out."

"I'm afraid to say something." My grip of the steering wheel was as tight as the one over my lips. "I'm so fucking angry at you. And at Mason. Like you had a bloody affair with him." The pain of it pulled my glare, meeting hers.

Her chin bobbed back and forth with the sass out of her mouth. "I wouldn't fuck Mason Hunt if the survival of humanity depended on it."

It was almost cute if the reality wasn't that was one of the many things Mason would try to painfully do to her if he could.

"Daniel." She sighed. "I'm sorry I didn't tell you. But trust me, I was going to. I just didn't want to ruin everything. The premiere. The baby shower. The first time in your home. Meeting your family. If I told you, it would've ruined it all."

"No, Charlie. That's not how we're doing this. We aren't keeping things from each other."

I said it and hypocrisy tainted every syllable from my mouth.

She heard it clear. "Then what aren't you telling *me*? Because I can sense it. You're keeping something from me too."

Oh fuck, Pierce. You just mailed a golden invitation for destruction now.

"All right, then. Yes. I haven't told you yet that Friday I'm supposed to do a photoshoot at Logan's new store. And that Kathy will be there."

There. One secret revealed.

Hold your fucking lips tight before the other falls out.

"Is that what you're afraid to tell me?" The grin on her face lifted a stone off my heart. "Daniel, I don't care about Kathy. No offense. Or any of your ex-whatevers."

God, how I hoped she meant it. The love of my life had no bloody clue. We were equal with guilt. And this fight was done. Because I sure didn't want to start another.

I reached for her hand resting in her lap. "Will you come with me to the photoshoot?"

"Why? Do you need a chaperone? Are things going to get heated between you and Kathy?"

She joked. I didn't. "I can't predict what she'll do. But I'll need my best protection officer for whatever she does."

That tossed her neck up in a laugh. "You need a battalion of officers to protect you from the people who want to fuck you, Daniel Pierce." Her gaze flicked back to my eyes. "Okay. I'll go."

I did too. Turning onto the road, starting our journey back to London, we talked it through.

How she would go with me to the shoot. How I would join the next call with the FBI. How we'd do this together now.

During the conversation, I was thankful for the automatic drive of my car so my other hand wouldn't have to let hers go.

CHAPTER THIRTY

CHARLIE

His multimillion dollar London townhouse was stunning—four narrow floors of alabaster tile, dove-white walls with floating staircases of walnut wood steps and glass railing walls winding up to each. The modern design transformed what used to be a stable and carriage house into a magazine-worthy home.

Light poured through skylights at the back of the home, from the third-floor roof terrace, down through the glass-enclosed opening at the back of the ground level sitting room, illuminating the lowest level basement with a gleaming kitchen and dining table below.

Anyone would love Daniel's house.

Except me.

Something was wrong. I couldn't shake it.

All while Daniel gave me a quick tour. Later, while he opened mail and delivery boxes and I started their laundry.

And now, while he reviewed a script and I made final preparations for our trip to my home.

The energy of the gorgeous home pranced across my nerves, darting my eyes up to the calm around us.

Looking for something.

Even the delicious curry Daniel ordered from his favorite London take out couldn't satiate the silent mania I swallowed down.

Maybe it was that I was one of his many women visitors. Daniel had lived here for almost ten years. At the rate he could go, the math in my head added up a lot of fucking in these walls.

But no, that wasn't it.

Jealousy wasn't a meal I ordered.

Maybe it was Mason. His evil was my other travel companion.

I got another text from him today, answering my question about his favorite shade of red.

Unknown

For 120 days you will know

my bloody shade

The reference to that specific number was cryptic. I didn't know what it meant. This time I shared it with Daniel after we arrived.

The rage across his face was sudden. He deciphered it immediately.

"He's referencing the Marquis de Sade. The French nobleman and author imprisoned for his depraved sexual behavior and violence."

"How do you know about *that*?" I was disturbed by Daniel's quick knowledge.

"Because I was offered a role about him twenty years ago. I turned it down. Not the direction I wanted for my career." His feet had started to pace, fingers shoving back his tendril. "Are you going to reply to him?"

"Yep. I gotta keep him talking about himself. We only need one certain reveal to get him."

I knew what would tempt Mason.

Ego and sex.

Every man's cyanide.

Nose down, fingertips flying across the keyboard, taunting Mason had filled me with sick delight. The pleasure unnerved me. But my logic dismissed concern with reason—it was the only way to catch him.

What naked truth is there to
know about you?

Daniel read it over my shoulder. The heat of his temper pressed firm against my back. I had to give him props for his physical restraint, but he couldn't hold his tongue.

"I bloody hate this, Charlie. It's like you're fucking him while I watch."

The pivot of my frustrated heel turned, facing him.

"Daniel, welcome to my side of our world. You've only known fucking the pretty angels while it's been my job to protect them from the ugly fucking devils like Mason."

The harsh truth had silenced his gorgeous mouth, stilling his stance.

"This is why I keep warning you to be careful." My stare held his. "Why I'm afraid to stand in the light of your celebrity world because I know its darkness. This evil. You can't have one without the other."

"Are you the angel who travels between both worlds now, Charlie? My heaven and his hell? Because if so, I won't lose you to him."

"Well, if I'm an angel, then I'm the angel of wrath because so help me, God, I will end Mason Hunt."

That text, truth, and time sat between us now.

Like Mason was a guest at Daniel's glass dining table, sneering through bites of inferno-spiced lamb vindaloo, eyeing the tension between us with evil glee, delighted that he could shred my sanity, and tear our love apart too.

Daniel sat at the head of the table, eating his dinner, reading the script, while I sat opposite him, savoring pieces of naan bread while I made a call home.

It was a call to a young man who was nothing but an angel in my world.

Silas. I babysat him when I was a teenager and he was a boy. Nowadays, he took equal care of me. All the residents on Daufuskie Island, the almost three hundred I grew up with, they'd protect me and Daniel. They'd never leak our location or betray my trust.

It was the weekly tourists and day trippers we had to steer clear of.

Still, it was the safest place I knew to hide from the paparazzi or any *White Flag* threat that could come hunting for us.

Once we were back in the States, all I had to do was get us, unseen, from the mainland to my home. The risk would dwindle dramatically, from very high at one of the busiest international airports with thousands of passengers to almost null on a secluded island.

Our biggest threat along the journey? All the damn phones aimed at Daniel's famous face.

"I need my boat out of dry dock and ready for me by Sunday." I spoke to Silas on my phone. "I'm flying in that afternoon and driving down from Charlotte. I should be there by seven. I'm bringing someone with me, and I need your help, please. No one can see us."

With no bridges, no planes there, everyone arrived by boat.

We couldn't use the public marinas on the island. Too many tourists were there, recognizing Daniel the instant he strolled up on the floating promenade into public. The boat club where I moored my boat was the same. My home faced the Atlantic. It had no dock. But if I used Silas's dock on the sound, no one would see us. I knew exactly what had to be done.

"You bringin' another celebrity?" Silas asked. "We already got a rockstar here."

Yes, the island famously housed an American icon of rock music. Silas's tone didn't sound thrilled to be adding another celebrity to the list. "I know *who* you're coming with." Warning hummed through his low register.

"We need your help, Silas." I felt tears coming. Shit, I was holding back so much fear. "I'm serious. Please."

Daniel caught it in my voice. Glancing up from his script, concern creased over his handsome face.

It choked a sudden lump in my throat.

This felt like another cruel deceit.

It was.

I could never tell Daniel *this* secret, my darkest fear, the one that haunted me and my sanity.

How somewhere in my mind paranoia smeared with premonition... a threat much larger than Mason loomed.

Daniel thinks he's going home with you to share your world.

That's the lie. You're taking him home to hide in it.

Silas's voice smoothed in a tender tone over the phone, echoing my soft accent, gently assuring me. "I got ya, Charlie Girl. *Always.*"

CHAPTER THIRTY-ONE

CHARLIE

All the next day, through my laughing lunch date with Juliette and into Friday, the same eerie energy charged through me.

No reply from Mason.

Still, I knew he got off on it. Literally.

The only messages I got were from home.

Silas, confirming my boat was docked for me on the mainland. Pop and Evelyn, asking what groceries I needed, assuring me that the security cameras were running, and that the air conditioner was on, cooling my home in the sweltering August heat.

The barrage of texts about island life had my mind safely home, swaying relaxed there like the Spanish moss from the trees, washing away the sinister that had swirled around me for days.

However, Friday Daniel's phone alarm woke us early for the photoshoot and for sure drama.

Strap your boots on. You're gonna be standing in a pile of ex-girlfriend bullshit today.

I wasn't wrong.

Inside the historic white stone building with wrought-iron window balconies, decadence greeted us. Along with Kathy. Sipping champagne, she flitted her hand, directing Logan's staff about. Her whittled nose up. Her pouting lips griping demands. Her heels clicking across the floor, fingers combing through her blown-out tresses.

I kicked back on the tufted leather sofa, boots stacked on the ottoman, hair in a messy ponytail, mouth sucking on a stick of mint Rock candy, taking it all in. Because, damn, what a sight.

Not Kathy.

Daniel.

One of those surreal moments for me again, watching him through the scope of "Daniel Pierce."

Good God, the man could fuck a camera lens, reaching right through the glass to between my thighs and those of millions.

Daniel kept glancing over, catching my hungry grin. His smile rose for me before he slowly aimed it back toward the camera.

Then the photographer wanted his profile. While Daniel stood, hands in his pockets in front of a pristine row of Logan MacGregor suits, his eyes mounted over me in a wolf gaze. Second by second his aqua stare devoured me, silently describing how he would be fucking me in a dozen lurid positions tonight.

No, now. I wanted him right now.

Shredding my bottom lip with my teeth, I felt my clit screaming for him. Challenging his silent stare back, I shared with him how I wanted him to drop those wool pants and bend me over, taking me from behind, spreading my...

"More of this!" Logan shouted, cutting through the pulsing moment. "My dear, I want you in the shot with him."

His command shook my head from its mental fuck of Daniel ten feet away. "What?" Not sure what I just heard.

Logan proclaimed again, "I want you in the shot with him. It's palpable. The camera is aflame with his focus on you."

Daniel smiled, busted, and loving the idea. But my ego was already out the door.

Hell to the fucking No! No way are you doing a fashion shoot.

Kathy agreed. Hovering behind Logan, she said, "That would be quite off-brand, Logan. Not suited for our aims."

"Bollocks," Logan said. "Ms. Ravenel was shot in my dress last week at the premiere and this would be right on brand. She's perfect. They're perfect. The fiercest couple in the world. With my vision for the new women's wear line— a strong line equal to the men's—it's bloody gold."

Logan turned to me. "Just a few photos. One outfit. That's all. No different than the premiere."

His feet charged across the herringbone floors to the women's line. Fingertips reaching for a small black leather bodice, he said, "You'll love it. A look like the dress you wore but strong." One row down and a pair of dark-teal women's wool pants were also in his grasp. "What will it take to convince you?"

"World peace and the cure for cancer," I said.

Good girl. The only thing model about you is your smart-ass mouth and perfect aim.

"Hard luck, Logan." Kathy's smile at my refusal was

also pleased, loathing fashioned over her now. "Dull look and idea."

Oh, snap! Another insult. 100 *percent interest in a fight now.*

Aim. Fire.

"I'll do it." I stood up. "Donate a hundred thousand to a women's veterans charity of my choice, Logan, and it's a deal. One look. Three shots."

Fuck, the irony of my last statement. Like the one look I gave before I took three shots down my body.

But that was six years ago, and this was only a picture.

Considering the thousands of posts of my image now, why the hell not? At least these I could control; these could help other women.

Logan agreed to the deal. Kathy stormed out of the store while Logan's team moved into fifth gear, fitting me in the bodice and pants, his hair and makeup team jumping in.

While Daniel was whisked off for his wardrobe change —the excitement, the attention, the idea to do this with him —it all became fun for me.

Kathy's departure let me breathe easier too. Not that Kathy scared me. Unnerved me was more accurate. It was that same fucking feeling I got in Daniel's townhouse.

Maybe that was it.

Kathy was the last woman to share the space with him. Two years of her malevolent spirit still clung to the air. Why Daniel ever dated her, I couldn't reason. Was it just me or couldn't other people sense when someone was dangerous?

Nope, that's your own special curse and gift. Sorry and you're welcome.

Logan fashioned us for a gender flip and the camera clicked all my nerves away.

I stood, stance wide, hands in pockets, chin down,

confronting the lens with a soft stare. The pants were tailored perfectly for me, tight across my waist, hemmed to skim the top of my black leather boots. The black leather bodice revealed my abs, arms, and shoulders... and my shoulder scar. My hair was slicked in a severe fall down my back. My makeup was minimal except for the smoky look around my eyes.

Daniel stood behind me, muscles straining the threads of a cream Aran wool sweater. His carved calves popped naked under a dark teal and black tartan kilt. Only he could make a sweater and skirt redefine masculinity.

The heat off his body behind me, the heave of his chest pressed to my shoulders, desire charged through us in such proximity. Damn, the test pictures *were* fierce.

Logan wanted two more shots. One of us facing each other. No smiles. Only confident stares, fucking each other with our eyes. And one more with Daniel standing behind me. One of my adoring smile nuzzled into his dark waves while his head bowed, kissing the crest of my scarred shoulder, because I couldn't help it. God, I loved him.

How we made it home in the car without fucking along the way, I didn't know.

Logan gave us the clothes. We fucked in them the second we were through Daniel's front door. He took me hard against the wall of his living room in the same position, thrusting behind me.

"Show me what a man you are," I rasped, hands splayed against the wall. His mouth latched to my neck, biting down, spreading my thighs wider for his driving grunts.

"Like this?" He growled, ruthless with his kilt up and my pants down, proving it beyond a doubt. Making me ache. Making me teeter on the delicate tip of an orgasm.

"Show me you're the best, Charlie. The best pussy, the best fuck of my life."

His grip pinned me here, fucking my feet off the floor, no denying our equal union. My body, his love, the groaning passion we shared, while his grip turned my chin for a savage, claiming kiss, the proof streaming down our quaking thighs.

Leaving our high fashion clothes in the puddle on the floor, we found our way to bed, laughing at our impulse, adoring the instant photos the photographer let us keep from the day.

We ate Chinese take out in bed before Daniel set our containers aside, pulling me on top of him for dessert, moaning with loud appreciation for my long ride.

Finally, sleep curled over our intertwined bodies. But something woke me. What? Thirst so strong I wanted to gulp two cold bottles down.

My feet quietly took the two narrow flights, making sure I didn't slip down the stairs to the water beckoning me.

I didn't even close the refrigerator door. Standing here in its light, guzzling the first bottle, then the second halfway down before closing it, I glanced left to the sleek white countertops.

They were pristine—like no one cooked on the surface. Neither of us had since we arrived here. That's why I noticed. Immediately—

The carving knife?

Missing from its oak block.

A snap of my neck scanned around the room. Nothing except modern furniture and moonlight beamed in from the skylights two stories above. Yanking the dishwasher open to be sure. No knife in there. The sink was empty too.

My fists grabbed the weapons remaining—the chef's

knife and a chopping knife. My bare feet silently ascended wooden steps. The moonlight gave me enough vision to confirm. The next level sitting room? Clear. Opening the garage door. Only his car. Checking the front door? Still locked. Alarm blinking, activated.

The only way someone could get in Daniel's townhouse? If they already had access and awaited our arrival hours before.

Heart rate elevated, my quads flexed, climbing up the stairs. Sweat dampened my palms gripping the knives and the truth.

Daniel was unprotected, asleep in the owner's suite at the top of the landing. My feet entered the room. Slowly, I climbed into the bed beside him. The knives, hidden, tucked under my forearms.

Light from the moon and streetlamps outside glowed through the sheers over the glass doors to the terrace. The illumination fell on the floor-to-ceiling walnut wardrobe doors running the length of the wall opposite the large bed where they lay.

His body rested. Mine was calm, waiting, my eyelids disguised as closed, watching through the curtain of my lashes.

The wardrobe door. Its perfect alignment with the adjacent one.

Disturbed.

Opening.

No shock across my nerves.

I was certain of the presence. Of the energy creeping through the air. Of the quiet approach across taupe carpet. Of a blade, icy steel against the hot blood that pulsed through the veins in my throat, pressing against the exposed skin above my tender trachea.

The assailant's edge pushed against my flesh, pressure leaning with a reach so the other arm could— *snap*—the table lamp on the nightstand exploded light into my pupils. It startled Daniel to jump, to awake.

"What do you want, Kathy?" My voice was a perfectly calm hum against the razor-sharp threat across my throat.

The brown of Kathy's eyes shook, fractured with frenzy while her groomed auburn brows lay serene above them.

"I want back what's mine."

It took those seconds for Daniel to find focus. To awake to a real nightmare. The shift of his weight on the mattress beside me was my only concern.

"Daniel, don't move," I said. "We're fine."

"Kathy, don't hurt her." His tone swirled calm with urgent. The white sheet over his naked groin twisted beside me as he shifted on the bed, readying to pounce.

"Daniel, don't." I didn't want him near the lethal weapon trembling in Kathy's frantic hand. Never taking my aim off Kathy's irises dancing with no logic, I said, "Kathy, no one's getting hurt tonight."

Kathy leaned over me, auburn strands falling in a flaming cloak around me. "I got hurt." Tears fell from her desperate eyes, down grimacing cheeks. "Daniel and I, we were fine until you came along."

Out of the corner of my eye, I saw Daniel's hand rising to halt her and the lie. "Kathy, put the knife down. This is my fault. Not Charlie's." He twisted more toward shielding me, pulling the sheet off his naked body, naively taunting Kathy even more. "Hurt me. Not her."

The command of his velvet voice attracted Kathy's stare up to him. Everything about Daniel seemed to summon her. The weight of the blade shifted against my throat with

Kathy's draw toward him, the amber spice of her perfume fogging over me.

"Why, Daniel?" Kathy's glare clung to his handsome face before combing down his sculpted torso. "Why choose her and not me?"

The pain in her question threatened to pierce my throat. The grip of my hands released the hidden knives poised to strike. Nerves curling in now. Heat firing across my muscles contracting. Harnessing power…

Daniel started to assuage her. "Kathy, I never meant to—"

Strike! One inner block of my right hand bit Kathy's forearm, leveraging Daniel's distraction and Kathy's weight. The move, so fast it knocked the knife from her hand. In a blitz, I surged, twisting limbs around her, crashing our bodies down to the floor.

"Kathy, stop." The strength in my arms and skills pinning Kathy's wrists against the carpet—no match for the struggling woman. "Kathy, please. Calm down. I'm not going to hurt you, but I will not let you go until you do."

Daniel was up, throwing the knives to the opposite corner of the room, standing in front of the weapons. He grabbed his phone charging on the nightstand. His gorgeous nudity in my periphery only salt in the wound of the woman thrashing under me.

I stopped him. "Don't call the police." Kathy's wrists forced back in vain against my restraint. But the distress pummeling Kathy's face looking at him? The pain twisting across her cheeks? The mania attacking her eyes? My heart broke. "Call Jeremy from my phone."

No one would be served by sirens wailing outside his door. Kathy needed help, not handcuffs. Her resistance to me waned while Daniel woke Jeremy, who immediately called a friend, an officer who would send an unmarked car over.

Her buttress against my control relaxed under my grip. Kathy's eyes finally found mine. Searching for clarity, for control over her mind. Taking in the sad spectacle around her, the powerful words mellowed from Kathy's mouth. "I'm sorry."

The return to lucidity. I knew its painful journey too coming back to find my mind after a PTSD shock to my system. Different reasons and emotions assailed us, but we shared the same travel through mental hell.

Compassion ruled me. Those who've never known real suffering judge others with such lofty malice. I never hated them for it. No, I pitied the righteous. Knowing that everyone will be humbled at least once in life. I certainly had been. Many times.

Releasing my hold on Kathy, sitting back on my knees, the woman under me searching for her sanity saddened me.

"It'll be okay, Kathy. No one's getting hurt," I said. "No one's pressing charges. We're just gonna get you some help."

I swung my leg back over to sit down beside her. Kathy drew her body into a tragic ball, sobs racking her.

It overwhelmed me, seeing any woman suffer. Soothing Kathy with rubs to her back, I could only offer words of assurance, of understanding.

Daniel sat on the edge of the bed looking in shock at the sight. He finally stood up to get dressed. I did the same while we waited for the officers to arrive.

Once they did, Kathy had nothing but apologies through tears during her departure. Daniel had found her bag in the wardrobe. He had called her best friend to meet Kathy at the hospital. Kathy would have a team of professionals helping her.

And the mystery was solved.

How did the paparazzi know when Daniel was arriving in London? Where his townhouse was located? Kathy confessed to it all.

She worked for the same PR firm as Daniel's publicist. For years, she said she'd secretly gained access to their company drive where Daniel's private schedule was kept in secured files. She'd been tracking his professional travel daily.

And Daniel forgot.

Forgot that Kathy had asked for a key and code to his townhouse two months into dating her. Under the ruse of helping him with his busy life, her request didn't alarm him. All the while, she admitted that she'd been sneaking in when he wasn't there, pretending that if she was in his home, she was still in his heart.

After her quiet departure, we couldn't sleep. We curled up on the sofa, talking through Daniel's shock. He wondered aloud what he could've done differently, regretting over and over how I was almost hurt.

"When we first met, you asked me about the price I paid for this." He gestured to the luxury around them. "It's not worth it. It's arrogant to admit, but I know how I affect others. People like Kathy. How desperate some are to have a piece of me. They bloody cry at the rope lines, like they have no value and I'm their only affirmation of worth. It's humbling and heartbreaking at the same time."

"It's taken a toll on you." I held his hand. "I could see it feeding your ego in videos years back at the *Zeus* premieres. You used to love it. But you've changed, I can tell. How at the last *Druid* premiere, you were kind to everyone, but you didn't like it anymore."

"Because look. Look at the toll it's taken on you, on Kathy."

"Daniel, I'm fine. And it's not your fault. Kathy is not a victim. She's a grown woman who needs help. Women are full adults, no different than men. We're responsible for our choices. Our actions. Our health. Not even you have that sway. If we give away our power, it's our responsibility to get it back."

"You're right." His gaze went to the ceiling. "I guess I knew for some time that she was struggling, that she needed help."

"We all struggle in silence sometimes."

Yep, same goes for you.

CHAPTER THIRTY-TWO

DANIEL

PILLOWTALK by ZAYN

"You've opened all your boxes except that one." Charlie pointed to the large one sitting by the front door.

My pulse tripled.

Why I thought she wouldn't notice it when the woman noticed everything, especially after last night with Kathy? Of course, while we made a final sweep through my townhouse for items to pack, the box sitting there made her curious... and me sweat.

"Just leave it," I said. "It's nothing important."

She stood over it, her stare traveling the path down to the box, studying the packing label before landing on my nervous eyes.

"Something large mailed to you last December and you say it's nothing?" She grinned. "Want to change your answer to the truth?"

Fuck's sake, Pierce. When are you going to learn? You can't fool her.

"I know what it is. It's a belated Christmas gift from my brother Samuel. A joke because I told him that Kathy and I were over. That my single days were back. It arrived and I never opened it."

"Then how do you know what it is?"

"Samuel texted me a picture of it from the online store, said he and my sister-in-law were loving theirs."

"Well, color me curious." Her head cocked to the side, eyes interrogating. "What is it?"

I didn't know if she was going to set me or the box on fire with her intent on catching me in a secret. "It's a sex swing." But I stepped into the blaze anyway.

Her eyebrows shocked up. "Your brother sent you a sex swing for Christmas?"

"Yes. You've met my siblings. It's all filthy jokes between us, particularly about sex."

"Why didn't you want to tell me?"

"Because I worried it would make you think of Kathy." Shame sighed from my lungs. "Or make you think I was some sex-crazed perv. It arrived before the New Year, before I left to shoot in Madrid, and it's been sitting there ever since."

"Daniel, do you really worry I'll judge you like that? Over an ex-girlfriend or some kinky sex toy?"

"Yes, Charlie, I do." Scratching at my fear, at my secret buried below. "I can't go back and change my past. I've told you, I'm not proud of it. And I don't want anything from it coming round to wreck what we have now."

"But you deal with my past all the time. It's written across my cheek. Hell, down my body. And with my PTSD? I know it's not easy, and I love you for it." Her hands wouldn't leave her hips, challenging me. "Why don't you trust me to love you and deal with your past too?"

My feet stood firm in the fact. "Because our pasts are opposite worlds. You were a hero off fighting a war, sacrificing everything, and almost died doing it." Another scratch, revealing. "While I was a spoiled prat, going from a movie set to revelry at a bar, to a posh hotel every night, and getting paid millions to do it. All for my ego and wallet."

I couldn't look at her, only at the floor. "I can't ask you to love that part of me. Not when I don't either."

"Too late, Daniel. I already do. Whatever the hell you did." Her small, bare feet stepped my way. "It made you who you are today. Humble. Wise. Grateful."

Her toes touched his. "The shit with Mason," she said, "that I should've told you. I shouldn't have kept that a secret. But the stuff from our past? The painful stuff? I know how it hurts, why we keep that guarded. That you have to be ready to tell. And I trust you. You'll tell me in your own time, when you're ready."

Trust me?

She did more than that.

She loved me. So much that I felt it seeping into my bones, forging me into a new man, even stronger and better for her.

But ready to tell her my greatest sin?

No. I couldn't do it. It would hurt her, and that would kill me.

"I don't want to lose you." Remorse, humility, guilt. It all crushed me. "If I tell you, you'll leave me."

"No, I won't. Don't treat me like some innocent angel, like I haven't seen real hell." Her fingertips reached out, tracing over mine. "I'm just as lucky to have you."

I looked up, overwhelmed, my hands reaching out,

cradling her cheeks. Nestling my nose next to hers, I stood wounded and redeemed at the same time.

"In this world we share, you may not be an angel, but I sure feel like a lucky devil."

"No. Mason is the devil. You're the man. The beautiful, caring, flawed one I love." She pushed back, confronting my gaze. "We're not playing this whole saint-with-the-sinner bullshit love story. That's fiction. We're real. Like this—"

She reached for the nape of my neck, drawing me hard against her soft, assertive lips, our tongues stirring, warming me, blaze building.

God, I could get lost in her. And all I'd find along the way were the best pieces of me, the only man I wanted to be, sharing the most incredible breaths with her. Her kiss rescued me from guilt, dragging me into desire. Moaning for her. For our love. Always.

"Besides." She pulled back for air, fanning the flames, one eyebrow up at me with that sexy twinkle in her eyes. "I'm the devil who wants this sex-craved perv to fuck me in that swing."

"Are you serious?" I couldn't believe my luck, but my dick was already throwing chips down on the table. "Even after everything that happened?"

I feared Charlie would run screaming after Kathy's attack. I was shocked she stayed another day here with me. And now she wanted to make love—hot, kinky love at that—in my townhouse? In a sex swing?

Well done, Pierce. You may be a devil now, but you must've been an angel in your past hundred lives to deserve this woman.

"Daniel." The grip of her small hands over my scruffy jaw took my full attention. And heart. And my rousing stiffy. "I told you, I'm not leaving you. Nothing is tearing us apart. We stay connected, on our terms, in every shameless way we can. That's how we'll get through this."

She was right. No matter what threatened us, if we stayed together, cherishing everything that bonded us... we could survive it.

"And it's a gift, right?" Her palms landed on my chest. "How dare we not try it? God knows, I'm curious. And I suspect... we're only living once."

And if we didn't survive it? What a helluva way to go.

"Well, Happy Christmas in August." The magic hit me instantly, lips dusting over hers, all else forgotten. This was *our* gift. "Were you naughty this year, Charlie? Does Santa need to come down your chimney to give you a spanking?"

"Ho, ho, hell yeah." Her grip kneaded my hardening present. "Hang it up, big boy."

I did. So bloody fast I'd impress the London Fire Brigade. The heavy bag that hung by the edge of my sitting room that normally took my pounding lay on the floor. In its place, a black swing dangled sturdy from its silver hook and industrial spring.

Charlie disappeared upstairs. I could hear the shower as I gazed at the arched harness hanging from the ceiling, black straps where she would swing back with her legs wide open, feet in holds, all before me. Trusting me.

Despite what she said, she was my angel. One I'd never stop worshipping. I'd repent for my past by spending the rest of my life on my knees for her, making her future the best it could be.

The typewriter chime buzzed in my back pocket. Speak of the horny angel.

Her contact name?

My love, Charlie

Come for me

Yes, I would. I didn't know what she had planned but my trainers took the wooden steps so fast my toe almost tripped over the landing at the top.

She watched me take a shower through the glass enclosure. She pointed to my crisp white button-up and dark-gray trousers on the bed. She told me to get dressed then go downstairs, pour some drinks, and wait for her.

No instructions needed down here. I knew the drinks to pour, the music to play. Pulling the curtains closed, I left the lights on. Neither one of us liked fucking in the dark. There was too much carnal beauty to be witnessed between us.

The click of her stilettos down the stairs lifted my eyes. Only for such erotic occasions did she wear them. Her black robe draped open. The reveal underneath almost dropped the crystal highball glass from my hand.

Oh. Hell. Fucking. Yes.

Her skin was bound tight in a black cupless bondage bra with matching knickers and bondage suspender belt—all luxe silk bands of gentle restraint for my control.

It flexed my breath against my ribs, lust firing across my nerves. When she drew near to my lips, her nipples grazed erect against the starched cotton of my shirt. She dizzied me.

"Who's the devil now, Pierce?"

Her scent was carved into my brain forever: chocolate, praline, and dark musk. A sweet, smoky flavor traveled across our tongues after our sips trimmed with rum. It summoned her name and a slew of my curses in awe after our kiss.

"Where did you get this?" It stunned me, this vision of

her dressed like an elegant BDSM cover girl. Good God, it weakened my knees and hardened everything else.

"In New York." The tips of her nipples, hoisted even higher by the straps, kept teasing against my heaving chest. "See, it was my little sin of a purchase days before I knew about your pervy sex swing. Don't underestimate how kinky I want to get with you. I've waited too long for this. To love a man and trust him like this." She tossed back her last sip. "Where's your phone?"

The blood to my cock emptied my brain of coherence. "We're doing a video?"

"No." Her robe floated to the floor. "We're doing our own photoshoot."

All the close-ups. Her nipples, dripping, melting the ice cube I took from my glass. My hand, wedged underneath the straining black straps across her firm, high bum. Her high heels, pushing taut against stirrups. Her blonde chandelier of locks swinging back over wood floors. My knuckles disappearing between her rosy lips. Her tiny waist, belted in elastic straps, arching. My hand, all my fingers, taking both her craving holes while my Hugot watch dripped from her and my efforts.

"Fuck's sake, Charlie." My chest huffed standing over her first puddle on the floor. And at the sight of her. "Spread your legs wider for me." I took more pictures of black straps, tan flesh, and pink lips, all glistening, all ready for me.

"You like taking pictures of me, don't you, Daniel?" The stirrups strained, all of her open, swinging with a shameless grin of satisfaction for my phone.

"Fuck yes." I lifted her heel in the stirrup to my lips, watching how it stirred in her eyes. Her exposure. Her trust.

Helpless in front of me, she held sway over my entire world. Goddamn, she was my sun, my essential light.

She swore, "I can take you, Daniel."

My lips skated over her ankle; she already had. "What do you want me to do to you tonight?"

Hanging in my living room, dangling every beautiful space I desired in the air before me. Yes, this was trust. I knew what I wanted. All of her. But no matter how many times we shared it, the sound of her affirmation? Of her desire for me? Pure opium.

"I want everything," she said. The strength in the svelte muscles of her arms hoisted her up while her legs hung at my mercy, her compliant posture not matching her demand with a smile. "I want you to show me what a naughty perv you are for me."

On my knees with her sanction, my tongue had to go first. Traveling the journey over every opening I'd tunnel next, my path paced up and down, unyielding, until the stirrups securing her feet shocked straight. With a loud scream of my name and clatter from the metal coil at her shake, her orgasm filled the air and my mouth.

She panted quietly. "Oh God, I'm sorry."

My hand glazed over her shaking thigh while I pressed my lips to it, licking up her drops. "Why are you sorry?"

"Your neighbors. We're so close they can hear us."

"Let them hear. I feel no shame with you. Only love." I stood and picked up her jewel plug from the end table before covering it with lube. "This is for us, remember? No one else matters." Carefully, I teased, pulsing it in and out against her tightest hole. "Let's fuck so loud the whole street can hear us."

Her gorgeous ass finally took it while a throaty "yes" fell

from her mouth. I had to stop at the sight. For my control. For my phone from my back pocket to take another photo.

"How do you feel, Charlie?" I aimed the lens, clicking while I said, "Tempting me with a jewel in your ass, your pulsing pink little hole, and everything framed by naughty black straps."

She grinned, having no idea how she was the most seductive sight I'd ever seen. "Like I want you to show me what a hard devil you are, Daniel."

Fuck, she was heaven, stunning… and all mine.

I obliged, putting the phone down, taking off my shirt and dropping my zipper. The pressure of the plug pushed against my cock while I entered her, making me groan back my release. My cadence was slow, grabbing the straps harnessing her hips, witnessing her breath deepen along with my tempo and our sway.

Sweet disbelief filled me—we were doing this. That I was so blessed with her. All I could do was love her, satisfy her, care for her until my end. And I did. With each sliding plummet, each gratifying slap between her thighs, each smack against her clit, each tight tug of her down my cock, my grip clenched the straps, reining in my control. But she lost hers with another scream.

The sight of her undoing, her complete surrender to me —it ruled me.

My hand gripped the straps pushing her breasts into my pinch. Then my fingertips squeezed a gentle clamp over her nipple while my cock started to pound with a fierce momentum into her. I didn't need a photo to remember…

Of how I'd always love her. Of how her beautiful body twisted for me in lewd gratitude while I cherished her next scream, rattling the harness.

"Do it, Daniel." She huffed. "Please. Fuck my ass."

Oh my God, I could die happy. Breath hammered over my lips, holding back. Everything I'd give to her: minutes, days, blood, breath. Redemption resided here. Waiting for her. Always. I found more lube. More control. No condom this time. She insisted.

With moans and praise, she urged me in, her hand guiding, accepting my gentle entrance until I was here, nothing left of me to take. I watched it all. "Oh fuck, this is going to end me, Charlie."

She swayed, panting, eyes heavy for more. "Use more lube and end us both."

I did and with a slow plunge, our moans filled the air followed by her begs not to stop, to do it again, over and over.

I gave her my all. My heart, my body—hers. Grabbing on to my only salvation, her. I knew her body, her shaking thighs. Knew she was arching for it. Knew the clank of the chain above harnessed her coming tsunami of lust. I marked time by her tide.

My throat strained, holding it all back, teeth clenched. This time I couldn't say it. I couldn't speak. The immense pleasure in her eyes, in her body, swelling only for me. With one more thrust, a low roar filled the air—hers—along with a gorgeous, thundering gush of her lust over my trousers, still on and soaking my thighs.

Grabbing the harness of the swing, I hung on for strength while I guided my cock out. Sound escaping, rocketing from my throat along with my creamy splatters across her belly, drops dappled all the way up to her pert, bound tits heaving for air.

Who was I anymore? No one without her.

Our last photo of the night? It was of my love for her, written in my oath across her body.

ANONYMOUS

The trail is cold.

It stops in New York. At their last seductive public display.

And then... nothing.

No fan posting in London under #danielpierce.

No sightings of him walking with her, hand-in-hand in Knightsbridge, or with shopping bags in tow.

No paparazzi catching them at a distance, chasing the couple down, shouting their names and getting their gazes to turn toward the lens to confirm their identity. To take the shot.

I'll wait. I have all the patience in the world for her. For my plan.

I know they'll emerge.

Their celebrity? The public demand for them? It's at a frenzied, fever pitch. They can't escape it.

Or me.

CHAPTER THIRTY-THREE

CHARLIE

I handed my carry-on to him to stow in the bin across from our business class seats.

"This is perfect," I said. "You're starting the journey to my home slumming it with the masses."

The brim of his Carolina Panthers baseball cap couldn't hide his grin at my smart-ass comment.

"You said you hated those first-class pods." He clicked the bin shut. "So this way we can sit closer together."

The center-aisle dual seats were cozier. We nestled in and took out our books. I focused on the pages until I heard a gasp before a symphony of giggles hit my ear, darting my eyes up.

Two twenty-something women had boarded the plane almost late, spotting Daniel immediately on their journey back to coach.

I warned him—even disguised in jeans, T-shirt, and a ball cap—he hid like a circus show in a library.

Now, their delight was all I could hear. And worry over.

Please don't post it. Please don't post it. Please go on airplane mode. Pronto.

At least I had the foresight to call ahead to the Charlotte airport for off-duty police officers to escort us from the plane to our car. I'd wanted to charter a private flight, but Daniel grew frustrated with my security demands.

He refused, saying it was excessive, declaring, "We're not posh bastards thinking we're better than everyone else. We're on holiday. Commercial will be fine."

I really think it was his pride, not wanting to let Mason dictate a damn thing about our life.

So I insisted on four guards for our detail, but Daniel's jaw clenched hard against that request too. Traveling with one guard max was his comfort zone.

"Look, I agreed to more protection at events." His stubbornness defied mine. "And to refrain from stopping for fans in public. But I'm not walking through an airport or standing in immigration with four guards, me, *and* you. It'll only draw more bloody attention."

"Yes, well, I'd rather cover my ass than stick it in the wind."

"I'm sorry." He smiled from ear to ear. "Any mention of your ass and I'm off on an entirely glorious train of thought."

"You know what I mean." Fuck this man and his seduction. And I had. Many times. But not then. "Better safe than sorry. Does that translate?"

"I'll compromise with two. Two plain-clothes security at the airport gate and to the car."

"Fine." I wasn't happy. Our careers mixed like oil and water. "The car at the airport will take us to the garage where I stored my Jeep. When I left to work *The Druid*, I was in a rush. I could only get a flight from Charlotte, so we have a four-hour drive home. And Captain Charlie will be in charge the whole time."

"Sounds crackin' to me." Yes, it was possible for him to tease me even more.

"Give me their names again." He leaned over now, asking about my almost-family.

"For a man who's paid millions to remember lines, you sure are forgetful with a few names." The cabin lights dimmed.

"I don't want to make a bad impression."

"Daniel, you could stand up in a virgin's church wedding and object and still make a swooning impression on the whole damn congregation." More giggling. I glanced back down the aisle. A peeking head snapped back behind a seat. My attention pivoted back to him. "They're going to love you."

"Well, my family wants to adopt you." His hand reached for mine. "No pressure on me now."

"Mine are easy too. Pop and Evelyn are like my mom and dad. They were best friends with my parents and have been by my side through everything. Quincy and Silas are like my brothers. Quincy had a stutter when we were kids, so I got suspended twice fighting some girls who bullied him."

"Is there ever a time when you're *not* protecting someone?"

"Yep"—the nerves in my stomach tickled up at our departure as I squeezed his hand—"when I'm sleeping or fucking you."

The roar of the plane's engines drowned out his chuckle. Hours passed with naps, movies, books, and a little banter. When we touched down in Charlotte, almost nine hours later, the plane wound its way to the terminal while *pings* and *dings* filled the air of phones back in use.

I was equally guilty.

My screen glowed...

Unknown

Welcome home

Terror gulped into my lungs.

Two taps and it was here. Four fucking "We're flying with #danielpierce" posts. Selfies of the two women in coach, giving deuces and fish-lip kisses to the camera nine hours before. All tagged with our next location: Charlotte Douglass International Airport.

Shit, shit, shit! They posted the flight number too.

I tapped Daniel's arm. "It's Mason. He knows we're here." The confusion on his face dissolved once I offered him my phone to tap through the evidence.

The officers were waiting for us—two men dressed in khakis and collared shirts with sidearms on their hips. Our flight with over two hundred passengers, along with flights from Jamaica, Aruba, and Mexico, flooded the immigration lines.

I loved flying back home, but now I wished we had the same pretentious asshole, private VIP terminals as JFK, LAX, or Heathrow. Because even though phones in the immigration lines weren't allowed, I clocked three out, popping pics of Daniel.

Three *pings* and I got the notifications. More #danielpierce posts.

Goddammit, now his clothing and hat would be identifiable too.

There'd be a damn ticker-tape parade outside of the

terminal by the time we got through... and not a welcome one.

Numerous fans could hide in a crowd of dozens if not a hundred people waiting to greet their arriving loved ones, all gathered in the unsecured public baggage-claim area of the airport.

Daniel watched me. "What are you searching for?"

"I don't search." My head was on a swivel. "I look."

Every bone in my body jolted, muscles charged with tension. While we waited at the carousel for our bags, I knew better than to be weighed down with luggage for this last transition through a high-risk space.

I scanned the crowd.

Three hundred and more were coming in behind us. If a tenth of these passengers had someone waiting for them outside the terminal, the crowd would be too much to handle, no matter how many officers guarded us.

"Hey, guys, change of plans." I huddled with the officers and Daniel, who tried keeping his face down.

"Once we clear our bags through customs and get close to the exit, you"—my chin nodded to the younger officer while I took a roll of quarters out of my backpack—"take our bags and meet us outside Zone Two. We'll drive around and come back for them.

"You"—I snapped my focus on the beefier-looking offi-cer, noticing his side-arm was on his left hip. That meant he was left-handed, would fire and defend with his dominant arm. I put the roll of quarters in mine, clasped in my right fist, adding weight to any punch I had to throw—"cover his left and I'll cover his right.

"And you"—I aimed my eyes for Daniel's—"take that hat off, they'll be looking for it, and do not stop. Keep your hands free and out in front. Be ready to defend yourself. I'll be fine."

I cursed having to sacrifice a guard to cover our bags, but we had no choice. Curious eyes were on us. Mine scoured the room and didn't see any other police around. No porters either. We couldn't leave our bags unattended. That'd cause more of a ruckus.

If the three of us—me, Daniel, and the officer—could move fast, we could make it right past the crowd... as long as no one recognized Daniel.

The long white corridor with burgundy carpet out of the terminal sloped up, creating a blind ridge on the horizon before the awaiting public appeared on the other side.

The beefy cop said, "Looks like a bunch of innocent bystanders to me."

"They're innocent bystanders unless I clock them"—my eyes scanning—"then they're not."

I assessed the sea of faces for either a guilty gaze averted or a direct, threatening stare. By the depth of bodies, there had to be fifty or more people, a horde of eyes staring directly at us.

Some wouldn't notice Daniel, their vision filtering for their intended. But all it took was one person shouting his name, turning necks, and a small mob would descend upon us.

My pulse soared the second we stepped into open air, my lips terse, my crosshair pupils scanning faces and hands.

"Daniel! Daniel Pierce!" The shriek of a woman sounded over the warning buzzer of a moving baggage carousel. "Daniel, over here!"

Left. My periphery caught it—white woman, thirties, blonde hair piled on her head, pink phone in hand. No risk. Behind her. More bodies stepping forward.

"Daniel! Daniel! Can I get a selfie?" Young Asian man. With a teen girl. Phones up. No risk.

The cop flanking Daniel's left pushed them back.

Daniel held his head down, thundering a firm "no" with a voice even I cringed to when he was mad.

My right arm was out, blocking, guarding, keeping two feet clear in front of us.

More bodies closed around us. "Daniel! Daniel!" filled the suffocating air.

"Get back!" I shouted.

The crowd crushed in. My bicep braced, charging them back. Daniel's palms were out, pushing back too.

The cop, mirroring me on Daniel's left, echoed, "Back!"

My focus was deployed in front of us.

To three heads back.

There. A flash. Green eyes, staring. White skin. Camouflage jacket. Black baseball hat. A deer on it with rifles crossed.

"Eleven o'clock!" I shouted to Daniel and the cop to look up and left.

The man charged through the crowd, a white Styrofoam cup rising in his left hand. The cop lifted his arm up to block it. Too late. A splash from it defiled my face, for seconds, blinding me with foul liquid stinging my eyes.

Still, I pushed back blind.

The man pressed against us. His scent, pine. His breath, tobacco. My left shoulder was pushed back against Daniel while our bodies urged forward.

My eyes fought for focus through the stench down my face. My blurred sight returned. Up to the man's face. Above it, Daniel's right fist, cocked high to punch it.

A gleam. A silver blade rose in front of my gaze. Stabbing up from the man's right hand, threatening Daniel.

My weighted fist circled, hammering down on the man's forearm, disrupting the aim of the knife and knocking it to the floor while Daniel's fist crunched down into the man's jaw.

An audible *snap* of bone took the air over the screams of the crowd. The man's mandible broke at Daniel's crushing blow.

The cop shoved the guy to the ground. His fall back cleared a small path as he disappeared under feet and bodies crowding forward.

"Get back!" I yelled, shoving chests while Daniel did the same.

We had twenty feet to go. Through the double sliding glass doors. I could see the car waiting, the make I always ordered—a nondescript white sedan. I urged Daniel, "Go, go, go, go!"

One more man stood at two o'clock, phone rising in hand, blocking our path through the glass doors sliding open. He took one step toward us. Protecting Daniel, the ball of my booted foot rammed his kneecap. He stumbled back, falling to the pavement with a yelp of pain.

The cop caught up to us, flanking our left while we ran for the car. With one fast grab, I snatched the door handle open and Daniel jumped in. I jumped in behind him.

"Drive," I told the driver, locking the doors behind us. "Go around and stop at Zone Two."

Fuck, the smell in my nostrils, the taste in my mouth.

Daniel asked, "You all right?"

"I'm fine. You?"

"Fuck no! I'm going to bloody fucking murder Mason Hunt."

This had Mason written all over it. I saw it. The flash of white draping from the man's hand clutching the knife seeking blood. The white pillowcase in his hand would chronicle the violence to Daniel.

Our car jerked and stopped, braking then moving, urging its way through the airport traffic, gaining speed, and preparing to circle back around.

With one quick rip, I took my T-shirt off to wipe my face. To clear the disgusting liquids from my nose and lashes. Not caring, but thankful I had a sports bra on underneath.

"What's that smell?" Daniel's breath huffed like mine from our fight.

"Piss and cum." My sticky eyes were on him. His face, still red with rage, stared back with eyelids wide, shocked by the insult down my face. "I'm fine," I said. "I've suffered worse in a latrine."

"Charlie." His hand reached out to my cheek. "I can't—"

"Daniel! You're bleeding." The outside of his left forearm, curving around to the underside had a long deep cut, dripping blood.

"What?" He lifted his elbow to examine it. "I can't even feel it."

"Here." I handed him my T-shirt. "Use this."

But it wouldn't stop bleeding.

Not while we circled around, and I darted out of the car. Not while I threw our bags in the trunk. Or while the cop who guarded us helped me, telling me that the man, the stabber—he got away. Or while the cop gave me his card, knowing it wasn't safe to stand and debrief.

All this while the blood wouldn't stop.

Daniel's stubborn resistance for care was as strong as the pressure he applied to it. But garnet weeps saturated the T-shirt and started dripping onto his jeans.

My stubborn streak bested his, telling the driver to take us to the nearest hospital. We waited for three hours in the emergency room for Daniel to get seven stitches and for a police officer from the airport office to meet us, getting our statements.

Daniel didn't want to call them, fearing the publicity would make our situation even worse. It would. But a stab wound in an emergency room summoned the cops anyway.

And I wanted to press charges. Wanted to open a case and to tell the FBI agent working the *White Flag* crimes about it too.

Every square inch of that airport had surveillance. There had to be multiple sightings of our attack and the guilty party.

By the time we wrapped up the horrific circus of a day, it was dark. The garage where we needed to pick up my Jeep was closed, and we were stuck in Charlotte for the night.

CHAPTER THIRTY-FOUR

DANIEL

Just Breathe by Pearl Jam

My gaze caressed the curve of her breast. Up the firm peak. Over the pink nipple blooming in the cold air. Back down the arch to gently lifting ribs. Then to breath falling from her button nose. A constellation of little freckles across its bridge sprinkled cute across her striking face.

This vision was my world.

Upon first blush, the sight of Charlie coursed visceral lust through my veins. But now? Waking up to her naked beauty, to her warmth, her vulnerable surrender by my side.

So. Much. Love.

The stinging in my arm woke me. Pain I was thankful for because it offered this moment, watching her sleep in our hotel room.

We needed the sanctuary of the luxurious bed in our

Ritz-Carlton suite. She'd said we didn't need such opulence. I reminded her that exclusivity also bought us safety.

The soft hum of the air conditioner filling the space gave me this moment, reconciling the last forty-eight hours. Hours that made my bloody head spin. But my life could twist in a tornado of drama with violent winds wrecking my world—as long as Charlie stood with me— I had my calm center.

Watching her the other night while Kathy lay next to her in a sobbing, unhinged mess—the contrast between the two women altered my soul.

My past was a numb, uninspiring chronicle of dating and fucking the Kathys of this world. The vain, the wealthy, the entitled women whose beauty could blind me for weeks, even months, until their inner ugly was finally revealed.

I never saw it until that moment that bent time. The moment I met Charlie, everything—my days, weeks, and months—they ceased to exist.

My life became every moment with her. With a woman who would sit naked on the floor, comforting another who had just put a knife to her throat. A woman who would risk death, protecting innocent girls. A woman who shared her body with me with no shame and then placed it in harm's way, fighting to protect me with no regard for her own safety.

There was only one time for me—a precious future with her.

"Wake up, beautiful." The tip of my finger combed over her silky dark eyebrow. "Let's get you home."

Her arms coiled up in a long stretch with a low growl before she turned her ocean-speckled eyes my way. She cooed, "Good morning, sexy." Those were often the first words out of her mouth. Bloody hell, her smile was the dawn in my world. With a curl toward me under the sheets, she asked, "How's your arm this morning?"

I lifted it up, inspecting it. "It's fine." The dull ache of the stitches was nothing. I looked back at her, at my everything. "Just a scratch."

My dismissive words contorted her face.

"It's not just a scratch, Daniel." Energy shifted. She was suddenly alert beside me. "And none of this is fine. I'd rather have an army of Kathys coming for us than what we fought off yesterday."

She turned her gaze and body away from mine, staring at the ceiling, eyes stirring with fear.

I could tell. She was auditing the terrifying events of the day before. Her cheeks winced, squeezing her eyelids closed, pain creasing down her face.

"Babe, I know it's been hard." The gentle pinch of my fingertips set aside a lock of hair from her frightened face. "It's been a bloody whirlwind these past couple of weeks, but we're almost home. We're almost out of the storm."

"For how long?" Her eyes, still suffering, wouldn't meet mine. "How long do you think we can hide safely in my home? We've got two months till you have to report to the studio in Wilmington. Then what are you gonna do?"

"We'll sort it then, Charlie. We don't have to think about it now."

If we were two sides of the same world, this was our fault, our dividing line. I had hope on my side. She had fear on hers. And our two damn careers kept shaking our world, slamming and quaking us together with tectonic violence.

"We always have to think about it, Daniel. Every next moment, to the next month, to the next year, we have to stay safe from Mason and his *White Flag* clan. Yesterday was only piss, cum, and a knife. Next time, it could be"—a quiver shook her bottom lip, anguish tightening across every muscle in her profile—"it could be a gun."

A sudden soft cry left her lips like she was staring down the barrel of one. A tear slid from her closed lashes. Her chest freed a silent sob, shaking her head no, to whatever tragedy ricocheted through her mind.

I'd never seen her like this before.

So afraid.

"Babe"—I rolled up on my elbow, poised over her suffering, trying to wipe it away—"I know we have to be careful. And we will. We'll catch Mason soon and all this will be over."

Her eyes opened to mine.

All I could see was terror in them.

She peered over my shoulder, like something more lethal threatened our way, bigger than what she feared now.

Her eyes met mine, flaming blue with tears.

"Daniel, I can be so strong. I can fight for us both. And I will. But if something happens to you. If I lose you..." Worry bludgeoned her beautiful face. "I..." A shake of her head refused whatever terror plagued her. "I know I'll live, but it won't be a life. It will beat me, and I won't live defeated. I'd rather it be me to die."

Fuck, her pain was killing me *now*.

God, this side of her. The one she guarded with her sharp sword of stubborn and strength.

I was one of the few allowed to pass through, marveling at what hid behind her spectacular walls. Here I found a love, a vulnerability I'd hold until my last breath. And beyond.

"The only thing that will end me, Charlie, is if I lose you." I nuzzled my nose and lips to hers. To share our breath. Tears and seconds fell here. "I know time will take us one day. Even then, there will still be our love. I'll never leave you. I'll always be by your side."

With one reach, she crushed me down to her. Fear and love bound us together while my strength turned our bodies, securing her to me in an embrace over my chest, over my heart.

"We'll be all right," I said. Her golden strands tickled my lips. Certainty flexed my defense, the muscles I wrapped around her. "I'll protect us, I'll fight for us too."

But I knew.

This wasn't a bloody fairytale of castles, knights, dragons, and damsels in distress.

This was real.

Real love.

One threatened with real violence and pain.

ANONYMOUS

The vanity of the average. Believing their days, their meals, their opinions matter.

They don't.

Arrogance makes them believe their travel is of interest to others too.

It is. Only to me.

Social media—a platform serving up insecurity, and thankfully, information too.

Seeking the drug of affirmation, posts trample a digital trail I can follow.

One hashtag leaves a drop here. Another drips there. A photo snaps like a fresh tree limb marking where they passed through, location pins tracking their last location.

All it takes is obsession and the will to keep my nose down, hunting their trail.

My scope narrows to an international airport in North Carolina.

Oh, the spectacularly foul yet failed attempt that afternoon at the airport. It's a noxious, viral sight. One I devour though I crave to be the one who actually attacks them.

If it were me, I wouldn't fail. Her blood would be my reward.

But that threat got closer, proving proximity garners fatal success.

Press reveals that Daniel Pierce will be shooting a film in Wilmington, North Carolina, in two months.

The game thrills me.

It's my turn again, prowling new territory, searching for where they will seek cover until then.

CHAPTER THIRTY-FIVE

CHARLIE

Driving my mom's old Jeep along with my "Going Home" playlist filled the four-hour drive and lifted my spirits. But the lull of the road dragged Daniel's lids down to sleep most of the way.

I glanced at him.

Sweat glistened over his placid brow, wetting his hair into loose curls. I grinned with an "I told you so" smile at the sight.

He thought I was crazy with all the shorts and shirts I bought him in New York. But I laughed, warning that he'd drench at least two a day in the oppressive heat of my home.

When I slowed to turn, it woke him up. Blinking at the light, he took in the same view—a humble home on the edge of a waterfront high over navy-blue water swirled with fields of marsh grass.

He stretched, looking around. "Where are we?"

I stopped the Jeep outside of the garage in the backyard.

"We're on the mainland in Bluffton, South Carolina. This is Quincy's house. He used to live on Daufuskie but moved here years ago. He lets me use his dock and van when I need to come into town."

Turning off the engine, I gave a honk in case Quincy was home. A smile took my face at one of my favorite sights bobbing on the water below—my powder-blue and white console boat moored at the dock.

With a lightening jump, I was out, grabbing a couple bags while Daniel did the same. His footfalls clunked behind me down the steep metal ramp.

"Just throw them in the middle." Our luggage landed with a thud on the fiberglass of my boat. I swatted his ass before climbing back up the ramp to fetch the next round.

"Hey, Q!" I shouted out to the wiry man on the screened-in porch. All skin across him was tanned leather while his brown hair in a ponytail begged to be blond by the sun.

He sounded back, "Hey, babycakes!"

Stepping outside, he was bare chested, wearing ripped cargo shorts stained with marine grease. He lit the cigarette hanging from his mouth, letting the flimsy screen door slam behind him.

The first familiar face from home had me running to give him a relieved hug.

"What sneaky shit you up to, Charlie Girl?" Quincy's grin loved the intrigue. "You pull into my drive with a man in your mom's Jeep and Silas pulled your boat in here a couple of days ago? You're up to somethin'."

Damn right you are. You're hiding from the whole world gunning for y'all now.

Folks only knew me solo all these years. To see a man by

my side warned of change. The last man I brought home was Kai and that was over ten years ago.

Quincy tugged a patient drag off his Newport, waiting for my answer. "Come meet him and you'll see."

Ten steps closer to Daniel, and Quincy jerked his head back with a laugh. "Holy shit! It *is* you. You're fucking Zeus, dude!"

Daniel smiled, shaking Quincy's weathered hand. "Nice to meet you, mate."

"So, no formal introductions required," I said. "Daniel, this is Quincy. And Quincy is gonna keep his sweet mouth shut, right?"

"Yep." Smiling at Daniel, he took another drag. "Y'all both are all over the place online. I 'bout lost my shit this morning when I saw the news. What the fuck happened at the airport yesterday, Charlie Girl?" He pulled another drag, eyeing me. "Ain't like you to seek the spotlight."

I didn't check social media or online. Neither did Daniel. I could only imagine what was posted everywhere.

"I know. It's a long story," I said. "And now... we need to hide from it."

Daniel's publicist blew up his phone all morning.

Every media outlet wanted a piece of us. Most were spinning us as a viral love story between celebrity and soldier. While some extreme sources proclaimed our relationship was a political statement: anti-gun, pro-military, pro-American, anti-American, you name it.

All wanted a statement about what happened at the airport. Was Daniel okay? What was thrown at me? Who attacked us? When would we give an interview? Dozens of questions fired our way, and none were taking "No further comment" for an answer.

Fins were in the bloody water, sharking for more.

"Well, y'all came to the right place to hide," Quincy said. "Just tell me what you need." With a practiced flick, his cigarette landed in the sandy driveway. "Silas is coming for your Jeep next week for the barge over, right?"

I tossed Quincy my keys. "Yep, and he's meeting us at his dock in a bit."

"Sounds like a plan." Quincy dropped them in his pocket, following us down the ramp one last time. "Hey, dude, seriously, I'm a big fan of your movies." He offered a pat on Daniel's back after we threw our last bags on the boat. "Happy to have you here with our Charlie Girl."

"Yeah, mate. Thanks for everything." Daniel gave him a hug and back slap. "Come by one night and have a beer."

"Yeah, come by next weekend, Q." I untied the boat. Daniel stepped over port side, grinning.

"Will do." Quincy lit another Newport and waved us off before walking back up the ramp.

Closing my eyes for a second, I started the engine.

Damn, how I loved the low roar. It was like a choir singing in my nautical church. Sudden joy filled me. Easing the throttle down, I started weaving through the twisting water lanes between the marsh grass like a city kid walking down a familiar concrete block.

Daniel's arms wrapped around my waist. Salt and pine hugged the air. Scorching sunlight danced in diamonds on the water, its heat defeated by the breeze that cooled our skin. I inhaled this one sacred moment of bliss.

"How long until we're there?"

The turn of his neck swept in both directions, taking in the sea island panorama of homes along the waterway with golden-to-green grass and glassy water for miles along shores of pines and oaks.

"Thirty minutes or so."

"Who's this Silas bloke you both talked about?"

I throttled up. We slowed, entering a blind twisting passage through the grass, only wide enough for one water-craft. Standing on my toes, checking over the grass, I waved. "That's Silas over there."

Deftly aiming the bow of the boat, I snaked through to the other side, tugging back to neutral. "Hey!" My boat slowed to bob alongside a similar one.

"Hey, Charlie Girl, I was coming to help you."

Silas always looked the same. No shirt. Black board shorts. Bronze skin over defined muscles slicked with sunscreen and sweat. And always with that same comb of his hand through a silky mop of long, sun-bleached hair.

I checked over my shoulder, making sure no one approached from behind. "I thought you were gonna meet us at your dock."

"The tide is out. I was coming to help you with the bags." That meant the ramps were super steep and hazardous for carrying anything. His gaze landed on Daniel. "I was gonna help you like *I* always do."

"Ah, thanks. I had other help today." I turned to the quiet man looming beside me. "Silas, this is Daniel."

No, this is awkward.

Silas recognized Daniel, but I didn't want to be rude. How do you introduce him to people? They'd either shock back at his celebrity face or stare ignorant of his name, still awestruck by his beauty.

Chalk another tick in the surreal "Daniel Pierce" column.

Wonder how it felt for him all the time?

Silas nodded his chin. "Hey, dude, nice to meet you."

I clocked the irritation in his scowl, the way Silas puffed up his smooth, carved chest at the greeting.

Daniel stepped to the edge of the boat, offering his hand. "Hey, mate. Nice to meet you too. Thanks for helping us. I appreciate it."

Silas released the steering wheel, stepping portside to return the gesture, veins straining in his forearm. "Yeah, sure. Anything for Charlie Girl."

I spotted a pontoon boat headed our way. "Let's go." Slowly throttling back down, I steered on while Silas turned and followed us home.

"Do they breed fucking fit people on this island of yours?" Daniel asked.

"What are you talking about?"

"He's one hunk of tan, half-nude muscle that looks like your surfer twin. You do know that young chap is in love with you, don't you?"

"Eww. No, he isn't. I used to babysit him. Talk about too young."

"Babe, your expertise is great on many things. But mine supersedes yours on young men and lust." The next right turn through the grass made him grab a bar for balance. "How old is he now?"

Massive power lines running across the water on huge pylons filled the horizon. "He turned twenty-five this past January."

"Take it from one who remembers. He fancies you, and we just gutted him. He had to have seen posts of us these few weeks. He came to help with the bags *and* to see it for himself."

"Daniel, that's 'bout ridiculous. Silas doesn't like me. He has at least three women at any given time. He's our island heartthrob. And I'm too old for him. He helps me on projects around the house and stuff."

"Just go easy on him, Charlie Girl." He sounded funny

using my local nickname, reaching out to cup my hand on the throttle. "You really have no idea how beautiful you are, do you?"

"I'm about as beautiful as you are sounding sane right now." With one last hard right through the grass, I sighed.

The shoreline on the horizon? The topography had its own crease in my brain. Immediate recognition.

Home.

Straight ahead.

"I brought your cart over for you," Silas said while I tied my boat up minutes later and Daniel handed him some bags. "And I fixed up your landscaping while you were away."

"Thanks, Silas." With a sure leap, my boots landed on the dock. Walking behind him, all of us laden with bags, I chewed on what Daniel had said. "You need to give me an invoice or something." No way I'd exploit anyone's affection.

Silas set our duffle bags down on the back seat of my cart. "Don't worry about it, Charlie Girl." He wouldn't look me in the eye with my shoulder perched beside Daniel's. "I hope you like what I planted."

Damn, Daniel was right.

How did I not see it until now?

"Seriously. I'm gonna pay you for all the work. I know you're saving up for that Kawasaki, so let me. Okay?" I conjured a big sister look. "Please. We need your help. No one can know we're here."

You couldn't grow up with someone without them hearing more than words from your mouth. The urgency, the fear in my voice perked Silas's ears.

"Dude, you gonna tell me what's going on with you, Charlie Girl, or make me fuckin' guess, 'cause it don't look good." I'd never seen him this agitated before. "I saw all the posts and news. That bullshit yesterday at the airport ain't normal fandom. You're fuckin' lucky he wasn't carrying." So protective too.

"No shit." His mention of guns twisted my gut. "Just be another set of eyes for me. You know who belongs here and who doesn't. While you're hanging around the marina, if anyone don't look right, snap a photo and text it to me, please."

"Mate, seriously," Daniel chimed in. The surgical bandage around his forearm and the posts Silas saw would add up to severe risk for him lightning fast. "Please help us."

His posture softened. "Okay." A blinding white side grin slid across his face. "I have to admit, dude. It's pretty fuckin' lit to be standing in my backyard with Daniel Pierce. I'm a huge *Druid* fan. Love the show. And I grew up loving *Zeus*."

"Thanks, man. It's a lot of fun and hard work. I'm honoured you're a fan."

The genuine warmth in Daniel's regard for Silas relieved me.

I wasn't in the mood for a jealous Daniel. We had enough trouble than to be worried over Silas being hot for me.

"Y'all need anything else?" Silas asked.

"We're good for now, thanks," I said, taking a seat beside Daniel on the cart. "Just keep your eyes on the lookout and help us hide. We got some sick fucks after us."

I turned the key in the golf cart and stepped down on the pedal.

A sudden odd breeze seized my lungs, starting down the sandy road before us. Familiar scents—pine, salt, and the clean-smelling, fragrant Spanish moss—filled my being... but a foreboding sizzled across my mind.

It made the hinge of my jaw tingle, crackling down to my fingertips, shuddering an ill tempo of beats across my heart.

It happened. Something you swore never could.

Daniel Pierce is here on your island. Your two worlds have collided in a supernova—the sun and the moon in the day sky.

Oh God, what have you done?

CHAPTER THIRTY-SIX

DANIEL

T couldn't believe my eyes. "You only drive bloody golf carts here?"

Our cart putted down a lane with a carpet of pine needles along each side. Spanish moss hung in blankets above us from live oaks while low windmill palms stood dwarfed by tall pines in between.

Nature still ruled this island. Most signs of humanity were tucked back, humbled by the subtropical canopy.

It was magical here.

The cart bounced down the road before she took a right onto a narrow paved one, answering, "Sometimes I drive the cart. Once my Jeep is here, I prefer it, especially in the rain. If it's mild, I ride my bike. Everything here depends on the weather."

I expected the white egrets and herons flapping high in the trees, but I was surprised by the small, rolling golf course dotted with ponds surrounded by cattails.

"Do you play golf?"

She laughed. "Daniel Pierce, what of all you know about me screams golf player? Besides, this course is closed anyway."

Weaving through the small community, we had the humble road to ourselves. She pointed to the alligator in the pond, to the small deer hiding in dense cover.

The cart slowed and turned, pulling into a cobblestone drive.

"Bloody hell, is this your house, Charlie?"

When she said "slumming it" about her home, she was taking the piss. It was beautiful—an elegant, large two-story oceanfront home tucked underneath a massive canopy of live oaks.

"Yeah. This was my dad's gift to my mom." She wrapped her arms over the steering wheel, gazing up at it. "Sometimes it's a warm home. Other times it's a lonely house."

She turned to me. "Kai was only here twice, a few years after my parents died. It was still very much their home then. That was ten years ago, and I didn't like being here. Every time I stepped in the door; their absence greeted me. I couldn't help it. I had to get away for a while."

"Do you still feel that way? Like you want to run away?"

I couldn't imagine it. This island was a tranquil paradise. But I was struck with its initial beauty, not with the painful memories.

"I made peace with it when I came home after I was shot. I was scarred skin and bones, a fucking shell of a person for a while. The Watsons—my like family—they took turns staying with me. I could barely get out of bed for months. But I got stronger. Jax and his wife, Ara, started coming by too. They live in Beaufort, about thirty miles away."

"Jax? The one you served with? The one who got shot the same day as you? He lives that close?" Pieces fell into place for me. "That's a small world. From Afghanistan to here."

"Tell me about it. Sometimes it's a million miles away. Other times, it's right on my shores." She looked up at the house. "I have to admit, my dad outdid himself. The house is beautiful." Jumping out of the cart, she reached her hand out for mine. "Let me give you the nickel tour."

We climbed the circular front staircase. "I like the blue doors," I said.

"It's called 'haint blue'. We locals believe it wards off evil spirits." She winked, unlocking it. "I sure as shit hope that's true now."

If I had to point to Charlie's style in a magazine, my finger would land here. Her house was very "beach Zen," as she called it. Simple white slipcovered furniture. White oak floors. Minimal but cozy informal design with no clutter but plants everywhere.

Almost every room took advantage of the view. One of a pool before a grassy backyard, flanked on both sides with tall pines and palms. Beyond the yard, sand dunes led to a beautiful raw beach and the steel-blue Atlantic beyond.

She explained how she bought the lots to her right so they would never be developed. The neighbors on her left were only here in the winter.

The home sprawled with five large bedrooms and six bathrooms. The feature was the modern kitchen and a magnificent breakfast room, flowing into two open living rooms, separated by a massive fireplace—all rooms with spectacular views.

Her second-level bedroom had a vaulted ceiling with French doors onto a covered balcony deck with the best view. Two guest bedrooms enjoyed similar vistas. She noted the rooms she spent most of her time in: the second story library with a window view, and the fully stocked gym.

She saved the best for last, ending our tour on the large covered back deck. Below was the pool with a wrap-around patio. It sat low behind the dunes with complete privacy from the beach.

"Oh my God," she exclaimed, eyes wide at the long, wide row of pink, maroon, and white calla lilies blooming between the pool's patio and lawn. "Silas planted all those."

"I told you he fancies you, Charlie Girl." I squeezed her hand. Impressed. Jealous. Mostly honoured to be here. "And so do I."

She pecked my lips before tugging me back inside. "Let's unpack then I'll start us some dinner."

"Show me how to make shrimp 'n' grits."

"You really are trying to blend in, aren't you?"

We lugged our bags upstairs. Honour hit me again when she offered half of her dresser and closet for my wardrobe.

Later, I explored the kitchen, nosing around until I had the lay of the culinary land. We made a proper mess during my cooking lesson.

Only a few times did I want to stop, kiss down her neck, and make love to her right here. But she busied herself, all smiles while peeling prawns and cooking our feast.

The patient hours we took settling in, enjoying the night, left our fear at the door. I could feel it here, why she had protected her home like a sacred shrine to everything she'd lost.

I did feel safe.

Even though our world balanced on the edge of bubble, I knew it. This was as secure as we could find.

And now she let me in, sharing her sanctuary.

I ate the delicious dinner we prepared, humbled, content to hold her in bed until dawn woke us both.

But she surprised me. After dishes were put away and lights turned off, she tugged my hand out to the pool deck. "Let's go for a swim." She stripped nude, offering me a beguiling sight in the twinkling deck lights.

My naked body plunged in behind, nearing hers at the shallow end of the pool. Her gaze was on the calla lilies. Even at night, the white ones glowed.

I realized it then. "They're your favorite, aren't they?"

"Yes."

"What else does Silas know about you that I don't?"

It was more than jealousy. It was a deep need to know everything about her past and to share every moment of my future with her.

"He knows that I love pecans. That I didn't shave my legs when I was a teenager, and everyone teased me about it. And that I can spit ten feet. It's my record." Her wet hand took mine, pressing it to her cleavage, over her heart. "No one but you knows this. You're the only one allowed in."

My knuckle lifted her chin, mouth offering a grateful kiss, my tongue gently flexing over hers, lips sure of how their soft suck and skate would ignite her.

The stitches on my wrist burned too, never letting me forget—a threat drew closer to us.

It stopped my heart. Fearing—I could lose her.

Pressing my ring finger to her lips. "We always stay connected. Right, Charlie?" So much menaced us, I had to be sure. "We stay together."

"Yes." She sucked my finger while a breeze thrilled her wet breasts. Circling her tensed nipples with my warmed fingertip, my tease didn't stop until it unleashed her first moan, tension dropping from her shoulders, seeking the pleasure, the escape we needed now.

A gentle tug at the nape of her neck pulled her to peer into my eyes. I teased her firm tits more, asking what I already knew, "What can only I do to you?" Still, I needed her affirmation.

Through the part of her lips, she answered, "This, Daniel."

Sliding my hand between her thighs, oh yes, she was slick for me. My fingers played, knowing how to open her stance to demand more. Wrapping her hands around my neck, she held on for what I was about to give her.

Two of my fingers beckoned, curving inside her, pressing my palm against her clit, offering her exact rhythm and ride. "Oh fuck," she groaned.

The fact that my touch could always lure her here, to her breath changing, to my hand coaxing her harder and faster, with the writhe of her greedy hips. "Goddamn, babe," I sighed at the way I could claim her sex. Maddening. Addicting. Liberating.

I gripped the nape of her neck, harder, securing her gaze to mine. "Only me, Charlie." The answer was in her eyes, but she didn't reply. "Say it." I murmured, needing to hear it, my jerking hand summoning her carnal contraction over my fingers. "You only come for me."

The answer lit across her eyes as she gasped, "Yes, Daniel!"

Spasms buckled her knees, but her clutch around my neck secured her here, quaking. I held her up until she found her breath and strength.

"Come here," she said. Taking my hand, she led our dripping bodies up to the pool deck. Like a boss, she pushed me back onto one of the poolside loungers. "Lie down."

It thrilled me. Though I could crush her with my bare hands, I loved it when she took charge. Feet planted on each side, I reclined back on the chair while her nude path stepped over, straddling the lounger.

"Is this what you want?" The soft smack of her fingers teased into her glistening pussy, fingering herself inches from my face.

Holy fuck, how she just turned the tables on me. And spellbound, I craved it. The submission, the sight, "Fuck yes," it made me groan.

She moved, hovering over my mouth. "Do you want to taste what's yours, Daniel?" She smeared her slick fingers over my lips. "Do you want to drink it?" They pressed at the seam of mine, demanding my suck. Her lust coated my obeying tongue while her other hand continued the show, dipping inside her, hypnotizing me into pure greed for more.

I'd take it now. "Give me every drop," I growled. Cupping her ass cheeks, my hands spread her open for my mouth, for my tongue taking savoring dives and licking for more.

Her hands laced through my waves; her groan escaped at the command she took over my face plunged between her legs. Swimming through her had me stroking my cock to her taste.

I needed no air, breathing in her desire, dipping and curling my tongue to taste more. Tremors shook her thighs, delicious vibrations quivering against my cheeks. Her scream filled the night air while her lust filled my mouth.

Thirsty swallows I took of my reward while some trickled down my chin.

I barely let her catch her breath. "What else is mine, Charlie?"

Grabbing her waist, I pulled her down, plunging her onto my hard cock. A gritty sigh seized my throat to be wrapped tight by her drenched sex.

Her feet landed next to mine. Strength flexed across her abs while she took me with all her force. "This pussy is yours," she said like she was home, home with me inside her and taking charge.

Two of my fingers wiped her lust from my chin and reached around, gliding down between her cheeks, easing my way in and filling her ass.

"This is mine too, Charlie," I demanded, watching the gorgeous vision of her carnally obliterate me from above.

She cried out to my stretching presence in all of her, bracing her hands on my chest so she could milk my cock with slamming rolls and a twisting, brutal grind of her hips.

"Because you're all mine too, Daniel." With a hard grasp through my waves, she pulled my chin to hers. "Say it." She bucked hard against my shaft. "Are you all mine?"

I was more than hers. "Yes, Charlie." I was nothing without her.

"Is this my cock, Daniel?" Her eyes, so beautiful, fiery and shameless. "Are you going to come for me?"

Fuck's sake, I revered the sight, the sound, dismantled by it.

How it was getting her off, fucking me as hard as I'd fucked her so many times. The chair gave her the power, the position, giving her all she needed to possess me no matter how I penetrated her everywhere. She ruled me. "Fuck yes,

I'm yours." And I needed it, needed her. She was my survival.

I pulled her down, latching my lips over her nipple. Her breast engulfed my mouth, her nipple hard against my suck. To be full of her, of her power, plunging me over the edge, a muffled roar rose from my depths. Still, I wouldn't let her go, my fingers and cock thrusting, my mouth clinging to her with a ferocity that made her scream out in luscious pain.

It exploded through me, into everything I loved above me. My release, it let go of every body, every fuck, every moment before her. Mouth gasping over her nipple for my next breath, reborn with her, another groaning pulse shook me, blinding me with the only light I craved now—stars of spasms from our love.

My lips let go, crying out to her relentless ride. "Oh fuck, Charlie." Even as I met my sweet end, she wanted more of me.

"Take me again, Daniel," she huffed.

I did, my mouth locked over her other nipple with a cinching suck, delivering pleasure and pain. My fingers pounded her ass while my cock was still hard inside her, firm for her savage ride.

Her fingernails carved pleasing scratches across my chest, screaming my name with convulsions before throwing her head down on my shoulder, gifting me with a strong bite. Every muscle in her petite, moaning body tremored over mine.

I withdrew, reaching both arms around, holding her tight, finding vision again, gazing at the night sky.

"God, I love you." I guided her lips to mine. Finally, I was here, so alive in her, in her home, in her world.

Saline filled our kiss along with a muffled sob from her throat.

I pulled back, finding her eyes. "What's wrong?"

Tears poured from her smiling eyes as she kissed me with soft lips, with a soft whisper. "Daniel." Sharing my breath. "I can't believe you're here with me. I used to be so alone here. So sad. It hurt so much." Her salty lips drifted over mine. "And now... I love you so much."

"You're my home, Charlie. No matter where we go. I belong with you."

CHAPTER THIRTY-SEVEN

DANIEL

Our path led through dunes topped with patches of golden beach grass matching the hue of Charlie's hair. A horizon smeared in coral and pink dissolved into clear deepening blue above. Sparkling low waves reflected the dawn's magnificence.

The sunrise welcomed me to Daufuskie Island.

"Wow!" The word bolted from my mouth along with my feet.

Charlie wanted me to experience her ritual. How every morning at dawn, she ran on the beach. This morning we had the glorious expanse to ourselves.

My shirt was soaked within minutes. Here, the suffocating August air would punish me into adapting for my next role—a torture I relished.

Hiding under our baseball caps, we neared the farthest point of the beach before turning back. I was aiming for three kilometers a day, plus a full kilometer swim. But I knew on day one and in this heat, I had to pace himself.

Frustration powered my steps knowing we had to guard themselves too. Why? A text woke us this morning.

Mason sent one at an ungodly hour. It robbed us of a peaceful first morning here, filling her screen with more alarm than the one set for our run.

Unknown
Ever thirst for more?

The evil taunt made me want to slam the phone down, smashing it into pieces against her bamboo nightstand.

Instead, I tossed it on the bed, knowing what she'd do next.

The reach of her hand yanked it up from the bedspread. Blasting with her own taunt, she replied:

You could never satisfy
my thirst

"What the fuck, babe?" I sat naked beside her, watching her fingertips fly across the screen. "That's not very cryptic. And getting too bloody close to him."

Whoosh.

Too late. Done.

"I'm tired of fucking around," she'd said. "I know what will entice him. It's gotta get sick and personal." Throwing the sheets off, she headed toward her closet. "We've got a call with the FBI at ten. Until then, I need to run this fucking fury off."

We circled back around to her home. I ran inside, threw on the board shorts she bought me, and took off over the dunes for a swim. The heat climbed with every minute. No wind or white caps to stop it.

She followed, dropping beach towels on the sand before dunking under the barely cresting waves while I took off in a breaststroke down the shore.

This was not my preferred stroke, but what the SEAL Physical Screening Test required. I had two months along with the back strength to dramatically improve upon it.

And with my rage at Mason along with the salt burning my stitches, exertion burned my lungs. Charlie had told me not to swim in the ocean with my wound. But I was as furious and as stubborn as she.

I asked her to join me, but she declined. She said she had to keep watch from the shore in case I got into trouble in the current.

I knew... she was watching for more than that.

Minutes later, I shook out my hair, emerging from the water, winded and smiling, feeling better.

"Give me a hundred, Pierce." She planked to do push-ups with me, not letting me catch my breath.

I dropped to my knees beside her, "Yes, Captain," giving her a salty, wet kiss.

I set the goal of a hundred in two minutes and almost met it. She was far kinder to her shoulder.

The effort collapsed me onto the striped towel. The sun was a blowtorch on my skin without a breeze. Squirting the last bit of water from my bottle on my face, I declared, "I'm knackered."

She leaned over for a kiss, but stopped, glancing up from my lips.

"We gotta go inside," she said. "Quick."

I turned.

A couple was walking their dog—eighteen meters out—and headed our way.

Later, Charlie sat behind her desk, checking emails on her laptop until the call from the FBI agent.

I waited. Staring out the window, a slight sway of rage rocked my shoulders while my feet stood firm in her office.

An image filled my head of a video I'd seen online of a silverback gorilla. His one body stronger than twenty humans combined.

The gorilla reclined, calm behind an enclosure at a zoo until people started tapping the glass, taking pictures, entertained by his prison.

The animal turned his heavy brow toward the provoking audience. Slow at first, his gargantuan approach made his fans shout. Then he burst up onto his back legs, charging the glass. With one leap and pound of his colossal fists, the glass was shattered by his brute force.

The spectacle marred.

My heart sympathized with the caged animal.

All I wanted to do now was smash it all too—the prison of my celebrity life—escaping, running wild with a stampede for Mason, ripping that evil fuck's limbs from his torso once he was in my demolishing grasp.

The chime from Charlie's phone paused my show.

"We're going through the surveillance footage," Agent Cooper updated us. "Seems the airport police were overwhelmed by the event. Witnesses left the scene, but a few gave statements confirming it was a white male, six feet tall in a camouflage jacket. Four said they saw him waiting for you with a pillowcase and a cup in his hands."

"So now what?" Charlie's question strained impatient.

Normally, she had monk-like restraint. But this week? Something changed for us.

Time was whipping our lives down a swirling tunnel with ever narrowing spirals of fear.

"We need something," the agent said. "If we can connect Mason Hunt to your attack, we have him on conspiracy to commit a felony. And if that man who assaulted you is connected to other *White Flag* crimes—I have a hunch he is—then we have both Hunt and the attacker on federal hate crimes too. Gives me a lot to throw at them."

It blistered me. What the fuck? Were we just supposed to wait for Mason's next attack? "What else can we do to help?"

"Stay safe," the agent said. "I'm not sugarcoating this. There's no telling how many of Hunt's fans will act on his behalf. Is it one or dozens? We don't know. But this I do—they are as cruel as they are determined. It's about more than a victim. They're making a statement, and they want it made as publicly as possible. That makes you two very high-value targets."

"What if we get nothing?" Charlie asked. "Then Daniel has to work in Wilmington. Can the bureau help him with protection there?"

"I'm afraid you're on your own for now," she answered. "I can't do anything until we prove the connection. The airport attack was a misdemeanor. Simple assault on you. Assault with a deadly weapon against Mr. Pierce. Both under the jurisdiction of the local police." The agent sounded equally frustrated by the law. She added, "Just keep doing what you know to do."

I cocked my eyebrow at Charlie. Did the agent know? Know that Charlie was replying to Mason? If so, she didn't seem to mind. Was she encouraging it?

We wrapped up the call and Charlie stood up, wrapping her arms around me.

"We're safe here. And that asshole isn't ruining this day

for us. Promise?" She gazed up at me, her embrace dripping relaxation into my veins, lowering my pulse and my lips to hers.

"Promise," I said before giving her a soft peck, then another. Willing to be led out of this mood, I turned to the bookshelves, pointing to a picture. "This is your father, right?"

One glance at the framed shot and she said, "Yeah, that's Dad."

Charlie's dad was a striking man, intimidating with his angular jaw. Tan raw-hide skin over defined muscles. Blond hair in a crew cut. Ice-blue eyes charged your soul with one stare. And that was just from a photo.

But the picture put a grin on my cheeks.

It was a stunning teen Charlie with her dad's arm over her shoulder, a rifle resting on her other. Her dad held a trophy in his other hand, adoration beaming from his eyes. Charlie had more than his hair and mouth. She inherited the steel in his determined eyes too.

"And that's mama." She pointed to the shelf beside it.

Bloody hell, it was her mum who gave Charlie the visceral beauty: long, wavy caramel hair; confident hazel eyes that knew no intimidation; bronze skin and full lips in a fearless smile; and definitely Charlie's nose, eyebrows, and high cheeks.

The sight wrested an "ahhh" from my lips.

It was the two of them flamenco dancing together in Madrid. A young Charlie looked adorable with her confident little body mimicking her mum's commanding stance.

Then she pointed to a photo on my right. "And you've seen that one. My wedding picture with Kai."

I had seen it. She kept a copy on her phone.

"I have to admit," she said, "it feels kinda odd standing

with you here in my home, looking at a picture of Kai, my late husband. Like maybe I should take it down or something."

"Don't ever take it down." The tip of my finger traced a path down the image of her happy face in the photo. "It's a beautiful moment and a man you should always remember."

"It doesn't bother you?"

"If you can put up with rubbish from an ex-girlfriend like Kathy with the grace you showed, then I have enough maturity to celebrate this photo of you with your late husband."

The tug of her small hand yanked my gaze her way.

"You sure can give the perfect answer, Pierce."

"I hope it makes up for all the times I cocked up with the wrong one. You should have a bloody list going by now."

"Speaking of cocking up." With a grin, she went for the pun and my dick.

I chuckled, my grasp wrapping full around her wrist, stopping her play. "We have a lunch date with your family in an hour. I don't need sex on my mind right now."

Searching for her name—Captain Charlotte Roberts.

Or for his—Daniel Pierce.

Anywhere in the Carolinas? Or nearby?

I find mothing.

No social media posts. No hashtags or locations to follow.

Their trail?

It's dead cold.

It leaves me here, calloused, numb fingertips hovering over my keyboard, more than a plan forming now.

I close my eyes, summoning an evil invocation written in the stars.

Yes, I can see it...

Blood in her blonde hair. Pouring down her face slack with death. Blue eyes still open. All life, all revenge, taken.

Scarlett splatters seeping through his shirt. Shot after shot riddling his muscular frame helpless and dying beside her. The last look in his eyes? Seeing his love beside him, holding her cold hand in his.

Pools of blood puddle under their contorted limbs, lifeless famous, frames twisted on the ground.

The world's heroic couple?

Dead.

For all the world to see and suffer.

I open my eyes... and smile.

CHAPTER THIRTY-EIGHT

CHARLIE

"Hand me that skimmer there, son." Pop pointed to the long-handled mesh scoop.

Daniel obliged with a smile. He stood by the outdoor fish fryer in the Watsons' backyard getting schooled on frying flounder, the island, and my extended family.

Even with Daniel's impressive size, Pop was a bigger man with dark-brown skin, his silver hair still high and tight from his years in the Navy. It took two seconds after meeting before Pop grabbed Daniel into a back-slapping hug.

Evelyn had greeted him with the same warmth. Smaller than me, she wore her long salt-and-pepper locks pulled back from her umber skin and eyes under striking black eyebrows. She wasn't slowing down for anyone, still working as an obstetric nurse at the hospital in Savannah.

Pop filled Daniel in while we guzzled iced tea—tale after childhood tale of my stubborn adventures.

I kept glancing over at them, catching Daniel's eye.

God, the man stopped my heart, making me question why I ever had an ominous fear about bringing him home.

His presence here only felt natural.

Fated.

"How long are you home, Minnow?" Evelyn asked, snapping the lid off a cold bowl of cucumbers and onions in vinegar-mixed sugar water, spoiling me with my favorite dishes. Pop even went flounder giggin' the night before knowing I was coming home.

"Until November or so." I set four plates out on the picnic table. "I'm going to London for a couple of months to visit with Juliette while she's filming. Of course, to be with Daniel some too."

Shit, this is real now. More than a calculated tactic keeping you both safe. Feel your chest warm? Yep, that's called "family". Again.

"Did you meet his folks already?"

"Yes, ma'am. Last week."

I beamed, sharing with Evelyn all I knew about Daniel. The real man with a big, loving family, not the celebrity splashed on the screen.

"Y'all seem quite taken with each other." Evelyn nudged me. "I quite like him too. Your mama would approve. I can hear her now. 'Es muy guapo,' she'd say."

"Yes, he is handsome." My cheeks were burning. I wondered if Daniel's ears were too. "He reminds me of Dad in a way. So powerful and strong but he'd never hurt a soul. Not unless he was protecting someone."

Evelyn fussed with the napkins, folding them into triangles, then changing to rectangles. The silence between us grew tense, heavy with what I knew weighed Evelyn down. She was the closest person I had to a mom, and full of worry.

Finally, Evelyn asked, "Does he know everything?"

It suddenly seized my throat—terror so tight it burst through the surface, splashing over my face.

Evelyn searched my eyes. She could read me in one look.

"Almost," I said, holding back the fright. "He knows what I did for those girls. How I planned it."

"But does he know the rest? How it's been for you since?" Evelyn dropped the napkins, wrapping her fingers tight around mine. "You've got to tell him. I can't have my girl suffering one of her spells and then the man she loves not know what's really going on with her. What's been troubling you all this time."

Yes, Daniel knew some of my fear. Of my past. Of my hallucinations.

But the depths of it?

The madness of it?

Every time I tried to tell him that I feared more than Mason, more than his *White Flag* fanatics. That it didn't start weeks ago. That a fatal prophecy had played in my mind every day for six years.

The words formed in my mind but never left my lips because I could hear their lunacy.

"Listen to me." Evelyn lowered her voice to a hush between us. "Your PTSD. It can do a number on you. I know you've gotten better, but it can be scary for the person by your side. When you're having one of your episodes, talking to ghosts, talking like someone's coming for you. I know it's part of it, the paranoia, but he needs to know how bad it gets for you. He needs to be able to care for you if it happens again."

Evelyn was right about one part. The episodes I could have—they were like scars on my mind. They had faded but remained.

But I couldn't tell Daniel. Hell, I couldn't tell Evelyn the whole story. That it wasn't PTSD or paranoia.

My instinct wasn't on a list of side effects you look up online or read in a pamphlet at the psychiatrist's office.

It's real, Charlie Girl. Someone is coming for you. It's the same certainty you had about Mason. About Kathy. So many damn times.

I'd always had this ability—able to sense danger coming.

It moved through me like electricity across a wire, eyes filtering for peril, neck twisting to my gut when evil approached. My right eyebrow shot up minutes before shit went south, tensing my muscles to protect others at risk.

My instinct never failed me when it came to guarding others.

But when it came to myself, could I trust it anymore?

Maybe I sacrificed that part of myself saving those girls in Afghanistan.

Maybe that's why I was a natural at my job. My instinct would always protect others. Perhaps though... it was lost on myself.

"Let me think about it." I glanced up. Daniel was still talking to Pop with his smile cast my way. It put one on my face. Then my eyes flicked down to his bandage, to the stitches from the attack. Fuck, my logic was a tornado. "We just got so much going on."

It was like Evelyn could slice my tension with a knife, knowing almost every layer of my torment. She patted my hand. "Y'all just catch your breath for now. You'll tell him one day. All in due time."

A buzz in my back pocket jolted my nerves—my phone.

Please not another damned text from Mason.

I checked it. The relief I exhaled laxed my ribs, the name on the screen delighting me.

"Excuse me a few minutes, please," I said to Evelyn. "It's Juliette. I gotta take this call."

Evelyn nodded while my steps wandered across the back lawn.

Answering one of my favorite ring tones, I said, "Oh, my favorite bitch, I miss you so much."

"I miss you too, bitch." Juliette's voice always made me smile. "But what the bloody fuck was that business at the airport? Are you two all right?"

"We're fine. Daniel got seven stitches, and I got a face full of man fluids I didn't kneel for."

"That's not funny, Charlie. This shite is all over the news. I've been trying to ring you, but it was going to voice-mail, like you're out of range. You had me bloody worried."

"I know it's not funny. And I know we're fucking viral. That's why we're hiding here, at my home." I shook my head, staring at the massive oak above and blue sky beyond. "I'm worried, Jules. Scared, actually. We've got serious threats against us. The airport was the tip of the iceberg. I can sense it. Something bad is going to happen, and it's driving me crazy."

"You're not crazy, sweetie. It's the life. Daniel's life. Do you not remember all the shite you had to protect me from?"

It gave me pause.

Yes, I did remember.

Juliette suffered constant threats. Her list of stalkers and demented fans was a mile long.

How are you going to do this, wrapping your mind and life around three dangers?

One certain threat—Mason and his *White Flag* extremists. Another was Daniel's obsessed fans. And the third? The haunting one I didn't tell anyone about? It was the one that stole my sleep.

"Hang in there, love," Juliette continued, soothing my nerves. "You're in the spotlight now. It just takes a while to get used to it. I promise, it won't feel maddening forever."

"I hope you're right. I don't know how you've put up with this hell for so many years."

"I have lovely people like you keeping me safe and sane, that's how."

"Well, who's helping me? I'm trying to stay safe and sane, but it ain't workin'."

"Do you need me to fly over there and drag your arse into a good time? Into relaxing the fuck out? Because I bloody will." Juliette's tone was only half joking. "You're Charlie Ravenel, for fuck's sake. Put your big-girl panties on and deal with it. That's what you told me when I whinged about it."

I kicked a pinecone across the yard. "Hey, who's the best friend here? Quit serving me my own damn medicine."

Juliette was right.

I needed to suck it up.

"Look, bitch." She wasn't done preaching. "You're finally happy. Finally in love and, dear God, yes, finally getting your leg over, with Daniel Pierce, nonetheless. So fucking enjoy it."

How I loved her. "I am fucking enjoying him. Hell, at least once a day. But if I fuck him every time I get a nervous twitch that something's wrong, I'm gonna break his massive dick off."

That had us laughing. At the absurdity. And the reality. Sometimes it was all you could do.

I peeked up, checking my audience. Pop and Daniel were setting the basket of flounder on the table. Evelyn was pouring more iced tea. All three were looking at me.

Shit, I hoped they couldn't hear me too.

"Not that he's complaining." I dropped my tone to dirty and discreet levels. "You'd be proud. He's tried breaking it off in every part of me."

"Yes!" Juliette wasn't lowering the volume on her end. "Welcome to the no-shame game. You've got to suck it and see, try before you buy. Told you you'd catch up to me one day. Perhaps a threesome is next on your menu."

"Oh, he likes it, all right. So do I. But we're not in the sharing mood."

My body responded on impulse, to the memory, flushing me everywhere then making me nervous. This was not the place or time to get horny.

Juliette cooed, "Alistair likes it too."

"What?" It surged my smile. "Are y'all a thing? For real now?"

"Oh, we're doing all kinds of things for very real now, thanks to you and Daniel. I think you two snogging love-birds are contagious."

"Same goes for Rob and Joaquin. They are all lovey, fuck-dovey too."

"That's it." Juliette's voice stomped its foot. "The six of us are going on holiday next summer. Until then, get used to the crazy, my love. This is the new normal. Might as well have some fun with it."

A whistle took the air—a whippoorwill bird call. I glanced up. Pop used it to call me and the other kids in from playing in the woods. It was suppertime.

"Hey, chica. I gotta go. Thanks for checking on us. We'll plan something soon. Love you."

"Love you. Cheers."

Our call ended, and I took a breath, reconciling it all.

Yes, I had a bloody past and scars I had to face. And I had a fatal instinct I trusted—most of the time. And I loved a man that seventy million people did too.

Sure... this is real fucking normal.

Not.

Walking toward the picnic table, toward three people I cherished so much, I wondered...

Or is this just a new nightmare?

CHAPTER THIRTY-NINE

CHARLIE

How odd was it? Staring at a picture of three people, knowing that now... one of them was gone.

Sitting in my office, my eyes cherished the photo on my desk. It was taken before the triad of tragedy.

Standing in our cammies, I stood in the center with my husband, Kai, on my right, and Jax on my left.

The image was a sea of beige. Light clay gravel on the ground at Camp Leatherneck in Afghanistan, our boots crunched over the matching rocks. Cammie pants, jackets, and lids, all a pixelated palette of beiges camouflaging us into our surround.

The only thing we couldn't conceal under the brim of our lids? Our big smiles.

Our buddy had snapped the moment right after a rapid-fire exchange of smart-ass jokes.

"Where we squattin' today, Roberts?" Jax had asked,

giving me a hard time for the times he'd guarded me while I took a piss.

"Don't know, Colonel Mustard." I reached my arms around my husband and my friend. Jax and I were headed out with our platoon that day. "Where you gonna spray your little yellow?"

Kai had given me a firm squeeze, the strong grip of his hand comforting. That day was another goodbye—an all too familiar ritual for us.

Kai quipped, "You're both full of hot piss and vinegar."

Snap. The photo captured our laughs.

Now Kai's body was buried six years ago and a thousand miles away in the Santa Fe National Cemetery. And Jax was only thirty miles away.

Jax lost his left foot months after the picture. On our patrol through the bazaar in Marjah. On the same fated day I was shot.

A day when the painful reality of what was happening to two girls at the hands of a malicious man collided with the call of something transcendent I had to do to stop him. I taunted the evil man to take a shot at me so I could fire back. Sure my aim would end him even if it meant my own death too.

No one else was supposed to get hurt that day. It was to be my sacrifice alone.

Fate had other plans.

Finding him in my sights, I aimed and eliminated the threat to those girls.

But then another one stood up; the evil man's older brother readied to fire on my body dropped to the ground by the three bullets I took in the attack. But Jax suppressed that man's aim, turning it on him, taking two close-range bullets to his ankle.

My heart still served penance for Jax and my plan. My soul still felt called to atone for Kai's death. Because the day after, a hundred kilometers away, Kai was killed in action.

The scars down my body, the ones in my mind too, they fused new tissue that day.

Fused a new truth in me.

I'd shared every part of me with Daniel but this one.

This war inside me, he could never know.

I needed him to trust me. I couldn't risk him questioning my logic. If we wanted to survive this stalking threat, we had to stay strong, tethered together, anticipating the other's tactic and touch.

My instinct stood beside me, just like the weight of the storm blowing outside the windows—certain but unseen —telling me...

You're still in the line of fire. From seven thousand miles away and six years ago.

Something more than Mason Hunt is scoping for you.

Searching. Hunting.

The *pings* of my phone startled me back to the soft cacophony around me.

Rain pelting the windows of my office. Clanking steel of the Olympic bar Daniel was lifting down the hall in the home gym. A gust of wind whipping through the pines outside shifted the air with a barometric pressure I could feel in my bones.

Unknown
I can satisfy whatever I crave
I want you in a slow shred of sanity
I want you in a ripping apart fuck

Sure as shit, I was right. My last taunt, challenging Mason's ability to satisfy my thirst—it pushed him.

He was getting visceral, sadistic with his texts, standing two steps closer to his edge.

I gave another shove with my reply:

> Where you're going, they
> will be feasting on you

Mason's arrogance reigned as dominant as his evil. He assumed he'd never get caught or see a day behind bars or six feet under in hell.

I clamped my fangs into his Achilles' heel.

His weakness? His compulsion to control others. Ironically, it controlled him.

My rapid second reply:

> Soon you'll have no control over
> any fucks or your sanity

Unknown
Where are you hiding for this feast?
Wherever you are, others will dine
with us

Of course, he was crazed trying to find us.

After the airport incident? We'd disappeared, off the grid. And I'd do anything to keep it that way.

A smiling Spanish face and tune lit up in my hand right as my finger held poised to reply to Mason's last text.

The screen redirected me to "Rob Vasquez."

I answered, grinning, like he was standing in front of my desk. "Sup, fucker."

"Sup, fucker. Am I interrupting something inappropriate, I hope?"

"Ha! You wish. No, he's down the hall, grunting and groaning that hot body into even more shredded muscle for me to enjoy. And I'm in my office, fucking with Mason."

I stood up to stretch my legs.

"Bitch, that's a threesome not even I'm turned on by. You and Daniel with me? Hell yes. Mason joining you two? Fuck no. I'd swear to celibacy before fucking with that man's perfectly wicked body."

My path led me to stare, nose inches from the window, looking at the gray stormy horizon smearing into the matching ocean.

"The only thing I'm fucking with is Mason's ego. I'm getting closer to proving that it's him stalking me."

"Yeah, I saw how close it got at the damn airport. It fucking terrified me. That was way too close, mi prima. We're not in Europe or Oz anymore. This is home, where real weapons reside. Knives you can stop. Bullets you can't."

"You don't need to fucking tell me. It's Daniel I'm trying to school, and he's learning, seven stitches at a time." Another clank of weights down the hall sounded his proximity to my conversation. "That's why we're hiding here for as long as we can."

"How do you know Mason won't find your house? Your name is on public property records, right?"

"Nope, it's not. I signed the house over to Pop and Evelyn before I left for Afghanistan in case something happened to me. Since Kai was serving too, we thought it was the smart thing to do and I never changed it back."

This was another tactical advantage I planned to keep.

Unless we were spotted on the island, no path led here.

One would have to go way back and use my family name, Ravenel, not my military one, Roberts.

That name—Ravenel—was a needle in a haystack. I had hundreds of distant relatives populating the Lowcountry with the same one.

Hell, one of the longest cable bridges in the world, right up the coast in Charleston, had my family name on it. Following the Ravenel road would only lead you heart-droppingly high across the Cooper River.

Never to me.

"When y'all comin' down?" I asked.

A clunk of dishes on Rob's end of the call almost drowned out his response.

"Not sure, mi prima. My mom is elbows deep making empanadas for me and Joaquin. She has a month's menu planned for us. Since we've been here, we've gained five pounds."

"How's your dad with Joaquin?"

I worried. Rob had been out to his family for years. But they'd never welcomed his love into their home before, particularly Rob's dad.

"Oh, Joaquin won him over with talks of Sammy Sosa, and it was done. We've been staying here with them in Brooklyn since. What about you? How'd it go meeting the Pierce family? Are they all beautiful like him?"

A cobweb in the corner of the window caught my eye. "Yep, it's in the DNA. His whole damn family is impossibly gorgeous and kind." It was old. Dusty and empty. Like it was built years ago and abandoned.

"Well, bitch, you scored the pick of the litter. And you deserve it. That's all I know."

More clatter on his end.

"You and I both earned the love of our lives. On our

terms with no apologies, right? Fuck the rules. *That's* what I know."

"Speaking of knowing," Rob said, "I want the dish. All the games you played with the toys you bought at my favorite Upper East Side sex shop, using the lessons I gave you to prepare. You're welcome, by the way."

With one quick jump, I reached up, knocking the old web down. "Thank you, and yes, I was well prepared for lots of games. And toys. A playground, actually. One with an adult swing."

A splash of shock. "Bitch, what? Hang on. I have to process." More water splashing. "You? Got to fuck? That sexy-ass man? On a sex swing?" Another wet clunk of ceramic. "I just can't. I mean, I would. But your lucky ass was in the stirrups instead."

Rob could joke all he wanted about how hot he thought Daniel was. Hell, millions of people did. It never bothered me. I knew where Rob's real love resided—with Joaquin.

I saw how natural it was.

How their love had flourished the weeks they all worked together on *The Druid*. First, it was a professional respect. Then, it was long talks about everything. Finally, they took their own secret vacation during hiatus and came back in love too.

I couldn't imagine them apart. Where Rob's good humor stopped, Joaquin's quiet care began, making them the perfect match.

Delighting Rob with a few hints and details only brought me joy too.

"Well," I said, "I want a trophy because I made him take pictures too. I've gone from not showing my scars, to starring in my own amateur porn shots. Quite the proud, horny achievement."

"You Olympic tramp, who do I send the money to for copies?"

"I tell you what. I'll leave the pictures for you in my will. Because over my dead body will anyone but Daniel and I see them."

"See what?"

The bass of Daniel's voice spun me around.

His ears and body stood hot, glistening with sweat in the doorway.

This truth I could share with Daniel. Our little friend group—me, Daniel, Rob, and Joaquin—had no secrets. Especially when it came to romance and sex. All four of us were guilty of it on the job when we weren't supposed to.

I brought Daniel up to speed. "Rob wants copies of our sex swing photos."

Rob chimed in, loud enough for him to hear, "Or just tell Daniel that he and I can make our own together."

Daniel sat on the edge of the desk, shirt off, wiping it across his laughing face at our exchange.

I answered Rob, "Tell you what, Vasquez, you can have Daniel Pierce once I'm done with him."

"Yes, bitch! When will that be? I'll mark my calendar now."

My gaze groped the alluring topic of our conversation with a smoldering half grin back at me.

My certain reply, "Never."

CHAPTER FORTY

A silky leg rubbed against mine.

I looked up from the page. A wicked recipe cooked in her eyes promising something delicious.

"Bored with your book?" I asked.

Our legs intertwined across the leather sofa while rain pattered against the window of the upstairs library. Cool drafts from the air-conditioning vent billowed over my waves, still damp from my shower after my workout.

"Not at all."

She showed me the cover. Last I saw, she was reading about Cleopatra. My nose must've been down when she picked up the Tantric Sex book from the coffee table instead.

I smirked. "A real page turner?"

"Oh, it's an inspiring read."

"Really? How so?"

Setting my book down, I reached next for her foot. My

thumbs massaged her arch, causing her eyes to close. Her head fell back with a deep moan escaping her lips. Oh, this woman. I'd stop a rugby match to have her. Indulging her sole with one hand, my other slid under her sundress. I started kneading her calf, seeking a path upward. She shifted, opening her thighs for more.

Speaking with her eyes still closed, she said, "I'm inspired to finish something we started at your home. It's your turn to share this time."

"My turn?" I massaged her other foot, letting the relaxed one rest on my crotch, against my twinging cock.

She circled her sole lightly down upon it, making heat rise across my skin. "You said last week there's nothing of yours you wouldn't give to me. So now I want us to be equal. I want to see you enjoy it too."

Her eyes opened, challenging me. "Have you ever shared yourself, Daniel?" Her foot pressed down harder, parting my lips at the sight of it massaging my hardening cock. "Have you?" she asked again before biting her lip.

"Not yet." My will complied to the image in my mind— of opening myself to her, more than to anyone else.

"Do you want to?" More foot friction against my cock. Fuck, the desire in her eyes. It captured me. "Do you want to share yourself with me?"

"Yes, Charlie."

With two simple words, I surrendered to the same vulnerable pleasure. I took her in my home. She could take me in hers. Anything to secure her to me, I'd give.

Minutes later, I sighed into the pillow, lying naked and prone on her bed. Her oiled fingertips lavished forever over my flesh, kneading my back, gliding wide across my lats.

Every sensation filled me. Deep relaxation. Tempting

pleasure. Intoxicating vulnerability. Carnal anticipation. She branded my every, aching nerve.

Her journey across my senses tingled up my calves, to my hamstrings. I moaned when her touch finally thrilled across my ass. The promise of all she could do to me here made me grind into the bed, desperate for more.

She kissed my muscular cheeks, teasing me with licks and gentle bites that made me stifle another low groan into the pillow.

"God, your ass is incredible." Her words murmured over my flesh. She bit my sides, the cut into my glutes flexing for her touch.

Finally, she opened me, curious for more. I trusted her, spreading my thighs to help her, lust melting any resistance.

Fingers sliding down my crevice, she nimbly played across my virgin desire, never fully taking me, only tantalizing me into lungs breathless with lust.

"Is this mine, Daniel?" The heat of her breath steamed over my most vulnerable flesh before her flicking tongue put me in a frenzy.

Eyes rolling. Jaw clenching. Fierce desire seized my reply. "Yes, Charlie." I was ready, crazed to receive her.

"Your body. Your cock. Your ass." Her finger circled, tempting me with the same demands, the same possession I took of her the first time I had her ass. The erotic reciprocity binding me to her. "Your heart. Your fucks. Is it all mine, Daniel?"

With complete commitment, I succumbed. "Yes, Charlie."

"Roll over."

I turned to the vision of her nude body straddling me.

She massaged my shoulders, chest, and abs while my

gaze relished the sight of her splayed pink and swelling, open to me.

Fucking hell, she was lightning across my sky.

Then she moved to kneel beside me, floating her tease up my legs, across my hip bones, over my abs.

It made me arch my back, my abandoned, engorged flesh aching for her touch, sending sweet begs over my lips "please suck my cock, babe" though we both loved the long torture she lavished upon me instead.

With a satisfied "oh fuck, yes" I finally rejoiced when her hot, wet mouth plunged down on me. Another moaning affirmation lulled from my throat when her hand descended between my thighs while her other tight, oiled fist grasped my length, pumping.

Her fingertips started teasing over my ass with no reprieve. The agony for her, so sweet. It twisted my spine. I writhed under her onslaught "fucking take me, babe," demanding more.

She granted my wish, propping her head up on pillows. "Straddle my face." I did, kneeling to worship before her mouth, bracing myself against the wall behind her headboard, gazing down to witness it all.

How light kisses from her glistening lips teased my swollen crown. How her small, firm hands caressed up my thighs, across my ass. How her tongue lapped me up, long, from base to tip, darting to taste my early drops.

I groaned at the sight searing into my memory forever.

Good God, how she would lick, then take me into her mouth. Lips tight with a thrilling wet glide down my long shaft. Then she'd stop, pull off, and lick again before taking me even more.

Marveling at her slow spectacle—her taunting, leisurely

descent closer to my base. Until yes, finally her mouth, her throat, all of me she savored.

"Fuck, Charlie. How do you do that?" It made me shake. My girth bulging in her dripping mouth. "Fuck, you drive me mad taking my cock so deep."

She held me here, moaning with vibrations, I could feel them, the pleasure down to my base. Pressure engorged me, ready to unleash right then.

My stammering breath betrayed me.

She pulled off, drips falling from her lips while she reached for the lube on the towel resting on the bed, intended for her later.

While she slicked the liquid over her right fingers, her stare clung to me, up from my heavy dick to my desperate eyes, staring back at hers. "Tell me how much you want," she said as my chest pounded for her.

Craving this new appetite, this new thrill, she had me fucking ravenous, desperate for it. "Take all of me, Charlie."

She purred the command, "Watch me own you, Daniel."

I obeyed, lust defeating my ego. With her eyes locked on mine, her mouth took most of my measure again, making me sigh her name. One of her tight hands indulged my cock along with her lips, her throat delivering those deep, glucking sucks she introduced me to—they ruled me now.

She traveled her other hand underneath me. Playing and toying, teasing my rim, forcing me to beg, "Do it." Her finger entered, making a hiss of "yesssss" escape my lips. Then another pressed slowly inside, gently stretching me, her fingers beckoning me up to a new plane of lust.

"Oh, fuck!" I cried out at the sensation, at the screaming new intensity. How her gentle pressure coaxing inside of me made her tight mouth sucking drizzles so thrilling, so sensitive over my cock, the sensation maddening.

Opening my thighs, "more, Charlie," I submitted, softening myself to receive her. The ferocity of her mouth and fingers taking me grew.

I wanted to share this with her, wanted the same pleasure for her. "You like it, Charlie, don't you? Sucking me off like this and taking my ass." She moaned in agreement. "Then play with your naughty pussy and show me how you like it. How you like being the only one to fuck me like this."

Bloody hell, the dirty talk she liked was going to take me too.

The fist that was pumping my shaft descended between her thighs. My lips stilled, gaping, while I listened to our sounds. The sweet smacks of her lust getting off on taking me like this drove me and my thrusting hips wild. The gulps from her throat. The slaps of her hand. The breath from my lungs.

It made her press farther in, harder. I roared at the divine spot she found, massaging it in circles with her fingertips. The magnitude of the pleasure was relentless, making me gasp with abandon. Holy hell, this felt so good. I begged her for even more, fucking her mouth and slamming my hands against the wall to steady myself. I couldn't take it and I didn't want it to end.

She took me with fierce sucks, and yes, another pounding finger. The exquisite stinging probes inside me had me searching for breath, gazing down at the sight, at her gorgeous face and sexy, teary eyes, at the corners of her mouth dribbling with her dedication to my pleasure.

To give this to her. To have me like this. To share what it feels like to be penetrated and pleasured to insanity. It was the most fucking erotic thing I'd ever experienced. God-damn beautiful. And so alive.

Only her. Only with her. Only letting her. Only she could be inside me like this—in every possible way.

It surged up in me from a deep, new place.

Trembling my thighs, shaking my hands, convulsing my hips thrusting into her mouth, into her probe, she ripped a loud cry ripped from my heart. The burst of gratification blinded me with flares of light. I wailed her name, exploding again into her sweet mouth swallowing my every drop.

I grabbed the headboard with gulps, seeking for air and focus to return while her fingers gently left me. "Charlie, my God."

My head rested on my forearms, trying to find vision again. She kept gently licking and tasting me, her palm still playing between her thighs.

Indeed, she owned me now, and I didn't know whether to celebrate or cry in the vulnerable certainty of it. I fell beside her. "Bloody hell, that was fucking intense."

"In a good way?" she asked, her body twisting with its own demand.

"Fuck yes," my lips professed before they sought hers for a deep thankful kiss and even deeper connection, tasting my pleasure in her mouth.

Joining my hand with hers between her thighs, together our fingers shared the slick effort. With a hard, ruthless jerk of my hand and my commanding suck of her nipple, her back snapped with a scream and a lush stream over our hands.

My fingers could feel her pulsing while I drifted my lips over hers, swearing through her gasps for breath, "I want everything with you, Charlie."

They simply vanished.

Grinding my molars in fury, my nostrils flex to find a scent. My brows tense down in a seething search. Where are they?

Sound? Nothing but a deafening high-pitched hum of a void.

Taste? No drops of blood.

Touch? Mine alone, rapacious across my nerves.

How long must I wait?

Nothing else in my life enjoys such patience.

Everyone submits to my power. To my demands.

Resist me? Refuse me?

It's not a reality in my world. It won't happen. I want her.

Their retreat from my control? From my hunt? From my divine plan?

It takes every breath of discipline I have to persist.

One reaches a point in every pursuit where there is no turning back.

You follow until the vile limit. Even if it takes ceding pride. Summoning yet another accomplice to pursue your aim.

I will do it.

Nothing will stop me from having their bloody spectacular end.

CHAPTER FORTY-ONE

CHARLIE

Sick of my phone exploding into my life, I'd left it downstairs.

For this exact reason.

Jeremy called last night. And if my boss was calling... oh shit.

"Ravenel," he answered. "Sorry to trouble you on your holiday. Or hiatus. Whatever it is you're doing now."

"Right now, I'm in need of a cup of coffee." I pressed the button on the machine to brew a full pot. "Let me have it, boss. You only call for a reason, and I know it's not a good one."

"I sent you an email with some links and photos. We caught these at the office monitoring you and Daniel. Thought you should know about them."

"So, you're monitoring me now?"

"After that bloody incident at the airport? Literally. I'm not leaving one of my officers exposed. One who's with a high-risk mark like Daniel Pierce. There's Mason Hunt's

White Flag threats. And a few of Daniel's unhinged fans. Get used to it, Ravenel."

"What'd you find?"

"Shite online. Posts from accounts within a three-hundred-kilometer radius of your home. You need to be aware in case they cross your path one day."

I stared out the window. "What kind of posts?" My imagination swimming.

"Pretty disturbing ones. The usual nutter fan stuff, but I don't take chances. I wanted you to know."

Welcome to the jungle. You thought you were being hunted before? Now you're in an Amazon of trouble. Predators everywhere.

"Okay, boss. Thanks for the heads-up. Keep sending them. It fucking pisses me off, but I asked for it, didn't—"

"Asked for what?"

I jumped.

Daniel walked into the room with his question.

Fuck, he needed to stop doing that. He had no idea just how pulled to snap I was.

I put a finger up for him to wait a second. "Gotta go, boss. I'll check the email. Thanks."

"Hey, Ravenel." Jeremy wouldn't let me end the call.

"Yeah, boss?"

"I've known you too long to let you clear off with that comment—about you asking for it. I know you fancy me as just your boss, but I'm also a husband and a father. One who wants you to know that you're not asking for anything. You've sacrificed enough. You've worked for me for five years, and all you've ever done is care for others. You deserve to be happy too, without apology. So sod off with the guilt over it. Just watch your six and give my regards to Daniel."

It almost, almost made me cry. "Thanks... boss." I ended the call.

"That was Jeremy?" Daniel asked. "What's going on?"

I reluctantly tapped my email icon, opening Jeremy's message. "I'm about to find out."

Pressing one of the links, it took a moment before I pushed the screen away, disgusted. "Good God, Daniel. Look at what some of your supposed *fans* are posting about me."

I held my phone up for him to see the twisted image.

It was a meme of the picture from when I was passed out in his arms with the words added...

Fill the bitch with more bullet holes
for fucking our #danielpierce

His eyes lifted from the screen to mine. "Charlie, I'm so sorry. Those aren't fans. Those are cruel, lonely people."

"Cruel and lonely? No. It's demented and dangerous. And this sick fuck lives within two hundred miles of here."

Fury made me go back for more. Fuck these assholes, I'd know it all. Daniel came around and watched over my shoulder.

I pressed another hyperlink in Jeremy's email. It opened a chatroom dedicated to everything Daniel Pierce for years. It had over 5,652 pages of posts from fans volleying gossip with facts.

This link landed on a page from the night of his film premiere. I scanned, reading dozens of foul comments about me.

They speculated about everything: my scars; my past; how we met; how we fuck; how I staged the passed-out gym incident so Daniel would save me; how I'm a poor veteran using him for money; how I'm a whore, wanting the media attention, and more.

Shaking my head the whole time, I was appalled. "They don't even know me but assume the worst. Only a few are kind. But the rest? It's like they hate me because you love me. Like they own you and want you all to themselves."

"They've been doing this for years. You wouldn't believe what some have said about me." He caressed my shoulder. "Please don't let it get to you, babe."

"It doesn't. I feel sorry for them. If they're this cruel to a stranger, imagine how they really feel about themselves."

Tapping another hyperlink, to an Instagram account someone created in a version of my name, the grid filled with posts of me and Daniel. Those were sweet. Along with scantily clad women in military uniforms, tits and ass out. Those were degrading.

Dismay rolled my eyes at the insult to women who sacrifice and serve.

Another link. Another Instagram account. Another version of my name. This one had images of me and the carnage from the Afghanistan war. Bodies and bombings. Rubble and ruin. The most recent post, I opened it.

A little Afghan girl appeared on the screen. Looking at the journalist's camera, she stood shocked beside a U.S. Army soldier. No face to the soldier. Just their firearm strapped to their thigh beside the traumatized brown eyes of the helpless child.

An innocent little girl.

The weight of it dropped my phone from my grasp. It crashed to the floor along with my knees.

Fuck, no, don't cry. My hands shook. My mind tunneled. *Too late. It's got you.*

Tears fell down my face. A sob wrenched up from my throat. My eyes closed to the grief.

"Charlie." I could hear Daniel's voice next to me. The weight of his arms around me.

All I could see though...

A helpless little girl by a soldier's weapon. My weapon...

Balance tilted. Sliding. Pulling me down. Mind hijacked. Going...

To a memory archived.

To smell.

To a tandoor.

The smoke from the clay oven in the home cooked mouth-watering bread. A musty dog sniffed, tail wagging, patient with the chubby hands of a toddler girl grabbing its fur. Her young mother told her to be gentle with the dog.

I understood their exchange of language and love. My eyes snapped up to the man skulking behind the mother and daughter. The glare in his eyes—it scratched my scalp, soured my stomach with a twisting certainty, branding my soul.

This girl and baby are in danger.

For minutes upon minutes, I guarded them, one hand resting on my rifle while my other reached out to pet the dog too. Watching the toddler play, I smiled at her innocent laughter. The bitterly young mother's delight warmed my heart, until I saw bruises on the girl's wrists. I protected their moment's joy until the toddler and girl were yanked back into his violent clutch.

Squaring my shoulders, tightening the grip on my weapon, I lowered my chin, aiming my eyes at his.

"I'll kill you." The words came from my lips.

Sensing someone behind me, staring at me with the same evil intent, I didn't care.

"I know you're coming for me," I said to its looming presence.

A voice called from the distance. From miles away. Shouting my name. Not "Roberts". Not from outside the compound.

Something warm cupped my cheeks. The smell filling my senses? Apples, cedar, and clean musk.

More sound approached. "Babe." It drew closer.

The evil man. The girl. The mom. They blurred.

"Babe, please. Come back to me." The soft command was in my skull. "Come on." It pressed to my lips, nuzzled the side of my nose, resting against my forehead. "Charlie, it's Daniel. Come on. Don't leave me. I love you. Please come back."

The hold of that voice over me—a heavy anchor.

It pulled me up from the dark ocean. Prickles from beard stubble tickled across my lips. "Come back to me, please." Darkness dotted with more light. Aqua eyes stared back at mine.

"Daniel," I gasped. I was back. To him.

His eyes. Tears welled in them. "I'm so sorry." His shoulders heaved, holding back whatever he dammed inside. "I'm so sorry."

We were kneeling. I knew the floors—my kitchen. I couldn't focus on much else. All that filled my vision was his pain.

"What's wrong?"

"You blacked out on me. *Because* of me." A twist of his neck nuzzled his face against mine. A tear fell down his warm, stubbled cheek. "I don't know if I can do this to you anymore. *Good God*, I won't hurt you like this."

The fog over my brain kept lifting. Logic started dropping back into my mind. Memory followed. What happened? A call to Jeremy. Oh fuck, the email. The posts.

The Afghan girl.

It tugged at me again, threatening to pull me back down.

No! Stay here.

I reached for him. "Daniel, I'm okay." *Hold on to him.* Kneeling, pressing my palm to his bare chest. *Don't let go.* The soft hair over his hard pecs. The smell of his soap. A shower. He just took one. I remembered that too. "I'm okay."

His arms wrapped around me. "No, Charlie, it's not okay. Loving me. Asking you to suffer with my bloody fucking life. All the pain it brings you. I'm not worth it."

More than cruel social media knifed my heart. This truth stabbed me—he was right. His celebrity life? It was my hell.

Even if he walked away from his career. Today. His face, his beauty, his celebrity, it would hunt us across the globe.

It brought us to our knees. Right here on my kitchen floor. Like we were already defeated by it.

He let go of me, pain creasing over his face.

"You don't see what it does to you, babe, for almost an hour this time. You're overcome by some hell, and I can't save you. I call out for you, but you look dead in the eyes, talking about killing someone, about someone coming for you. And I don't know if you'll ever come back to me again."

His fists clenched over his thighs. "And it's all my fault. *I'm* doing this to you. *I'm* the reason you're suffering."

"What are you saying, Daniel?"

"*You* said it. That I fuck your life sideways. That you were safe before me. Not anymore. Since you met me, all

I've done is bring you fear. And risk. No one knew you before me. Now the whole world does, and you bloody hate it. I know you do. And one day, I know, you'll start hating me too."

"No, I won't. Don't tell me what I will and won't do."

"Don't be naïve, Charlie. You'll resent me because it won't stop. And what if you agree then that I'm not worth it?" Strands of his hair ripped out at his fist's yank through it. "I'd rather you leave me than hate me."

"So you're leaving me?"

The fear in that one small sentence. It overwhelmed me. With the familiar. With the pain of losing love. And the betrayal of it happening yet again.

"You're willing to just walk out on us, Daniel? Because it's my past coming back for us?"

"We don't have the same pasts."

"No, we don't. But I won't ever hate you. Or leave you. I love you no matter what horror is in yours. Whenever you finally tell me about it, I'll still fight for you."

The aim of my words hit the target. I saw it strike his chin back.

Yes, I knew his secret was a ghost as dark as my past, and he held silent vigil over it like a damn death sentence.

"Whatever it is, Daniel, I won't let it end us. So don't you dare let my past, my PTSD do it."

He opened his mouth. "I—"

"No, not now"—I could see it, poised on the tip of his tongue— "not like this. I mean it. I don't care. I love you no matter what." The grasp of my eyes held his, hard. "Just tell me. Are you giving up on our future because of our pasts? Are we over?"

"No, Charlie." His warm hands returned to my cheeks. "I'll never be over you. I'll have no love, no life without you.

But I won't keep you trapped in mine. I can't bear you suffering this fucking shit pain because of me. You've suffered enough. And you didn't ask for this life, I did."

"Yes, I've suffered, Daniel. So don't make me do it again. I've endured far worse than a goddamn Instagram post. Devices don't breathe and bleed. They don't matter. We do."

With a huff of breath, I tried explaining how the wires in my mind get zapped. "It just caught me off guard. I'll be immune to it now. It won't happen again. I'm strong. I'll get used to it."

My fingers curled over his grasping my face. Pulling them down, holding them firm in my grasp where our knees touched. "And you're not making me do a damn thing. Good fucking luck with that."

That hitched a smile up on his face, unburdening his eyes.

"I'm here because I love you, Daniel. You keep being all pretty, flawed, and private. And I'll keep being all pained, fucked up, and paranoid. And we'll be fine. And fuck Mason, your fans, and the social media bullshit. They can't touch us."

The lines on his forehead softened. "I know it's bloody sick what some post," he said. "That's why I don't look at it anymore. But I hate how they target you." He cradled his palm over my cheek. "All I want to do is love and protect you. At least *one* of those I have to get right."

"Just love me and I can survive this, Daniel."

My declaration?

Really, a prayer.

CHAPTER FORTY-TWO

DANIEL

"You're looking for a shape." Pop pointed in front of his boat to the shallow water illuminated by the lights he rigged up. "That there is an imprint where one laid."

I looked through the dark night into the water lit clear and green, learning to hunt for something I'd never seen.

Pop explained, "Sometimes they're buried up but sometimes you can't miss 'em."

"There's a pair." Evelyn shined a spotlight on them. Two figures trying to hide in the Lowcountry tide— just like me and Charlie.

Charlie eased the boat into neutral. Pop showed me how to hold the gig like a pool stick, letting the spear slide through one hand, while the other delivers the force. In one deft move, Pop got it.

"This bank is usually full of 'em on a night like this," he said.

He pointed again. I recognized the spade-like shape of

the flounder now, the dark color and light spots of the older ones in particular.

"There, son." Pop indicated where, and I followed his instructions. With one quick plunge, small splash, dust up of sand, I did it. I turned, showing Charlie my first catch, feeling like a kid at Christmas.

"Let's see how many we can get!" Pop patted my back. "We're limited to twenty."

We spent a couple of hours on the water. I got better at spotting them. Evelyn gigged two. Charlie got two more for old time's sake. But they let me fill the rest of our catch.

"How do you say it, sexy?" Charlie grinned at me after I put another flounder in the cooler.

"Giggin'!" I nailed it, leaning in for a kiss with a wink.

Pop laughed while Evelyn teased me, "We'll have you talkin' right in no time."

When we headed back home, Pop let me take the helm while Evelyn and Charlie sat up front.

Our pace was slow through the shallow current until we hit open water and waves. Then I throttled down, chatting with Pop about the shore fishing I did at home.

Pop interrupted me with a touch to my back, using the roar of the engine to mask our words.

"You know, son, I approve of you with my Minnow. You're a good man. And you're good to her. Evelyn showed me on her phone the pictures of you two. My girl looks so happy on your arm, but I gotta say, it crushed me seeing her passed out in 'em too."

I turned, witnessing the love in Pop's eyes. It almost crushed me. "I promise you, sir. I won't let anything happen to her."

"I know, son. And she can take care of herself. We've just been through a lot. First, her parents. Now, she's our lil' girl while they watch over us. Then her service. I still remember her call after she was shot. I 'bout fell to my knees, thankful she was alive, but then in tears that Kai was killed. I'll tell ya, when she came home, it was hard seeing her like that. Barely able to move. But the hardest part was that I didn't recognize her. She was lost in a storm of pain."

Imagining Charlie like that, wounded, weak, and grieving; it knotted my throat. I knew that look in her eyes. It was the same one she got when she hallucinated.

"It took months to see glimpses of her again," Pop said. "Years almost. But then she brought you home and I could see it true. My Minnow with that fast, shining light she has, you brought her back."

"She brought me back too, sir. To everything that matters. I love her. So much."

"I know you do. So I care and fear for you both 'cause it seems this world is hell-bent on taking a piece of you two."

Suddenly, a small swell pitched the bow up high before it dropped the boat to its trough. Charlie jolted up with the next lurching dive, vomiting over the railing.

Evelyn jumped up, holding her hair back. "Bless your heart." I could hear Evelyn ask over the engine, "Since when do you get seasick?"

Pop called out, "Y'all all right, Minnow?"

"Yeah," Charlie replied, "too much potato salad."

Pop returned to talk fishing with me. I steered the boat, my focus on the center bow, but also on the sight in front of me, distracting me.

Evelyn sat huddled with Charlie. Their conversation set an odd look in Charlie's eyes. And then she avoided mine the rest of the night.

With hardly a word to me, she was out within seconds after we showered for bed. I watched her lashes tremble while she slept, deep in my own thoughts until exhaustion overtook me too.

The loud light of morning through the bedroom windows would wake the dead. It did me, but she twitched, still asleep. The sun traveled up the wall. An hour later. I couldn't wait anymore.

I played with a lock of hair over her face, gently brushing it away. She lay on her back, finally fluttering her eyes open.

"Good morning, beautiful."

"Mornin', sexy." She yawned. Her chin turned toward me with a soft smile. The sunrise on her face made her eyes blue pools of light.

"Charlie, can I ask you something?"

"Sure." She twisted to mirror me, lying on her side.

"What did Evelyn say to you last night on the boat?"

I saw it flash across her eyes. A look I'd witnessed from her before. She was scared of the answer, smashing her pink lips together.

"Can I tell you what I *hope* she said to you last night?" I knew she'd be afraid to tell me.

Like she was strangled silent, she nodded her head yes.

"I hope she said that you're pregnant." Those words fluttered my heart, catching, full in my throat when I dared saying them aloud.

We'd joked about this weeks before in San Diego. Now, it wasn't a joke. It was my most vulnerable wish.

She nodded her head yes again, tears falling from her lashes.

Joy flooded my face and heart. "Is it possible?"

CHAPTER FORTY-THREE

CHARLIE

Swallowing through the strangling fear, I made myself speak.

"I'm sorry. I fucked up, Daniel. I thought the implant worked up to five years, but Evelyn told me last night it was only three. I don't remember much when I had it put in. I just wanted to stop my period while I recovered and started work. God knows, I didn't need it for birth control. And I certainly didn't test it until now... with you."

His fingertips lingered, tracing gently over my brow. "Please don't be sorry. I think it's beautiful, glorious. But I don't know how you feel. I hope it's the same way but it's not my decision to make."

"I don't know how I feel," I confessed with more tears. "I feel like an asshole saying it, but I have to be honest. I guess I'm happy, mostly, if it's true. But I'm scared as hell too. Real scared. This isn't what I planned."

"Babe, nothing between us was planned." His thumb

gently swiped a tear off my cheek. "Why are you scared? I'm not leaving you, Charlie. And to have this with you..."

He didn't finish his thought, reaching out and touching my belly instead.

I cherished the hope in his eyes, wanting to share his happiness. I couldn't. Not completely.

"Daniel, my life has been a hurricane for as long as I can remember. I've only known losing life and fighting for my own. I lost my parents. My husband. Kai wanted kids but I didn't. At eighteen, I buried my mother. It hurt too much thinking about being one myself. I never dared to imagine having a child. I never wanted to love someone that could be taken from me again."

The raw truth pouring from my lips almost made me sick again.

I held it down, continuing, "And to do this now? I love you so much. And it feels like we've lived a lifetime in the months we've been together. But still. It's early in our relationship. *We're* still getting to know each other. I mean... *I* don't even know what I want."

My hand rested over his on my belly. Protective... because one sure thought I did know. "And we have real threats against us. There's too much risk. You really think it's wise bringing a baby into our world? Do you really think we're ready for this?"

I could keep pushing with a barrage of questions and reasons why not. The list was long.

The rub of his hand over his hope stilled my lips and opened his.

"Charlie, listen to me. I'm as certain as the breath I draw lying next to you. I felt it, from the moment we met, how we recognized each other's souls and I've loved you since. The only surprise is how it deepens every day. I've always wanted a family, but it was never right, nothing was right until you. I don't need more fucking time. I know exactly what I want, what I'm ready for. I want *you*. And I'm willing to risk it all for a chance at a family with you, no matter what we call it."

He leaned over, kissing me again and again, like his passion could impart how certain he was.

The purity of the moment I couldn't deny. His confidence and joy? Contagious.

I tried inhaling in his love instead of my fear. Resisting that dark space inside of me. The omen that stole my happiness. If I didn't stop letting it ruin these moments, it would ruin my life.

"No matter what?" I snuck the ask between our kisses.

His smiling lips answered before his next kiss. "No matter what."

And if the fear, if that dark space, didn't exist? If I could breathe in only this love? Only dare hold his precious hope that we might share this?

Then yes... I wanted this too.

"Look here, Sex God." I made my choice—diving into the joy with him. "We don't know yet what we're dealing with. I could just be sick from bad potato salad. And my boobs are probably sore because you've been having a lot of fun with them lately."

He looked down at our nude bodies. The spread of his hand rubbed sunny warmth over my flesh.

"I don't know, babe. I'm the one who's been drinking Guinness, not you. But you're the one who has a little belly now."

"Uh! Fuck you, Pierce." I laughed, looking down at his hand rubbing my belly like a fortune teller over a glass ball. It looked flat to me. Maybe a little bloated. Hell, I didn't know. "I do *not* have a beer belly. That's your wishful think-ing. You'd be so proud if you knocked me up."

"If you're not knocked up yet, I'll sure enjoy trying. I tried seventeen times in our first week together. And that was just the fucking. Not everything else."

"Did you count how many times we fucked in the Seychelles?"

"Yes, I fucking counted. Counted fucking." He rolled back, laughing. "You threw Tantric sex and that fit body on me. And you were starved for sex after six years. I could barely keep up with you. It was seventeen times." His gaze fell back on mine. "If fucking were an Olympic sport, we won a gold medal that week."

"You're unreal. Of course you counted. How many times since that week? Until now?"

"You've blown my mind and cock so many times I've lost count." He roared back at his joke. "Your curious, horny pussy keeps me busy."

I shook my head, infected with his laughter. "What do you think me being pregnant will do to your Olympic fucking career, Mr. Pierce? It may slow you down and put you into early retirement."

He bent down, showering my bellybutton with kisses. "I'll think it's beautiful. You know it's true. Sharing this with you, it will only make me want you more."

His chin traveled down to kiss between my thighs.

I gently grabbed his raven curls. "Hold your horses, Pierce. Later." No way I could focus on anything else. "Now you got me wanting to call my doctor to see if she can come to me, instead of us having to sneak onto Hilton Head."

CHAPTER FORTY-FOUR

CHARLIE

His grasp held a now familiar spot—my hair back from my perch over the toilet while I spewed up my breakfast.

"You sure seem pregnant to me."

"Daniel, please." The flail of my hand found the lever to flush it all down. "I can't think about that right now."

"Well, we're supposed to leave in an hour on the boat to get Dr. Patterson on Hilton Head. Should we reschedule?"

I pushed back against his helping hand and urgent timeline. Yes, I wanted to pick up the doctor. When I'd called Dr. Patterson the day before, she said she understood our special circumstances and agreed to the trip out to Daufuskie.

But right then, the dual focus overwhelmed me—a pregnancy test and our call from Agent Cooper this morning.

It spun my head and world.

Sitting at the kitchen island, I'd put the call on speaker phone so I could enjoy the pancakes and scrambled eggs Daniel served up.

At first, I was starving, shoveling it in. But once the agent started her update, I lost my appetite.

"There was an attack on the young woman in Virginia," the agent had reported.

Oh shit, the same one Jeremy told you about.

The agent continued, "She's a college activist working on gun control and human rights campaigns. She was in the parking lot of her apartment complex, and someone attacked her."

I blurted, "Oh God, is she okay?"

"She will be," the agent said. "She sustained broken ribs, facial trauma, and a laceration with a knife. A deep cut across her scalp. He went for as much blood as possible."

We all knew it: scalp cuts bleed profusely. And the blood? It was for the *White Flag* pillowcase proof of target attacked.

"I'm paying all of her medical bills." The statement flew out of my mouth, desperate to help the young woman and feeling like a hypocrite because I was hiding for my own life.

"I'll put you in touch with someone at the hospital if that's your wish," the agent had replied.

Then, a long pause.

One that had held Daniel's worried look at me. One that lurched my stomach. The escalation of violence? It raised heart rates and alarm.

"Ms. Ravenel. I mean, Ms. Roberts." Another brief pause from the agent. "Forgive me. I want to respect your name but don't know which to use."

"Please just call me 'Charlie'." I didn't give two shits about surnames and symbolism right then.

"Okay. Well, Charlie, I feel compelled to tell you, I'm concerned. The young woman in Virginia looks eerily like you. And the tactics? They match the assault on you and Mr. Pierce. It's the same. She was doused in urine and semen too."

That was all it took. Hearing the unique marker of that crime had me jumping up in a mad dash for the guest bathroom in the front foyer as Daniel told the agent we'd call her back.

"Babe, should we reschedule with the doctor?" He knelt by me now, offering me a cup of water to sip.

I leaned back against the wall, the grasscloth wallpaper snagging my long hair. "I don't know what to do."

Something shifted inside me.

Something I never reconciled before.

No matter which way I turned, so much more could be at stake.

"Well, I do." Daniel put a cool washcloth to my face. "We are going to get the doctor. We will have our appointment and we will go on with our lives. Sitting here helpless plays right into his bloody hands."

He didn't need say who.

Mason's shadow stood in the doorway, smiling down at the havoc he wrecked over our joy.

I never heard back from Mason. After our last, perverse volley of texts with him asking where I hid. And with whom. That was six days before and no wicked pings since.

He was going dark. The attack on the woman in Virginia would scan a spotlight over Mason's life, investigating his every move prior and next, for a time. It would give us a perverse break because I knew he'd be back.

"Come on, babe." Daniel's imposing frame gracefully rose to his feet, offering his hand out to me. "Are you ready?"

Yes, you are. I grabbed his hand. *Get the fuck up. If you are pregnant, get ready to fight like hell.*

One Way Or Another by Until the Ribbon Breaks

The tragic list is gloriously long—celebrities who have been murdered.

Leave it to Hollywood.

Turning their stories into award-winning films decades later.

And leave it to America—buying tickets and popcorn to watch fictitious fodder be made from real pain and horror.

But for a few? Like me?

It's inspiration.

The ultimate statement.

Yet again—a beautiful blonde. Even better. This one was a Marine. Their treasured heroine.

Yet again—a powerful screen icon. Even better than a singer or a designer. This one is a beloved blockbuster hero.

One can only wonder... but be sure... oh, the movies that will be shot decades later.

I will certainly buy a ticket for that show.

CHAPTER FORTY-FIVE

DANIEL

The doctor's visit went by fast. She removed Charlie's implant, drew blood, and gave her a home pregnancy test to take first thing in the morning. And she scheduled us for an office visit in two weeks if it was positive.

Charlie slept like an exhausted angel while I tossed and turned.

Waiting until the morning was bloody torture.

I'd tried every sexy ploy to convince Charlie to take the test right after we got home from taking the doctor back.

"Seduce me all you like, Pierce." Her voice had cooed while my lips trailed down her neck with kisses. "I'm following doctor's orders, not your desire."

When her head fell on the pillow later, it went right to sleep while mine swam with excited plans. I lay awake on the mattress beside her, watching her dream.

If it was positive? No. It was. I was sure we were pregnant. Wow, that hit hard.

Fuck's sake, Pierce. This is what it's supposed to feel like. So overwhelmed with love that it humbles you. Finally. Actually wanting a child and not fearing one.

God, my parents would be thrilled. They loved Charlie. My entire family did. I didn't know if they would be more overjoyed about the news, or more relieved that I finally got it right this time.

Be it faulty or fickle choice, or fate, I spent two decades and never found anyone remotely proper to start a family with.

Quite the opposite, I was ashamed to admit.

Now... with her... it was all I wanted.

What she had said the other day? It hadn't gotten past me. How she knew I hid something horrible.

I did.

Yet she still loved me. Not asking. Not caring what secret lay between us. This was how strong we were together.

And I'd almost told her.

Part of me wished I had before we had the hope of this. A hope I wouldn't destroy now. Not when I could see a new joy sparkling in Charlie's eyes too.

I wasn't protecting myself. I was protecting her.

All the bullets I'd take to keep her from getting hurt again.

My past would stay hidden, where it couldn't hurt her.

This was our chance. Hers to have a family again. To have someone to love her, because, dear God, I did.

And it was my chance too. To start over.

The maths kept me awake, running calculations of weeks. She could be due as early as next February.

We'd need to tell Lorraine, *The Druid*'s showrunner, and the studio. My shooting schedule must be rearranged because I wasn't going anywhere without Charlie and our baby.

Our baby. I beamed in the darkness.

Falling into dreams of our future claimed me for minutes, maybe short hours, before excitement woke me up again.

In less than two months, I'd leave for Wilmington to start shooting the Navy SEAL film. The production would have me working nose to the ground to get through since I'd asked the producers to shoot me out quickly.

I'd barely have spare hours to sleep much less spend with Charlie. I'd figure a way. Maybe she'd stay in the house I rented in Wilmington.

It was a lavish one on the waterway. She would love the views. It was in a gated community, so we'd be safe there. Simon returned in October for my detail too.

We could make this work.

No, Pierce. You WILL make this work. This time. Whatever cross you must bear. Whatever cost you must pay.

You will never abandon her or your child.

She finally stirred awake. Once her lashes started fluttering, bliss fired through my nerves.

The back of my index finger lingered down her cheek. "Wake up, beautiful. I've been waiting all night."

She smiled over at me with a stretch, swearing, "Damn, Daniel. For a man who was so patient with me before, you sure are rarin' to go this morning, aren't ya?"

"In more ways than one." I grinned, feeling the pulse in my morning wood and excited heart.

"Well, settle down, Sex God. All in due time. Let a woman wake up first."

She paused, her gaze studying my eager face.

Twisting hers into a more serious expression, she said,

"You know, I may always be barefoot around here, and you may have gotten me pregnant. But let me be clear, Daniel Pierce—I'm not gonna *be* barefoot and pregnant. Not even for your hot ass. We're in this together. I'm not going to stop working. And I'm sure as shit not going to do all the parent stuff by myself either. A man doesn't babysit his own children. Mothers aren't primary, and fathers aren't second wheel. We're equal in this."

I chuckled at her soapbox disclaimer.

"Tell you what, Ravenel. I'll keep count and make sure we're always even. Fifty-fifty. I'll even buy us both aprons because I bloody well know you don't own one."

"We ain't countin' shit but go ahead with the aprons. You'd be so fuckable in one."

Another pause coiled concern over her face. "Just give me a kiss and promise me you'll be okay if it's negative."

"If it's negative, I told you, it won't be for long." I mounted over her, sharing a passionate kiss. Lips still dusting over hers, I swore, "I'll enjoy many, many times trying to get you pregnant," reaching between her legs.

She jerked my hand away. "Don't. I really have to pee."

I leapt out the bed, handing her the white stick on the nightstand. "Then let's do this."

"Good God, Daniel Pierce, you're a fucking sight! You've got a pregnancy test in your hand and a screaming hard cock ready to make another."

She threw the bed sheet off her. I handed her the stick.

Rushing toward the bathroom, she proclaimed over her shoulder, "I never saw this coming, drinking Guinness with you the first day we met."

Fast on her heels, I followed. "Yeah, well, I've seen us coming, Sex Goddess, many, many times."

"That's ten points on the board for that pun, Pierce."

She pivoted to me before entering the loo, nose inches from my chest. "Um, I don't need an audience for this part. We can do all kinds of kinky shit but this ain't one of them."

She grinned, pushing me out and closing the little door in my face while I waited outside.

I set a hand towel down on the countertop in anticipation. She returned with the test in hand a couple of minutes later, setting it on the towel before washing her hands.

Pulling her into an embrace, I held on to more than her warm body. Clinging to her and to every prayer I sent up or to the good Karma she espoused to so much. Something. Anything.

Please give us this one precious joy.

I didn't need a timer, desperate to see it with my own eyes.

It only took eighty-seven seconds (I counted) before it clearly read "Pregnant".

Oh God, Pierce. My soul burst. With what? *No words. Just an ecstatic awakening.*

The gasp from Charlie made my arms scoop her up.

She didn't protest. Wrapping her arms around my neck and burying her face in my neck, her happy tears wet down my chest while mine welled up.

I laid her on the bed, descending upon her with all my love, suggesting, "Let's make another one now just in case."

CHAPTER FORTY-SIX

CHARLIE

"My God, she looks grown up."

I marveled at the screen in my hand, watching a live shot of Kierra Williams smiling at the camera, sitting in the studio of *Wake Up, America*. "It's only been a month since Comic-Con, but she looks like she's matured five years... in a good way."

Daniel held my other hand, sitting beside me in the back seat of Quincy's van while Pop and Evelyn drove through the summer tourist traffic on Hilton Head Island.

Two pulse-raising events were planned this morning: Kierra's live interview and our first ultrasound.

The show teased that Kierra's exclusive with Meg Wiseman on *Wake Up, America* was coming up next—after the break.

Publicists for the cast of *The Druid* had prepared for this. It was time for Kierra to speak up, to share her side of the story, taking the power back from Mason.

My heart pounded with pride. How Kierra sat up

straight in the chair, looking ready for battle in a black pantsuit trimmed with leather lapels.

"Turn it up, babe, so we can all hear it." Daniel leaned over, smiling at the phone too.

I clicked the volume up to max. From the front seats, Pop and Evelyn tilted their ears toward the sound. They were a much-needed help this morning, ready to run advance when we arrived at the doctor's office, making sure all was clear in the building before we entered.

Because if we were spotted entering a medical office, we were fucked. It would fire up another media frenzy.

BREAKING NEWS

Daniel Pierce caught holding Captain Charlotte Roberts's hand entering an OBGYN's office. We got all three of them now!

That's why I took no chances.

Kierra's interview started with confidence. Her comments focused on awareness for teens about stalking, about the emotional abuse of it as well as the danger.

Then the strength in her voice wavered when she shared the toll it took on her. Kierra didn't reveal details about Mason's tactics, but she confirmed that, yes, it was Mason who took the creepy, viral videos of her on set.

I watched Kierra's eyes. Eyes I could read without a word.

How Kierra struggled with the reporter's next questions. How she pursed her lips, nervous, and tucked her hair behind her ear at the inquiry.

"Now, Kierra, what can you tell us about Captain Charlotte Roberts?" Meg Wiseman asked.

A photo split the screen. Their live interview on one

half. A picture of me guarding Kierra on the July Comic-Con stage on the other.

The picture went viral five days before. Close-ups on the fresh bruise and cut on my face started a wildfire, scorching more accusations about me.

Daniel's publicist told us how people were in chatrooms and on posts commenting upon our obvious on-set romance. Some loved it. Others criticized me, accusing me of exposing Kierra to even greater risk because I was involved with Daniel while I led Kierra's protection team.

A random fan account for *The Druid* had ignited it all.

Like hell it was random.

It was Mason.

He messaged someone the Comic-Con photo, encouraging the #danielpierce post, knowing exactly what to aim for in getting a measure of revenge against me.

Kierra swallowed the obvious lump in her throat, answering the reporter's question with her chin up.

"Ms. Ravenel, I mean, Ms. Roberts, protected me. She'd never let anyone hurt me. She kept me safe and taught me a lot. And she made me stronger, braver. I'm quite inspired by her, actually."

Fuck, Charlie Girl. She said "Ravenel".

Kierra just dropped your other name. Your maiden one, and the only one leading someone here.

But Kierra didn't know better, and the name leak was inevitable. Anger didn't hit me. All I felt was pride watching her on the screen.

The reporter asked, "What about Ms. Roberts's relationship with Daniel Pierce? Do you think it put you at greater risk?"

Kierra tugged on her jacket. "Anyone who claims that is thick in the skull and doesn't know Ms. Roberts. She takes her work seriously. I caution anyone who stands in her way. Believe me, she'll take them down."

Cocking her head with a triumphant smile, Kierra conjured what only a few had witnessed a month before.

How I beat Mason, no matter how hard he fought me. How I choked him out. How I stood over him, ready to do it again if he threatened Kierra.

Kierra smoothed her pants. "Ms. Roberts and Mr. Pierce have been nothing but professional and kind to me and everyone on our show. I think it's grand they're together now. That's all that needs to be said." That concluded the interview.

"I can't believe how people accuse such foolish things," Evelyn chimed in from the front seat. "But you trained her right. She's just like you. Puttin' them in their place."

The phone in my hand lit up with a distinct ring. "Kierra Williams" appeared on the screen.

"Hey, chica," I answered. "Strong job on the interview."

"Charlie, I'm so sorry. I had to answer those questions."

The mere sound of her voice made me miss her. "I know, and it's fine. No, it's ironic"—I grinned as we pulled into the parking lot of the medical building—"it looks like you're the one protecting me now."

"You know I always will. It's rubbish what they're saying. Makes me worry what else Mason will do."

"Well, he's been busy awaiting court. Filed a lawsuit against me and HGR Security. Refused to sign nondisclosures. And now he's appealing his protective order from you." Our van parked. "You gotta stay strong. Mason will keep taunting us. He gets off on it."

Daniel sucked his teeth at my side of the conversation, muttering, "That fucking arsehole is demented."

"I will," Kierra replied. "And I'm safe. Taneesha is a

badass protection officer like you. She's loving the pints and oysters here. How about you? How's Daniel loving your Southern life?"

"I think he's loving a lot of things here." He grinned, able to hear Kierra's question. "I've got a happy secret for you, but you've got to keep it."

"You're married!"

"Nope."

"You're pregnant!"

"Yep."

"I'm going to be Auntie Kierra!"

Her voice screaming from the small device filled the entire van. It made Pop and Evelyn smile while they exited to scope the path for our entrance.

"You'll make a wonderful auntie," I said, clicking my door open. "Speaking of, I gotta go. We're at the doctor's office now."

"Good luck and kisses. Ring me soon."

Holding Daniel's hand, joy filled my steps into the building. Pop and Evelyn checked, peeping into the elevator before signaling for us to follow. No staff greeted us in the empty doctor's office. Only Dr. Patterson reading a book, waiting for our lone entrance.

"Oh, that's cold!"

I flinched minutes later when Dr. Patterson squirted gel onto my belly. The doctor just smiled, turning dials on the ultrasound machine.

Standing beside the chair, Daniel wouldn't let go of my hand. His sweated, making me glance up at him.

The sight of the raw knife scar on his arm filled me with sudden anxiety. It was on his face too—worried, watching my little belly.

With all that threatened our world, we needed this tiny joy.

A rhythmic *whoosh-whoosh* of a baby's heartbeat filled our ears and the morning's trouble disappeared.

A sudden gasp came from Daniel's smiling lips before he gazed down at me and squeezing my hand.

"Everything is looking and sounding good." Dr. Patterson moved the wand over my belly.

I turned back to watch the blissful process.

The doctor paused in one spot, then another with the beautiful whooshing sound in the background, making clicks and measurements.

Then she stopped. For a long time.

Exploring a certain area.

I looked anxiously at the monitor; didn't know how to interpret what I saw swirling in colors on the screen.

The doctor's poised silence swelled my terror.

The concentration on the doctor's face was eerie.

The cool, sterile smell of medical air took my senses, skyrocketing my heart rate with fear.

I hated hospitals, anything medical. All it ever brought me was loss, devastation.

Something's wrong. Horrible news again that will rip your life apart.

Told you. Don't fall in love. Don't hope. It never works out.

"I think..." The doctor's eyes didn't leave the screen.

I inhaled, preparing for the shock.

Like it would hurt less if I braced for it. Like that one breath could protect my heart from the devastating shatter that was coming.

"Yes"—Dr. Patterson turned to me, smiling—"we have two."

The statement hit my ear like a foreign language, one I didn't know.

Daniel exclaimed, "Oh, wow! I had a twin. My mum is a twin." He looked down at me with the purest smile I'd ever seen on his face.

"Twins?" I asked, my mind finally translating fear into joy. "Are they okay?"

"They look and sound great." Dr. Patterson continued with her measurements. "I think about thirteen weeks now. Everything is fine, dear." She patted my hand while addressing Daniel with a smile. "That's not quite how the science works, if you were a twin too. It's simply a beautiful coincidence."

Laughter burst from my lungs while Daniel started smothering me with soft kisses.

"Leave it to you, Sex God," I said, "thinking you gave us twins." I warned him through kisses and grins, "I'm gonna get huge."

He grinned, nose to mine. "After my film, I'll drink pints of Guinness, eat burgers and fries, pasta and pizza, Christmas pudding too. I'll get huge with you. We'll both be a beautiful sight."

"That's a fifty-fifty deal, Pierce."

With over ninety million posts a day, it requires no effort.

A #danielpierce post of an interview this morning with Kierra Williams does the work for me.

Leave it to fans with nothing else to do but dig down the virtual rabbit hole.

Most fanatic followers celebrate, even defend, the relationship. Happy that their god found another to love. Heralding the woman, her service and sacrifice. And her beauty.

A few malign their union. Obsessive, vicious, wicked posts and rumors. All aiming to shred reputations and ruin careers. Demanding blood from the woman who their hero dares to love.

The sentiment driving the most traffic?

#captaincharlotteroberts is also #charlieravenel.

Fans connected the dots so I didn't have to. Revealing

that the former Marine was hired by HGR Security for #thedruid, hired to protect a beautiful girl.

Who wouldn't fall in love with a woman like that?

Their super-god hero certainly did.

The intrigue of it all.

That Daniel Pierce is in love with a woman of formidable strength and stunning beauty—a woman with two names and mysterious scars.

It's perfection. I couldn't have written the tragedy better.

The soaring press of the romantic story only adds potency to their ultimate ruin.

A fresh crimson drip lands on the trail.

One search of that name revealed—Ravenel—and a very specific location filters my search to far fewer targets.

Picking up her scent again.

I start to scope the Lowcountry of South Carolina.

CHAPTER FORTY-SEVEN

DANIEL

"How many y'all want?" Jax, Charlie's old Marine buddy, called over his shoulder, slapping raw burgers down on the grill.

"Three," I answered.

"Five," Charlie joked.

No more morning sickness. Her spitfire energy had returned, barely slowing her down.

Now though, her tan belly was obvious, and the most captivating sight. Especially when she kept walking around the house with her cut off, jean shorts unbuttoned and unzipped, like an invitation for me to drop them to the floor.

"*This* is a beer belly, Pierce." She rubbed the special oil Ara, Jax's wife, had brought over for her growing mound. "Looks like I swallowed a cantaloupe."

"Need help with that?" I poured a puddle into my palms. She reclined on my lap in her bikini while the glide of my hands swirled over the swell of her belly. I murmured,

"You make Guinness proud." She swatted my arm. I whispered, "You're so beautiful, babe." She nuzzled into my lips.

Jax plopped on the pool lounger next to us. "Daniel, man. Sucks you can't have a cold one with me."

I toasted with my iced tea, another Southern delicacy I was growing to love. "I promise, once I wrap this film, I'll buy a bloody keg for us both."

Jax and Ara had come over two days before and the laughing hadn't stopped. Jax was a riot, and Charlie and Ara were like sisters. With Ara at seven months pregnant and Charlie at four, we had plenty to share.

The first night we sat around the pool while Jax and Charlie swapped tales at each other's expense. Seems it wasn't easy being a Marine on patrol *and* a woman who had to pee.

Puffing his cigar, Jax had joked, "Daniel, I gotta tell ya. I didn't know what my mission was—Afghanistan or guarding Roberts while she squatted by the Humvee."

With a slosh, Charlie had tossed the ice water in her glass on him, making Jax jump up cackling and I howled at the joke.

"Charlie, don't encourage him," Ara warned. "We've got one kid on the way. I don't need another grown one."

Jax declared, "All right, then, woman. Take me upstairs and make me a man." He pulled a giggling Ara inside the house to their guest room.

Charlie sat back down on my lap. "Just you wait. You'll hear them for the next hour. They're the reason a sound machine is by our bed."

It had only made me equally inspired, kissing her neck, humming the words in her ear, "You know what *I* want to hear, babe." And we did, making our own muffled moans by the pool all night.

After three days together, the bond that Charlie and Jax shared rubbed off on me too.

Jax and I woke early the next morning to go fishing with Pop.

I was impressed with how fast Jax walked on a prosthetic foot. The only issue? His balance sometimes. But we all had to steady ourselves over the waves. Pop took us out far today. It was September and that meant Tarpon time.

"So, what has Charlie told you?" Jax cast his line, staring out at the rolling water.

"Everything." I wound my line. "I know she still blames herself about you and Kai."

I looked over at Jax. He wore the kind of tan that looked perpetually sunburned. The brown hair under his camo baseball cap with a fishhook on the bill was still shaved like a Marine. There was a lot of grit to him, but his playful brown eyes revealed a kind heart.

Jax shook his head. Pop did too. He stood on the other side of Jax toward the stern.

We all knew the real story about that day. The one when both Charlie and Jax were shot.

"I don't know why she blames herself." Jax tugged at his rod. "I never did for a second. We're both fucking lucky to be here. Ain't no use in blame or guilt."

The question swelled in me. "Do you think she planned it? Letting herself get shot so she could kill that man?"

Because I had to know. Given the twins, how much risk would Charlie take, how far would the woman I love go to protect someone else?

The glance Jax gave me said it all—to the bitter, fatal end.

"I don't know man," Jax said. "It's the weirdest fuckin' thing. What I remember of that day? Mostly... it's in the official report. And that fucker shot at the wrong Marine. She dropped him faster than any of us could."

Jax stared at the water. A twitch took his cheek with the memory.

He explained, "But I felt it. Like a premonition. Then it happened so fast. I heard the first shots, turned and saw her taking the bullets, leaning into them, like she was ready for 'em. All while she fired back, dropping that man fast with perfect aim. Then she fell.

"That's when the other man stood up, aiming for her too while she was on the ground. I tried getting a clean shot at him, but I was at a bad fuckin' angle. I got him in the thigh. So, he turned and got a lucky shot on me."

Jax gestured toward his prosthetic foot. "I went down. Miller and Perez fired to suppress him, but he got away. Charlie told me yesterday about remembering who he was —the one who tried to kill her next but he shot me instead. We'd been watching him, suspecting he was Taliban and moving weapons. I didn't make the connection 'til she told me it was him, the oldest brother from that compound with those poor little girls."

Jax reeled his line in for another cast. "But that's ancient history. Gotta let it go."

I imagined Charlie as Jax had described. Witnessing myself how she was the same with Mason. Hell, with every-one. How she brought the fight to her to help anyone.

Yes, there was deep tenderness to her in most moments.

But she was a whole other woman when protecting someone. Like a vengeful hurricane that couldn't be stopped. Best to take cover. Especially if a rifle was in her hands.

Yes, Pierce, she planned it. Willing to die. That's the woman you love.

Was her stubborn courage a treasure or terror?

With all we could lose now, I didn't know.

Later, I sat with Charlie on my lap while Ara reclined next to Jax. A cool night breeze by the lit fire pit rewarded us after the waning summer day.

Jax started playing his acoustic guitar. He was a great musician with a melodic gravel voice singing a Zac Brown Band song about being free.

The lyrics gripped my heart given all that imprisoned us. Silence from the lack of Mason's texts. No leads from the FBI on *White Flag* extremists. Vicious gossip online from a few of my zealot fans. It tried caging us on this tranquil island, trapped by my fame and her fear.

But it wasn't strong enough to erase our joy. We only shared more laughs, love, and lazy afternoons napping in the shade of her balcony deck. The promise in her belly freed me from any damning worry.

Nothing could take this from us.

Wrapping my arms around her tighter, thinking of our story, I kissed her bare shoulder.

She got up when the song was done, joking that she needed to pee and for Jax to guard her. When she came out minutes later, my phone was in her hand.

"Hey, sexy, this thing is blowing up."

She handed it to me without checking—another thing I loved about her. How she told me she wasn't the kind of woman who checked a man's phone.

I unlocked it. Three calls from Elaine. One from Simon. My assistant and my detail were calling late from London? What the fuck?

The pit of my contented stomach dropped. Charlie sat back on my lap while I called Elaine back.

"Hiya." Her voice filled my ear. "Sorry to keep ringing you at this hour. Everyone all right?"

"Cheers. Yeah, we're fine. What's going on?"

Elaine was enjoying her months off before returning in December to help me juggle a dizzying press junket promoting season two of *The Druid.* Until then, she managed the business of my career from London.

"Simon rang me. Tried to phone you too," Elaine said. "He got a call from the property manager in Madrid. There's been a terrible fire at your house there. No one was hurt but it's in ruins."

"What?" I sat up. "How did it start?"

"They're not sure. The manager mentioned something about the garage. I assume they'll investigate but have nothing yet. We need to find you all someplace else and get started now. I'll pull some listings and send them over tomorrow."

Shock shook my head, relieved to hear no one was hurt. I didn't own the estate, just rented it. All my stuff was packed and sent back to London in July when the season wrapped.

Still... it felt personal.

The Madrid house started to feel like a home to me.

With Charlie on my lap, remembering our first intimate moments together there, the sudden destruction disturbed me.

CHAPTER FORTY-EIGHT

CHARLIE

It soared my heart rate listening to Daniel's end of the conversation.

When he told me the rest, I closed my eyes, running it back through with an exhale.

Daniel dismissed the fire at his Madrid home as caused by something electrical or chemical in the garage.

No, it wasn't.

When I was there, I never noticed flammable cans in the garage. The house was relatively new with proper wiring. And garages were easy to break into, offering concealment while the property is accessed.

Many people who lived in the area around Daniel's Madrid home knew he lived there while shooting *The Druid*, with his loud and proud Ducati zooming in and out of his drive. If that didn't confirm his location, all one had to do was ask at the café near the studio or any restaurant nearby. You could find him.

He slept like a baby all night while I lay awake. The

haunt I tried forgetting rolled in again on a tide of fear, lapping waves over my mind.

Someone is trying to get to Daniel. Or trying to get to Daniel... to get to you.

One #danielpierce threatened crosshairs now. Searching for us. Burning through each confirmed location.

Would it find us here?

Fear got me up. Sliding my maxi dress on, I wandered out to the pool deck for air. Salt and sea always calmed me.

"When was the last time you slept for more than four hours?" Jax's voice rose from the darkness, lighting his cigar with quick puffs.

I plopped down on the lounge chair beside him. At four a.m., we were wide awake.

"When I finally had fucking sex again." I smiled at him, always telling him the truth. "Daniel rocked my world to sleep."

I had no secrets with Jax. He and Ara knew about my years alone, all my ghosts, and my fight back to life. Jax's path was like mine.

He laughed, taking a big puff, and agreed. "I hear that."

With a serious look, he paused and held my gaze.

"I like him, Roberts. The love in his eyes for you almost makes that man too fuckin' pretty. But it ain't an easy life with him. I don't know 'bout his bullshit celebrity y'all gotta deal with. No fuckin' way I could handle it. It'd keep me awake too. I wouldn't need anything else making me feel more on edge than motherfuckers chasing us, huntin' for a picture of me, Ara and our kid, every damn time we left the house."

I sighed, relieved by his validation, rubbing my little belly, staring up at the darkest hour of the night and bright stars above.

"You know what's fucked up, Jax? Six years ago, we would've been sitting here, and these would be Kai's babies."

The familiar constellations above comforted me into confessing, "But would that have been an easier life? I changed and so did Kai. I loved him so much but the last time we were together? The sex was great, but we were emotional strangers. Distant from even ourselves. I think it's a delusion. The words 'easy' and 'life' don't belong in the same sentence, no matter who you are."

"What's changed?" Jax puffed the smoke of his cigar into perfect rings.

The smell pleased me, wishing I could take a puff. "Truth is, I'm an asshole for admitting it, but I love Daniel more than Kai, 'cause I love me more than I did back then. Kai wanted kids. I couldn't see it. It felt like we were still kids ourselves, busy surviving. And I was too afraid to have a family, since mine was ripped from me. But I grew up. I love the woman pain forged me into. And now..."

Resting back against the chair, I turned my head. "It's all I want—a life, a family with Daniel. I love him and I don't give a shit about the rest. People can take all the pictures they want, say what they want. It's just the fear I can't shake. Like something bad is gonna happen."

Jax stared up at the same night sky humbling us from above. "You gotta lot of feelings you need to shake, Roberts." Tapping his ashes onto the cement pool deck, he cut me another soft but stern look. "You need to quit with the fear and the guilt."

We stared each other down in a brutal, safe dance of raw truth.

He broke the silence. "Roberts, I love you, but I ain't

holdin' the burden of your guilt anymore. About me getting shot that day too."

I huffed a humble chuckle. "It's done?"

"Yep, it's done." He reached a hand out to hold mine while his other offered up another satisfying puff to his lips. "If the guilt is gone, then what are you so damn afraid of?"

I squeezed his palm. It was sandpaper in my grasp.

"I'm afraid I'm so fuckin' paranoid now that I believe folks will always come back hunting for what they want, for what they hate. Once ambushed, always ambushed."

He squeezed my hand back before letting it drop, nodding up to the moon, fully understanding.

CHAPTER FORTY-NINE

DANIEL

This was the first time I cursed my career. While packing my bags, resentment twisted my nerves.

Before Charlie, I always looked forward to the next project, working hard to prepare, enjoying the challenge of something new. For decades I chased the ever-elusive next best role, best paycheck, best deal, or best anything.

Whatever the bloody hell for? None of it fucking mattered to me now.

Why did it ever?

Still, I did my job.

I was prepared for this role. After two months of punishing sweat, sun, sand, water, and training. With both Charlie and me eating healthy for four and my strict regimen. No drinking. Deep sleep. Long workouts. It put ten more pounds of pure muscle on my frame. I was tan, strong, and shredded—more than ever before.

And for the first time in my life... my heart actually

hurt, tasting a small flavor of the pain of leaving your family behind for the job.

I felt as bloody close to being a Navy SEAL as I could ever get.

Charlie had been having fun with my long waves, moaning with them buried between her legs. She'd have to kiss my locks goodbye. My first stop would be with wardrobe, then hair and makeup. The coming buzz cut pleased me. It would cool my scalp. It was the first day of October, but this place knew no autumn.

I packed all the clothes she bought me. No need for much else in Wilmington. I'd come back to her as much as I could. But when I looked at the schedule for the next couple of months, I didn't know how.

She sat quiet on our bed, handing me folded T-shirts while I stewed in the ache.

"This makes me sick." I shoved running shoes into my suitcase next. "I bloody fucking hate leaving you and the twins. Why won't you come with me?"

"Daniel, you're right on the Intercoastal Waterway in that house you're renting. Talk about living in a goddamn fishbowl? It's a beautiful view and home, and yeah, it's in a gated community, but it's also a wall of windows two hundred feet from open water that anyone can access."

"What about here?"

I gestured to the vast view of the ocean from the windows of our bedroom in her Daufuskie home.

"These are hurricane and bulletproof glass." She mirrored my motion. "I had them replaced last year. And you saw the surveillance in the office downstairs. I know every goddamn squirrel on this property. It's not the same."

"Babe, I have a brutal schedule since I asked them to

shoot me out fast. I don't know how often I will get home to you... if at all."

"I know." She reached her hand out for mine. "But you'll be so busy and so tired, you'll blink, and it'll be done. We were spoiled this summer. We have to get used to this. You'll go for a time for your job. I may go for mine. We have to adapt."

Shaking my head, I refused her hand or that plan. No. She had lived military life. She accepted it. Not me.

Never would I desert her or my children.

The thought—the plague of abandonment—it burdened my soul.

The magnitude of the strain pressed down upon me then, threatening to open my lips to explain why. Why I couldn't do this. Again.

She stole the silence between us, halting my confession.

"Daniel, think about it. They know you're coming to Wilmington. They'll be waiting for you there, looking for us. No one is looking here yet." She explained her strategy. "Between me, Silas, Pop, and Evelyn, no one can get on this island without notice. We have the advantage here. We're watching for *them*."

Bloody hell, her logic. On the one hand, I was always impressed with her. It was her job, her training. But sometimes she sounded obsessed. Like she was preparing for an ambush that would never come.

And to give into this? To what Mason had threatened with his barrage and then dearth of texts and other *White Flag* attacks?

We were doing exactly what she had insisted we not.

We were letting fear tear us apart.

"Charlie, we can't live secluded here forever. Even if I

give up my entire career. Or you do. It's a matter of time. Time we're letting Mason control if we let him bloody win."

I tossed the final pair of socks into my bag with the force of the hole I wanted to punch through a wall.

"I'm going to miss you, babe," I said. "I've waited too long to have this in my life, to have this with you and I don't ever want to leave you or the twins. Never will we choose our careers over our family. Especially when the distance is this close, this easy. We have to make this work."

I sat down next to her on the bed, kissing her hair, crushed by a grief I couldn't explain.

You can now, Pierce.

The logic of my burden would be obvious. But the truth would implode our beautiful world. The pressure crushing her, our children, everything I loved.

Don't do it. Don't take this from her. She's lost enough.

My head bowed in shame, resting it against her silken strands beside me. "Please go with me. Fight for us and compromise. Come with me to Wilmington. Check the house out. Have dinner with me, Greg, and his wife tomorrow night. They invited me over. If you don't want to stay, Simon will get you back here. Is that fair?"

She dropped her shoulders and sighed. "Okay. I confess, I'll miss you too. I don't want to go back to living in this house all alone." She nuzzled me, cheek to cheek. "I'll go with you tonight and check it out." She whispered in my ear, "But it's going to cost you."

Relief freed my muscles. *Yes, Pierce. The right way this time.* My lips traveled toward hers. "I'll pay you back all night, Sex Goddess."

"*That* and a foot rub, Sex God, with lots of oil."

I sealed our deal with an eager kiss.

My upper lip snarls, tension pulling at the singular muscle above my frustrated seethe.

I can't find them.

There are too many targets.

Searching for "Ravenel" is like firing at stones in the mountains. They are everywhere across the landscape.

There is nothing on the trail but screen silence from them... hiding somewhere.

I inhale and grit my teeth.

Not for long.

Duty calls Daniel Pierce back. Back to the studio. Back to the screen. Back to the limelight.

His Instagram account reliably brags about it.

Patience pours down my face, exhaling my breath, taking the moment to be sure to find my target this time.

One sure terrain to hunt next.

The Wilmington film studio where Daniel Pierce will

finally emerge. His celebrity face will lead my soldier directly to her.

CHAPTER FIFTY

DANIEL

Falling Like The Stars by James Arthur

This felt right.

Our bags were unpacked, our toiletries lined up neatly in the shower, the oil I rubbed every night on her belly sat on the nightstand. This Wilmington waterfront estate was stunning, but it was home because she was here with me.

For ten years it had festered inside, what I did, who I left behind. It was the ultimate act of love, the ultimate sacrifice. And the grief, the secret, it's been poison in my veins ever since.

But now, I was cured.

Every job, every move I'd plan around Charlie and our family. Nothing would keep me from making everything perfect for her.

Our compromise seemed to suit her too. She glowed, admiring peeks of the ocean between the houses while

Simon drove us through the palatial community we were renting in, pulling into the driveway of Greg Miller's rented home.

Over dinner, Charlie relaxed, enjoying the evening with Greg and Margaux.

Greg was my co-star on the film. We talked about bikes, mainly Ducatis, during dinner. Margaux, Greg's wife, was a producer and screenwriter. She talked long into the evening with Charlie while their two-year-old daughter slept upstairs.

Afterward, we ventured into the backyard. Greg lit the firepit. I sat, watching Charlie's face in the firelight, transfixed by the stories she told Margaux, stories I never knew.

Margaux asked Charlie questions about her service. She was fascinated with Charlie's work on the Marines' Female Engagement Teams.

It surprised me how forthcoming Charlie was with her story. Then again, Margaux was a writer. She had a way with her questions, putting Charlie at ease.

Marguax took a pensive sip of wine before asking, "How do you think they perceived you there, a female soldier in Afghanistan?"

"Like people do here," Charlie answered. "Some don't welcome women with power. At first, they didn't trust me. Didn't understand how I was twenty-six at the time, married, but had no kids. A truly foreign concept to them. But I was one of the few women interpreters the Marines had. I gave people lots of patience and smiles until they came around." The sincere one across Charlie's face was ironic to me. "They always do." Ironic because she lifted a Mason jar of lemonade up to her grinning lips.

The moment stilled me, marveling at her with humble pride.

Margaux spoke from a place of pity for the Afghan women. There were horrific stories Charlie shared, but she told Margaux it was a mistake thinking of the women as only victims.

"We're all alike," Charlie said, combing her fingers through her long mane. "We all do what it takes to survive, to live safe with our families."

"Speaking of..." Greg flicked the end of his cigarette into the fire. How he could maintain his physique and still smoke, I had no clue. But I liked the guy, looked forward to working with him. He was no bullshit, through and through. "How are y'all handlin' all this? That attack at the airport? Did they ever catch the guy?"

"Not yet." The reply strained up through my neck.

"Man, we had some run-ins," Greg said. "When Margaux was pregnant and we were in New York, fucking photographers and fans stalked us through SoHo every day. I swear they were around every corner. But no one ever came at us like that, not with violence."

"It's not photographers or fans we gotta worry about," Charlie said with her eyes on me. "It's Mason Hunt's *White Flag* zealots that are stalking us."

Something sounded hollow in her assessment, striking my ear.

And the look in her eyes?

It's like Charlie didn't believe all of what she just said. Like there was more she wasn't saying. The oddity stirred me.

"Well, shit," Greg sounded out, lighting a fresh Marlboro. "How do y'all guard against that? Those *White Flag* fucks can come from anywhere."

Greg and his no-bullshit observation pushed the difficult topic. He and Charlie spoke the same language. Greg was from Georgia, echoing her accent.

It fascinated me.

How people from the Southern states were all manners upon greeting them but get them drinking and rolling up their verbal sleeves on life and their poetic tongues took no prisoners with the truth.

"Yeah, they can come for us from anywhere." Charlie set her Mason jar on the arm of the white Adirondack chair she and her beautiful belly reclined in. "That's what I've been trying to explain to Daniel."

She left it there. In the air. The obvious conflict between us.

Margaux picked it right up. "Security and celebrity love together? Trying to join their opposing worlds? Now that's an interesting story too."

Indeed, it was.

It wasn't like I didn't appreciate the material threats against us. The fresh scar down my forearm reminded me every day.

"I've made concessions for her." I smiled at Charlie while I squirmed in conflict and adoration at the same time. "No more stopping for fan selfies or impromptu autographs, no matter how hard they beg."

"That panty-melting smile doesn't help my mission either, Pierce." Charlie's beautiful face hitched up in a half-cocked grin. "It always keeps 'em coming for more."

Her toying critique threw a log on the flames between us, sparking cinders up on what would surely be continued later at home.

"Tell me about it." Margaux pointed to Greg who was another big dose of masculine catnip.

Greg and I cast together on the Navy SEAL film was

designed to attract the demographics of yahoos who get hot for muscle heads and the fans who get wet at the sight. And all four of us laughed at the obvious industry ploy that paid us millions to do it.

"YOU NEVER FAIL to have me in awe of you, Charlotte Sophia Ravenel."

I stood behind her, cherishing our nightly ritual of a shower before bed. "I never knew those stories you told Margaux tonight. Watch. She's going to make a movie inspired by you."

Her head tipped back, trusting my expert shampooing of her tresses.

"Yeah, right. I'm no victor or victim. Just did what I had to."

She turned to face me. I ran the nozzle over the crown of her head, watching how water cascaded through her strands, how her eyes closed in complete trust of me.

The moment stopped my heart.

I put the nozzle up then hooked my finger gently under her chin, lifting her lips to mine.

"You're an incredible woman. I'm bloody lucky you love me." I cherished one soft kiss after another before nestling my nose down to hers. "Do you remember our holiday, on the beach that week, when you said we didn't have to say goodbye or forever, that we could just live in between?"

"Yes."

Her gaze joined me in the memory.

"I want you to know... there is no in-between in my love for you. It's going to be forever for me, Charlie Ravenel."

The admission. The promise. It brought my lips to hers again.

She returned my deep kiss before pulling back with a smile, the one she gave from her heart that crushed me every time.

"Then marry me, Daniel Balthazar Pierce, and promise me forever."

The words bloomed my sudden smile from ear to ear. "Did you just propose to me, Charlie?" It thrilled my heart. Pulling her and our belly closer, the joy made me wind her up. "Isn't the man supposed to do that?"

"Really?" Her eyes rolled with a big grin. "Since when do those bullshit roles apply to us?"

"So does this mean I'll have you barefoot, pregnant, *and* my ball and chain for life?"

I could do this all night, teasing the fuck out of her, knowing it pissed her off to the point of pleasure.

"Uh-huh. That'll happen, Pierce. You'll make water dry and fire cold too." She chuckled, resting her palms on my chest. "You can knock me up, but you can't knock me out."

I rubbed the tip of my nose against hers.

"Will you change your name to Charlotte Ravenel Pierce?"

"I'll change my damn name again if you change yours." Her eyes were laughing, pushing me right back. "I'm sure your agent, manager, and publicist would fucking love it if you did, Daniel Pierce Ravenel."

"Will you make our bed every day?"

Bloody hell, excitement coursed through me at the promise of so much more than shared house chores with her.

"All right, you lucky man, you'll be marrying a Marine, not a maid, so maybe. If I fuckin' feel like." The muss of her fingertips through my chest hair gently pulled me even closer. "Will you cook dinner and have it ready for me when I get home from work?"

"Who's been cooking for you the past seven months?"

"Will you do the laundry?"

"Who's been finding their clothes washed and folded at the foot of the bed every week?"

"Will you wash my hair every night?"

"Yes. Will you kiss my back and hold me from behind like you do?"

"Yes. Will you keep picking me up and carrying me all over the damn place? 'Cause secretly, I kinda love it sometimes."

I hovered my lips even closer. "As long as you keep being a cute smart-arse with this mouth I love."

God, happiness ruled me.

I'd held this wish in my heart for months. Hell, from the first night we met—I only wanted her for the rest of my life.

"Did we just write our vows?" she asked.

"You tell me. You're the one who proposed." I wanted to play with her forever. "Shouldn't you get down on one knee with a ring?" And now, I could.

"I don't have a ring, but you're the only man I'm willing to kneel to, Daniel Pierce." She grinned, swimming in the joy of our eyes.

I nudged her gently back up against the shower wall with my mouth. My hand sought its home between her sexy legs.

She said, "You still haven't answered me."

I didn't stop with my hand while I whispered in her ear, "I'm going to make us both moan yes."

CHAPTER FIFTY-ONE

CHARLIE

Black Sea by Natasha Blume

"This is gonna get ugly."

I watched the shitshow of Daniel, Greg, and the Navy SEAL cast taking shots of tequila the executive producers ordered for the cast party in honor of Halloween.

Sitting next to Margaux, counting how many times Daniel's lips met the glass, I knew too well how such parties end.

Not pretty.

It only amused me. Daniel had been a monk of devotion and discipline for two months. And damn if his body didn't show it. Millions of fans who watched the film would enjoy the fruits of his hard labor on the screen.

I sure enjoyed it now in the flesh.

"Greg's usually good about this." Margaux tossed back her last sip of wine. "Rarely does he blow off steam and get a little crazy with the guys, especially since Matilda's been born. But tonight is fine."

I dipped a carrot in hummus, sticking to my nutritional regimen.

"It's fine if we get to do the same. I swear, once I'm cleared from breastfeeding, I'm calling you for a mom's night out and these two cute fuckers can give us our turn."

Margaux and Greg had a babysitter while I nursed a ginger ale for me and the twins, kicking my heels up in a booth at the private club the production had reserved.

It was a swanky spot beside the river, tucked into an alleyway of the historic Wilmington promenade of bars, restaurants, and shops.

Daniel was all smiles and laughs. Coming over to lavish me with kisses, his sweet lips slurred words. Greg was the same.

Once they started throwing darts, I feared eyes would be lost by the end of the night. A night Margaux called done to get back to the babysitter.

"I'll go with you," I offered. The soaking bathtub at the house called my name. "Simon can get Tweedledee and Tweedledum home."

With a glance, I noted Simon at a cocktail table. Earbud in, a cup of coffee steaming under his nose, he was watching a cricket match on his phone.

When I told Daniel of my plans for an early exit with Margaux, he protested. "No, babe. Simon's taking you home."

Funny how Simon's name had four syllables with all the tequila in his blood stream.

"Hell no, handsome. Simon's bringing your drunk asses home whenever they kick you out." With a quick kiss to his Don Julio breath, I smiled. "Love you. Have fun."

With a few quick goodbyes, Margaux and I walked out the door, stepping into the mild fall night.

Even under night skies with ghoulish decor and costume-clad college students around, the air was mild. I didn't even need a sweater. With my body temperature up for three, I wore a fitted black long sleeveless maternity dress and flip-flops—fashion heaven for the pregnant.

Margaux led our path down the sidewalk toward the parking garage a few blocks up the street. We pointed at the costumes. There were a good number of pirates around which I appreciated in this port city to the Cape Fear Coast.

Concrete crunched lightly under the slide of my shoes.

Then I heard it...

Steps behind us.

The muscles along my spine tightened.

Someone was following us.

Pockets of people dotted the sidewalks on the holiday night. But the tingle across my earlobes told me the steps behind us were intentional, aimed at us on a night when I was already on edge.

Because for the first time in almost two months... I received a text today.

Unknown

Miss me?

Talk about adapting.

It took weeks—first of Mason's feast, then his famine of torment, along with my haunting instinct that kept constant vigil—for it all to take residence in my nerves.

It lived in me.

The turn of my chin wasn't required for me to be scanning the periphery. The cells in my body were constantly deployed, biologically wired, protecting more than myself now.

At first, I reacted with pure apathy at the words on the phone's screen. Calm and numb. Running the logic.

Mason's restraint had impressed me. But never would he be satisfied with leaving me alone.

His court date approached. The frustrating talks he must be having now? His lawyers presenting him with the mountain of evidence I'd collected against him, proving without a doubt that he stalked and tried to rape Kierra Williams.

It had to have Mason going home in fits of mania, itching for revenge.

But my apathy morphed into anger hours after. Getting ready for the evening, I caught a glimpse of my expectant belly in the mirror.

The idea of any threat to my children? It rasped my breath, filtering through my lungs, then my teeth with seething rage.

This waiting game tried the patience of all who played. With my body on a clock, ticking down, it dropped a veil of impatient fury over my eyes. Tired of fucking waiting, I wanted to fight, to end Mason.

I replied with a stream of texts to Mason before we left for the party.

You're the one texting me.

Missing me.

You can't stop yourself,

can you?

Proof = I control you

Margaux commented on the group dressed like Wonder

Woman across the street while I tuned in to the stalker behind us, stepping in cadence to our footfalls.

Turning down another block, one that was empty, the shadow still followed.

It flared my nostrils, clenching my jaw, ready to bite.

"Damn, baby, can I get some tasty fries with that hot-ass shake?"

The voice over my shoulder told me Mr. Wordsmith lurked about four steps behind. Another shuffle.

And he wasn't alone.

I glanced in the reflection of the window of the closed sub sandwich shop we were walking past.

Two college-aged guys. No costumes. Only drunken sneers dishing out street harassment to me and Margaux.

Margaux wore a velvet duster jacket with no display of her cute shaking ass. It had to be mine the dickhead was admiring. With my back to him, he didn't know I had more shake up front being five months pregnant with twins.

"Fuck off, little boy." I tossed the words over my shoulder.

That exchange got Margaux's attention. She glanced back at them.

I clocked the four-story parking garage up the block where Margaux had parked. And the security cameras at the entrance gate and pay station, recording our approach. The distance? Too great to quickly escape the creepy company stalking us.

"Fuck you, blondie. Your hot ass is mine. Like it or not."

My steps halted. Words like that? It poised the needle above my flesh. Sweating, I needed a drop of this.

Margaux took more steps away from the confrontation.

Oh, yes. Please. This drug. But the ball of my foot

pivoted, curling my cheek up in a cocky smile, swinging my aim toward the taunt.

"Clearly, dumbass." The presentation of my pregnant belly and angry eyes shot right through him. "None of me will ever belong to you."

Quick assessment—typical handsome college boy: arrogant, entitled... and drunk.

A dangerous mix to most young women.

A naïve underestimation of me.

The look of him tasted like Mason on my tongue.

His eyes and his friend's shocked back at the pregnant sight before them.

I stood here, nose down, leering at them, nostrils inhaling wafts of beer sweating from their AXE body spray pores.

"Damn, blondie. Hell yeah. I like me some kinky MILF action." The rise of his tanned left forearm, tracked by my pupils, reached for me. "Goddamn, you're hot. Especially with tits like this," grabbing my breast.

Pop! The heel of my right palm struck his nose, throwing his chin up, opening his neck to my lightning-fast left hook punching hard against his throat, taking his balance and breath away.

He staggered back, cupping the fountain of blood bursting from his nostrils. He fell, landing askew against the brick wall to his left, almost hitting the sidewalk.

I aimed my eyes next at his friend. "You want some too, asshole?" His hands were balled up tight while he glanced down at my full breasts. "The only thing you're fucking tonight is your fists or mine." I raised them fighting stance.

His palms flew up in surrender. "All right, bitch. I ain't hittin' no pregnant woman."

"Fuckin' right, you're not."

With a quick turn, I walked toward Margaux who stood, chin dropped at the sudden spectacle before her. "You okay?" Her eyes were wide. I followed her gaze, glancing back at the duo in shock on the sidewalk.

"Oh yeah," I said. "That felt good."

And it did.

All night while I soaked in the tub and then crawled into bed, the justified outburst released the tension from my nerves. The euphoria lasted into the next morning when I found Daniel passed out on the sofa where Simon had safely deposited him the night before.

The smell of breakfast cooking woke him. He walked into the kitchen, grabbing his skull like a vice grip crushed it, but with a smile on his face.

Yep, he had needed to blow off steam too.

Satisfaction tasted good to me in the morning until Daniel, sitting at the dinner table, took a call from Greg.

"She did what?" The tone in Daniel's voice lifted my eyes up from my orange slices. His aqua irises glared at me; chin cocked at whatever filled his ear. "Margaux all right?"

Oh fuck, Daniel was getting an update on my little ass-kicking adventure last night. Margaux must have told Greg, who was amused by. But the praise about me from Greg's mouth was not singing happy into Daniel's ear.

"Yeah, mate. See ya tomorrow." Daniel ended the call, setting his phone down on the table calmly while the veins in his neck rose with ire. "You want to tell me what happened last night, Charlie?"

"Don't talk to me like you're my father. Like I'm in trouble or something."

"No, I'm not your father." The stillness of his body demonstrated how he could act, holding one performance while another raged across his nerves. "But you will be my wife in a few weeks and the mother to our children, the three people I love the most, who it seems you took into a fight last night."

"Damn right I did. I popped some asshole's nose and throat. That's what he gets for fucking with me."

Bits of pulp burst delicious, sweet juice in my mouth while my bite ripped more flesh from the rind.

"Were you hurt?"

"Nope. He didn't stand a chance. Once he grabbed my tit, it was on, and he went down."

That lifted his shoulders off the back of the chair. "Some man grabbed your breast last night?"

"Yep. Dumb college boy, little fuck. He started harassing me and Margaux. When I confronted him, he tried to grab me."

"Goddammit, Charlie. Why did you confront him? Why didn't you just walk away and ignore him?" The clench of his fist never pounded down on the table, but I could tell he wanted to punch something. "There's too much at stake now for you to go fighting every time something comes at you. Or anyone else."

"Daniel, do you think because I'm almost a wife and mom that I'm gonna stop fighting? Stop defending myself or others? Hell no. In fact, I'll get worse. If someone comes at me, my kids, or you... they're fucking dead. I'll rip them apart, rearranging their guts and DNA too, all with a fucking smile on my face."

Visions of last night weren't in my head. Twelve hours ago was a distant flash across my mind.

All I could conjure then? Mason.

And something else even more distant scratching through my veins, rewiring my senses.

"It's one thing to defend yourself, Charlie. It's another to provoke a fight."

"I didn't provoke it."

You're full of shit, Charlie Girl. You could've kept walking and not saying a word.

The squint of Daniel's eyes called it out too. The man knew me too well.

"Are we going to get a visit from the police today?" he asked. "Or a call from an attorney suing you for assault?"

"No. He committed sexual battery, and I was justified. And it's on a surveillance camera. Besides, I like to read. I'll sit in jail and read books till I die. Or pay every damn dollar I'm charged in fines to do it again to that asshole and all like him who keep grabbing women like they fucking own them."

Daniel shook his head, rolling his eyes. That made him wince with the headache that clearly danced in his brain. But he was a grown man. He could suffer his consequence while I would mine.

Yep. You were itching like a million mosquito bites for a fight last night. No sense in denying it.

Scratching his fingernails across his hot-as-hell buzz cut scalp, he declared, "I don't know whether to be pissed off or proud."

"Both is kinda fun."

I took a bite of eggs, chewing and unapologetic... and starving for more.

"Yeah, it's only fun for *you* when you go all *Charlie* on some bloke."

"So, my name is a verb now?"

"Yep. I'm adding it to the Charlie-ism list." His handsome face flashed a hungry smile, eyes sparkling my way. "Because I'm never going to change you."

Reclining back, I wiped my lips with a napkin. "Do you want to change me?"

The look he gave told me exactly what he wanted from me... in probably less than hour.

"Never."

He knows he's being hunted.

Daniel Pierce was spotted leaving the film studio a few times.

But attempts to tail him failed, losing his black car in the congested highway traffic.

And then.

Nothing.

The black car hasn't returned to the studio. Each car driving in or out of the studio gates shows no sign of his famous face behind a car window.

But he must be there.

Last week, he was spotted leaving the nearby local coffee shop, a watering hole for the cast and crew at that studio. It was a quick shot, a flash of his face ducking into a white sedan with two paper lidded cups stacked in his hand. Then the car disappeared, darting down nearby streets.

A few days ago, Daniel Pierce was spotted on the beach, running with Greg Miller, his co-star and apparently his workout companion now.

But her?

No sightings anywhere.

She must be there too. Daniel Pierce will never abandon his mate.

A hunch hit me. Ah, this was too easy. I was almost going to miss.

Because there's one sure spot to hunt.

The over-priced, locally sourced organic grocery store. The one near the multi-million-dollar waterfront homes in that exclusive gated community.

The store is like a Mecca for the rich and famous.

Watch and wait.

One of them or that white car will be spotted there.

And then?

Follow the trail home to its bloody end.

CHAPTER FIFTY-TWO

DANIEL

everything i wanted by Billie Eilish

"Babe?" I called out across the darkness of the house, setting my duffel bag down on the foyer floor. "You left the front door unlocked."

What the hell? I couldn't see a bloody thing either.

I knew she was here. Simon told me that he'd taken her to that posh grocery store earlier. That Charlie was getting stir crazy and needed to get out, saying she wanted to cook a fancy late dinner for me.

Was she playing a sexy game?

The thought thrilled me as I walked down the dark foyer into the living room with a vaulted ceiling and massive windows to the waterway.

The golden silhouette of her hair shone against the faint lights twinkling across the water.

"Hey, beautiful." I used my playful voice, my steps traveling around to stand in front of her, excited for what I'd find.

She sat on the upholstered chair, staring at the windows, cute in one of her pretty maternity sundresses.

But my sudden glance down punched my heart.

A gun, it was in her hand, resting in front of her beautiful swelling belly.

"Charlie?" The sight flooded me with sick fear.

Her eyes were wide open. The stillness of her body, bizarre.

She turned slowly to peer up at me.

I could tell by her stare back... she wasn't hallucinating.

"Keep the lights off," she calmly instructed.

"Charlie, what are you doing?" The black weapon in her lap. Should I fear her... or be worried for her? "Where did you get that gun?"

"It's my gun, Daniel. Someone's out on the water. Two o'clock."

She sounded sane.

What she said wasn't.

I turned and looked out over the inky dark waves.

A faint green starboard light on a boat twinkled at two o'clock on the horizon. You could barely see it bobbing in the darkness, but it loomed there.

"Charlie, boats are always out there." I looked back at her. Understanding. She was on guard, not taking her eyes off that green light. "Babe, you're scaring me. Put the gun down. It's just someone taking a stop, fishing or anchored for the night."

"No. It's a bad place to fish or drop anchor. And it hasn't been there before. I know every fixed light on this horizon now, just like I do the ones at home. It came in tonight, and I saw it. It's masking its masthead and stern lights. I think there's tape over the duo light in front, but I still see it. I've been watching it all night."

CHARLIE

I WAS STANDING in the kitchen, cooking dinner.

With a quick flick of my eyes up from prepping some shrimp for the grill, I spotted the green light on the water.

Suddenly, pieces from the past year dropped into place like bloody drips across a calendar.

May. The viral photo of my distinct scars passed out in #danielpierce's arms at the Madrid gym.

June. The feeling I got in Menorca when they shot *The Druid* there, sure someone stood in the shadows, following Daniel's trail to confirm it was me.

July. The New York film premiere and press, his global interviews with my battalion photo and my Marine name, confirming our connection.

August. The attack at the airport, the Comic-Con photo of me working security on his show and the leak of my maiden name.

September. The fire at his house in Madrid where they shot *The Druid*.

And all the evil internet trolls searching for Daniel year-round to now, November, and shooting a film in Wilmington.

It wasn't only Mason and his *White Flag* fanatics hunting like sadistic bloodhounds, trying to find our scent.

It was my instinct for six years, telling me... more were on the same lethal trail.

They followed Daniel... and they found you.

I had turned off all the lights in the house, pulling my gun from its holster in my backpack.

When it was me alone, I waited for them to come for me, making it easy by unlocking the doors.

All someone had to do was try to enter and I'd take the shot. And I never missed.

But now with him home, I didn't want to scare him.

Gently, I set my gun down on the floor. It was close enough though—with the safety off—for a one-second reach.

Daniel

I LOOKED AGAIN.

She was right.

It was a dangerous place to anchor. The other required lights would be lit on the boat if they were fishing.

Someone was hiding out there. Probably paparazzi trying to snap pictures.

Simon already had to drop three tails on us my first week leaving the studio. The paps had parked down the street, watching for my car exiting the gate, following us down the highway until we lost them.

So now Simon drove two different cars. Charlie refused the obvious big black SUVs that the principal cast typically use. Instead, she rented a used white sedan and a sport 4x4 with no rental decals. They looked like a car a crew member would drive. She even put local bumper stickers on them.

Now I rode up front with Simon, lying down in the seat until we were blocks away from the studio gates before I sat up. It was bloody insane, but Charlie had insisted, and Simon agreed.

"All right, babe. Yes, I see them. What do you want to do? Call the police?"

"No. It's international waters. They can be out there if they want. But they know we're here. This is why I didn't like this house for you, for us. We need something inland, in this gated community but not open like this. We're sitting ducks here."

"Fine. I'll call Elaine and rent something else. We will go to a hotel tonight or to Greg's down the street. I don't care. But why the bloody hell are you sitting here with a gun? Have you been hiding that on you all this time?"

I trusted her more than anyone. But I didn't know she had that gun. It unnerved me. Yes, I used them on sets. Hell, I used one in character now.

But that was fiction, a fake gun.

This was my pregnant fiancée, sneering with a loaded one in her hand.

I never grew up with a gun in the sanctity of my home. To see a real one in her hand or resting by her feet, in front of her pregnant belly with our children, it was disturbing. Especially with the obsessive, deadly look she had in her open eyes.

Like she was coaxing their next move to attack.

"I keep it at home in a special strap hidden under my nightstand," she said. "I only take it out to clean it. I never took it with me." She looked up at me, touching her belly. *"But I do now."*

"Charlie. They're the paparazzi, not the bloody Taliban. You don't need to carry a gun around. It's bloody insane."

She stood up fast with a rush of anger down her face.

"That's not fair, Daniel! I know this isn't Afghanistan. And it isn't fucking London or Madrid either. You don't know how it is here. There's a lot worse that can hurt you than a damn knife. We grow up fearing it. It's everywhere. Presidents. Politicians. Celebrities. Concerts. Dance clubs. School children, for God's sake. This isn't a fucking film, Daniel. It's dead fucking real."

"I know." The taste of regret was sudden in my mouth. "I'm sorry. I didn't mean it like that." Her face was full of pain, her words full of truth. "Guns aren't a part of my life at home. I know they're a real threat here."

I looked back at the water, back at the green light floating there, waiting for the lights in our home to come on so they could get a good shot at us.

If Charlie or I stepped outside of the house, the picture would be legal. But they couldn't publish anything taken of us inside the home.

Still, they would be watching us the whole time.

Fuck, now I understood why she didn't like this house. Elaine didn't know better renting it. Neither did I.

"Let's call Greg and Margaux tonight." My arms reached out for her. "We'll stay with them, find a place nearby tomorrow, and get Simon to help us pack up."

"Thank you."

Her shoulders relaxed in my embrace.

"But, Charlie, you've got to let this go. I know the press is hard, that some of my fans are bloody cruel towards you. And I know Mason and his fucking texts disturb us. But keeping a gun under a nightstand in case of something is one thing. Sitting with it in your lap or by your side is another. It's like you're obsessed."

I stepped back, holding her arms, searching her eyes. "I won't live like that. Afraid all the time with guns around our house, around our children. Fucking hell, I look at your beautiful face every day and see what they've already done to you. I hate them."

CHARLIE

I SEARCHED his eyes and saw his resolve.

But I had mine too.

"Daniel, I'll always be safe and discreet with a firearm. I'm fucking trained. If I use it, there will be a good reason and I'll end it in one shot. And I don't care if they're just your zealot fans. Or Mason's crazy followers. I have to protect us at all times."

"I can protect us too. Between the two of us, we don't need guns to be safe all the time."

I scanned his hulking, muscular arms holding mine, the tight tan T-shirt he wore hugging his massive carved pecs, stretching over his tapered, shredded abs.

He had no fucking clue.

"All it takes is one bullet to change everything," I said. "All the muscle, workouts, and martial arts in the world can't protect you from it. Yes, you see the evidence on my body every day. And now, this—"

I gestured to the boat bobbing on the water, mocking me, shattering our peace and bliss.

His nostrils flared. "Babe, they're bloody photographers. They are going to hound us for years. And I'm sorry for that. To bring you, to bring our children into this. This was the part of my life I feared you'd hate. That you'd want to leave. But you said you could survive it. So you need to make peace with it. Quit fighting everyone and carrying guns around. They're not going away."

I sucked my teeth, stubborn determination storming through me. "Yeah, well, me, my fists, and my .380 aren't going away either."

He dropped his arms.

"Fine. You be fucking stubborn and so will I." Punching his finger toward the boat hunting for us. "I bloody refuse to live in fear over this. We're going to get married and have a normal, happy life as much as we can. We're going to play on the beach with our children, take them for ice cream, and drive them to school without living on guard all of the goddamn time."

Anger rose on his face along with his voice. "Your fear isn't imprisoning our lives any more than my fame already does."

"It's not living in fear," I insisted. "It's living safe."

One sure thought kept firing through me, forcing my sudden tears and words to fall. "Daniel, I can't bear the thought of..."

I stopped—remembering funerals and hospitals—holding it back so tight behind my lips with saline drops of my terror trickling over them.

His gaze bore into me. "Charlie, what is it?"

He took a half step back, scrutinizing my stance, my silence.

"I can see it in your eyes," he said. "I've heard it in your voice before. You're not telling me something. You don't need a gun to protect us from fans or photographers or online bullshit. You're the strongest, smartest person I know, so tell me now. What are you really fighting? What are you so afraid of?"

I looked out of the window into the dark water—staring past the green light stalking us—seeing through the night into my darkest fear.

Tell him. Tell him about your lunatic moon in the day sky. The one that's hunted you for six years.

"Daniel. It's more than that." My chin nodded toward the boat lurking on the water.

When I lived alone, I knew it to be true—someone was coming for me. So, I hid by myself, ready for the ambush. Ready to end it all.

But now with him? With our love? With the hope of his babies growing inside of me, sharing my heartbeat and blood pumping through us all?

It changed me.

Maybe it wasn't real. Maybe it was like what Evelyn said. It was my PTSD. I needed to make peace with it. If I didn't, it would rip us apart—my mind and family gone.

With a deep breath, letting the tears burst from my heart, I turned back to him, anchored to his aqua eyes and let my storm assail.

"I'm afraid that something bad is going to happen. I know it is. For six years now, it's been warning me. Like I knew about Mason, knew about Kathy, or knew at the airport, or other times in the past. I can always sense a threat coming, and I've always been right."

I huffed my next confession. "But my PTSD. I know my mind can play tricks on me. You've seen it yourself."

His gaze wouldn't leave mine—listening to my truth. Could he handle more?

"But I can't make it stop, Daniel. It's haunting me. Every. Single. Day. And I never told you about it, how bad it is, because I know it sounds crazy."

The look in his eyes turned to torment. Like when we were on our knees in the kitchen after my last hallucination.

But I wouldn't hold back, not anymore.

I couldn't carry our children and this burden anymore.

If this was my ruin, today was its birth.

"Daniel, since the day I was shot, the only emotion I felt was fear. I never wanted a family or to love again. Because I knew it would be taken from me. But now? Since I met you? I do want it. I want this love with you. It's so beautiful. Our children. Our marriage. I want it all. Your love almost makes my fear go away. In your arms, it's the only time I feel sane, or feel safe. And I can almost have hope and be happy…

"But then shit like this happens." I pointed toward the boat. "And I don't know if I'm correct or crazy."

No stopping it. The dam broke and all my terror flooded out.

"Either way"—I wiped the streams from my cheeks—"I suffered it in silence, because I love you and I didn't want you to think I was crazy. But I can't help it. I'm living every day with you in a wonderful dream and a deadly nightmare, all at the same time."

"Oh my God, babe." He wrapped his arms around me. "This? This is what you've been feeling? What's been hurting you all this time?"

"Yes." The smell of him was pure comfort. "But I don't know anymore—is it my truth or my trauma? And I couldn't tell you if I didn't know myself."

"Charlie, please. You won't suffer or merely survive. Not anymore. Not alone. We're doing this together, loving each other, getting married, having kids. I'm in this with you." He pulled back, cradling my jaw in his hands. "You're always so strong, so brave, so I had no idea you were this afraid too."

"I don't know what to do anymore." I let him—only him —see this truth. "I need help." It trembled my lips, this vulnerability only he could hold. "I'm tired of feeling this way. I want to be happy like you, like everyone else."

He pressed his forehead mine. "I've bent my heart and my life in circles for you, and I've cherished every moment of it and I'll never stop changing for you. I'll do whatever. Whatever you need to feel safe. To be happy. And I'll never think you're crazy." He smiled. "I'll just keep thinking that you're the real hero, the sexy badass between us."

He said the last part to make me smile.

It worked.

That and the suffocating burden lifting off my fractured heart, of finally confessing it all to him.

Relief started filling in the cracks. I inhaled. Hopefully, happiness and peace followed next.

And he believed me, holding me again. He didn't think I was crazy.

Then I felt it—the hammering of our hearts pressed together.

Did it mean I was correct?

CHAPTER FIFTY-THREE

CHARLIE

"Juliette sent this special delivery." I set the global parcel box down on the kitchen table. "She texted, said we had to open it together."

We shared a rare night off for Daniel, cooking dinner, enjoying it to the fullest in our new inland rental home down the street from our old one.

Simon had taken me to the grocery store again today. I was craving salmon, the little potatoes Daniel liked to roast, and all the fixings for a salad.

One more week and we were done in Wilmington. Maybe a few more days if they needed Daniel for reshoots. But so far, it looked like we would be home with days to spare before our November twenty-fifth wedding.

"Who gets the honour of opening it?" Daniel rested his hand on my waist, the other took a healthy gulp of Guinness.

"It's your turn. I opened the last two your parents sent over."

Setting the beer down, his grip seized the box, ripping the perforated ribbon. Inside was a gift box, elegantly wrapped in white paper with an incandescent blue pearl ribbon.

Ah, if Juliette didn't note every detail. Knowing exactly what blue pearls meant to us. The matching necklace Daniel gave me months before dangled from my neck.

With gentle rips and tears, he opened that box, peeling back the gossamer tissue paper. Two perfectly folded white infant onesies rested side by side. One with the Stars and Stripes. One with the Union Jack.

It was the cutest, most perfect present ever, making us chuckle with "aahs".

Daniel's fingertips cherished down the tiny garments. "Question is, who wears which one?"

I nestled against his bare arm, grasping his hand. "Equal and sharing, remember?"

"It looks like something is under them." He pulled out a blue velvet ring box hidden by the baby gift. It made me gasp while he lowered to his knee beside me, opening the lid.

All my sudden assumptions were right—Juliette had schemed with Daniel to make this moment happen. One that had my heart pounding to see him on bended knee. Only the look in his adoring eyes was more dazzling than the jewel before me.

"I've been wanting to do this for months," he said, taking my hand, "but per our custom, I waited for you. And you were worth it. These past months with you, Charlie, they make all my years before grey. You saved me; you colour my days with love and all I want now is every brilliant, bright moment with you."

His words, his love. They were perfect. But the ring. It

was too much. The grand, circular diamond was an obvious estate piece, something cherished and from his family, humbling me. "Daniel, it's too beautiful. I can't—"

"Yes, you can." He read my mind, lingering the ring over the tip of my wedding finger. "It's from my family, from my heart so it belongs with you, like I do." My hand trembled in his.

"Charlotte Sophia Ravenel." His was clammy with nerves. "Will you honour me and let me be your husband? Forever?"

He switched the traditional ask for me, making me laugh through happy tears. So, I did the same, respecting the ritual for him.

"Yes, Daniel Balthazar Pierce. I would be honored to be your wife."

The ring slid down my finger while more tears slid down my face. He stood up, cradling my wet jaw in his shaking hands, sealing the moment with kiss after kiss, melting away my every last piece. Only love. Only joy now.

He nuzzled his nose to mine. "Forever fifty-fifty. Promise, Mrs. Pierce?"

Winding me up with his cocky smile, it always worked, making me fire back. "Yes. I promise. Forever equal, Mr. Ravenel."

Something about the evening, about daring to more than imagine, it was real for me. This was happening. The onesies, the ring, his proposal. We'd be married in two weeks and parents in over two months.

Years I could finally see, surrounded by family, engulfed in his love.

A new feeling dawned in my world—bliss and hope. Fear diffused into nothing. Gone.

I couldn't remember the last time... no... never had I been this happy.

Later, while Daniel washed my hair, standing in the shower, my gaze went up to his. Regarding him with this new focus, it healed my heart, it molded me even more into his curve, into his love.

I'd say the words later, over rings, in front of loved ones. But I felt it then. The full circle. Born into love and light, I was thrown into hell, a freezing isolation. Until him, my warm, wet spring, a renewal, a love I earned again.

It had me reaching for him, needing him, but finding him limp in my grasp. Not his usual state naked beside me.

He jolted back, surprised by my touch. "You need to get your sleep, babe." His eyes didn't meet mine, focused instead upon returning the shower nozzle to its hold above our heads.

The crush was sudden. One I'd never felt before. His innocent rebuke trampled my ego. Smashing me so small. Taking my breath, my confidence.

"You don't want me now?" The words emerged insecure, unfamiliar across my lips. Where they came from, I didn't know. But it was real, washing over my naked body standing before his.

"Babe, what?" His looked down at me. Surprised. Confused.

"Because I'm so pregnant, you don't find me sexy anymore?"

It was too powerful to hide. Because all I saw before me was his beauty. One I wanted. Beside me. Inside me. Always.

The wet clasp of his hands around my cheeks lifted my eyes to his.

"Is that what you think? That I don't find you sexy

now?" A peck of his lips landed on the tip of my nose. "I'm just worried I've been waking you with all my early alarms, that you need rest."

His lips reached for mine, gently taking my bottom one before his tongue, intimate at first, then hard, dominated my senses, radiating a surge through my body. Sinking even deeper into him, a hunger, a craving for him, it ached between my thighs. His lips, his tongue, they took my mouth, giving back all the breath I needed.

God his kiss, how it reached for me, pulling me to him with no shame. Securing my body to his, to whatever he desired, to whatever I craved. His tongue over mine promised an erotic ride, a sure, orgasmic end.

The length of him, not limp anymore, it pressed, urging against my hip. "Can I show you how sexy you are to me, Charlie?" His mouth barely left mine, skating over my lips, relishing our connection. "How I'll never stop wanting you." His hand, gliding down my back, teased over my crevice. "How years from now, I'll wake my wife, wanting to fuck you hard." His other swirled over my nipple. "How I'll take you on a date and eat your pussy out 'til it's dripping wet and not care if we get caught." His hands didn't stop. "Will you let me show you?"

Hell yes, I would. I put my back to him, offering my hands up against the wet tile. He curved behind me, his palms cupping my breasts, fingertips swirling firm and wet over my sensitive nipples. The heat of his breath and words steamed through every pore of my being.

"You're the sexiest woman I've ever seen." His fingers played, seeking under me, the tip of his middle finger teasing circles over and again, igniting my clit. A moan left my lips, my body responding to his hard cock sliding between my cheeks. "And you'll be my fit woman, forever to fuck." His firm crown pushed, urging in. "Feel what you do to me? How much I want you, Charlie?"

"Yes, Daniel." Wife, mother, Marine, protection officer —whatever role I chose to play—none could shame me into giving this one up. Woman with so much lust. Desire for him—I was equally entitled to that too.

The beautiful power of it. Wrapping his body around mine, pressing into me, his palms over my hands, holding them tight, every part of him gently took me from behind. Knowing with his exact slow, guiding tempo how to take his time and take me with him.

There was no part of me, no nerve, no cell, no breath that wasn't joined with his, fused to him.

"I love you like this, Charlie." His whisper not leaving my ear. His cock rubbing against that perfect, exquisite spot he found inside me months back, promising relief, pleasure only he could provide. "So much." The rasp in his breath held me, drawing me up, sure and ready for a lush shower over him. "Do it, babe." All I needed; he knew. He had. "For me."

And he gave it to me, everything I ever wanted.

CHAPTER FIFTY-FOUR

CHARLIE

The next night? A different craving.

"Pretty please." I teased him, tickling my big toe up his thigh on the sofa across from me. "I can't sleep tonight without chocolate in my mouth."

"So, it starts now?" he asked. "The nightly cravings?" Annoyance failed him. The look on his face was only amused.

"Yes. Heads will roll if I don't get something sweet and sinful in my mouth."

"We don't need to go to the grocer's for that." His fist clutched his generous package under his pants. "I got something for your mouth right here."

He was joking because exhaustion creased his smiling face. Still, he always made me laugh.

"No offense," I said, "but for the first time, I'm not craving you. I need Snickers. Now."

He patted my foot, starting to rise. "What else is on the order for tonight?"

This man was the delicious one. Tired after a four-a.m. call time and a twelve-hour shoot, regardless, he was up and willing to satisfy me.

"Let's go to the pharmacy," I said. "I need to pick up my vitamins anyway. And they have a frozen section too."

I started to get up and had to pause, shifting my weight to stand. My growing belly was a drill sergeant now, dictating which way I had to turn and twist.

"Oh, now we're adding ice cream to the order?"

An even bigger smile lifted his lips while he offered me his hand. Okay, maybe I did need a bit of help to stand.

I took it. "We'll stock up tonight to avoid a run tomorrow. Let's call for Simon. He's got to get used to this too."

"Can we not, babe? It's just to the CVS. Not the studio." The tension in his deep tone signaled another potential impasse. "The poor chap was up at three thirty to fetch me. Let him sleep."

Most of me wanted to refuse. We needed Simon. That was part of the deal. At a minimum, we'd have at least one guard with us, even on personal outings. Between Mason's texts and my fear, Daniel had agreed.

But this new part of me—the one with impulsive cravings, joy, and hope—it felt guilty, understanding why Daniel didn't want to summon Simon for a fifteen-minute trip to the store and back.

"All right," I said, reaching for my backpack by the front door. "No Simon."

Daniel would know the signal. If my backpack came with me, so did my gun. No extra bodyguard meant I had to be armed.

Another term he had agreed to.

We took the white Toyota sedan we'd rented. It screamed "grandmother" not "A-list celebrity."

I drove, of course. Daniel made me nervous with his driving—one side of the road in the UK, the other side here. As a result, he hugged the center line, making me grab the "oh shit" handle like any minute would be our last.

"Hey, Curtis." I waved to the guard at the gate to our community, having memorized everyone in the guard house.

With a quick step out of his booth, he waved back. "Evening, Ms. Roberts. Mr. Pierce."

The gate quickly swung open while my impatient foot eased the gas pedal down, seeking chocolate.

During the five-minute drive, habit found me checking the mirrors every thirty seconds, finding only quiet local traffic on a Monday night. I added aloud more sweets to our shopping list while I parked the car in the lot outside the lone, square building.

With a click, I unbuckled my seat belt.

"No. Stay here, babe." Daniel did the same. "You'll only slow me down and bankrupt me in the candy aisle if you come in too."

"God made you hot so you could say shit like that to your pregnant fiancée and get away with it."

Sitting there, grinning sexy with his Carolina Panthers baseball hat over his shorn head with woodland cammie pants and a black T-shirt on, Daniel really did look more like local military than an A-list celebrity. Making us both relax since he finally blended in.

I noticed his gait had changed too since he started filming. He walked like a proud soldier, not a smoldering model for the camera. He even did that thing with his chin, jutting it up in a "wassup" recognition instead of aiming it down with a wolf-gaze at his intended.

Votes on going back to the sexy-model look instead of

puffed-up dude were unanimous on my part. But it was part of his performance. He'd drop it soon enough.

"Anything else?" With a lean over the console for a peck, he asked, "Or shall I nick the entire ice-cream section too?"

"That's it." I planted a soft kiss on his lips before my reminder. "Don't forget my prescription, please. I need chocolate but these two need their vitamins."

With a quick smile, he was out and closing the car door. His peacock pecs strolled across the parking lot with two fluorescent streetlights zapping above.

I swooned, watching his massive V-tapered back and incredible peach of an ass enter through the sliding glass doors.

A *ping* shattered the happy air. I glanced down at my phone on the console.

Unknown
Is it time yet?

Goddammit. I couldn't even have this moment—a rare one when I was actually relaxed. Yes, by my measure, relaxed required a .380 in my backpack, but it was progress.

Fuck him. What did he mean by "time yet?" Mason couldn't know about my pregnancy. He was just fucking with me.

My reply:

You're the one who should
be concerned with time.
Soon. Behind bars

The triple blinking dots thrilled me, like having a shark on the line.

Unknown
No matter where I go, my
reach will find you

I kept reeling him in.

> Do it and I'll reach my hands
> around your neck. Again

Adding the middle finger emoji before I sent it.
The tension building. Dots blinking.

Unknown
I will take much more from
you than your hands on my
skin.
You will be mine

Impatience wasn't pumping through my veins. Certainty was. Mason dangled right here, ready on the hook.

Do it, Charlie Girl. Yank his ass in the boat with you.

> You'll never control me &
> you'll never have me,
> Mason Hunt

•••

The blinking lights of his coming reply made me smile, ready for him to emerge.

Unknown
I will take everything from
you, like you took from me.
You & that cunt Kierra. I
control you both. To the vile
end

Got him. The screenshot I took of his text was sent with a fast *whoosh* to Agent Cooper.

That was too easy. I stared at the phone screen, at his guilty reply. *Yes, Mason can be taunted. But why now? Why reveal himself now?*

A shiver shocked down my spine. The phone lit up in my hand, ringing with a call from a local area number.

"Hello?"

"Ms. Roberts?"

"Yes."

"It's Curtis at the guard house. You just drove by, ma'am?"

"Hey, Curtis. What's up?"

My eyes stared out the front windshield, watching a truck pull into the almost empty parking lot. Only a few employee cars were parked at the far edge. The black Ford F-150 creeping by captured my attention.

"I'm sorry to bother you ma'am. But you drove out and I forgot to give you a flower delivery that was dropped off a couple of hours ago."

Lately delivery trucks had trampled a trail to our house from friends and family sending gifts for our pregnancy and wedding announcement. Usually, though, they were left at our front door.

"Curtis, why didn't you let them through to the house?"

"It wasn't a marked delivery truck, ma'am. It's our policy to collect such items at the gate and contact the resident for pickup."

Something darkened inside me... and in the parking lot —the truck's lights a couple of rows back. It lurked out of the glow of streetlights, turning off the engine.

"Hey, Curtis." I reached for the handle of my backpack, setting it on the passenger seat.

"Yes, ma'am?"

"Who are the flowers from, please? Go ahead. Read the card."

"Yes, ma'am." The sound of ripping paper filled my ear, along with the opening zipper on my backpack. A small pause held my breath while my stare held the rearview mirror. "It just says, 'Congratulations.' Nothing else, ma'am. Doesn't say who it's from."

The breath I held dropped from my lungs. "What color are the flowers?"

"It's a big bouquet, all yellow."

Mason! *Oh fuck! He found you.* The same color of flowers he hid in Kierra's bag when he stalked her on set in Spain. *And he knows you're pregnant.*

"What kind of truck was it?" My thumb unsnapped the gun holster.

"Black F-150, ma'am."

"Curtis, call the police now. Tell them we have a suspected break-in. Possibly armed. Have them check the house."

As I ended the call, my stare flicked to the doors of the

pharmacy. Daniel was still inside. Fuck. He left his phone on the passenger seat.

A shadow darted. Out of the corner of my eye. Across the rearview mirror. It disappeared behind our car.

Never taking my eyes off the mirror, I pulled the weapon from its holster. My palm wrapped around the familiar ridged handle, thumb flipping the safety off, the first round of six already racked in the chamber.

My other hand called 911.

With a glance around my periphery, nothing but black filled my vision punctuated by the two streams from the streetlights and the fluorescent glow through the high commercial windows and front glass doors of the pharmacy.

Those sliding doors opened. Daniel's strapping silhouette, always known to me, appeared in the doorway.

"911. What's your emergency?"

Shit. No time. I needed three fucking hands. One for the gun. One for the phone. One to open the car door. To protect Daniel. He stepped out of the building, onto the sidewalk, heading toward our car.

I set the phone on the console. With a glance in the sideview mirror, I hit the automatic button, lowering the mirror to scan to the ground. Driver's side? Clear.

"Hello? 911. What's your emergency?" The operator asked again.

"I need police. Now. I'm six months pregnant and I have an armed man stalking me. He's outside my car right now. At the CVS at Gordon and Market."

There. That would bring backup.

Daniel approached, thirty steps away and closing toward the car. My left hand popped the lever of the car door. My left foot kicked it open while both hands secured my target, aiming my weapon at darkness down the side of the car. Both feet hit the pavement, with adrenaline coursing through my pregnant body, I stood quickly, steps and target gunning toward the back of our car.

Like a slow-motion lightning flash, it always happened.

A large figure. In a camouflaged jacket. Leapt out from behind the car. Toward Daniel.

My aim tracked the sudden movement, sights and quick steps following the path to him.

"Daniel!" was all I could scream as the threat approached him.

The white plastic bags in Daniel's hand dropped to the pavement; his large figure eclipsed by the man charging toward him.

The hitch in the man's right shoulder rose with his fist, a twelve-inch hunting knife gleamed in it, stabbing for Daniel.

The tip of my index finger poised over the trigger, tendons in my second knuckle pulling, the pressure against it, building...

My aim; front sight tracking the assailant's moving head, back sight, framed the shot, ready to fire.

Over the assailant's left shoulder, Daniel's right fist, it fired down first. The strike powered by his bruising arm bombed the man in a thud to the pavement. Back down on the ground, but curling up again, he surged, striking again, the hunting knife still clenched in his fist.

But Daniel dropped his massive thighs, crushing his left knee over the assailant's arm, pinning the weapon down while he unleashed his across his face, bashing the man's head with a rage I'd never seen.

The knife dropped from his grasp, but Daniel's fists wouldn't stop. Left hook. Right hook. Left hook. Right hook.

Over and over. Deploying a frenzied, bloody retaliation. The man? Out cold to Daniel's inferno assault.

"Daniel! Stop!" My aim covered him. He didn't hear me. "Daniel! Stop it! He's not worth it."

Fuck, he was going to kill him. The strength in Daniel's demolishing fists across the attacker's face was enough to lethally swell a brain too big for the skull he pounded.

Sirens neared. I closed the distance. My aim pivoted, still on the attacker. One pull of my trigger finger and sudden death was certain.

"Daniel! Stop! Stop now! You're going to kill him."

Staying clear of his swinging blows, my left hand touched his back. The muscles flexing in fury under his T-shirt dripped with raging sweat. With a heave from his shoulders, breath huffing, his momentum stopped to my touch.

My aim kept protecting him while he found his sanity, kneeling over the assailant while two police cars with tires squealing raced into the parking lot.

The only thing I feared now was my pulse, so high. Then and over the next hour while I sat in the passenger seat of our car with the door open. Giving my statement. Waiting patiently while the officers conducted their investigation of the scene. Answering the same questions over and over. I offered Agent Cooper's contact information to help their investigation.

The white pillowcase in the sleeve of the assailant's jacket was all they needed.

That and the immediate recognition from me that it was the same man from the airport who had cut Daniel.

Surveillance video from the airport would match his appearance. But it wasn't the sight that confirmed it. It was his scent—tobacco and hunting pine—wafting up my highly-acute pregnant sense of smell. Then I scoped his face and clothing. Same hat. Same jacket.

Once we were cleared to leave the scene, Daniel insisted on taking me to the emergency room. He wouldn't take no for an answer or my reluctance to being a passenger this time, though his knuckles looked like they needed more medical care than my expectant belly.

Indeed, the ER doctor confirmed.

I was fine.

Because my heart rate dropped to a calm certainty lying on the crinkled white paper over the hospital bed, arm pressure cuff constricting then releasing over my bicep, cold jelly across my belly while the wand searched to confirm...

We were more than fine.

Because Mason Hunt was done.

CHAPTER FIFTY-FIVE

The Fear by The Score

All that was in my sight. Pounding my heart. Fueling my fists.

Charlie. Our twins. My family.

Nothing but rage at any threat against them had possessed me, unleashing my fury. I had no thought, just a sudden attack to protect everything I loved.

I felt it seize me—the brute, primal urge to end the menace. A bloody outburst of a madness to kill.

Mason's face had spewed blood under the explosion of my fists across his pretty face. Every hook, every swing across my target, crushed the torment, all the torture these past months.

Now? I finally understood Charlie on a cellular level.

How it felt to fight for something—no, someone—and to forget yourself. All I wanted in that moment? To protect everyone I loved.

Never would I think she was crazy.

No. I respected her even more, knowing now what it was like, willing to sacrifice your life for someone else's.

And Charlie did the same for me. She stopped me. The gentle, electrifying brush of her fingertips across my back seized my attack. She protected me from killing that man, from carrying that burden on my soul.

With her singular touch, I was alive, my senses returning, vision realizing... it wasn't Mason.

It was the man from the airport. His noxious smell was distinct to my nostrils.

Charlie brought me back. To her. To our twins. Were they okay? I'd looked up and all I could see was the black muzzle of her gun aimed at the threat against me, protecting me, protecting our babies, our future.

And it was done.

The ambulance took the man in cuffs and the nightmare away.

I stood, holding Charlie's hand in the emergency room at a different hospital, watching the white wand press into the glistening gel across her miraculous belly... making sure.

We were finally safe.

Clicking and checking, the doctor took measurements but kept glancing up at me, a glance I knew too well.

The doctor recognized me, had already placed my face and name but didn't want to say it aloud.

I could read it in the nervous tension across his shoulders under his white lab coat. The doctor was fanning, almost distracted by my presence looming protectively over Charlie and the two secrets the young physician was legally required to keep, no matter how it might burst in him to tell.

Even the local television reporter that showed up in a news truck to the flashing police lights at the pharmacy honoured her profession. I gave her a polite statement off-camera but begged her, please, don't disclose Charlie's pregnancy. It was still a matter of safety. The reporter, true to her word, guarded our secret.

After twenty years, I could predict it like tomorrow's weather.

Who would be giddy around me. Who would cry and overact. Who would blast it online. Who wanted something from me, hoping I'd sign the lucrative deal they offered.

And then there were the ones I liked the most. The ones who didn't give a bloody hell that I was Daniel Pierce. Those people were few and far between.

The doctor's glance returned to where it belonged. From my bloody famous face back to the screen, delivering his assessment of Charlie's state.

"They look fine," the doctor said. "Sister is a little bigger than brother, but nothing to be concerned about."

Her eyes rolled far back with a groan. Not in peril. In frustration.

We didn't want to know. She had insisted at every visit. "Don't tell us what you think their sex is. All that matters is their health."

God, how we had a long conversation about this a couple of months before. "Why can't we know, babe?" I had been dying to know. "So we can get ready for them. Buy the right clothes and stuff."

Secretly, I was hoping for two girls because I loved the idea of doting daughters since I grew up around boys and turmoil.

"Daniel." I knew by her tone, her mind was set. "No matter how brief, let them just be *babies* and not *girls* or *boys* and all the bullshit expectations that come with it."

She'd even refused pink and blue anything. I had to

admit, I liked the ocean theme and mural she'd picked for the nursery. She kept saying, "They're two island kids like us. That's all that matters."

She'd shared so many stories of her growing up as a girl. "Trust me. When you're raised with a name like 'Charlie' and people expect a man to enter the room, I can see the esteem drop in some people's eyes when I enter instead. All I've ever known is people and their dumbass gender stereotypes. I want our kids to be free of it, as much as we can."

With a squeeze of her small hand, I gazed at her now, silently acknowledging her disappointment... to know before they were born...

We were having a girl and a boy.

Still, I couldn't stop the big smile on my face at the intel. And the assurance that they were okay.

The next day, we got news that was almost as welcome. Mason Hunt was arrested again, this time with no bail.

Agent Cooper called to confirm it. Yes, the assailant had been working with Mason. They'd used messages on burner phones to conspire. But they'd found a few direct ones on Mason's Instagram account that introduced him to the man. The messages were cryptic but enough along with Charlie's evidence to make a solid case against him.

The assailant cut a deal too. One that allowed him to confess to his other attacks. All, he swore in a statement to the FBI and would later before a judge, were at Mason Hunt's evil *White Flag* directive.

CHAPTER FIFTY-SIX

DANIEL

"They'll sort it," I insisted to Elaine on the phone while I stood in our hotel suite booked at the New York Palace for sentimental reasons.

"My wife is seven months pregnant with twins. I don't bloody care how they pressure me; I'm not making her suffer through a long screening and premiere party. I'll do the ensemble shots, work the rope line, and talk to the press. Then we'll quietly leave out a side door. The studio can sort the rest."

My gaze was on the sun setting over the Midtown winter skyline, but my mind was on one thing—my family.

One I patiently waited on while Charlie had been hiding with Logan MacGregor and his glam squad for over two hours in our bedroom.

"I'll tell them again," Elaine said. "Maybe they'll finally listen."

She shared my frustration with the demands upon me for the season two premiere of *The Druid*. She'd helped me wrap up a two-week long press junket promoting the show. We were ready to be done and home for the holidays.

She asked, "Is Charlie all right? Does she need anything?"

"She's fine. Logan's properly spoiling her right now. She's been all smiles with her lunches with Kierra, Anders, Maja, and everyone here this week. Juliette even flew in for the night for a surprise visit." I pulled a long blonde hair off my dark-gray suit. The remnant of her made me smile. "She's been an ace about all this, but she needs rest."

"The interview was lovely," Elaine said. "And the photo proofs of the cover are breathtaking, so beautifully done."

This was why I was ready to get Charlie safely home to Daufuskie Island.

She had agreed to a couple's interview with Meg Wiseman of *Wake Up, America*. The questions to Charlie about Kierra and Mason's attack on us were tough, but she didn't flinch. Guarded with her comments, she refused to be baited into trash talk about Mason.

And after our *GQ* article and photos a couple of months before, the demand for more our interviews and photos was ravenous.

So, she agreed to shoot the cover of *Vanity Fair* with me if our interview also focused on causes she was passionate about—helping people escape violence and women veterans, of course.

The proofs of our black-and-white cover shoot with my hands wrapped around her naked, pregnant belly did truly take my breath away. The cover and interview would run in February, when the twins were due.

"Yes, it was splendid." I agreed with Elaine. "And now, after this, we're finally done." My sigh was deep. "See you in a bit then. Cheers."

After tonight, I'd ask no more of Charlie. It was her turn to have her life back, to have our privacy for a few sacred months with the twins.

And it was my turn to finally tell her.

I had it all planned. The picture. The video. The NDAs. The evidence of my secret, my shame—I was going to share it with her when we got home. Before the twins were born, before our future began, I had to tell her about my past.

When I first met Charlie, I knew it would destroy our love. I needed a chance with her. To be a better man. To love her like she deserved. To honour this woman in a way that transformed us both.

Now, I'd swear on my last breath... nothing could threaten us.

All this time, I wanted to protect her, swearing I'd never hurt her again. But after what we survived together? I believed in us, that every part of me she knew. No matter how damning my truth, I gave her my heart; laid bare for her, she could see through to my soul.

My sin would pale to our love.

She was right—I rolled my eyes, grinning—always. Yes, we could survive anything.

The bedroom door clicked open. I turned around.

Logan entered, pronouncing, "Your Warrior Goddess," ushering Charlie into the room with her hand held high in his. Logan's grandiose gesture made her laugh, rolling her eyes.

But the beauty of my wife entering the room conquered me, my allegiance sealed.

Indeed, Logan's dress fit a goddess.

The design, fearless. The flowing empire waist gown in blush pink matched my shirt. The dress was fashioned with long slits showing off Charlie's strong, tan legs. An intricate belt of purple, blue, and gold pearls glistened high across her ribs, matching the pearl straps over her sculpted shoulders.

Logan's team left her thick blonde waves natural to her waist, adorning her tresses with a simple, gold triple-ribbon headband.

The makeup on her gorgeous face was minimal, only playing up her arresting eyes with a smoky look, leaving her lips a blush pink, beckoning me to kiss them over and over.

The sight tightened my throat as she walked toward me, hitting my heart with a million cherished blasts of rapture. How did I get so lucky? Like our angels winked down on us and trusted me to cherish this gift, to cherish her.

"Are you going to say anything?" Her steps drew near.

I could barely speak. Could barely believe the blessing of her gorgeous, powerful body. Could barely find any shred of my ego left in the presence of the three of them—my wife and children—making me feel blissfully insignificant.

"Charlie," I sighed, cupping her face for a kiss full of awe. The knowledge that I'd worship her even more when she brought our daughter and son into the world in a couple months' time, it stopped my words while my lips took hers.

She returned my kiss, cradling my jaw in her hands, glossing her lips over mine. "You're making me cry."

"Don't mess your face, dear," Logan called out.

I could hear the emotion in Logan's voice too.

"Come here." She pressed my hand to her right ribs.

I felt the ripple, my whole world moving underneath my palm.

"Little fuckers won't keep still," she said, eyes beaming up at me. Another strong kick flicked her glance down to my hand resting on her belly. "You're wearing my dad's cuff links again."

"They're the only ones I'll wear now."

Pop gave me the mother-of-pearl cuff links for our wedding. He said they were a gift from Charlie's mum to her dad for their wedding forty years before. I wore them as a proud blessing of Charlie's family of our marriage... one I'd never forsake.

"I got this for you to wear too."

I reached into my jacket pocket, presenting her with a white velvet jewelry box. Opening it, I said, "Gold for you, purple for the twins and blue for me."

She fought back tears again, putting on the custom earrings I had made for her—platinum strings dangling with the smallest pearls of rare colors.

There weren't enough gifts in the world to thank her for all she blessed me with.

But fuck's sake I'd sure try.

CHARLIE

I RUBBED MY FULL, firm belly.

"Yeah, Mama's nervous."

Between little feet pushing into my ribs and my apprehension about the night, my breath shallowed. Then the other one gave me a good flutter kick above my right hip, making me wince. Then grin.

Daniel held my other hand to comfort me. It worked. We didn't need to exchange words when he caressed my hand.

Yes, I love you too.

His other held the phone to his ear, wrapping up a call with Elaine. They were working out our final exit plan while Elaine waited for our arrival on the red carpet around the block.

I glanced out the car window.

The holiday lights of New York City made it magical. The weather added to the charm. It was an unusually warm December evening. So warm that I didn't need a wrap, not with two babies raising my body temperature to an almost sweltering degree.

"Babe, you don't have to do this." Daniel was still on the phone with Elaine but focused on my nervous comment. My hand was trembling in his. "We can just keep driving."

"Daniel, I'll be fine."

"Yes." He was wrapping up the call with Elaine. "We're around the block. See you in a minute."

Tapping the screen, he tucked the phone into his jacket pocket. The look on his face twisted with concern.

"Elaine said it's bloody mad out there. There's more press and fans than they anticipated. With the interview about our wedding, the twins, and the news about Mason and the attacks, she said it's insane. That when Kierra arrived, they erupted in screams so loud it made them flinch."

"Is Kierra okay?" The mention of her only raised my galloping heart rate.

Kierra and I already had two lunch dates this past week in Manhattan. Kierra had been all laughs and hands on my belly like a doting young aunt. But still... I'd never drop my guard. I'd never stop protecting her.

"She's fine. Elaine said she's taking it like a pro. And they're all waiting for us."

Simon turned our car around the block. The blast of

lights and screams shocked me back in my seat. "Holy shit." I couldn't believe the crowd gathered outside the theater, lined down the block and pouring into the street.

"See what I mean?" Daniel held my hand even tighter as he looked up the block too.

A rhythmic drum, a chant in the air seeped through the windows. "What are they shouting?"

"CharDan." He rolled his eyes. "That's our supercouple name."

"What?"

Supercouple? All I felt was a super love and super need to pee.

He stared at the mob of bodies. "This is going to be madness."

It was madness indeed. Like Daniel didn't even need to do a press junket to promote *The Druid*. The press was at a fever pitch for us—demands for photos and interviews were insatiable.

We'd been lucky these past few months. No one knew about my Daufuskie home. Our wedding with friends and family there was wonderfully intimate, very private.

But I'd clocked photographers outside our hotel the moment we arrived in New York. It seemed they'd camped outside every luxury hotel in Manhattan waiting to spot us at one.

And once they had our location, they wouldn't leave and I was trapped. So, I never left our suite. Everyone came to visit me while I hid safe inside the hotel.

Until now.

With this premiere, there was no turning back.

We were about to step into a supernova of spotlight. The ultimate fame reserved for only a few cursed couples.

"Babe, we can just keep driving." Daniel offered one

more escape while Simon slowed the car into the security line for our approach. "I don't care about this. I only care about us."

"No," I said while the car steered through the sea of bodies threatening to drown us. "Let's do this now. Give them their last shot and satisfy them for a while. I don't want them hunting us once the twins are born."

My gaze found his with that last statement.

It stopped my heart.

The care in his gorgeous eyes was focused only on me.

Yes, his skyscraper shoulders wrapped in a perfectly tailored gray suit from Logan MacGregor were a heavenly sight. Especially with two buttons undone on his shirt underneath, revealing my favorite, sexy-as-hell resting spot.

But Daniel looked at me now like he stood in front of a firing squad, not hesitating to take any punishment to protect me and our babies from pain.

It made my soul smile, despite my rocketing anxiety.

"Besides," I said, "it's only an hour now and then I have you all to myself for months."

CHAPTER FIFTY-SEVEN

DANIEL

Our car pulled forward, stopping in position in front of the red carpet. Simon would circle around for us, waiting outside the side exit in an hour.

I spotted Elaine and my team waiting there.

Rob and Joaquin stood there too. The premiere had their own event security, but this was our new protocol—Rob would cover Charlie and Joaquin would cover me.

Yes, by the book, they'd told me they were too close to us to be our permanent personal detail.

But I'd insisted.

I wanted our team on the carpet. I trusted no one more than Rob for this job, to protect Charlie and the twins. And Joaquin's stealth and expertise made me equally confident in his protection.

I knew we were stronger together, a fated foursome who would always love and protect each other.

Still, I'd known fame for decades... but not like this.

It pulsed through the air like a predator's heartbeat on the hunt, chasing, fangs bared and ready to take.

This night? This past month? The appetite for me, Charlie, and our story was madness.

Only a few other celebrity couples had suffered this flood of insanity.

And now... we were swimming in it too.

The press demands for Charlie surpassed my celebrity.

My ego didn't mind. I was beyond proud of her.

But the loving husband and father in me was terrified by it, my instinct on alert.

A familiar adulation, a performance awaited me on the other side of the car door.

I'd done this countless times. Smile. Wave to crowds of screaming strangers, shouts of my name. Hit my mark. Talk with the press. Answer the same questions. Sign the autographs. Take the camera-high selfies with fans. Adjust my hair and suit for the next round. Give more prepared answers, perfect smiles, and big waves, always finding the lens with my practiced smolder.

That Daniel Pierce was a million years gone.

I didn't know him anymore.

All I was now—a proud husband, a blessed father.

The click of Joaquin opening the door hit my ear.

I leaned over, giving Charlie one last passionate kiss, resting my hand over hers, cherishing our future before speaking my truth.

"I love you"—I promised to her marine eyes with the same vow from our wedding, the word engraved inside our matching wedding bands—"forever."

She answered me with that smile that was my dawn, blessing my every day. "Forever."

The door opened and screams poured in.

I turned, stepping out into the deluge. Rising, adjusting my jacket, I gave a nod to Joaquin, then to Rob who stood behind him, ready for Charlie. After a quick peck on Elaine's cheek, I turned to wave at the line of press and fans shouting from behind the long line of stanchions with *The Druid* banners draped over them.

With a pivot back, I turned, offering my hand to Charlie.

Her palm landed in mine.

I paused, grinning, searching her eyes. "Are you ready for this, Charlie?"

"For you, sexy?" She winked, cheeky-like. "Always."

She set one graceful foot down in front of the other. Her feet with golden Grecian sandals touched the ground, traveling me back to memories of her, water, and sand. Her refusal to wear high heels bewitched me. She wore a red-carpet version of flip-flops instead.

I smiled.

That's my stubborn, stunning wife.

CHARLIE

MY GAZE LIFTED from watching my feet step out of the car up to his aqua eyes smiling down at me.

Then... the screams hit me. "CharDan! CharDan!" And rapid-fire shouts of "Daniel! Charlotte! Captain Roberts! Captain Roberts! Daniel! This way! This way!"

The volume pelted my senses and flesh, seizing my breath while Daniel held my hand firm.

As he guided me, we took more steps into the hell tunnel of paparazzi and wall of hissing lenses aimed at us.

All I could focus on—breath for our babies, my feet moving, his touch on me. Hanging on, I clenched my teeth behind smiling lips. My grip anchored to Daniel as he led us to our first mark.

A shout rang out.

"Daniel! Charlotte! Give us a kiss!"

He turned to me. I knew the look in his sparkling eyes. He was jubilant to oblige.

If only the world knew what one kiss meant to us. No photo, no post could capture how we had waited for it. Waited for our passion to bloom into a love so strong no storm could ravage.

How we waited like we knew that once we joined, in the fiercest collide of lust and devotion, we would be forever.

That story was sacred, private, and for us alone.

Not this moment.

It was for all to see, to take from us.

I only wanted him, not this world, but I proudly walked through it to support him. His celebrity was our reality, not our truth.

Our love was the truth.

"Can I please kiss you, Charlotte Ravenel?"

His deep voice soothed through the noise, taking all sound, taking my heart. His side-grinning request for my consent was sexier than any entitled take he could have of my lips.

"Forever, Daniel Pierce."

I gave everything to him as he gently kissed my right cheek, my scar, before his supple, full lips seized mine.

For a breath... I was at our wedding, standing on the beach, promising before everyone we cherished, and in the memory of those who passed away, to love him beyond my last exhale.

I was back in his arms while he carried me into the low waves after we said, "I do." Everyone on the shore laughed at the sight of us in our wedding attire, of Daniel's white shirt soaked through while my white dress, wet with salt water, hugged my silhouette. He had waded chest-deep into the brisk water before we took the plunge. He never let me go as we emerged with one pure kiss.

That moment—captured in our favorite photo—it sat on the nightstand beside our bed in our island home.

This moment—his hand cradling my cheek while his soft lips caressed mine in a sultry kiss—it sent the crowd into a feeding frenzy.

Frantic shouts hurled toward us. "Again! Charlotte! Daniel! Captain Roberts! Captain Roberts! Mr. Pierce! Daniel! Again! More! Daniel, this way! Another kiss!"

Daniel's eyes sparkled at mine, his bowed lips leaning down for one last kiss.

God, how I wanted to hold him here and just disappear into this sanctuary, the bliss of him connected to me.

But reality stole him away. I squeezed his hand as his lips left mine.

That was it.

The world had taken enough from us.

No more.

His kiss could stop time for me, but when I turned from his gaze, looking back into the crowd, seconds passed like years.

A publicist approached, pointing, telling Daniel who was first to talk to on the carpet. He had to do his round of interviews and then his ensemble photos with the cast.

I looked to my left. Rob stood there. I nodded, mouthing, "Sup, fucker." He laughed, nodding a "sup, fucker" chin back at me before turning his eyes back toward the crowd, watching.

One of the twins kicked. Making the other do the same. Making my heart pound. Making a full breath impossible.

I closed my eyes, grabbing an inhale. Holding it in, I guarded so much love in my heart.

Flashing blasts of light fired through my eyelids. A rattlesnake hiss of camera shutters sounded a threat to my ears.

I exhaled and opened my eyes, glancing down at Daniel's hand wrapped around mine with his wedding band on his finger, feeling the sacred molecules between his skin and mine, and all we created.

His grasp unlaced from mine to follow the publicist down the red carpet, heading toward the crowd while I would go inside.

"I'll meet you on the other side," he said, eyes brimming with love, holding a smile only for me, his touch letting go.

From my depths, I smiled back, teasing, "Don't forget about me," watching him turn away.

But when his touch left mine, an annihilating void filled it.

Suddenly, I felt cold.

Fear.

Exposed.

I heard no sound.

Only, "Ravenel! Ravenel!"

Following the tidal pull of its call, I turned.

It shot across my mind, a glare of recognition. Of a nightmare I had months before, lying beside Daniel. Of a prophecy fulfilled.

Scanning across the evil white lights, I inhaled,

searching through the screaming crowd, through the feral faces and eyes scoping me.

There.

Your target.

The moon in the daytime sky, the haunt and the hunt aligned.

I stared the sight down with a long exhale. I'd seen this before.

A man coming for me.

A gun aiming for me.

Murderous eyes hunting me.

Piercing me.

I fell.

"Charlie!" Daniel shouted.

Sign of the Times by Harry Styles

DEAR READER,

In honor of Charlie...

If you do share/review/post, thank you so much.
While you do, please help me protect this ending.
Books must end. Stories don't.
It continues in *CHASE HER*.

As always, thank you for reading *HUNT HER*, and thank
you for your reviews, posts, and shares! I read as many as I
can, and I just smile, often with humble tears.

Get CHASE HER now.

And get free bonus scenes, sneak peeks, the stories behind this story, and more at
KellyFinley.com

ALSO BY KELLY FINLEY

Come for Me Trilogy

Protect Her, Prequel Novelette

Pierce Her, Book One

Hunt Her, Book Two

Chase Her, Book Three

All for You Duet

After Him, Book One

With Him, Book Two

And more coming very soon...

Get more from Kelly Finley on Amazon

ACKNOWLEDGMENTS

The beginning of this writing journey was humble for me, as it should be.

Now, I'm so honored, so touched by the readers, followers, friends and fellow writers I am meeting along the way.

Y'all keep me writing. Keep me inspired. Keep me tapping away on my keyboard, determined to deliver heroines we love.

The only way I can write great love is to know it. Thank you, Kevin, for being man enough to love a woman like me.

To my family, who I keep warning not to read the steamy pages, thanks for your support and blushing faces.

Always mad love to my alpha readers: Sarah and Melissa. I know you love these characters as much as I do. To my beta readers, same goes. Your encouragement keeps me writing. To the ARC teams—I can't do this without you! Hugs.

Once again, to all my friends and family who indulge my research and interviews. I'm honored to know people who served, people on set, and people who kick ass for a living.

Serious thanks to my editors, my designer, and proofreaders who help me realize this dream.

My humble gratitude goes to the women who have or do serve. This beloved character is inspired by you.

Above all, thank you again to my readers.

Keep reading. Keep swooning. Keep trusting.

ABOUT THE AUTHOR

Kelly Finley hates writing bios but appreciates you made it this far. So here you go...

She lives in the Carolinas with her sexy husband and cherished family. A rebel with many causes, she fancies black leather, dirty jokes, big hearts and smart mouths.

Thrilled by a flipped gender script and ticked off by women portrayed as weak, she noticed how many steamy, sexy heroines were missing, particularly from romance pages.

Her friends shared the same frustration and told her to practice what she has taught for over twenty years—women who kick ass.

Dedicated to writing books featuring heroines we champion and love—ones with shameless heat, brave hearts, and whip-smart minds—she's most likely at her keyboard putting the next one on the page for you.

amazon.com/author/kellyfinley

patreon.com/kellyfinleyauthor

goodreads.com/goodreads_kelly_finley

bookbub.com/authors/kelly-finley

instagram.com/kellyfinleyauthor

tiktok.com/@kellyfinleybooks

facebook.com/KellyFinleyBooks

9 781737 451655